D1246896

Advance Praise for Full Bloom:

"*Full Bloom* is an unforgettable story of family ties, turmoil, and finding the things that truly matter in life. Deeply dramatic and undeniably funny, Judith Arnold's latest will have you up all night reading."
—Susan Wiggs, *New York Times* bestselling author

"Judith Arnold's delicious novel about a family running the best deli on New York's Upper West Side has it all: wit and wisdom, intelligence and heart, drama and laugh-out-loud comedy, gonifs and mensches, knishes and wine. In short, this wry look at the conflicts and joys that constitute family life is the everything bagel of novels, and I happily devoured it."
—Judith Claire Mitchell, award-winning author of *A Reunion of Ghosts*

"I'm starving! You will be, too, as you read Judith Arnold's latest, the story of Bloom's Delicatessen and the three generations of Blooms who fill it with pickles and bagels and ever-engaging conflict. With her trademark combination of warmth and wit, Arnold shows us what happens when the needs of the individual trump the needs of the family. If you're anything like me, you'll finish *Full Bloom* wishing you lived only a block away from the deli and its cast of intriguing characters."
—Diane Chamberlain, *New York Times* bestselling author of *Big Lies in a Small Town*

"I love the Blooms! *Full Bloom* is warmly written and fiercely funny, the characters real, flawed, and sympathetic."
—Virginia Kantra, *New York Times* bestselling author

"You'll smack your lips and wish you had your own Seder-in-a-box as you read *Full Bloom* from Judith Arnold. Manhattan's most lovable dysfunctional family faces trials and triumphs set around Bloom's, their popular West Side deli. With sass and savvy, Arnold captures not only the physical geography of Bloom's and its urban neighborhood, but the emotional geography of the Bloom family, too. Eat it up."
—Emilie Richards, award-winning author

"*Full Bloom*, Judith Arnold's new book, is chock full of high points: snappy dialogue which reveals the main characters' personalities and furthers the plot; the fascinating details of running a New York Jewish deli, even if you've read and enjoyed the other Bloom books, as I did; the picture-perfect dynamics of a big family. But it's the organic humor that grows out of these elements that will keep you reading. Arnold's ability to make us laugh (a talent from her earlier books) is even sharper, wittier and, most important, still touches our hearts with poignancy. Most writers can never measure up to her comedic touch combined with pathos. Kudos to Judith Arnold all around! I hope you keep the Bloom books coming."
— Kathryn Shay, *New York Times* bestselling author of The Hidden Cove Firefighter Series

Full Bloom

Story Plant Books by Judith Arnold

Love in Bloom's
Blooming All Over

Full Bloom

Judith Arnold

This is a work of fiction. Names, characters, places, and incidents either are the product of the author's imagination or are used fictitiously. Any resemblance to actual events, locales, organizations, or persons living or dead, is entirely coincidental and beyond the intent of either the author or the publisher.

The Story Plant
Studio Digital CT, LLC
PO Box 4331
Stamford, CT 06907

Copyright © 2020 by Judith Arnold

Story Plant hardcover ISBN-13: 978-1-61188-287-2
Fiction Studio Books E-book ISBN-13: 978-1-945839-43-6

Visit our website at www.TheStoryPlant.com

All rights reserved, which includes the right to reproduce this book or portions thereof in any form whatsoever except as provided by US Copyright Law.

For information, address The Story Plant.

First Story Plant printing: June 2020
Printed in the United States of America

To Carolyn, who taught me how to read,
how to write,
and how to be a sister

Chapter One

Julia Bloom believed pickles were the perfect metaphor for life. They could be sweet but were usually sour—a tasty, gratifying sour that only rarely lapsed into an overload of vinegar that made her tongue double back on itself. Pickles could be cut into ripply round slices or long, aggressive spears. They could be crisp and firm or limp and soggy, a lustrous green or a jaundiced yellow-beige. Their skin could be smooth or mottled with wart-like bumps.

Life was sometimes smooth and sometimes lumpy with warts, too. Sometimes sweet, sometimes sour, sometimes acidic. Sometimes nourishing. Sometimes nauseating.

Seated in her office on the third floor of the Bloom Building, she gazed at the plate of pickles on her desk, her phone pressed to her right ear and her left ear absorbing the din outside her open door. She kept the door open because, despite the existence of telephones, cell phones, computers, and legs that could carry people from one place to another, the folks who worked in the executive suite of Bloom's generally communicated by remaining at their desks and shouting from office to office.

Her mother, Sondra, a vice-president of Bloom's because Julia felt she deserved an exalted title, was currently shouting to Deirdre Morrissey—another vice-president, because she actually knew how to run the business competently—about various tea towel designs. Myron Finkel, the accountant who'd been with Bloom's practically from the day Grandma Ida and Grandpa Isaac had moved their operations from a sidewalk pushcart into this brick-and-mortar building, was shouting to anyone who would listen that he couldn't figure out how to do multiplication on his Excel spreadsheet. Uncle Jay was shouting to Julia's sister Susie about the placement of Bloom's Seder-in-a-Box promo in the *Bloom's Bulletin*—he wanted it on the first page, and Susie was shouting back that since Passover was more than a month away, a page-three mention was adequate. Uncle Jay was yet another vice-president, because his brother Ben, Julia's father, had been the president until he'd died from eating tainted sturgeon, and after a year of mourning, Julia's Grandma Ida had bypassed Uncle Jay and named Julia the president of Bloom's. No way could Uncle Jay have run the place, but anointing him with a fancy title made him feel better.

Julia understood that it was her job to make everyone feel better.

Susie wasn't a vice-president. She often said that if Julia dared to dump that much responsibility on her delicate shoulders, she would bolt from the building and not stop running until she reached the Pacific Ocean—quite a distance, given that Bloom's was located on the Upper West Side of Manhattan. Susie's shoulders were not the least bit delicate, but Julia believed the running-to-the-West-Coast part of Susie's threat.

The vocal cacophony outside Julia's office swirled around her like background music while she talked on the phone with Bernie Koplowitz, her new pickle supplier. He'd recently bought out her former pickle supplier, Murray Schloss, who had packed up his barrels and retired to Boynton Beach. The quality of Bernie's dills was a little less dependable than Murray's had been. "Some of them are mushy, Bernie," she complained, gazing at the plate of pickles resting on her desk. They ranged from as stiff as a man who'd just popped a megadose of Viagra to as limp as a man in the deep throes of erectile dysfunction. "You bite into them, and it's all seeds and brine inside."

"Pickles have seeds in them," Bernie's voice blasted through the phone. Like the Bloom's executives occupying the third floor, Bernie was given to shouting. Of course, he was not just a few feet down the hall from her but in Bayonne, New Jersey. Julia wondered whether she'd hear him just as clearly if she opened one of her office windows and tilted her head in the direction of the Hudson River. "Cucumbers have seeds in them," he bellowed. "That's not my fault. God stuck those seeds there."

God probably had more important matters to attend to than sticking seeds inside cucumbers. "It's the consistency I'm worried about," she explained. "Not just the consistency of the pickles themselves, but consistency from one pickle to the next. People who buy pickles from Bloom's should know what they're getting. It shouldn't be a craps shoot whether they get a crisp pickle or a mushy pickle."

"But that's the nature of pickles," Bernie insisted, his booming baritone echoing painfully inside Julia's skull. "Some are crisp. Some aren't. You never know. You take your chances and hope for the best. Like cantaloupes."

This was one reason Bloom's didn't sell cantaloupes. The store sold cheeses from every country that cultivated milk-producing mammals. It sold olive oils so expensive, you might as well dab them behind your ears and call them perfume. It sold bread sticks from Italy and saffron from India, smoked salmon from Nova Scotia, dried porcini mushrooms from wherever dried porcini mushrooms came from, and bagels from Casey's Gourmet Breads in the East Village, six miles downtown from Julia's office above the store. And pickles from Bayonne, New Jersey. But no fresh produce. Fresh produce was too iffy, and it didn't store well.

Murray Schloss's pickle enterprise had been located in Brooklyn. Maybe God sent less seedy cucumbers to Flatbush than to Bayonne.

"Look, Bernie. We're a big client. You get a lot of money from us. We offer pickles individually from the barrel, pre-packaged pickles, and pickles garnishing our custom sandwiches. I don't think I'm being unreasonable when I ask for crisp pickles. I don't want soggy ones. They look like..." She deleted the Viagra analogy from her mind and said, "Overcooked spaghetti."

"They're green."

"You've never seen green spaghetti? We sell green spaghetti." Spinach linguini, actually. It was a big seller, much more popular than the orange carrot farfalle.

"I tell you what." Bernie's voice took on a wheedling singsong quality. "I'll give you a deal, ten percent lower price, and I'll send you only my crispest pickles. You can tell me in a month if you don't like the quality."

"Fair enough." Julia ended the call, lowered the phone and issued a whispered "Yes!" Unlike her family and Bernie Koplowitz, she wasn't big on shouting. But her primary goal in contacting him had been to get him to lower his price. No one liked mushy pickles, but most people accepted that sometimes a pickle couldn't get it up, as it were. You couldn't tell from looking at a cucumber whether it was going to be overly seedy. You simply had to take pickles on faith. Like life itself.

Like life itself, however, paying ten percent less for faith ought to be viewed as a major triumph. And Julia had accomplished that. She deserved a moment to bask in her victory.

Susie swung through Julia's open door and into the office, interrupting Julia's basking. She wore an oversized black sweater, black jeans, black ankle-high boots, and black mascara. She looked like a refugee from a grunge funeral, except for her bright smile and her buzzy energy. "I finished this week's *Bloom's Bulletin*," she announced, "and I don't care what Uncle Jay says. It's too early to put the Seder-in-a-Box promotion on the front page."

"You're the editor," Julia said. In the two years she'd served as president of Bloom's, she'd gotten better at delegating—including delegating to her flaky younger sister. When it came to important matters, like negotiating lower wholesale prices for pickles, Julia believed there was no one better than Grandma Ida, but Grandma Ida was too old and imperious to be delegated to. She was inching toward her ninetieth birthday and no longer terribly active in the business, except to cast a shadow over the place so large it was like that cloud of volcanic ash that altered the entire planet's climate back in the 1800's. Julia aspired to be as shrewd a businesswoman as her grandmother had been, although without the volcanic ash. If she'd wanted to chill everyone, she wouldn't have given so many of them the title of vice-president.

She had started her professional life as a lawyer in a large, stultifying law firm. Lawyers were control freaks. They knew that a misplaced comma in a brief could mean the difference between a multi-million-dollar settlement and a dismissal with prejudice, so they tended to pay close attention to commas. Susie was a poet and seemed to have a general disregard for commas, but she did put together a terrific weekly circular, complete with limericks about Bloom's merchandise. Julia would love to have her sister working full-time for the company, but Susie refused—partly on principle, she claimed, but mostly because she was also working at Casey's Gourmet Breads. Casey was her boyfriend.

"What are you so happy about?" Susie asked, eyeing Julia skeptically. "You're never this happy."

"Thanks a lot." But Julia was too happy to take offense. "I just got Bernie Koplowitz to lower his pickle price."

"Oh, joy. Break out the bubbly." Susie grinned, too, but shook her head. "The things you choose to get happy about..."

"What do you think should make me happy?" Julia asked.

Susie shrugged. Her shoulders definitely weren't delicate. She was slight in build, but sturdy. That she was relatively flat-chested made her shoulders look bigger by comparison. "I'm happy because I finished writing this week's *Bloom's Bulletin* and I can get the hell out of here. Plus, I came up with a rhyme for kugel."

"What rhymes with kugel?"

"Read the bulletin. It's in the shared file." Susie flounced around the office, paying brief homage to the framed print of the World Trade Center Julia had hung on one of the walls—Susie thought it was tacky, but it always made Julia tear up when she looked at it—and the old wooden desk in the corner of the office. Their Grandpa Isaac had used it when he'd been alive and running Bloom's with Grandma Ida. Nowadays, the desk was never used, except as a perch where Susie usually sat when Julia hosted her weekly executive staff meetings in the office. The desk was battered, but it was as much a fixture in the office as the equally battered leather couch and the window and the computer humming on Julia's desk, which was newer than Grandpa Isaac's desk but still pretty old.

"I've been thinking," Susie said, turning back to Julia, "of getting back to doing poetry slams."

"Do you have time for that?" Julia asked. Between working at Bloom's and helping out at Casey's bread bakery downtown, when was Susie going to find time to write poetry?

"That's not the point. I stopped doing the slams because they're usually at night and Casey has to go to bed ridiculously early, so he can get up at four o'clock and start the ovens at the bakery. But I realized I don't need him to go to the slams with me. I'm a big girl."

"You're a woman," Julia pointed out.

"Let's not get carried away."

"Is everything all right with you and Casey?" When a woman wanted to spend her nights in gloomy clubs reciting poetry and drinking bad wine instead of going to bed early with her boyfriend, it could be an indication of trouble.

"Everything's fine. I just told him I missed doing slams and he said, 'So go and do some.'" Susie hesitated, her smile losing a little of its wattage. "Do you think that means things aren't okay?"

"You're the one in the relationship. You're supposed to know if things aren't okay."

Susie ruminated on this for a moment, then shrugged her robust shoulders once more. "Things are okay. Are you going to eat all those pickles?"

Julia nudged the plate toward Susie. "Help yourself."

Susie took one and bit into it. It wasn't crisp enough to crunch, but at least it didn't collapse and dribble seeds all over Julia's desk.

"Mmm. Delicious," Susie said around a mouthful of pickle. "I like these pickles better than the ones we used to sell."

"Really?" Julia smiled. Maybe they *were* better. Maybe she wasn't the best judge of pickles. And now she'd be getting better pickles for a discounted price.

Susie popped the tail end of the pickle into her mouth, and Julia closed her eyes to erase her Viagra-influenced images of stiff pickles entering orifices. "Excellent," Susie declared. "Notes of dill and garlic, with a nice finish of salt. I gotta go. I have to write some poems that aren't limericks about Bloom's food."

"No kugel rhymes, huh." Julia clicked her computer keyboard, searching for the shared file where Susie had saved the latest *Bloom's Bulletin*. "Tell Casey he's charging me too much for his bagels."

"Yeah, right," Susie said before vanishing through the doorway.

She might be flaky, she might believe Bayonne pickles were tastier than Brooklyn pickles, but she did write a superb advertising circular. Julia opened the file, read Susie's limerick, and grinned.

The specials from New York's best deli
Will delight both your wallet and belly.
We've got knishes and kugel
For shoppers quite frugal
And a discount on fresh vermicelli.

"Hey."

Julia swiveled her chair toward the door to discover her brother Adam perched on the threshold. For a moment, she thought he was her father. He was, in fact, a young, skinny, hirsute version of her father. He had Ben Bloom's height, his slightly S-shaped posture, his narrow nose and piercing eyes. But Adam's hair was definitely not anything like the late Ben Bloom's TV-anchorman coiffure. Julia often urged Adam to make an appointment with a hair stylist for a cut that would give his untamed waves some shape, but he said he had better things to do with his money. Maybe he was angling for a raise. He wasn't a vice-president—not yet, anyway. And Julia was subletting her old apartment to him at a great price, which was arguably a better financial deal than a mere bump in salary.

He stepped into the office, blinking like an animal emerging from its den after a long winter of hibernation. Despite her insistence that he dress like a *mensch* instead of the slovenly college student he'd been less than a year ago, there was still something unformed about Adam. Something sloppy. His shirt might have a collar, but the shirt's tails were untucked. His trousers might be clean, but they were cargo pants, with strangely bulging items in their pockets. Julia didn't want to know what those items were.

Still, he was a genius. He'd been accepted into a doctoral program in mathematics at Purdue when Julia had persuaded him to join the company, instead. She'd put him in charge of inventory management, and he'd done wonders, computerizing everything, reorganizing the basement storage spaces, coordinating delivery schedules, and all in all making things run much more smoothly. If he didn't want to tuck in his shirt...well, at least the shirt wasn't a ragged T-shirt with some death-metal band or political slogan silkscreened onto it.

"Susie rhymed kugel and frugal," she told him.

"Susie deserves a Pulitzer," he shot back. "Listen. I've found some retail space available for not-too-obscene a price-per-square-foot on Lexington Avenue."

"That's an oxymoron," Julia said. "There's no such thing as retail space on Lexington that doesn't have an obscene price."

"It's doable."

"It's not doable. We're not doing it." When he wasn't handling inventory, Adam was pestering her about opening a satellite Bloom's outlet somewhere else in the city. The Financial District, maybe. Or Gramercy Park. Or near the Skyway, or a stone's throw from Beth Israel Hospital. Last week he'd suggested opening a Bloom's bodega in Washington Heights. "Ethnic people like ethnic food," he'd argued. "It doesn't really matter what ethnic. I love plantains. Latinos love smoked whitefish."

He and Uncle Jay shared an obsession about expanding Bloom's, opening a second retail center, selling franchises, setting up kiosks in subway stations... God knew what they had in mind, but whatever it was, it wasn't in Julia's mind. Bloom's was an Upper West Side institution. It belonged where it was and nowhere else. It was in and of its neighborhood. If tourists could travel all the way from Berlin and Tokyo and Nairobi to the Upper West Side to shop at Bloom's, surely people who lived in Gramercy Park or Washington Heights could make their way to this location.

"I don't know why you won't consider it," Adam said. "You're leaving money on the table."

Those were Uncle Jay's words, not Adam's. Adam couldn't care less about money or tables. He was a math geek. He was a twenty-three-year-old guy, high on his freedom, his bargain-sublet Manhattan apartment, his discovery that he had outgrown a fair amount of his nerdiness and was now, for some reason, considered desirable by desirable women, and probably on his frequent recreational use of marijuana.

Uncle Jay had been agitating for an Upper East Side Bloom's outlet for as long as Julia had been the president, and he'd found an ally in Adam. Uncle Jay lived on the Upper East Side; ergo, he believed the Upper East Side was the place to be.

And he cared about things like money on the table, which Julia considered a pretty Upper East Side attitude.

"Why is this such a thing with you?" Julia challenged Adam now. The joyful fizz she'd experienced after extracting the ten percent discount from Bernie Koplowitz was going flat like day-old seltzer.

She loved Adam. He was her brother, so she had to love him, even if she didn't want to, and usually she wanted to. But she was tired of hearing him go on and on about opening a new Bloom's somewhere that wasn't in this building on upper Broadway. Surely he could find something else to obsess about: computer games, or chess, or all those skinny little ballet students from Juilliard who kept throwing themselves at him because he was straight and did a reasonable job of pretending to like ballet. "Our bottom line is fine. Things are moving along. I've been running the place for barely two years. Give me a break."

"You don't want to expand because Grandma Ida doesn't want to," Adam said, digging his hands into two of the less bulging pockets of his pants and leaning against the door jamb.

Well, there was that. Grandma Ida was firmly opposed to expansion, and Julia deferred to her. She might be elderly, but she was still Bloom's CEO and a formidable force. Julia could cajole Grandma Ida, but she couldn't confront her. Nobody could, really. Business decisions that went against Grandma Ida's preferences were generally implemented behind her back. But there was no way opening a second branch of Bloom's could happen without Grandma Ida's knowledge.

Besides, as Julia said, she'd occupied the president's office for barely two years. During that time, she'd left her job at the law firm, fallen in love with Ron, and married him—and sublet her apartment to Adam, the thankless turd. She'd provided emotional support to her widowed mother and her mercurial sister. She'd gotten to know her father posthumously, for better or worse. And she'd kept the store and the entire multigenerational Bloom family functioning, despite the turmoil following his death.

Her shoulders were arguably more delicate than Susie's. She wasn't ready to add any additional weight to them right now. "Why do you keep *noodging* me about this, Adam?" she asked, gesturing at the plate on her desk, one pickle short thanks to Susie. "I'm dealing with other challenges at the moment."

"You're in a pickle, huh."

Bad joke but Julia forced a laugh, hoping that would encourage him to go away.

"I'm *noodging* you," he answered her question, "because growth is a healthy thing."

"Adam, *bubby*, you don't know what you're talking about," Sondra hollered from her office. Evidently, she'd been eavesdropping.

Adam attempted to dismiss their mother's comment by rolling his eyes and grinning, but Julia could see he was hurt by it. "Of course you know what you're talking about," she said, hoping to stroke away his resentment with a few kind words. "It's a good idea. Growth is good. But just not right now, okay?"

"If not now, when?"

"I'm thinking about it," she assured him. "I'm not ignoring you. Just don't be a *noodge*, okay?"

"Okay," he said, although he clearly didn't think her position was okay. Still, he seemed vaguely mollified. She'd made him feel better. Later, she'd have to talk to her mother, tell her not to interfere and not to listen in on conversations that didn't involve her…and then say some nice things so her mother would feel better, too.

After Adam left Julia's office, she stared at the plate of pickles for a few long seconds, noting the puddle of brine that had formed in the plate's shallow curve. She was hungry—she hadn't bothered with lunch—but if she bit into one of the pickles and discovered it soggy and seedy, she'd be sorely disappointed.

She picked one up. It drooped slightly. Really, Susie thought these pickles tasted better than Murray Schloss's pickles?

Sighing, she put the pickle back on the plate, rose from her desk, and closed her office door. This simple act was certain to offend everyone in all the other offices, and she'd eventually have to do something to make them feel better. But she didn't wish to have her mother—or any other snoop—listen while she called her husband.

"My brother is driving me crazy," she said as soon as Ron answered his phone.

"I've got a deadline breathing down my neck," he warned her. "Talk fast."

"I don't want to talk fast," she said. "I want to whine about my brother. And gloat about the discount I got from our new pickle supplier," she remembered to add.

"You're a goddess. Anything else? If I have to beat Adam up, I'll do it later. I've got to get this piece about payday lenders done in the next half hour. You wouldn't believe the shit Kim is giving me." Ron was the business columnist for *Gotham Magazine*, and Kim Pinsky was his editor. In addition to the articles he wrote for the weekly print edition of the magazine, he wrote essays for the daily online edition and his blog. Obviously, writing daring, erudite pieces about economic trends and corrupt hedge fund managers and usurious lenders was far more important than listening to his wife bitch about her baby brother and brag about her pickle-negotiating skills.

"You're right. I wouldn't believe it," she said, feeling as wounded as Adam had looked when their mother had implied that he was ignorant. And there was no one to make her feel better, other than herself. "Get back to work."

"I love you," Ron said. He must have heard the hurt in her tone. "Bring some Heat-'N'-Eat home for dinner tonight, all right? We can pig out on stuffed cabbage and you can tell me all about the pickles."

"Fine." One of the ironies of being a Bloom was that, despite the fact that the most renowned gourmet delicatessen in the city, if not the entire world, had sustained the Bloom family for three generations and bore the family's name, no Blooms really knew how to cook. In fact, when they were growing up, Julia's family rarely ate food from Bloom's, even though her parents were running the business. Julia's parents viewed Bloom's food as merchandise. It was a profit center. If they were going to eat, they would eat food from the supermarket a few blocks away, which sold national brands filled with preservatives and high fructose corn syrup and artificial food coloring. Sondra used to cut coupons from the Sunday paper and boast about saving a dollar on a box of Cheerios, instead of letting

Julia, Susie, and Adam breakfast on bagels and bialys from the store their family ran.

But after Ron had met Julia while writing an article about her ascension to the presidency of Bloom's in the wake of her father's death, he'd convinced her to eat Bloom's food, and she'd discovered how utterly delicious it was. Sometimes she believed she'd fallen in love with Ron only because he'd wooed her with her very own store products.

Bloom's food was astoundingly good. Good enough to make her marry him.

"I'll bring home some Heat-'N'-Eat," she promised. "Go meet your deadline."

She clicked off her phone and sighed, then lifted another pickle. It looked relatively rigid. She bit into it and her mouth flooded with luscious sourness. It wasn't the crunchiest pickle in the world, but God hadn't put too many seeds in it. And one bite reminded her that she was starving.

She took another bite. This time her sigh was a happy one. Pickles might not be champagne, but they would do. She had scored a victory today. Some days, you got only one victory—and one was enough.

A tap on her closed door interfered with her evaluation of the pickle—better than Murray Schloss's pickles? Worse?—and she turned in time to see the door open. Uncle Jay stalked uninvited into the office, scowling.

Uncle Jay had been the better looking of the Bloom brothers. He'd been far more athletic than Julia's father, and far more cheerful. On him, a scowl looked like a mildly distorted smile. His hair was a blend of dark brown and elegant silver, and his apparel—tailored trousers, tailored shirt with his initials monogrammed onto the left cuff—was spiffy. His wife Wendy didn't know much, but she knew fashion, and she oversaw Uncle Jay's wardrobe. Julia wished she could hire Wendy to oversee Adam's wardrobe, too.

"Why is your door closed?" he asked.

"I had to make a call."

He eyed her phone, which was on her desk, not in her hand. She could almost hear his brain ticking as he added up the evidence and decided she was lying. His frown intensified, but he still looked as if he was smiling.

"Fine. Whatever. I just wanted to tell you I'm quitting."

"Quitting what?" He wasn't a smoker. He wasn't a heavy drinker, at least as far as she knew. He'd never quit golf, so that couldn't be what he was talking about.

"Bloom's. I'm quitting this place. Good-bye. *Adios. Shalom.*"

Before she could ask him what the hell he was talking about, he pivoted on the heel of one expensive Bally loafer and strode out of the office.

If Julia had had a bottle of champagne, she would have consumed it in a single non-stop chug, or else thrown it at her uncle's receding form. All she had was the pickle in her hand, and the three other pickles on the plate. If she threw them at Uncle Jay, he wouldn't even notice. Especially if she threw one of the limp ones.

He has to be kidding, she consoled herself. *He's just experiencing a mini-meltdown because Susie wouldn't put the Seder-in-a-Box promo on the first page of the* Bloom's Bulletin. Uncle Jay couldn't seriously be thinking of leaving Bloom's. He was a Bloom, for God's sake. Blooms didn't leave Bloom's. It would be like abandoning your own skin. This was all a joke, a snit, a momentary spasm of stupidity. Just Uncle Jay being Uncle Jay.

She popped what was left of the pickle she was holding into her mouth. She chewed. She savored the notes of garlic, dill, and salt. She swallowed.

He's not going to leave, she assured herself.

But she failed to make herself feel better.

Chapter Two

The time had come. Jay had had enough. And now—miraculously—he did have enough. He could do this. He could leave.

Everything had fallen into place last weekend, when he'd driven out to Emerald View Country Club for a round of golf. March was a bit early for golfing, but it had been a mild winter, and the ground, while spongy, wasn't covered with snow or mud. The club took superb care of the course. They hired top-of-the-line grounds keepers. If Jay lived in a house surrounded by acreage, he'd want members of the Emerald View Country Club grounds crew mowing his lawn.

His usual Sunday golf partner wasn't available. "But listen, Jay," Marshall had said. "I can set you up with Gil Jenners and Rupert Niles. Great guys, they're available, and they've been dying to meet you."

Anyone dying to meet Jay was all right with him.

Gil Jenners and Rupert Niles sounded awfully Wasp-y, but then, it was a Wasp-y country club. Marshall Wynn sounded Wasp-y, too, but Jay suspected that at some point early in his life, Marshall Wynn had actually been Moishe Weinstein. Jay could relate to him in a way he wasn't sure he could relate to people named Gil and Rupert.

But he was working on that. He'd gotten into the club on his first try, having been proposed by Stuart Pinsky, the attorney who handled his divorce from Martha all those years ago. If Emerald View Country Club had allowed Stuart in, they couldn't balk at allowing Jay Bloom in. He, after all, was the scion of the world's premiere delicatessen.

Or what had been the world's premiere delicatessen up to now. Things were about to change.

Gil Jenners and Rupert Niles were clearly two very wealthy fellows, if their addresses—Gil in Sands Point, Rupert in Manhasset—were anything to go by. Rupert had a British accent, although Jay wasn't sure if he was actually a Brit. A guy could grow up in the Bronx, make a killing, and take elocution lessons so his diction matched his bank account. He could change his name from Reuben Novitsky to Rupert Niles. Jay didn't have the guts to ask him whether he really was from the United Kingdom—and if not, how he'd gotten rich enough to afford that accent. To ask would be crass.

Besides, Jay was rich, too. Maybe not in Rupert and Gil's class, but he was rich enough to own a six-room apartment on the Upper East Side. He was rich enough to have jettisoned Martha and replaced her with Wendy, his beautiful blond second wife. It took a lot of money to keep someone like Wendy satisfied. As far as he could tell, Wendy was satisfied.

So he, Gil, and Rupert played a round on Sunday morning. Their shoes got a little damp, but they were ugly golf shoes, cleat-soled versions of saddle shoes, so what the hell. Jay and his new golfing partners talked. They laughed. Gil broke seventy and insisted on buying drinks in the clubhouse after the game.

The lounge in the Emerald View Country Club was a haven of pale paneling and broad glass overlooking the slate patio and beyond it the beautifully groomed fairway of the first hole. Something about the atmosphere—the plush carpeting, maybe, or the silk drapes, or just the fact that Emerald View's members were classy—muted sound. People spoke quietly. None of that crazy shouting like Jay was used to on the third floor of Bloom's.

"I wish I sold food," Gil said, once they'd been served a round of Dewar's in elegant cut-crystal glasses. "Portfolios are so dry. You can't eat money, am I right?"

"You can't eat without money, either," Jay pointed out.

Gil and Rupert laughed uproariously. Really, they were great guys.

"Well, Gil just piddles about at his hedge fund," Rupert said. "I don't find money all that dreadfully dry."

"Because your money is international," Gil said. "You get to fly all over the world and hobnob with the big boys. Have you ever flown first class on that Middle East airline—which one is it, Rupert? Kuwait? Emirates? The one where each seat is like its own little cabin?"

Rupert waved a dismissive hand. "I've flown all of them. One way or another, you still have to deal with jet lag."

"A lot easier to deal with jet lag if you're in your own little cabin. Am I right?" Gil asked Jay, seeking confirmation.

Jay was certain he'd have no trouble flying in his own little cabin.

"That said," Rupert continued, "Selling food must be so rewarding. You actually can see and feel and smell what you're selling."

"And taste," Gil added. "On those rare occasions when I venture over to the Upper West Side, I'll stop at Bloom's and pick up some treats. My wife loves that Australian cheddar you sell there. Also the Italian chocolates. She says they're better than the Belgian chocolates. She's a chocolate connoisseur."

"All women are," Jay said. All women except his first wife, Martha, who was a health-food nut. She was a tofu connoisseur. A lentil connoisseur. A steel-cut oatmeal connoisseur. Bloom's sold some costly gourmet oatmeal, but as far as Jay was concerned, oatmeal was oatmeal. Put it in a fancy container, double the price, but it was still just oatmeal.

Wendy, on the other hand, would live on chocolate if it wasn't so fattening. And he would gladly encourage her to live on chocolate, because he'd discovered that chocolates had an aphrodisiac effect on her. Especially expensive chocolates. When it came to screwing his wife, he'd gladly pay double for the fancy gold-foil packaging.

"I'll tell you," Gil said, "I'd love to sink some money into a food venture like Bloom's. If only I could find something new, a truly superior gourmet emporium, I'd invest in a minute."

"Half a minute," Rupert agreed. "I'd pull out my check book right now."

Jay was tempted to ask him if he spelled "check" with a *q*. He was even more tempted to ask him to pull out his check book, regardless of how he spelled it. "Frankly, I'm looking for investors," he said impulsively. Holy shit, these two very rich men had money to burn. And Jay was eager to break Bloom's wide, to expand to the East Side, to open a truly superior gourmet emporium.

Not just eager to open such an emporium, but to run it himself. He should be the president of Bloom's, but instead he was answering to his niece—whom he loved, of course, she was his niece, for God's sake—but she was only, what, thirty years old? An amateur. A fucking lawyer. What did she know about the food business?

Screw expanding Bloom's. If these guys truly wanted to front him, he'd open his own superior gourmet emporium. He'd compete. And he'd damned well win the competition.

"So...seriously, guys, if you're looking for a place to plant some money, here I am."

"You want us to invest in Bloom's?" Gil's manicured silver eyebrows shot up. "Don't tell me Bloom's is in financial trouble."

"Oh, it's not," Jay assured them. "My niece is running the place, with my mother behind the scenes pulling the strings. But I'm there, keeping an eye on things, making sure they don't make any mistakes. No, I'm thinking of branching out, starting my own store."

"What store might that be?" Rupert asked.

"Something classy," Jay said. Something on the Upper East Side, where he lived. Where classy people lived. "More refined food. Crumpets instead of bagels." He wasn't sure what a crumpet was, but it sounded British.

"Are we discussing a branch of Bloom's?"

"A separate entity. Something all my own. Something my mother wouldn't be involved in." Because his mother had screwed him. She'd stabbed him in the back. When Ben had died, she could easily have named Jay the president of Bloom's. She *should* have named Jay the president of Bloom's. Like the Royal Family in Rupert's home country, assuming he really was a Brit. Jay was second in line for the throne, and when Ben died, Jay should have ascended. He should have received the crown.

Except that if he was using the British Royal Family as his model, the crown would have been passed, upon Ben's death, to Ben's first-born. That would be Julia. Damn it.

Okay, forget the British Royal Family. Jay should have been named the president, because Julia knew *bupkis* about retail. She'd had to learn on the job—and Jay had been the one to teach her.

Of course, Sondra believed *she'd* been the one to teach Julia. But Sondra was a bitch. And she was a Bloom only by marriage, which didn't count when you were considering royal lineage.

If it weren't for him, Bloom's wouldn't have any online presence at all. Or its Seder-in-a-Box. He'd been the one to come up with that idea: pack an insulated box with matzo, ground horseradish, *charoseth*, jars of matzo-ball chicken soup, bitter herbs, parsley greens, yarmulkes, and a symbolic shank, and express-ship it to customers. "Just add wine and serve"—that was the slogan he'd come up with. Bloom's shipped Seders-in-a-Box all over the world. Passover was almost upon them, and Bloom's income would see a nice bump in profits, thanks to him.

He was a genius. Why his mother couldn't acknowledge as much…well, that was probably a subject for a therapist's couch, but Jay saw no reason to pay someone two hundred bucks an hour to listen to him complain. As far as he was concerned, playing golf was the best therapy. He ought to be able to write off his club membership as a medical expense on his taxes.

"I tell you what," Gil said. "Let us see what we might be able to do for your store."

"We can do a great deal," Rupert added. "We've plenty of money to invest. But let's be discreet, shall we? Let's keep this under our bowlers."

"Right," Gil agreed. "We need to remain behind the scenes."

"Strictly *sub rosa*," Rupert said.

Jay nodded solemnly. "Of course, *sub rosa*," he promised. He'd look up what *sub rosa* meant later.

"Because we can get you the funding you need," Gil said.

"We know people," Rupert assured Jay.

Jay assumed that by that, Rupert meant they knew *people*. Big *machers*, people who traded in Upper East Side real estate.

Little did he realize, during that amazing round of Dewar's at the clubhouse that past weekend, that his own nephew knew people, too—or at least, knew of available retail space in the neighborhood. But Monday, through the open office doors, he'd heard Adam mention this retail space to Julia.

She'd dismissed him. Said no and sent him on his way.

It was one thing to disrespect her uncle, but another to disrespect her brother, who was a genius. Hadn't he gotten accepted into a doctoral program somewhere? Doctoral programs didn't accept morons.

From his office, Jay listened through his open door and Julia's as Adam pitched the idea, and he listened as she rejected the idea. Jay was already pissed off at Susie for not promoting Seder-in-a-Box in this week's advertising circular. If Adam's retail space was anywhere decent—no way would Jay open his emporium on Lexington Avenue in East Harlem; it had to be the right neighborhood, near the Metropolitan Museum of Art and Carl Schurz Park and Gracie Mansion—Jay was done. He was gone. Screw Bloom's, and his nieces and his bitchy sister-in-law. And his mother, who never appreciated him the way she'd appreciated Ben.

He set down his golf club—he'd been practicing putts in his office—and waylaid Adam steps from Julia's office. Grabbing the kid's elbow, he ushered Adam into his office and shut the door. "Where's this retail space?" he asked. "Why didn't you tell me about it?"

"I just found out about it," Adam explained. "This girl I've been seeing mentioned it and I checked it out online. It looks okay."

"Is it in East Harlem?"

Adam shook his head. "Somewhere in the sixties. I've got the address..." He poked his hands into assorted pockets in his trousers and pulled out a scrap of paper, which he handed to Uncle Jay. "Here. You can Google it. It looks real good."

Jay took the shred of paper and tucked it safely into the chest pocket of his shirt. "You and me, Adam," he whispered. "Let's do this."

Adam looked bewildered. "Do what?"

All right, so the boy was a genius but a little slow. "Open an East Side food outlet."

"Julia said—"

"Julia isn't God. Just tell me—if I can pull this off, are you in?"

"In what?"

A lot slow. "Opening an East Side food outlet."

"A Bloom's branch? Like, a franchise?"

"We'll work out the details. Just tell me, are you in? Because I'm going for it."

"Well...sure," Adam said.

"Okay. Great. Don't tell anyone until I work out the details."

"But Julia said—"

"Trust me, Adam." He wanted to kiss Adam on his forehead, one of those kisses uncles gave their nephews when they got bar mitzvahed. But Adam looked a little alarmed, and Jay thought a kiss might spook him. "This will all work out great," he said, instead. "We'll be partners."

"Really?"

No, not really. Unequal partners, maybe. Jay would be the president. The head honcho. The *macher*. But he'd need Adam's expertise, and his youth. His energy. His strong, sturdy back, and his almost-PhD brain.

"I'm your uncle," Jay reminded him. "I'm going to make us both—" He cut himself off before saying "rich." He didn't think that would persuade Adam. "Proud," he said, instead.

Adam smiled. "Okay."

Jay gave him the uncle-of-the-bar-mitzvah-boy kiss then, which startled Adam but didn't seem to displease him. Then, with a swagger that seemed to originate somewhere in the vicinity of his balls, Jay strode down the hall from his office to Julia's to tell her he was quitting.

Chapter Three

In Sondra's mind, the terms "good" and "bad," when applied to food, had nothing to do with how that particular food tasted. They had to do with how fattening the food was. By that measure, celery sticks were clearly "good," and butter pecan ice-cream with hot fudge sauce and whipped cream was clearly "bad," even though it tasted a hell of a lot better than celery sticks.

The adjectives used to describe food applied to Sondra as well. Last night she'd been bad. She'd consumed a dinner of mac-and-cheese from a box—after many years of making boxed mac-and-cheese, she remained in awe of the fact that cheese could be reduced to a dusty orange powder and then reconstituted to gooey, cheesy sauce in a pot—accompanied by two very large martinis, and for dessert a bowl of butter pecan ice-cream and plain chocolate syrup, because she didn't have any hot fudge sauce or whipped cream handy.

Bad food. Bad Sondra. Very bad.

So today she was munching on celery sticks like a rabbit and hoping to redeem her soul, and while she was at it, her tush. She wasn't fat, but her bottom spread out from her pelvis like two round blobs of yeasty dough. Luckily, it was behind her so she didn't have to look at it very often.

If she ate enough celery sticks, maybe her tush would flatten into yeast-free matzo.

A strand of celery wedged between two back molars. She dug around in her purse for the small container of floss which she'd gotten for free from her dentist at her last check-up. Ice cream did not get stuck in her molars, she thought ruefully as she threaded a length of floss between her teeth and loosened the piece of celery. What did people who didn't have private offices do at such times? Did they floss in front of their co-workers? Or did they just not eat celery while they worked?

Her molars restored, she discarded the floss and returned her focus to the payroll print-out on her desk. Julia had named her a vice-president when she herself had been named president—the position Sondra ought to have received, given that she'd worked at Bloom's pretty much her entire married life, without pay, without recognition, without anything but the knowledge that she was helping her husband. She'd done it for the family, and bless Julia for finally acknowledging her contributions to Bloom's, not only with the title and a generous salary but also with a floss-worthy private office. Back when Ben was running the place, Sondra used to work either on the couch in Ben's office, her papers spread on the scuffed coffee table in front of her, or upstairs in her apartment on the twenty-fourth floor of the Bloom Building. It was a fabulous apartment—three bedrooms, not counting the maid's room off the kitchen, which Susie had taken over so she and Julia wouldn't have to share a bedroom, and also so she could have her own bathroom. Because Sondra was a Bloom by marriage, she got to pay the family rent, which was absurdly low and went into a family trust, so in a sense she was paying rent to her kids, her ghastly mother-in-law, her equally ghastly brother-in-law, and also, indirectly, herself.

Her apartment was directly below Ida's, which had always made her uneasy. Not that she expected her ceiling to break abruptly one day, causing Ida to plummet through the shattered plaster and land in Sondra's living room. Prewar buildings like the Bloom Building were built to last. Also, Ida was a Bloom, which meant that she, like her sons and Sondra's children, were blessed with the kind of metabolism that enabled them to eat all the butter-pecan sundaes they could possibly wish for, without having their tushes puff up like unbraided *challah*. Ida simply didn't weigh enough to fall through her floor and into Sondra's apartment.

But when Ben had been alive, Sondra had always been afraid of arguing loudly with him. What if Ida could hear them through the ceiling? What if she spent her evenings on all fours, with her ear against a glass pressed to her parquet floor, listening while Ben and Sondra bickered about how much time Ben spent at the store, how he was too busy to attend Susie's third-grade play—a bowdlerized version of *Alice in Wonderland* in which Susie played the Queen of Hearts and got to shriek, "Off with her head!"—and how he seemed more receptive to his mother's edicts than Sondra's polite and invariably brilliant suggestions? There was just something icky about living below your mother-in-law.

Martha, Jay's first wife, also lived on the twenty-fourth floor, just down the hall from Sondra. Martha wasn't a Bloom, but it wouldn't occur to her to eat an ice cream sundae unless the ice cream had been made with unpasteurized milk from cows that had been fed only organic alfalfa. And anyway, Martha wouldn't give a damn about the size of her rear end. She wore baggy clothes and spent much of her time taking classes on esoteric subjects at the New School and hanging out at her women's club, where, Sondra assumed, all the other women also wore baggy clothes. But although neither she nor Martha were any longer married to a Bloom brother, they got to keep their apartments in the Bloom Building, which was something.

Sondra deserved more than something. She deserved the presidency of Bloom's. At least her daughter had gotten the nod from Ida. It could have been worse. Ida could have named one of Jay's sons the president. And God help them all if she had. Those boys knew nothing about how to run a store, let alone a landmark emporium like Bloom's.

When Julia had made Sondra a vice-president, she'd requested that her mother run the store's Human Resources Department. As far as Sondra was concerned, "human resources" was just a fancy name for "personnel," which was where female executives used to go to die, before feminism allowed them to become presidents of companies.

On the other hand, Sondra was good with humans, and with resources. And really, other than being a little resentful and envious of her daughter's effortless svelteness, she was very proud of Julia. Susie, too. The business was flourishing. The showcase windows Susie designed were funky and eye-catching. Julia's weekly meetings might not be precisely necessary, but they kept everyone in the executive offices on the third floor communicating and aware of what was getting done and who was doing it, and they were always catered with bagels from the store.

Another plus about being the vice-president of Human Resources was that Sondra knew how much everyone earned. Jay and Deirdre were not earning more than she was. That was important.

And her responsibilities notwithstanding, she still had input into other facets of the business. Like the tea towels Bloom's was selling in the second-floor house-wares department. Sondra had nothing against tea towels, but they seemed a little too adorable to her. Dish towels were thicker, textured. A tea towel was just a dish-towel-sized rectangle of starched muslin with a cutesy design on it. Sondra had seen people use tea towels as dish towels. But dish towels worked better. And she'd never seen anyone use a tea towel to wipe up spilled tea.

Deirdre seemed to believe the store should carry more tea towels. She'd found a supplier who printed tea towels with colorful still-life images. Suitable for framing, Sondra had thought as she'd checked out the supplier's website, but really, who'd use them for tea time? Who in America even observed tea time? The only "tea time" people around here cared about had to do with golf dates.

Tea time—and tee time, too—both seemed *goyish* to Sondra. Which wasn't a negative by any means, but *goyish* wasn't in the genetic make-up of Bloom's. True, the store sold plenty of gourmet teas. But she imagined those teas were consumed like coffee, with meals or at a person's desk while at work. They weren't brewed for special sit-downs with cucumber sandwiches at four in the afternoon. At that hour of the day, Bloom's customers were toiling at their jobs or else wandering the store's aisles, shopping for that night's supper.

Let Deirdre deal with the tea towels, Sondra decided. Deirdre probably should have raised the subject at that morning's meeting—during which Sondra had consumed a pumpernickel bagel with only the thinnest *schmear* of cream cheese, so it ought to qualify as a good food, even if the bagel was as dark as chocolate.

A chocolate doughnut it wasn't. Bagels weren't sweet enough to be a bad food.

But the meeting had been dominated by Adam's report on the warehouse space Bloom's rented in Long Island City. "With other retailers considering locating in Queens," he'd said, "we should probably lock into a long-term lease. Rentals are going to go up."

"Or else we could find warehouse space over the bridge in Fort Lee," Deirdre had suggested.

"Have you seen the traffic on the bridge? Our merchandise would rot by the time it got here," Jay had argued. Since he was the only person at the meeting who owned a car, he knew a lot more about traffic jams on the George Washington Bridge than anyone else at the meeting.

"Maybe Staten Island," Susie had said.

"Sure. And we can rent rowboats to get our inventory up to the store. Or maybe gondoliers." Jay had been particularly negative at the meeting. But then, he was chronically negative. How he and Ben could have been brothers... Well, Ben hadn't exactly been an angel, either. As the spawn of Ida Bloom, they were both genetically flawed. They hadn't chosen their mother. It wasn't their fault. Or so Sondra told herself.

She plucked another celery stick from the self-sealing bag she'd stashed in the top drawer of her desk. She had just bitten down on it when Julia's voice interrupted her. "Mom?"

She spun in her chair to find Julia entering her office. Julia could have yelled from her own office, but clearly she'd come bearing unpleasant news—perhaps news too awful to scream from office to office about. She looked so stricken, so pale and wide-eyed, Sondra almost choked on her celery. Another fiber got trapped between her molars. "What's wrong?"

Julia entered the office and flopped into the visitor's chair beside Sondra's desk. "Uncle Jay is gone."

Was that all? Big deal. Not worth getting celery stuck in your teeth. Sondra wondered if she could floss in front of her daughter. "He likes to leave early," she said, trying to keep the tip of her tongue from toying with the trapped strand of celery. "God forbid he should put in a full day."

"No, I mean he's gone."

"Golfing, probably," Sondra said, swallowing a bubble of bitterness. It irked her that Julia—her own beloved daughter—had given Jay the same title as Sondra, even though Sondra was smarter, more capable, and much more diligent. Sondra took care of humans and resources. What did Jay take care of? The store's website? Adam could have done Jay's job as a high school student. He understood computers better than anyone else in the company.

"No, Mom. Listen to me. He's gone. He quit."

"Quit what?" Sondra asked.

Julia smiled faintly. "That was my first thought, too, when he told me he was quitting—what did he quit? But he quit *us*. He quit the store. He said *shalom* and walked out."

Sondra took a moment to process this. Had Jay actually given up his position? Had he actually left Bloom's for good?

And said *shalom*? That seemed pretty passive-aggressive.

She couldn't believe what Julia was saying. Jay Bloom would not abandon a job that paid him far too much—she knew exactly how much, thanks to the personnel files she had access to—for working so little. He would not walk away from the company that sustained the entire Bloom family. As exasperating as Ida Bloom could be, he would not betray his mother that way. Ida wouldn't let him. She was the puppet master, pulling all the strings

He lived an expensive life. He had his cute little trophy wife, who liked the finer things in life. He had his ex-wife Martha, who still received alimony. Until recently, he was still more or less supporting his son Rick, the *auteur* filmmaker who for years had lived on handouts despite his fancy degree from NYU's film school. Thank God the kid had finally landed a job with an ad agency, filming TV commercials. That was one expense Jay could remove from his budget.

But there were so many more. His hotshot sports car, and God knew what it cost to park the thing in Manhattan, let alone insure it. His fancy-schmancy country club membership out on Long Island. His co-op in the East Sixties. Unlike family members who lived in the Bloom Building, he didn't get any discounts on his housing costs.

She added things up and shook her head. "No, Julia. He wouldn't quit. He can't afford to."

"I don't know what he can or can't afford. Maybe he won the lottery or something."

"We would have heard. You think there are any secrets in this family?"

"I'm just saying—he quit. He's gone."

All right. Assume for one crazy moment that he really had quit and he really was gone. Was that such a loss? The guy was a *putz*. He wasn't exactly necessary to the running of the business. Adam and Susie could handle the online stuff, Adam the technical side of things and Susie the content. She did such a fine job with the *Bloom's Bulletin*. She was so artistic, and Adam was so computer savvy. And Julia was so responsible. Sondra had to admit that her children had turned out magnificently, all things considered. Since she'd done about ninety-nine percent of the child-rearing, she deserved credit for that.

If Jay was truly gone, Sondra's standing in the company would be enhanced. She'd be the only representative of the generation between Ida and Isaac, on one side, and her children on the other. Martha wanted nothing to do with the business, and Wendy was a bimbo. The Bimbette, her kids called Jay's current wife.

The hell with Wendy. The hell with Jay, too. Maybe with him out of the way, Julia would elevate Sondra to a co-presidency. Julia wouldn't have to worry about hurting his feelings, or keeping things fair between her mother and her uncle. Sondra's star could only rise.

"It's going to kill Grandma Ida," Julia said.

Another plus, Sondra thought as her tongue liberated the piece of celery from her teeth.

Chapter Four

Eight-thirty p.m. seemed too early to be feeling so tired. In the old days, Susie's nights used to be just getting under way at eight-thirty. She'd be energized, full of spirit, ready to pick a fight with anyone who looked at her the wrong way, ready to guzzle crappy booze and clap for the best poets of the evening, even when she privately thought that she was the best poet by far. She used to think that a lot.

When you wrote poetry, you had to be your own biggest fan. No one else was going to cheer for you, so you had to cheer for yourself.

Tonight she had the crappy booze, a glass of red wine so dry, it practically chafed her throat going down. She had her cousin Rick and her former roommate Anna for company. As usual, Rick seemed more interested in Anna than in Susie. Rick had been carrying a torch for Anna for so long, he ought to have third-degree burns on his hands by now. Anna found Rick periodically interesting, and now that he had a real job at an ad agency, filming the sort of schlocky commercials that only insomniacs watching local TV stations in the dead of night would ever see, he seemed to have risen in her esteem.

He and Anna didn't have much in common, though, other than Susie. Anna played the cello and worked as a substitute teacher while she waited for someone in a symphony orchestra to retire or die so she could take that musician's place. Unfortunately for her, cellists seemed to have long life expectancies. The substitute teaching gigs kept her solvent.

Rick had never professed much interest in classical music. But the fact that Anna was Chinese-American blew him away. "She's got the most incredible cheekbones," he'd gush to Susie. "And her fingers are so slender."

"That's probably from playing the cello. Her fingers get a lot of exercise," Susie explained.

"Did you ever notice how straight and black her hair is?" he'd add, ignoring Susie's comment about the cello.

Of course she'd noticed Anna's hair. They'd been roommates for a few years. Susie had noticed Anna's straight black hair in the shower drain enough times not to be anywhere near as enamored of it as Rick was.

Anna wasn't seeing anyone else right now, so she'd agreed to join Susie and Rick at this dreary basement club in the Meatpacking District, where a poetry slam was taking place. It was Susie's first poetry slam since Casey had opened Casey's Gourmet Breads and their nightlife had turned into, if not night death, then night coma.

Casey's entrepreneurial ambition delighted her, but it sure screwed up their old routines. No more attending the late showing of some obscure art-house movie at Cinema Village. No more hanging out at dive bars into the wee hours with Casey's best friend Mose and his girlfriend LaShonna, or with Anna and Susie's other former roommate, Caitlin, and whoever Anna and Caitlin were with at the moment. Or Anna and Rick.

Thanks to Casey's Gourmet Breads, Susie and Casey were early to bed, early to rise, like monks.

Well, not quite monks. They still got to have sex. But it was evening sex, not dark-depths-of-night sex.

She used to love having sex with him at two in the morning. They'd both stir, as if awakened by a sound only they could hear: the sound of mutual lust. They'd go at it happily, giddily, wildly, and then she would melt against Casey's body like a pat of butter on a roll fresh out of the oven, and they'd fall back to sleep.

Ever since he'd opened his business, however, they had to make love in the early evening. He was usually fast asleep by nine or nine-thirty, and when he woke up in the middle of the night, it was to get dressed and head to the shop, to fire up the ovens and bake the up-coming day's inventory.

They wouldn't be having sex tonight, because she was here and he was back at their cramped apartment in the East Village, just a few blocks from the place she'd shared with Anna and Caitlin but a world away from his former apartment in Queens—bless him for moving to Manhattan so Susie wouldn't have to move to Queens. "Go to the poetry slam," he'd urged her. "You'll have fun. Just don't wake me up when you come home."

Like an old married couple. Like a couple that wasn't okay. Julia's words haunted Susie.

This awful wine was going to haunt her, too. It was going to give her heartburn and turn her tongue blue. She took another sip because it was all she had to power her through the evening. Even though it tasted awful, its alcohol content might do something for her.

Rick was quietly mocking the guy currently reciting. Susie couldn't hear Rick—his mockery was for Anna's ears only, and Anna was laughing. Susie had to assume Rick's whispered comments were the source of Anna's amusement, because the poem the guy was declaiming into the microphone wasn't the least bit funny. *"I saw you die. I watched you die. I lived your death as the firefly lives the fire."* That made no sense, but even if it did, it wouldn't be tickling Anna's funny bone.

Also, the guy was dressed like a street mime, in a tight-fitting, long-sleeved T-shirt with horizontal stripes, and trousers with red suspenders, and a slouchy fedora. Definitely not funny.

Susie drank some more wine and stewed. Was her relationship with Casey in trouble? Was it good or bad that she was here and he was home in bed alone? The alone part was definitely good—if he were home in bed *not* alone, their relationship would definitely be in trouble. But still, they were too young to be not spending their evenings doing stuff together. Thinking of the bed as a place to sleep instead of a place to have hot, sweaty sex was supposed to happen after years of marriage and children and arguments over money had worn them out.

Susie's parents' marriage hadn't been so great, and they'd spent all their time together, not just at home but downstairs at Bloom's. Susie's father had been the president of the company and her mother had been his assistant, his gofer, his keeper. The arrangement would have seemed claustrophobic to Susie if she'd thought much about it, but as a kid, she was happy to do her homework on the floor of her father's office, or to run up and down the aisles of the store, or sometimes to sneak downstairs to the basement, where inventory was stashed on towering shelves and meats, salads, and kosher-style entrees were prepared in a professional kitchen as brightly lit as an operating room, despite the absence of windows. Susie used to enjoy watching the ladies—they were nearly all ladies back then—dressed in yellow smocks and hair nets chattering away in assorted Eastern European tongues while they worked. Some of the women baked sweets—*rugelach, hamantaschen, mandelbrot*—and if they spotted Susie spying on them, they'd sneak her a treat.

How could she be bothered caring about the state of her parents' marriage when the ladies in the hair nets were slipping her a couple of *hamantaschen* stuffed with poppy seeds?

Only as an adult did she realize her parents might not have been the happiest husband and wife in the universe. But married couples working together was the way Blooms did things. Grandma Ida and Grandpa Isaac had founded Bloom's together. Susie's parents had run the place together. She was simply following Bloom family tradition by working with Casey at his bread shop.

The thought that she was following Bloom family tradition was even scarier than the possibility that her relationship with Casey might be in trouble.

It wasn't as if she worked at Casey's Gourmet Breads full-time or exerted any authority. She spent her hours there behind the front counter, bagging fresh loaves of rye or sourdough, counting out bagels, placing muffins in neat rows in boxes made of 100% recycled paper—she'd insisted on that—and handing out receipts when the customers slid their credit cards into the chip reader. Casey's carrot-bread muffins were a big seller. People seemed to think they were healthy because they contained carrots.

She liked working at the bakery. She liked chatting with the customers, and she liked helping to make Casey's dream come true. He had hired a couple of other clerks who rotated shifts with Susie, but his business was still fairly new, and not exactly drowning in profits. It wasn't drowning in losses, either, and Mose, who was also Casey's business advisor, assured Casey he was doing just fine for a new enterprise. But he wasn't doing as well as, say, a tech genius who developed a cool app and sold it to Facebook for five billion dollars.

Susie and Casey didn't fight about money, at least. She'd grown up comfortably affluent—the big apartment in the Bloom Building, private school, four years at Bennington. She received a modest income from the trust that owned the Bloom Building, and Julia paid her a decent salary for her work at the store, even though she was there only part-time.

Sex between Susie and Casey was still good, even if it happened a little less spontaneously and too early in the evening. He was still the best cook she'd ever met, thanks to his degree from the Culinary Institute of America. Looking at him still turned her on, and eating the meals he prepared turned her on even more.

But... Could they be in trouble? Could everything be not so terribly okay?

The guy who was alive like a firefly finally wound down. The audience greeted him with a polite smattering of applause. Rick and Anna continued to whisper and giggle. Was their relationship—which didn't even exist, really—in better shape than Susie's relationship with Casey? Anna had told Susie on multiple occasions that, while she thought Rick was a terrific guy, he wasn't the guy for her. On the other hand, now that he worked for the Glickstein Agency, he dressed better. He'd jettisoned the pretentious camera lens he used to wear on a cord around his neck, as if he needed it to frame every single thing that came into his field of vision, just in case he was moved to launch into a new film project that instant. He earned enough money to stop mooching off everyone all the time. Anna didn't have to pay for the drinks anymore. Maybe that was enough to win her heart.

The applause died down in time for Susie to detect a buzz coming from her purse. Her cell phone was alive like a mosquito, not a firefly. She pulled it from the depths of her bag, hoping Casey wasn't calling to tell her he thought their relationship was not okay.

Not Casey. A text from Julia: *Can you talk?*

Susie typed back: *No.*

Before she could get the phone back into her bag, it buzzed again, vibrating against her fingers. She read Julia's message: *It's important.*

Susie translated that to mean that even though she'd just told Julia she couldn't talk, she was going to have to talk. She sighed and interrupted the happy schmooze-fest between Rick and Anna. "I've got to call Julia," she told them.

"Everything all right?" Rick asked.

Nice of him to be concerned. "I'll find out," she said, waving her phone at them as she pushed away from the tiny round table. She wove a path to the alcove where the restrooms were located and entered one.

It was a one-seater, thank goodness. She locked the door, rested her hips against the sink because the toilet looked a little too scuzzy to sit on, and tapped Julia's number.

"I'm sorry to bother you," Julia said, sounding not the least bit sorry. "We're having a crisis here."

"Is Mom okay? Something with Ron?"

"No. Uncle Jay."

Uncle Jay? As far as Susie was concerned, nothing about Uncle Jay could possibly be important. "What happened? Did he throw a hissy fit because I wouldn't put the Seder-in-a-Box promo on the first page of the bulletin?"

"I don't know. Maybe that was it. Can you talk?"

They'd already covered the can-you-talk issue while texting. No, Susie couldn't talk. She was trapped inside an ugly, minuscule bathroom that smelled like a rancid blend of Pine-Sol and urine, and any minute, she might be summoned to the stage to demonstrate to the miming firefly and all the other thirty or so people in the room how poetry was supposed to be done. "I'm at a slam with Rick and Anna right now," she said.

"Oh—you're with Rick? I don't want you discussing this with him."

"I don't know what I'm not discussing."

"We'll have a meeting tomorrow morning in my office."

"We had a meeting today." Julia hosted her meetings every Monday. Susie couldn't recall ever having to attend a meeting on a Tuesday.

"Well, we're going to have another meeting tomorrow. We'll figure it out then. Nine o'clock. Don't be late."

Susie was finally pursuing an evening activity that didn't involve watching Casey fall asleep. She had thought she might actually take a walk on the wild side and stay out past eleven. She'd figured she could sleep in tomorrow. She'd gotten next week's *Bloom Bulletin* written. She wasn't even supposed to be at Bloom's tomorrow morning. She'd planned to write some poetry once Casey had left to bake his bagels and bread and she had the apartment to herself.

"Do I really have to be there?"

"Yes. It's a crisis," Julia said ominously. "I'll see you tomorrow."

Susie said good-bye, her words more courteous than her thoughts. Julia could be so bossy sometimes. Always the big sister, always lording over Susie. Now she was the hot-shot honcho of Bloom's, and Susie was fine with that—or she'd be fine with it as long as she didn't feel like Julia's underling, her frickin' *employee*, forced to obey her commands.

If this was really and truly a crisis, maybe Susie ought to cut her sister a little slack.

But if it had to do with Uncle Jay, how could it be a crisis? If he wasn't dead and hadn't killed anyone, Susie failed to see why she should have to rearrange her entire life—or at least her Tuesday morning—just to attend one of Julia's stupid meetings.

She took consolation in the understanding that there would be bagels at the meeting. Casey's own homemade bagels, since he was still under contract to supply his best-in-the-whole-damned-world bagels to Bloom's. That contract brought in a significant percentage of the shop's income. Susie should be grateful.

She was. Just not grateful enough to attend Julia's meeting without being pissed about it.

She'd go, if only to avoid becoming Julia's next crisis. But she damned well wouldn't be smiling.

Chapter Five

Myron Finkel was the first to arrive for Julia's Tuesday morning meeting. He entered her office, a bald, wizened man in a herringbone-tweed jacket that might have fit him back when such a garment was in fashion, but now hung on him as if his shoulders boasted the dimensions of a wire hanger. "No bagels?" were the first words out of his mouth.

"Deirdre's downstairs getting some," Julia assured him.

She knew Myron attended her meetings mainly because he wanted the bagels she served as an inducement. Given that he had little to contribute to the meetings, Julia felt a charitable satisfaction in feeding him a Bloom's treat. He was partial to fruit-flavored bagels and whined that his wife made him eat oatmeal for breakfast. "Not the fancy stuff they sell downstairs," he'd elaborate. "The stuff that comes in the round cardboard box. You're supposed to add salt when you cook it, but she won't. 'Blood pressure,' she says. Without salt, it has no taste. And God forbid I add sugar!" He would shake his head in dismay.

So he feasted on bagels at the meetings. Julia figured that what his wife didn't know wouldn't hurt her. The bagels didn't seem to be hurting Myron.

He lowered himself to the sofa, occupying the end nearest Grandpa Isaac's desk. Sondra usually occupied the other end of the sofa. But today, one of them was going to have to sit elsewhere. This meeting would not go well if Grandma Ida had to sit on a hard chair, and Julia couldn't imagine her happily wedging herself between Sondra and Myron. She'd demand at least half the sofa as her due.

The meeting would not go well no matter where Grandma Ida sat. But Julia figured that announcing Uncle Jay's defection to everyone at one time might be easier than informing them individually. Perhaps they could brainstorm a strategy to fill his position quickly. It wasn't as if Uncle Jay was the center tent pole holding up the entire company, but Passover was approaching, and online orders for Seder-in-a-Box were one of Uncle Jay's responsibilities. The store needed to hire someone who could take over Uncle Jay's job ASAP.

She gave Myron a phony smile, which was wasted on him as he stared dolefully at the center of the coffee table, where he'd hoped to find bagels. Barely a minute after he'd settled himself onto the couch's sagging leather upholstery, Deirdre transformed his despair into ecstasy, sweeping into the office with a large plate heaped high with bagels in one hand, in the other an insulated carafe of coffee, and two tubs of cream cheese wedged between her elbows and her waist, one on each side. After two years of working with her, Julia remained in awe of Deirdre, not only for her expertise regarding Bloom's but for her ability to deliver food like a trained waitperson while wearing shoes with three-inch stiletto heels. Deirdre didn't need the extra height her shoes gave her; she towered over everyone in Bloom's inner circle except Uncle Jay, who wouldn't be present, and Adam, who probably matched her inch for inch in bare feet but lost to her once she slid her feet into those precarious shoes. The high heels, combined with her snug-fitting slacks and bright pink sweater, gave her the appearance of a flamingo.

Susie arrived next, wearing a scowl that was undoubtedly much more genuine than Julia's smile. "Thanks a heap," were her first words.

Not wanting to ignite a conflagration before she dropped her bomb, Julia stretched her phony smile even wider. "You're very welcome," she said, although she had no idea what Susie was sarcastically thanking her for.

"I had to leave the poetry slam early last night," Susie enlightened her. "If I'd stayed as late as I'd wanted to, I wouldn't have been able to wake up in time for this stupid meeting."

"It's not a stupid meeting." Julia's cheeks were beginning to cramp.

"It's not a stupid meeting," Sondra echoed as she entered the office. Unlike the others, she knew about Uncle Jay's departure. Julia had confided in her yesterday. Julia would have confided in Susie, too, if Susie hadn't been at her poetry slam and unable to talk. As far as Julia was concerned, poetry slams were a lot stupider than any meeting she'd ever hosted.

Susie eyed their mother and her frown intensified. "You know what this meeting's about?"

"We'll all know soon enough," Sondra said. Her smile slid past Julia's on the genuine scale, although it hinted at smugness. Evidently, she relished the fact that she knew about Uncle Jay before everyone else did. Or else she was just plain thrilled that he was gone.

Susie plucked an everything bagel from the platter and carried it to Grandpa Isaac's desk. After hoisting herself up to sit on it, she took a fierce bite of the bagel and swung her black-denim-clad legs back and forth, kicking one of the drawers with the heels of her black canvas sneakers. Maybe once her breath was reeking of onions and garlic from the bagel, she'd feel better.

Maybe, like Sondra, Susie would feel better yet when Julia announced Uncle Jay's departure. Maybe Julia would be the only person upset about his resignation.

No, Grandma Ida would be upset. Very upset.

Grandma Ida was the main reason Julia had arranged this meeting. She'd been too cowardly to ride up the elevator to Grandma Ida's apartment and tell her about Uncle Jay, one on one. She needed the insulation of her executive staff. If Grandma Ida freaked out, if she started raging or weeping or had a stroke, Julia didn't want to be alone with her.

Sondra helped herself to a plain bagel, probably assuring herself it had fewer calories than the flavored ones, and dropped into Julia's desk chair. Julia could interpret that to mean her mother felt like leading the meeting or else she realized that Grandma Ida needed a seat on the couch. Julia hoped her second interpretation was the correct one. If ever she had to maintain her authority as Bloom's president, now was the time. She loved her mother but she didn't trust the woman. Sondra had never bothered to hide her disappointment that Grandma Ida had tapped not her but Julia to take over the top spot when Julia's father died.

"Where's Adam?" Susie asked between bites of her bagel. "If I have to be here, he has to be here."

"He said he'd be here." Julia peered through her office door, then glanced at her mother again. Sondra looked far too comfortable in Julia's chair.

Let her sit there. Julia would stand. Standing would make her appear totally in charge. She only wished what she was in charge of wasn't an impending catastrophe.

"I don't think Jay's arrived for work yet," Deirdre remarked as she handed Myron one of the two plastic knives she'd stowed in the back pocket of her slacks, and also a tub of strawberry-flavored cream cheese.

He helped himself to a blueberry bagel and smeared it with the pink-hued cream cheese. "So patriotic," he crowed, holding his colorful concoction up for everyone to view. "I've got the red and the blue. All I need is a little white."

"There's plain cream cheese," Deirdre said helpfully, nudging the other tub toward him.

Adam appeared in the doorway, mildly unkempt, his eyelids slightly droopy and his expression bland. Unlike Susie, he apparently hadn't chosen to curtail his late-night activities to attend this meeting; he looked sleepy and hung over. Hands buried in the pockets of his cargo pants, he shuffled across the office to Grandpa Isaac's desk. Instead of sitting beside Susie, though, he only leaned against it. Maybe he didn't want to run the risk of getting kicked by her kinetic feet.

"I'm here," he said, sounding less than thrilled. "Let's get started."

"We're waiting for one more person," Julia said, and then she saw Grandma Ida making her way through the open area connecting the offices, one hand securely hooked around Lyndon's elbow. Lyndon Rollins was Grandma Ida's personal assistant. He managed Grandma Ida's apartment, cooking, cleaning, running errands for her, and helping her navigate the many TV channels her cable service provided—"It's too much," she often complained. "Who needs to watch so many shows? They're all *drek*, anyway." He escorted her when she required escorting. He amused her when she required amusing and chided her when she required chiding. He was calm and good-natured, and he maintained his sense of humor around Grandma Ida, which was truly a remarkable accomplishment. If he weren't

gay, Julia would have proposed marriage to him. She
wouldn't have cared that he was black and Christian;
his partner was white and Jewish, so he wouldn't have
held those things against Julia. He claimed he did love
her, except not sexually.

He served as an island of sanity in the raging sea of
Bloom family *mishegas.* Even her own white, Jewish,
heterosexual husband was rarely an island. A beach-
head, maybe. A buoy. A bagel-shaped life preserver
bobbing on the waves. Not a whole island.

He'd barely even been a pair of inflatable water
wings last night. She had brought home some Heat-
'N'-Eat stuffed cabbage for dinner, and they'd opened
a bottle of wine, and then he'd spent most of dinner
kvetching about his stupid blog post, and his demanding editor, and how he was due for a raise. Julia had
mentioned Uncle Jay's abrupt resignation, and Ron
had said, "Good riddance. He was just dead weight,
anyway." Then he'd gone back to complaining about
his editor, comparing her to oleander. "She's pretty but
poisonous. Get too close to her, and she'll give you a
rash." As if asking him to write his blog post on deadline was a toxic thing for an editor to do.

Julia bet Lyndon would have been more sympathetic.

If he stayed for the meeting, she'd find out just how
sympathetic he could be.

But no. He offered a general smile to everyone as
he led Grandma Ida to her place on the sofa, as re-
gal as a father escorting his daughter down the aisle
to meet her groom. Then he kissed Julia's cheek, and
she thought once again about what a shame it was that
he was gay and she was already married. "I'm heading downstairs to pick up a few items," he said. "Shoot
me a text when your meeting is over, and I'll come for

her." Pivoting gracefully, he leaned down to murmur to Grandma Ida, "Have fun."

"Don't buy the Nova downstairs," she said. "They charge an arm and a leg for it."

Nobody pointed out that the body parts Bloom's charged for its smoked salmon meant bigger profits for the Bloom family—including Grandma Ida, who still drew a generous stipend from the business. Nor did Julia mention that the price Bloom's charged for its lox was in line with that of other delis, and their lox was of a much higher quality—and it was sliced tissue-thin, unlike the lox at other delis, which was often served in thick, greasy slabs. She simply directed her fraudulent smile at her grandmother, who sat rigidly on the couch and glowered at no one in particular.

As usual, Grandma Ida was dressed dowdily, in a prim blouse, an A-line skirt, and opaque stockings. Her wrists were circled in gold bangle bracelets, because she'd read somewhere that copper bracelets alleviated arthritis and figured that if copper was good, gold had to be better. Her hair framed her face like an ominous cloud. Lyndon diligently ushered her to a salon once a month to have it colored. Julia wondered if the stylist used India ink on her grandmother's tresses, which were uniformly black.

"What is this, bagels?" Grandma Ida asked, gesturing toward the platter on the coffee table, her bracelets clanging. "You said a meeting, not brunch."

"It's just a snack while we talk."

"They're delicious," Myron said as he devoured the last of his festively colored bagel. "Bloom's makes the best bagels, hands down."

"Casey makes them," Susie muttered, tearing off a piece of her bagel and popping it in her mouth. "And I should be downtown at his bakery instead of up here right now."

"A snack at a meeting? I never heard of such a thing." Grandma Ida clicked her tongue. "A meeting. When Isaac and I were running this place, we never had meetings."

"Well, we *do* have meetings," Julia said. Already the tension was escalating, and she hadn't even shared her awful news. "And I'm glad you're here, Grandma Ida. I called this meeting because I have an announcement to make."

"You're pregnant?" Grandma Ida squinted at Julia's abdomen as if searching for a bump.

"No."

"If it has to do with computers, I give up," Myron said as he reached for another bagel.

"It has to do with Uncle Jay."

"He isn't here," Deirdre unnecessarily reminded everyone.

"That *shiksa* wife of his." Grandma Ida sniffed. "She distracts him."

"He isn't here, and it has nothing to do with his wife," Julia said, steering the discussion in the right direction before it got hopelessly detoured. "He's quit."

"Quit what?" Myron asked.

"I never knew he smoked," Deirdre said. "Unless he's quitting booze. I know he drinks."

"He's quitting Bloom's," Sondra declared, her tone oddly triumphant.

"What?" Grandma Ida turned her hawk-sharp gaze toward Sondra. Her scowl deepened. "You can't quit a family. You're born a Bloom, you're a Bloom. *You*," she added, "were not born a Bloom."

Sondra scowled back at Grandma Ida.

"He's resigned from his position at the store," Julia explained. She heard a quiver in her voice, as if tears were planning to bubble up and spill out. Swallowing hard, she did her best to steady her tone. She was the president, after all. She had to behave presidentially. "He didn't offer any reason. He just said he was leaving. He said *shalom,* so I assume he was leaving peacefully."

"He left the store? He left *here*?" Grandma Ida pressed her hand to her chest, as if pressure from her palm could keep her heart from bursting through her rib cage and landing in a tub of cream cheese. "That's *meshuge.* He can't do that."

"He isn't a slave, Grandma," Adam pointed out. "This is a free country. If he wants to leave, he can leave."

"But he's *family,*" Grandma Ida retorted.

"Besides, he's a vice-president," Susie said.

"*Was* a vice-president," Sondra corrected her. To Julia's great annoyance, her mother seemed much too pleased about using the past tense verb.

"He was a vice-president," Julia said, "and he had certain responsibilities. He was in charge of our online business, our mail-order business, our Seder boxes. And he's just walked away from everything we counted on him to do." She heard that quiver in her voice again. God help her if she started to sob. She swallowed some more. Maybe eating a bagel would steady her—but it would probably also make her throw up. Her stomach twisted with tension.

"He didn't give notice?" Myron seemed so shocked, he had to stop slathering cream cheese on his bagel for a moment. "You're supposed to give notice."

"He didn't give notice," Julia confirmed.

"Isn't that against the law?"

"What, you're going to arrest my son?" Grandma Ida challenged him. "My only surviving son, now that my Ben is *in drerd*? You're going to throw my Jay in jail?"

Myron looked suitably cowed. "I only meant, he should have given notice."

"Well, he didn't," Julia said. "He walked out yesterday. He didn't even negotiate a severance package."

"A servant's package?" Grandma Ida asked. "What's that?"

"Severance. What people negotiate when they're leaving a job."

"But they have to give notice," Myron insisted. "You don't get a severance package if you don't give notice."

"I don't believe it," Grandma Ida said with finality. "I don't believe my son would do this, and so close to *Pesach*. It must be a mistake."

"He didn't come in today," Deirdre reminded her.

"Eh. He used to skip school, too. He still got his degree."

Julia wasn't sure that analogy worked. For that matter, she wasn't sure Uncle Jay had actually earned his degree. He'd gone to Boston University and, according to her mother, majored in partying. But after four years, a dean had handed him his diploma—whether or not he'd earned it—and he'd returned to New York City, married Martha, fathered two sons, divorced Martha, married Wendy, and through it all pulled down a fat salary for spending between twenty-five and thirty hours a week puttering around Bloom's, pretending he was essential.

So what if he wasn't in fact all that essential? He was essential enough—because he was family. He was a Bloom. The store, the business, the entire enterprise housed within this building relied on the unity of the family. And Uncle Jay had shattered that unity.

"Let me speak to him," Grandma Ida said, gesturing toward the phone on Julia's desk. "I can talk some sense into him."

"When has anyone ever been able to talk sense into him?" Sondra argued.

"I'm his mother. I can tell him this is cockamamie, his quitting. He probably didn't mean anything, what he said yesterday."

"He probably doesn't even know what *shalom* means," Sondra muttered.

"Of course he does. He was bar mitzvahed. Give me the phone, Julia. Let me talk to him."

Julia reached for her cell phone and tapped it to summon Uncle Jay's phone number.

"I don't want that one," Grandma Ida objected, wagging a bony finger at Julia's cell. "I don't trust those phones. I heard somewhere they give you heartburn."

"Brain cancer," Myron corrected her.

"Cancer, schmancer. They give me heartburn. Give me the other phone, Julia—the real phone."

Julia plucked the cordless handset from her desk phone, read Uncle Jay's number on her cell phone screen, and punched it into the handset. Then she handed it to her grandmother.

Grandma Ida tucked the phone to her ear and listened. After a while, she lowered it to her lap. "No answer. Maybe he's still asleep."

"Being asleep never kept him from coming to work," Sondra grumbled.

"All right, so he's not answering his phone," Julia said, moving things along. "We're going to have to hire someone to replace him."

"How do you replace family?" Grandma Ida lamented. "How is such a thing possible? Family is family."

"No one is arguing that," Julia said gently, trying to gauge Grandma Ida's emotional state from her appearance. Her face was neither flushed nor pale. Her hands weren't shaking. The corners of her mouth turned down, but they usually did. She didn't look like someone on the verge of a stroke, although Julia had no idea what someone on the verge of a stroke was supposed to look like. To be sure, Julia felt more agitated than Grandma Ida looked. "If he's gone, we'll have to hire someone to do what he used to do here."

"Practice his golf putts?" Sondra made a face.

True, he did spend a fair amount of time in his office tapping a golf ball across the carpet and into a sideways glass. "The website," she reminded her mother and everyone else. "He managed our online sales."

"So we'll hire someone else to manage them," Sondra said.

"Right. You're our human resources person," Julia reminded her. "Hiring a—" she caught herself before saying *replacement* "—person to manage our online sales will be your job."

"*Mine*?" Suddenly Julia's mother didn't look so smug. "I handle payroll. Time sheets. Vacation schedules. All that insurance crap."

"And hiring," Julia reminded her. "Deirdre can help you with recruitment." Julia eyed Deirdre, who nodded. She'd get the job done. She was so damned dependable.

"Well, we're not hiring anyone at a vice-president level," Sondra said.

"Of course not," Julia said. "Just a manager of online sales."

"You have too many vice-presidents," Grandma Ida opined. "Why do you need so many vice-presidents? Even the president of the United States has only one vice-president."

"We won't be hiring another vice-president. Myron, you can do some research on the salary range for the position. We'll come up with a reasonable package. In the meantime..." She turned to face Grandpa Isaac's desk and her two siblings. "Susie and Adam, you'll have to fill in for Uncle Jay until we've got a—new website manager," she concluded, once again stopping herself before she used the word *replacement*. Grandma Ida seemed to be doing okay, but Julia didn't want to take any chances. Right now, Grandma Ida was more likely to have a stroke because she couldn't figure out how to redial Uncle Jay's number on the phone handset. She squinted at the buttons, pressed one, held the phone to her ear, shook her head, and pressed another button. For all Julia knew, she might actually be phoning someone in Botswana. Julia needed to get the phone away from her.

Before she could contemplate the long-distance charges her grandmother might be racking up, Susie and Adam erupted in a chorus of protest so coordinated, it seemed almost rehearsed. "Why are we getting stuck with Uncle Jay's responsibilities?" Susie fumed. "I can't take on anything more."

"No way," Adam harmonized. "I'm not overseeing the Seder-in-a-Box thing."

"I'm also working at Casey's Gourmet Breads," Susie pointed out.

"I'm still trying to drag the store's inventory management into the last century, let alone this one," Adam argued.

Julia held up her hands, hoping to silence them. "It's just temporary, to get us through Passover. I don't know if we'll be able to hire anyone before the holiday. Adam, you can do the website. You're a tech genius. And Susie, you can oversee the content. You're so good at that."

"It takes time to be good," Susie retorted. "I don't have any time."

"Then just plagiarize stuff from the *Bloom's Bulletin.*"

"Plagiarism is a crime," Myron said.

"Not if she's plagiarizing herself," Julia explained.

"I'm not going to plagiarize myself," Susie said. She was actually pouting. "You're trying to get me to go full time here, and I can't do that. If I can't continue my work at Casey's, he may have to cut back on his bagel production."

Julia saw no reason Susie's spending a few hours less a week working behind the retail counter of Casey's bakery should affect how many bagels he could make. But the possibility that Bloom's might not be fully supplied in fresh bagels clearly struck Myron as tragic. He gasped, blanched, and grabbed another bagel from the platter, as if afraid the pile might vanish before his very eyes.

"We can work things out with Casey," Julia said. "We all just need to be flexible until Mom can hire a new website manager."

"*Oy,*" Sondra moaned. She no longer seemed thrilled about Uncle Jay's defection. "It could take a while."

"Then we'll have to be flexible for a while."

Susie pouted. "I don't want to be flexible."

"I don't, either," Adam said.

For a moment, Julia imagined she and her siblings were children again. She was ten, Susie eight, Adam four. She was practically a teenager, very mature, sprouting tiny breasts that never exactly developed beyond small, but at age ten she'd seen those tiny buds as proof that she was now crossing over into adulthood. Her siblings were still children, though, and they pestered her. Susie made fun of Julia's developing taste for rock music. Adam left his damned Matchbox cars all over the apartment, where Julia could step on them and bruise the soles of her feet. Both of them seemed utterly incapable of rinsing out their shared bathroom sink after they brushed their teeth. It was always caked with dried blobs of sparkly children's toothpaste. When Julia would yell at them to clean up after themselves, Susie would call her a creep and Adam would throw Lego bricks at her.

She didn't want to bicker with Susie and Adam now. They were all adults, responsible for keeping the family enterprise solvent. Summoning another forced smile, she said, "Okay, everyone. Fill your cups with coffee, grab an extra bagel, and let's get to work."

Sondra shot her a helpless look, as if to say, *Really? I've actually got to hire someone?* Fortunately, Deirdre would be up to the task. They left together, the two women Julia's late father had most depended on in the world. Myron snagged another bagel before heading out of the office. He seemed chipper enough, given that Uncle Jay's resignation wouldn't demand anything extra of him, other than researching salary ranges. Grandma Ida remained on the couch, futilely pushing buttons on the telephone handset. "Here," Julia said gently, easing it from her grip. "I'll have Lyndon come and get you. You can call Uncle Jay from your own phone when you get upstairs."

"I can't believe he did this," Grandma Ida said. "It must be a mistake. My baby may be a *putz*, but he's a Bloom."

A blooming putz, Julia thought, but she only placed the handset back in its cradle and used her cell phone to text Lyndon.

"And you two," Grandma Ida said, glaring at Susie and Adam as they shoved away from Grandpa Isaac's desk. "Don't be *shtunks*. Help your sister out. She's trying to run a big store."

"Oh, yes, she's so important and busy," Susie snapped. "Unlike me."

"What's a *shtunk*?" Adam asked.

"We're fine," Julia assured Grandma Ida. She knew she was the favorite grandchild. Grandma Ida didn't have to increase Susie and Adam's resentment by reminding them of that fact. "Lyndon will be here soon."

"Lyndon is dependable," Grandma Ida said. "Jay, Jacob, my *schmegege* son, I don't know. I don't know what he could be thinking, why he would leave like this."

"He wanted his stupid Seder-in-a-Box on the front page of the *Bloom's Bulletin*," Susie said. "Now he's throwing a hissy fit."

"So put the Seder-in-a-Box on the front page," Grandma Ida scolded. "Is that such a big deal?"

"Julia made me the editor of the *Bulletin*. That means I get to decide what goes on the front page. And the *Bulletin* is every bit as important as the Seder-in-the-Box. Probably more important. It brings in money every week, not just at Passover." She thought a bit and added, "*I'm* important."

"You are," Julia said, trying to make Susie feel better, not just because that was what Julia did but because she really needed Susie's help until Uncle Jay could be replaced.

"I'm important, too," Adam remarked.

Honestly. Did they want raises in their allowances? A gummed gold star pasted next to their names? "Of course you're important," Julia assured her brother.

She'd never been more relieved to see Lyndon sweep through her office door. He carried a Bloom's tote bag filled with his purchases, and he was smiling.

"We'll eat well tonight, Ida," he promised Grandma Ida as he offered his hand to help her to her feet.

"You probably paid too much," she said. "Did you buy halvah?"

"I bought marble halvah and chocolate-covered halvah."

"Okay." She curled her fingers around his elbow. "I have to talk to my son Jay. He's done something very stupid."

"We all do stupid things sometimes. And we learn to forgive one another. It keeps us sane." Lyndon shot Julia a quick grin and then escorted Grandma Ida from the office.

She wasn't sure anyone in this family was entirely sane. Reading the frowns on her brother's and sister's faces, she wasn't sure anyone was entirely forgiving, either.

"Guys," she addressed them, hating the plaintive undertone in her voice. "I need your support, okay?"

"Screw that," Susie said. "You need us to cover for Uncle Jay, who's an idiot. I don't have any time to spare. I'm overextended already."

That Susie could possibly think of herself as over-extended was ridiculous. She was a flake. She'd always been a flake. Before Julia had hired her, she'd been a waitress at a pizza parlor. She should be grateful to Julia for having hauled her into the land of responsible professional endeavors—so grateful she ought to volunteer to take on extra work until Uncle Jay's job was filled.

And Adam—just standing there, looking half-stoned. Julia wanted to smack them both, or maybe throw Lego bricks at them.

No she didn't. She wanted to cry. But she couldn't do that, either. She had to be strong. She had to be a leader.

A tear trickled down her cheek. Damn it.

"Oh, stop," Susie said, her voice brimming with impatience. "It's just a job. It's just Uncle Jay. Get a grip."

"If this business falls apart, it's my fault. The whole family—you heard Grandma Ida. We're family."

"What's that expression?" Adam glanced at Susie. "You can choose your friends, but you can't choose your family. Something like that."

"I sure as hell didn't choose this," Susie snapped, storming out of the office. With a shrug and a smile that struck Julia as inappropriate under the circumstances, Adam followed Susie out.

Julia wondered if she could quit her own family and join Lyndon's instead. A family of forgiveness and sanity, gourmet cooking skills, and serenity. It would sure beat being a Bloom.

Chapter Six

A dam was confused.

He was also kind of...well, not exactly angry. Vexed. Baffled. Maybe a little ticked off. When they'd talked yesterday, Uncle Jay had left Adam with the impression that they were going to convince Julia to open an East Side branch of the store. Adam had assumed that Uncle Jay would succeed where he himself had failed. He'd tell Julia about the retail space on Lexington Avenue that Dulcie had mentioned to Adam, near where her parents lived, and explain the value of opening a branch of Bloom's there, and if all went well, Julia would say okay, let's look into it. Adam hadn't known Uncle Jay was actually going to *quit*.

If he'd quit, he had no intention of launching an East Side Bloom's outlet. He wasn't interested in expanding the family business. He was starting something new.

And he wanted Adam to be his partner.

Adam had witnessed Grandma Ida's inability to reach Uncle Jay during the meeting, but Uncle Jay's phone would have identified the call as coming from Julia's office line, so he might have simply chosen not to answer. Adam left the office suite and ducked into the stairwell. Then he pulled out his cell phone and tried Uncle Jay's number. Sure enough, Uncle Jay answered right away. "Adam!" he said cheerfully. "You'll never guess where I am!"

He wasn't at Bloom's, which might be why he sounded so cheerful. "The golf course?"

"Lexington Avenue, checking out the property you found. It's fabulous. The rent is a bit steep, but I've got financial backers. This is going to happen, Adam. *Jacob Bloom's Delectable Food Emporium.* What do you think? Classy, huh."

What Adam thought was that five words were at least two too many for the name of a store. How would all that verbiage fit on a sign, or in an advertisement? It would look like text rather than a title.

What he also thought was that if they were partners, maybe it shouldn't be named after Uncle Jay. As if anyone ever thought of Uncle Jay as *Jacob.*

Finally, what he thought was that if they were partners, Adam would have to quit Bloom's, too.

Quitting Bloom's wouldn't be a wrenching step, at least not to Adam. A year ago, he'd had no intention of joining the business. He'd been planning to move to Indiana, to pursue a doctorate in mathematics at Purdue—"Is that where the chickens come from?" Grandma Ida had wondered. "Not that we would carry those chickens. They aren't kosher." Adam's girlfriend from Cornell had been planning to join him in West Lafayette. She'd expected to keep busy hugging trees and protesting environmental degradation while he collected a modest stipend for playing with abstract concepts under the guidance of a professor as obsessed with numbers as Adam had been back then.

One summer in New York had changed all that, however. Because Julia had asked him, he'd agreed to spend the time between his graduation from Cornell and his departure for Purdue working in the store.

He'd met his first ballet student from Juilliard and discovered that—call him shallow—he liked lithe women
who shaved their legs. He also liked eating meat and
junk food. Tash had been passionate about saving the
planet, and somehow she'd believed that Adam could
destroy the planet merely by snacking on Cheese Doodles. Or, for that matter, knishes and kugel and some of
the other delicacies sold at Bloom's.

If Uncle Jay opened a store across town, could it
possibly sell food as tasty as what Bloom's offered?
And if the food wasn't as good as Bloom's food, what
was the point?

The point, he realized, was independence. It was
proving to Julia that she'd been wrong about refusing
to expand the Bloom's franchise.

And for Uncle Jay, it was probably also about
proving to Grandma Ida that he could be every bit as
successful as his brother Ben had been. As a younger brother, Adam could relate. Younger brothers had a
way of being overlooked and underestimated.

Still...leaving Bloom's? Could Adam do that to Julia?

He realized Uncle Jay was waiting for him to say
something. "So the store for rent looks good?"

"It looks perfect! Wait—hang on." Uncle Jay said
something to someone, then returned to the phone.
"One of my backers. He's from London. International
money, Adam. This could be big."

Was international money bigger than domestic
money? And how had Uncle Jay found a London finan-
cier? "Is he investing or just loaning you the money?"
he asked. "Because if he's investing, he's going to want
part ownership. And if he's loaning, he might charge a
lot of interest."

"What was I, born yesterday? This guy is the answer to all our prayers. He's got more money than he

knows what to do with. He needs to park it somewhere. Trust me, this is going to be amazing. I can already see the front windows, displaying only the best. That could be our slogan, Adam: *Only the best.* I love it. We can do funky things with the windows, like what Susie does with the Bloom's windows, only classier. We want this to be a class operation. Class all the way. Maybe that could be our slogan: *Class all the way.*"

"That sounds kind of like 'Jingle Bells,'" Adam argued.

"You're right. *Only the best.* I'll tell my backers."

"More than one backer? Are they both from London?"

"Don't worry about that. I'll take care of financing. You'll take care of inventory. And hiring. We'll need a classy staff. Do they have a career office at Cornell? We should hire Ivy League graduates, or the equivalent. I'm not saying Ivy League schools are the only places we should recruit, but they set a standard, am I right? We want a very high standard here. There's another slogan: *We set a high standard.*"

"I think we should think about more basic things first. The slogan will come later."

"You're right. That's why I need you as my partner, Adam. You're so basic. First we'll rent this store. Fantastic real estate. That's why I need you on board with me. You found our location."

"Shouldn't we have, I don't know, a business plan or something?" Adam had been friends with a few business majors at Cornell. Tash hadn't liked them—they were too capitalistic, according to her, and of course they were, because that was what majoring in business was all about. But they were smart, and they threw excellent parties, with expensive beer. Not that no-name light piss-water stuff, but flavorful beers. Gourmet beers.

Maybe Jacob Bloom's Delectable Food Emporium could sell gourmet beers. How did one go about getting a liquor license in New York City? You probably had to sleep with someone. Or kill someone. Adam might be willing to do the former, but definitely not the latter.

Uncle Jay's exuberant chatter dragged him back from bleak thoughts about murder to the immediate issue of this new enterprise. "We don't need a business plan," Uncle Jay insisted. "Did my parents have a business plan when they sold knishes from a pushcart? Did they have a business plan when they moved into the Bloom Building? No. They had vision. They had *chutzpah.* That's all you need to start something like this, Adam—vision and *chutzpah.*"

And maybe a couple of international financiers, Adam thought.

Did the financiers really just want to park their money somewhere, no strings attached? Did Uncle Jay really want to make Adam his partner? If Adam became Uncle Jay's partner, would he have to leave Bloom's? If he left Bloom's, what would Julia think? What would she do? What would Susie do if Adam stuck her with Uncle Jay's entire job? Would she have to quit working at Casey's place? Would they break up? Would she blame their breakup on Adam?

His brain was overheating, redlining. He needed to slow down.

But Uncle Jay was going so fast. He was used to speeding, scooting around town in his super-revved Beemer Z3, even though there was too much traffic in Manhattan to put the coupe's engine through its paces. When it came to starting his own business, Uncle Jay was flooring the gas pedal.

"Grandma Ida seemed pretty upset about your leaving Bloom's," Adam said, wondering if that would be enough to get Uncle Jay to test the brakes. "So was Julia. I think everyone was. Like your departure is some kind of existential threat."

"What the hell does that mean? Wait, hang on." Uncle Jay conferred with someone, then returned to the phone. "I could spend years listing all the ways my mother has upset me. As for Julia, she's young. She'll get over it. I bet your mother wasn't upset to see me go. She hates my guts."

"No, she doesn't," Adam said, although he had no idea if that was true. His mother hadn't seemed particularly bothered by Uncle Jay's resignation, come to think of it. But family members shouldn't hate one another's guts. It made for awful holidays and expensive therapist bills.

"Not a problem, Adam. The feeling's mutual. Sondra and I will probably get along much better, now that I'm gone. Listen, these people here need me. I've got a rental agent, our backers, some guy from the tenants' association. There's a thirty-story apartment building above this store, did you know that? Oh, and someone from the city health department, because we're talking food. Bureaucracy, Adam. It sucks, but we've got to deal with it. If you want to come over and join this discussion, you know where the place is. Just hop on a cross-town bus."

"I don't know, Uncle Jay. There's stuff I have to do here."

"Right. You do what you have to do, and then we'll get together, have a drink, and make plans. You're old enough to drink legally. It's time you learn a thing or two about single-malt scotch."

Adam would prefer microbrewery beer. Or maybe just a nice, fat spliff, but he didn't think he should mention that to Uncle Jay. "Okay," he said, because debating the finer points of various intoxicants seemed like a subject for another time. "I'll talk to you soon."

"Keep your eyes and ears open," Uncle Jay said. "Let me know if anyone there is plotting against me. And keep your mouth shut. I don't want them to know what we're up to until it's a *fate-accompany.*"

Fait accompli, Adam thought, but he didn't correct his uncle. The inability to toss off a French expression was no indication that Uncle Jay couldn't run a business. He'd worked at Bloom's his entire adult life, after all. He'd grown up with it, just as Adam had. He had bravado. He had *chutzpah.* He had two financiers, and one was a Brit.

This would all work out.

After saying good-bye, Adam tapped the end-call icon and pocketed his phone. He took a few deep breaths, then exited the stairwell, retracing his steps down the hall to the suite of offices. Glancing around, he noticed that all the doors were open as usual, but no one was hollering back and forth. Either they were all shell shocked from the news of Uncle Jay's departure or they were hard at work figuring out how to replace him.

Hoping his mother wouldn't spot him, he eased past her office door and slipped across the threshold into Susie's office.

There was barely room for the two of them in the tiny room. No place for him to sit down, unless he sat on top of her desk or in her lap. She shot him a quick look, then scowled. "I am so pissed," she whispered.

Adam shut her door and leaned against it. "Because Uncle Jay left?"

"Because Julia thinks you and I should take over his job."

"It's only temporary," Adam assured her.

Susie's scowl intensified. He could almost feel electrons humming in the air around her, creating an aura of rage. "Just yesterday I told Julia that I was going to start doing poetry slams again. You know what? Writing poetry takes time. It takes focus. It takes energy. So what does she do? She dumps Uncle Jay's job on us. I don't want to do his stupid Seders-in-a-Box."

"They're pretty cool, actually," Adam said. "I mean, the concept—"

"I don't give a shit about the concept." Susie stewed. "I want my life back."

"Which life?"

"The one where I stay out late at night and have fun and watch cheesy kung-fu movies. How much of Uncle Jay's job can you do?" She gestured toward her computer monitor. "I was checking out the website. I don't know what needs to be done with it. I mean, it's all there. It works. You click on things. You put them in your shopping cart. You go to check-out and enter your credit card number. What are we supposed to do with it?"

"Keep it up to date?" Adam guessed. He had no idea.

"So, if we're discounting the blintzes, we have to change the price on the website. I don't know how to do that. I hope you do. You're the computer genius."

"I'm a mathematician, not a computer genius," he argued.

"Well, I'm a poet. I think you should be the one to change the prices."

"Are the blintzes on sale right now?"

Susie rolled her eyes. "That was just an example. This coming week, it's knishes, kugel, and vermicelli. I just finished the *Bloom's Bulletin*."

"What's vermicelli?"

"A kind of pasta."

"Why are we selling that? It's Italian."

Susie rolled her eyes again. If she rolled them any more, they might pop out of their sockets and spin across the floor, like two big brown marbles, staring up at him with each rotation. The image made Adam smile. Just a fleeting flashback. The weed he'd smoked last night had been pretty damned strong.

"Uncle Jay probably worked with a website geek," he said. "It's not like he knows how to do programming. I'll find out who his geek is and we can send updates to him."

"First you have to be able to reach Uncle Jay. If this morning's meeting is anything to go by, he's not answering his phone. I mean, really—what's his problem? He walks out, he gives no notice, he shuts off all contact. He blocks his own mother."

"He didn't know Grandma Ida was calling him," Adam said. "If he has caller ID, it would have shown her call coming from Julia's office. And let's face it, how many times a day would you like to block Julia?" *Good save*, he assured himself. Susie would never guess that Uncle Jay was taking calls from Adam, let alone *why* he was taking calls from Adam.

"Julia can be a pain in the ass," Susie agreed, staring forlornly at the Bloom's website on her computer. "There are so many products here. Maybe we can just move the Seder-in-a-Box to the first page of the website for the next few weeks. Once Passover is done, we can move it back again." She sighed. "Once Passover is done, maybe Bloom's will have someone new here to handle Uncle Jay's job. Because I sure as hell don't want to do it. If I'm going to do it," she added, gazing around the stifling space where she worked, "I should get his office, right? A window, a couple of chairs, room to move."

"Room to practice your putts," Adam joked. If he made teasing remarks about Uncle Jay, no one would suspect him of being part of his uncle's defection.

"*Putz* is right. I can't believe he's such a dickhead. Although, yeah, I *can* believe it."

If she believed Uncle Jay was a *putz* and a dickhead for leaving Bloom's, would she believe Adam was a *putz* and a dickhead for leaving Bloom's, too?

Probably.

But Julia was whatever the female equivalent of a *putz* and a dickhead might be. She'd stymied Uncle Jay at every turn. She'd stymied Adam, too. They were smart. Their idea of growing the store was brilliant. But she'd ignored them.

He recalled the excitement in Uncle Jay's voice when they'd spoken just a few minutes ago. He'd never heard Uncle Jay so psyched about anything. To be sure, Adam couldn't recall ever being as psyched as Uncle Jay had sounded. Maybe when he'd gotten his first smart phone, back in middle school. Maybe when he'd smoked pot for the first time. Probably when he'd lost his virginity. But never over a work situation. Never over the prospect of doing something daring and independent, something that required *chutzpah.*

He wanted to have *chutzpah.* Did that make him a dickhead?

Screw it. Screw Julia's bossiness and stubbornness. Screw Susie's whining. Screw his mother for hating Uncle Jay's guts. Screw Grandma Ida for deciding Julia was her only worthy grandchild.

Screw them all. He was joining the *chutzpah*/dickhead team.

Chapter Seven

"I hear my ex-husband has stirred the crock-pot."

Sondra looked up to find Martha standing in her office doorway. As usual, Martha resembled a refugee from a 1970's lesbian commune. Her dress hung from her shoulders like a deflated hot-air balloon, and she wore ribbed woolen knee socks and Birkenstock sandals. Her hair hung in a long, thick braid, drab brown liberally highlighted with drab gray. She clutched a drawstring sack of drab beige in one hand. Sondra's best guess was that it was a purse.

Martha rarely came to the third-floor offices. She didn't work at Bloom's, and she was no longer married to Jay, so she had no real ties to the store. That she still lived in her apartment down the hall from Sondra in the Bloom Building was a testament to the masterful lawyer she'd hired to handle her divorce. Or perhaps it was a testament to the fact that Jay was an ass, so eager to make an honest woman out of his cute blond girlfriend that he'd given Martha everything she asked for, including her spacious apartment in a grand prewar building, as long as she'd signed the paperwork and left him alone.

She hadn't exactly left him alone. She attended all the family events. And of course, she co-parented Neil and Rick, although now that they were adults, motherhood no longer made any demands on her. Until Rick had finally landed his current job with that schlocky ad agency, he'd required financial assistance, but that had been Jay's responsibility. He was the one being grossly overpaid by Bloom's.

Deirdre was seated on the opposite side of Sondra's desk, her laptop open. She'd been explaining LinkedIn to Sondra when Martha barged in. Sondra had only a vague idea of what LinkedIn was. Until Deirdre had enlightened her, she'd thought it was a dating service, which had piqued her interest. She believed she was ready to start dating, if only she could figure out how to go about initiating a social life after three years of widowhood.

Online dating services intimidated her. She didn't want to meet men as young as Adam and her nephews. She also didn't want to meet men who posted photos that made them appear young but were actually eighty years old.

"LinkedIn is where people get hired," Deirdre had told her.

"We've never hired anyone from a website," Sondra had argued. "People come in, they say they want to run a cash register or stock the shelves, and if we need someone, we hire them. For as long as I've been working here, we've never recruited."

"This is different," Deirdre had said. "This is an executive-level position. We can't just hire someone who comes in off the street and fills out a form."

Sondra couldn't decide if she liked or loathed Deirdre. The woman had had a long affair with Sondra's husband, may he rest, and practically under Sondra's nose, too. They'd all worked together. As it turned out, Ben had also been doing a lot of extracurricular work with Deirdre.

Once Sondra had learned about their hanky-panky, after Ben's death, she'd tried to figure out when this affair had taken place. During the hours she'd been upstairs in the apartment with the children? When she'd been in bed, drifting off to sleep, and Ben had said he needed to go downstairs to the Bloom's offices to review some records? When she and the kids had traveled across town to visit her brother and sister-in-law and the Feldman cousins? When she'd flown to Boca to see her parents?

The knowledge that Ben had cheated on her with Deirdre no longer irked her. Because she hadn't found out about it until after he was dead, she'd never had the opportunity to indulge in a dramatic scene of tears and rage and bitter condemnation. She'd never gotten to accuse him. She'd never thrown dishes at his head and forced him to sleep on the couch in the living room. She'd never had the satisfaction of having him drop to his knees and beg her forgiveness.

Not that he would have done that.

Ben Bloom hadn't been the greatest husband in the world, but they'd made a life of it. Now he was dead, and she was still making a life. Deirdre might be as tall and thin as a runway model, and she might have been blessed with a congenitally nice nose, unlike Sondra's, which had been surgically reconfigured by an expensive plastic surgeon when she'd been in high school. But the truth was, Deirdre was just a glorified secretary. A glorified secretary with a fancy title and a comprehension of LinkedIn.

Ordinarily, Sondra wouldn't have welcomed Martha into her office, but right now she was relieved to see her sister-in-law standing in the doorway. "I think the correct word is crackpot, not crock-pot," she said, smiling with pleasure at her own wit.

"So he's left the business?" Martha asked.

Deirdre's gaze shuttled between the two Blooms-by-marriage. She folded her laptop shut and rose. "Why don't I continue working on this while you two catch up?" she said diplomatically. Her ridiculously long legs carried her past Martha and out of sight.

Martha watched her go, then entered the office and settled into the now empty visitor's chair. "Those shoes she wears must be painful," she said.

"I've never asked." Sondra had wondered, though. Had Ben been turned on by stiletto heels? He'd never mentioned that particular proclivity to Sondra.

"She could fracture her metatarsals."

"Or get bunions." The woman deserved bunions for having screwed around with a married man. But enough obsessing about Deirdre, her footwear, and her wisdom regarding online hiring forums. Martha had apparently come to the third floor to discuss her ex-husband, and Sondra was eager to hear what she might say. "Did Jay talk to you about quitting Bloom's?"

"Jay and I don't talk about much," Martha said, apparently not terribly troubled by that fact. "I ran into Ida and she told me. I was up on the roof, doing my tai chi, and then I took the stairs down. Why take the elevator after doing tai chi? The whole point is exercise. Tai chi is excellent for your core and your balance. You should consider doing it."

Sondra's core and her balance were just fine. "So you saw Ida when you came down the stairs?"

"She and her factotum were just stepping out of the elevator when I came through the stairwell door. She asked me if I'd had anything to do with Jay's resignation. I knew nothing about it, other than the fact that Jay will leave anything if it doesn't suit him."

Like his marriage to you, Sondra thought, feeling a twinge of sympathy for her sister-in-law. She couldn't imagine that marriage to Martha would be a day in the park, but marriage wasn't supposed to be a day in the park. It was supposed to be years and years of wearying treks over rugged mountain trails choked by brambles, through fields of poison ivy, down paths slick with mud from constant downpours.

"So you have no idea why he decided to do this boneheaded thing?" she asked Martha.

"I thought *you'd* have an idea. You work with him." Martha sighed and shifted her bag in her lap. Mysterious clinks and clanks filtered through the canvas as the bag's contents collided. Sondra wondered what Martha would carry in her bag. Certainly not a tube of lipstick or a comb or a nail file. Maybe a book about Zen Buddhism, or a guide to wild mushrooms. Maybe one of those coin purses like Sondra's grandmother used to carry, a cloth sac with two brass beads that snapped shut against each other. Nobody under the age of sixty, with the possible exception of Martha, would carry such a purse. Most of them didn't even carry coins.

"Jay is a *schmendrik,*" Sondra said. "Why he does anything, who knows? He really upset Ida with his resignation, though." Ordinarily, Sondra wouldn't care one way or the other about how upset Ida might be. But if Ida's distress over Jay elevated Sondra in the old woman's eyes, that would not be such a bad thing. "I think Julia's pretty upset, too, although she's tried to put a good face on it."

"Maybe he felt he was working too hard," Martha speculated.

Not likely, Sondra thought. Whatever the opposite of industrious was, that was Jay.

"We all need balance in our lives."

"Yes. Tai chi. You said."

"*You* need balance," Martha informed Sondra with annoying certainty.

"My balance is fine. I can't remember the last time I fell."

"Not just physical balance, although that's important, too. You need life balance. Look at your life, Sondra. You work here all day. Then you go upstairs to your apartment and think about work. You need more in your life."

"I'm not complaining." To be sure, Sondra would welcome more work—the work that would come from being the president of Bloom's. If Julia decided she needed more balance, Sondra wanted to position herself so she could take over Julia's job. She wouldn't want Deirdre to find a replacement for Julia on LinkedIn. Even worse, she wouldn't want Deirdre to replace Julia herself.

That would never happen, at least not as long as Ida was alive. Sondra's last name was Bloom. That had to count for something.

"You should come to my women's club with me," Martha said. "Our next speaker is going to talk about work-life balance. I think you'd find it enlightening. And you'd meet some interesting women."

As interesting as you? Sondra thought uncharitably. Martha meant well. She was earnest to the point of dreariness, and her idea of a good meal was tofu cooked with bean sprouts and kale. She definitely wasn't interesting.

But maybe, just maybe, she was right. Sondra's life was not very balanced. Jay had always had more than work in his life. He had Wendy. He had golf. He had his sports car. He had long lunches during which he drank expensive liquor.

What did Sondra have? Her job, her apartment, a contentious relationship with her bathroom scale. Three wonderful children, but they were living their own lives, and one of them was her boss, which chafed a little. A lot, actually.

She did need something more. She'd like to meet some men. She'd like to feel like a woman again.

Maybe the women in Martha's club would be as earnest and dreary as Martha was. But some of them might be more adept at online dating than Sondra was. Maybe they could give her a few pointers. Sondra's mother had always urged her to go out, to mix and mingle, because, as she would say, "You never know."

Maybe Sondra should go to one of Martha's meetings and mix and mingle. You never knew—something might come of it. Something a lot more exciting than balance.

Chapter Eight

Larry Calabrese, formerly known as Fat Larry but currently using the handle "Phat Larry," was glowing like a full moon, thanks to the light reflecting off his shiny scalp. "Renee," Rick muttered, leaning away from his camera and squinting at the white glare bouncing off Phat Larry's head. "Can you do something about that?"

"Yeah, I could buff it up with some Turtle Wax," Renee said.

One of the things Rick liked best about working for the Glickstein Agency was that he had an assistant. Renee Terranova was a compact woman a few years older than Rick but small enough that he could pretend she was younger, which made ordering her around easier for him. She rarely smiled, frequently resorted to sarcasm, but always got the job done, whether it was as trivial as coiling cable or as creative as dressing a set.

Since joining Glickstein eight months ago, Rick hadn't filmed on too many sets. Today's taping was being done in front of a green screen at a small studio in Astoria. He'd already recorded footage of cars at Fat Larry's Auto Mart; those shots would be added to the commercial in the editing room.

Phat Larry kept glancing dubiously at the green screen. Twice he'd asked Rick, "You sure there's gonna be something behind me in the ad?" Twice Rick had sworn to him that there would be.

Phat Larry's bald pate wasn't the only part of him that was shining. Around his neck hung a brassy-looking pendant of a vintage Corvette convertible. He was aiming for a hip-hop look, right down to the bling. His eggplant-shaped torso was encased in a snug black sweatshirt; his legs sported green nylon warm-up pants with a white stripe running down the outer seam of each leg; and he was shod in black Converse sneakers. He looked about as funky-urban as a fat, bald Italian guy from Far Rockaway who sold used cars could look. But the ad was going to feature him rapping about his business, and he wanted to get in character.

Renee dusted his head with enough powder to fill Jones Beach, and it reduced the sheen to a non-blinding level. Rick had already adjusted the lighting so it wouldn't bounce off Phat Larry's necklace, and if the guy didn't move his hands too much during the taping, his diamond pinkie ring wouldn't spark.

After double-checking the teleprompter to make sure the lyrics for Phat Larry's rap were lined up and ready to roll, Rick smiled at Phat Larry in the hope of relaxing him. "Okay," he said. "The first time doesn't count. We're just going to run through it to get a feel for things."

"Hey, I'm ready," Phat Larry said, then sneezed as Renee dusted the residual powder from his shoulders.

"You need to blow your nose?" she asked.

"No, no, I'm really ready." He bounced on the balls of his feet, shadow-boxed a few jabs and grinned.

"'Cause we don't want any mucus in the picture," she pointed out.

Phat Larry gave her an annoyed look, then took a deep breath and turned to Rick. "I'm set. Let's do this."

Rick smiled and nodded. He planned to record the first run-through, because after producing three commercials for Fat Larry's Auto Mart, he'd learned that Phat Larry gave his best performance when he thought he was just practicing. Not that any performance he gave qualified as good, or even remotely mediocre. But that was the point of these low-rent commercials. They were supposed to look cheesy.

Rick cued up the percussion, hit the record button on his camera, and started the teleprompter. Phat Larry bounced on his toes again, jabbed his index finger into the air, and ranted:

> *You got some problems, you need some wheels.*
> *Come on down, I'm talking deals!*
> *I've got a car to fit every budget.*
> *Just give me a price range, I ain't gonna fudge it.*
> *You wanna talk trade-in, you know I'm cool.*
> *I pay top dollar, and that's my rule.*
> *So come on down and get your start*
> *In a car from Fat Larry's Auto Mart!*

While he recited the rap, he attempted a few moonwalk moves, some shoulder shimmies, and a dance step that vaguely resembled the Charleston. Rick captured it all with his camera. If Phat Larry had any pride whatsoever, he would pay Rick top dollar to destroy the recording.

But Phat Larry loved starring in his own commercials. He'd mentioned more than once that his wife thought he ought to go on some TV talent shows. According to her, this would be a fast track to stardom for him. Rick had met her when he'd first been assigned to the Fat Larry account. Felicity Calabrese was a *zaftig* platinum blonde with a lot more bling than her husband and a voice like Minnie Mouse's. Next to her, Rick supposed, Phat Larry was Harry Connick, Jr. Or at least Snoop Dogg.

Rick released his camera trigger and nodded at Phat Larry. "That was great," he said while Renee marked a white board "Phat Larry—Take One."

"You know what?" Phat Larry seemed mildly out of breath. Rick hoped he hadn't exerted himself to the point of a heart attack. He looked to be in his forties, but he did have a lot of extra poundage on him. "This is really bothering me, Rick. Two things, actually." He raised two beefy fingers. "One is, I'm having a little trouble finding my motivation."

"You did fine," Rick assured him.

"And the other thing," Phat Larry continued, his accent laden with several generations of pre-gentrified Brooklyn. "My character is Phat Larry, P-H-A-T Phat. But that sounds the same as F-A-T fat. No one's gonna know I changed the spelling."

"*You* know it," Rick pointed out. He'd learned, after months of assisting on other Glickstein shoots and then finally inheriting Phat Larry, that a director had to stroke the talent—or, in this case, the non-talent. Phat Larry might behave like a diva, but he was the customer, the person who paid the bills, and if he wanted to pull a little Stanislavski attitude, Rick would play along. And he wouldn't point out that no one used the term "phat" anymore.

Renee rolled her eyes, making no attempt to look sincere. "*I* know it, Lar. *I* know it's a p-h. Isn't that enough for you?"

"I love you, Renee, you know I do," Phat Larry gushed. "But I want my customers to know it. You aren't a customer, are you? You oughtta stop by, sweet-heart. I could put you in beautiful Miata, convertible hard-top. Very nice number. Under twelve grand."

"No, thanks," Renee said. "I'm too in love with the subway."

"I've gotta find my motivation." Phat Larry closed his eyes and frowned; the search for his missing moti-vation was obviously a deep internal struggle. His lips moved silently and he pressed his hands together in front of his Corvette pendant, as if praying for its Chevy soul.

Renee sidled up to Rick. Across her chest, her T-shirt read: Try It And I'll Kill You. Rick had no inten-tion of trying it. Renee might be cute in a stumpy sort of way, but his heart belonged to Anna Wong, his cous-in Susie's erstwhile roommate. Now that Susie was liv-ing with her boyfriend, Rick saw less of Anna than he used to. But according to Susie, Anna was still single and available—and he was going to see her after work that evening. Susie and Casey had invited him to din-ner and told him Anna would be there.

He'd been pining for Anna a long time. He dated other women, of course—he was only human, and beyond that, he was a guy. And Anna wasn't exactly throwing herself at him, so what was he supposed to do? Still, he hadn't given up on her. He loved her long black hair, her fine-boned physique, her exotic Asian features. He also loved her intelligence and her pa-tience. He loved that even when he was acting like a jerk, she never shut him down.

She never quite encouraged him, either. But now that he was earning a regular salary rather than trying to make ends meet by scraping together a little grant money here, a part-time gig at a daytime drama there, and loans from his father as needed, he didn't always have to split the dinner bill with Anna—or let her pay the full tab. Not that he could afford to escort her to swanky meals at four-star restaurants, but he could treat her to more than a meatball hero these days. He believed he might be making progress. He'd paid for her drinks at the poetry slam last night, and she'd said "thank you," several times. Each thank-you was precious to him, something to savor, something to raise his hopes.

Tonight he'd get to have dinner with her, and he wouldn't even have to pull out his wallet to enjoy a gourmet feast. Casey was a terrific cook. His store specialized in breads, rolls, muffins, and bagels, but he knew what to do with the other major food groups, too. Rick had once eaten a pasta dinner at Susie's apartment that had forced him to rethink his entire concept of spaghetti. Or it would have, if he'd had a concept of spaghetti to begin with.

"Okay," Phat Larry said, opening his eyes and taking a yoga-deep breath. "I think I've got the essence of my character now."

"Great." Rick sent Phat Larry his patented you're-a-wonderful-client smile. "Let's tape this one, okay?"

"Okay."

Renee held the whiteboard for Rick to record, and then he cued up the percussion. He saw little difference between this recitation and the last. Less finger jabbing, more hip swiveling—which was not necessarily a good thing—but all in all it went well. So did the other four takes.

"This is going to be your best ad yet," Rick predicted after calling it a wrap. Phat Larry loved when Rick used filmmaker expressions like, "That's a wrap."

"You think so?"

"Sure." Rick glanced at Renee, seeking confirmation.

She obliged. "They'll be knocking down your door. Storming the place. I predict riots."

"Riots? You think?" Concern flickered across Phat Larry's flushed, round face. He never knew how to take Renee.

"You're gonna make so many sales," she continued, "Glickstein should get a cut of the action."

Afraid that Phat Larry might actually take her seriously, Rick interjected, "Don't worry. We take a straight fee, as always. No cuts."

Phat Larry looked greatly relieved. "Good. 'Cause I've already gotta pay commissions to my sales staff. I mean, you know? Enough is enough. This business is bleeding me dry."

Yeah, right. "Bled dry" did not describe Phat Larry. His pinkie ring alone could support a family of four for a year. "Renee was just kidding," Rick said, then shot her a stern look. She shrugged and busied herself packing up her box of cosmetics.

Phat Larry eyed Renee dubiously as he crossed to the chair where he'd left his leather biker jacket, complete with a Harley-Davidson patch on the sleeve. Phat Larry looked about as much like a Hell's Angel as he did a hip-hop star, but if he felt like a real man in that jacket, Rick didn't mind.

He didn't mind anything, actually. So what if he wasn't directing features for the film festival and art house markets? So what if he wasn't being showered with prizes and distribution deals and offers from Hollywood? He was earning a living behind a camera. And in less than an hour, he'd be seeing Anna.

Life could be a whole lot worse.

Chapter Nine

"I shouldn't have lied to him," Susie said.

Casey stood at the counter of what passed for a kitchen in their cramped apartment, slicing vegetables so rapidly his knife blade was a blur. The kitchen was actually just a wall that contained a small refrigerator, a stainless steel sink that was, in fact, not at all stainless, a four-burner electric stove, an oven not much bigger than a shoe box, and connecting counter space, with drawers below and cabinets above. When Susie and Casey weren't preparing food, the entire thing could be hidden behind a wide drop-down shade constructed of plastic slats designed to resemble bamboo.

It was amazing, what Casey could do in a kitchen like that. When he'd attended the Culinary Institute of America, he'd worked in huge kitchens, although they'd been crowded with instructors and fellow students, appliances and utensils. At Bloom's, he'd had a spacious baking area to make his bagels in the food-prep area of the Bloom Building cellar. At Casey's Gourmet Breads, the bakery area was about three times the size of the retail store. But he didn't need all that square footage to create culinary masterpieces. Even in their teeny-tiny apartment, he could work magic when it came to food.

He continued chopping the onions for the stir-fry he was preparing. He'd already started a batch of sticky rice in his rice-cooker, an appliance Susie thought was far too specific, but one which sold quite well on the second-floor kitchen gadget section of Bloom's. "You're right," he said, fingers flying, knife pounding against the cutting board, everything so quick Susie half-expected to see blood spurting from one of his veins any second. "You shouldn't have lied."

"It's just, I couldn't invite him over and say, 'Your father's a dick.'"

"He probably knows his father's a dick."

"Maybe his father *isn't* a dick. Maybe he's quit Bloom's to do something fantastic, like sailing solo around the earth, or training to hike up Everest. Or joining the Peace Corps." That possibility was so far-fetched, Susie had to laugh, although she wasn't in a laughing mood. "The thing is, Julia's freaking out, and she's dumping on everyone else, and..." Susie shrugged. "I'm pissed."

"So you told Rick to come here for dinner and promised Anna would be here."

"Because he might not have come otherwise."

"If he knows I'm cooking, he'll come."

True enough. Even if Casey weren't cooking, even if Susie had told him she'd be making dinner—which would have meant microwaving something from Bloom's Heat-'N'-Eat department, or else local take-out—Rick would have come. He might have a real job now, but he was still a mooch. Free food was free food.

"Unless he knows what his father is doing, in which case, maybe he's pissed at me."

"Why would he be pissed at you?"

"Because I'm Julia's sister. Because I work at Bloom's. I don't know."

Having decimated the onion, Casey moved on to a zucchini, slicing it into paper-thin circles. Susie wished she could exorcise her anger by slicing something, although her zucchini circles would not be anywhere near as uniform as his. Cooking was his therapy; writing poetry was hers. But she couldn't stand at a kitchen counter and hack away at a poem. Poetry required focus, a meditative mind-set, and a whole lot of words, some of which she would use and most of which she'd discard, just as Casey discarded the parchment skin of the onion and the stem end of the zucchini.

"Do we have enough liquor?" she asked, swinging open the refrigerator door. A bottle of Pinot Grigio lay on its side on one of the shelves, too tall to fit into the door shelf, which held a row of beer bottles. She counted six. There was probably another six-pack of beer, unchilled, in one of the cabinets.

"There's not enough liquor in the world to make up for your lying to your cousin," Casey said.

Susie shut the refrigerator and glanced at Casey, unsure if he was joking. He was smiling, but it was a sly half-smile that didn't quite reach his eyes. He possessed an entire repertoire of smiles, only about half of which she could interpret. Which was fine in terms of her relationship—she liked a guy with a little mystery to him, and Casey had more than a little.

All his smiles were sexy, at least. This one—the left corner of his mouth quirked up slightly, a single dimple indenting his right cheek—was enigmatic. Casey probably thought she was about to destroy her relationship with Rick. She shouldn't have invited Rick over at all. She should have discussed his father with him over the phone.

If she'd done that, of course, Rick wouldn't have told her anything. As long as he was directly in front of her, however, and consuming food she'd served him, he was much more likely to share everything he knew about what his father was up to.

Once she had some information regarding Uncle Jay's abrupt resignation from Bloom's, she could go to Julia, calm her down, tell her that, hey, Uncle Jay was planning an ascent up Everest or whatever, and Julia should stop thinking the world had ended just because he'd left the family business. He would be back, assuming he didn't die of altitude sickness or hypothermia, and everything would be fine. Or he'd be gone for a year and Julia would hire someone a lot sharper than he was to manage the website in his absence.

The truth was, Susie had a little fantasy that Rick, feeling responsible for his father, would volunteer to take over the website. He could do it in his free time, when he wasn't directing ads for the Glickstein Agency. If Susie could work two jobs and—she hoped—squeeze in some time to write poetry, Rick could work two jobs without the poetry.

And really, why should Julia demand that Susie cover for Uncle Jay when Rick was right there? Let Rick take responsibility for his father's decision to abandon Bloom's. Susie and Adam shouldn't have to.

The buzzer sounded. "Well, he's about to find out his favorite cousin is a liar," Susie muttered, wishing Casey could be a little more supportive. If Casey was right, she'd destroyed her bond with Rick. The cousin who'd been almost like a brother to her—a twin brother, since they were less than two months apart in age—would hate her forever. This dinner was going to be a disaster, except for the food. When Casey was cooking, the food was guaranteed to be wonderful.

She pressed the intercom button. Rick identified himself, sounding ridiculously cheerful despite the metallic echo the speaker filtered into his voice. Susie buzzed him up, then opened the apartment door and watched as he climbed the stairs. He was beaming as he reached her landing. That grin, she knew, was meant for Anna. It would be gone soon.

"Hey, 'Cuz," Rick said, arms wide. He was dressed nicely, for him, in a button-front shirt, khakis, and leather sneakers rather than his usual scruffy sandals. Maybe he'd come straight from work—although he must have stopped by his apartment long enough to douse himself in some manly cologne. The scent emanated from him like steam off hot asphalt, practically making the air around him ripple.

"Hey," Susie said. "Casey's fixing stir-fry. I hope you're hungry."

"I'm hungry, I'm thirsty, and I'm ready to rock and roll," he said, sweeping into the apartment. "Hey, Casey!"

Casey greeted him with a nod, then fussed with his wok, arranging it atop one of the stove's coiled burners and muttering about the superiority of gas ranges.

"Anna's not here yet?" Casey gazed around the tiny apartment, needing no answer. It wasn't big enough for Anna to hide in.

"She won't be coming," Susie said, clearing up her lie as quickly as possible, then moving right along. "What can I get you to drink? We've got beer and wine."

"I guess you can get me beer or wine," Rick said, failing to hide his disappointment. "Is she okay?"

"Who, Anna?" Susie sighed. "She's fine. I told you she'd be here so you'd come. I wasn't sure you would, just to see me."

"And me," Casey called over his shoulder. Sizzling sounds emanated from the wok.

"Of course I'd come," Rick said uncertainly. There was no *of course* about it—except for the free food.

He accepted the bottle of beer Susie handed him and wrenched off the top. "I was hoping to see her, though." Disappointment coated each word like syrup.

"I know. And I'll get you both here for dinner soon." Her promise relied on Casey's willingness to cook, but he was usually willing. And really, he *should* be more supportive.

Rick took a sip of his beer, straight from the bottle, then asked, "So, what's up?"

"Your father," Susie said. She poured herself some of the Pinot Grigio and set the bottle on a spare inch of counter space, rather than sticking it back in the refrigerator. She had the feeling she'd need to refill her glass soon.

Rick looked wary. His eyes remained on Susie even as he tilted his head back and took a deeper slug of beer. "What about him?"

"We'll talk over dinner," Casey suggested. He was so diplomatic. Susie ascribed this to his upbringing as a good Catholic boy, raised to honor his parents and the local priest. His parents drove him crazy, just as her mother drove her crazy, but he always spoke respectfully to them. He and Susie had gotten together with them a few times at their row house in Sunnyside, Queens, with its neutral but well-polished furniture and its display shelves filled with fat little Hummel figurines. Each time they visited, his mother served something bland, usually boiled beef and boiled cabbage, or boiled chicken and boiled peas and carrots, and his father made subtly snide remarks about Casey's career as a chef, and his mother asked Susie about Jewish holidays, as if Susie was some kind of expert, and about growing up in Manhattan, as if it were a foreign country. But never, never did Casey talk back to them.

He was a gentleman. That was one reason she loved him, even though sometimes his gentlemanliness drove her crazy.

Rick kept his gaze pinned to Susie. The mention of dinner seemed to mollify him, but he still looked suspicious. He drank his beer and settled into one of the chairs at the bridge table Susie and Casey used for dining. Casey had found it in his parents' basement, blanketed in a good inch of linty gray dust. His parents had never played bridge, and he'd had no idea why they'd owned the table, but because its legs had folded flat, it had been easy to transport to his and Susie's Lower East Side apartment on the subway. Susie hoped to replace it with something a little nicer once she had some spare cash.

If she was going to have to do Uncle Jay's job, Julia had better give her a raise.

"So," Casey said amiably while he stirred the wok's contents, "what are you working on these days?"

"A new commercial for Fat Larry's Auto Mart," Rick said, a hint of pride edging his voice. "Only now he's P-H-A-T Phat Larry."

"How can you tell the difference?" Casey asked.

"That's an issue. 'Fat' sounds the same as 'phat.'"

"If it's printed on the screen during the ad..." Susie suggested, thinking this was a truly lame topic for discussion, but she'd abide by Casey's edict and not mention Uncle Jay again until they were eating.

"It's not. It's just in Larry's head. The business is registered as Fat Larry's Auto Mart, F-A-T. Even if he went on a diet and lost fifty pounds, he'd still have to call it Fat Larry's. You don't mess with a brand."

"People like to have a person's name in their business title. It humanizes things," Casey said. "My friend Mose thought calling my shop Casey's Gourmet Breads was a good idea. It would make customers think I was their buddy."

Susie gulped her wine and focused on the framed Bruce Lee movie posters hanging above the sofa they'd rescued from the sidewalk shortly after moving into the apartment. It had been relatively clean and sturdy, and after vacuuming the cushions and repairing a wobbly back leg, she'd tossed some throw pillows on it to dress it up. The posters she'd paid real money for: *Enter the Dragon, Game of Death*, and her favorite, which was written in Chinese so she had no idea what movie it was for.

Even though she wasn't looking at him, she felt Rick's gaze on her. He was waiting for the main course—not the dinner main course but the conversation main course.

She refilled her wine glass as Casey served the meal, scooping rice out of his cute little rice machine and spooning the stir-fried chicken and vegetables over the top. He put out plates of salad and a loaf of sourdough bread from his bakery, which didn't really go with the stir-fry but would taste delicious anyway.

Susie had no appetite.

"Okay," Rick said once they were all seated at the bridge table. "What's the problem with my father?"

"You tell me," Susie said.

"Tell you what?"

"Tell me why he quit."

Rick frowned. "He quit what? He doesn't smoke. Well, an occasional cigar when he's feeling pretentious—"

"He quit Bloom's. He walked out. He said *sayonara.*" She glanced at the Bruce Lee posters and recalled that *sayonara* was Japanese, not Chinese. Bruce Lee had been from Hong Kong. He wouldn't say *sayonara*. "Actually, your father said *shalom*, according to Julia."

"My father said *shalom*?" Rick seemed more shocked by the idea that his father had uttered a Hebrew word than by the guy's having ditched Bloom's.

"You don't know anything about this?"

Rick shook his head and devoured a forkful of stir-fry. "This is delicious, Casey," he said, then turned back to Susie. "When did he quit?"

"Yesterday, I'm guessing. Remember when Julia called me during the poetry slam last night?"

"Yeah. You went off and left me alone with Anna." Rick issued a lovelorn sigh. "And then you came back."

"Julia told me I had to go to a company meeting this morning. So I went, and she dropped this bomb on us. Your father split. He's gone. And she expects me to do his job along with my own job there. Needless to say, I'm not pleased."

"Wow." Rick chewed thoughtfully. "If he quit Bloom's...I mean, that's his life. His business. His family." He chewed some more. "His income."

"You think he has something else lined up? Because he has a pretty expensive life style. I don't know how long he can survive without an income. And it's not like Wendy is the breadwinner in their marriage."

"I don't think Wendy has ever held down a job in her life," Rick said.

"Unless you count being married to your father. I bet that's a tougher job than mining coal."

"Coal miners are unionized. Wives aren't," Casey noted. Susie was able to read his smile this time. He was joking, hoping to lighten the mood. She smiled back to show she appreciated his effort.

"Wendy's even more extravagant than he is," Rick said. He shoveled stir-fry into his mouth, eating as if he feared this would be his last meal. He could afford to buy food these days, but he was a bit extravagant, himself. Susie wondered if he was still hitting his father up for financial aid, despite his job at Glickstein. How much did he get paid to deal with people like Fat Larry? Did they pay him more for dealing with *Phat* Larry?

"So...he just said *shalom* and left?" Rick asked.

"According to Julia, yes."

"That's crazy." Rick ate some more. He drank some more. He ruminated. "I don't believe this. He wouldn't do it, not without a good reason. Did your sister do something terrible to him?"

"Julia? What would she do to him?" *Other than demand that he perform his job, which he might consider terrible,* Susie thought.

"She can be bossy," Rick pointed out.

"She's the boss. She's supposed to be bossy."

"Even when we were kids. She was always bossing us around. She'd say we were making too much noise. And she'd give us shit when we were watching a video, and she wanted to watch something else. She'd say we needed to watch something more mature."

Susie's eyes strayed to the Bruce Lee posters once more. Maybe that was why she was a kung-fu movie fan—because Julia had tried to steer her toward more refined cinematic fare, and Susie was a rebel. Julia would demand that Susie watch Shakespeare and Susie would insist on watching low-budget horror movies with tacky special effects, despite the fact that she loved Shakespeare.

"This is crazy. I can't believe my father would quit his job and not even mention it to me." Rick appeared shocked, although his shock didn't seem to affect his appetite at all.

"When did you last talk to him?"

Rick peered at the ceiling, as if the answer was printed there. "Saturday, I think. Or no, Friday. Saturday he went out to the country club to play golf. I don't know how he can play golf when the ground is still muddy. Although we didn't get that much snow this winter. I guess the golf course was in decent shape."

He was wandering astray. Susie lassoed him and dragged him back. "So you talked to him Friday. Did he say anything? Hint that he was upset about work?"

"He *kvetches* about Bloom's all the time," Rick said. "But so do you. So does everyone who works there. Even Grandma Ida. She's the biggest *kvetch* of all."

"She loves Bloom's," Casey said. He adored Grandma Ida. Easy for him; she wasn't his grandmother.

"You know what?" Rick lowered his fork. "I'm going to give him a call and find out what the hell is going on. It's probably just some stupid thing."

In Susie's mind, Uncle Jay was the stupid thing. But she was touched that Rick was willing to get to the bottom of Uncle Jay's stupidity. Obviously, he forgave her for lying to him about Anna. Or maybe he'd forgotten her subterfuge in the wake of her news about his father.

He pulled his cell phone from his hip pocket, scarfed up one more forkful of stir-fry, and then tapped on the screen to connect him with his father. He held the phone to his ear and shot Susie a smile that looked anxious. A pause, and then, "Hey, Dad? Yeah, hi.... No, everything's fine. I don't need money. So what's up with you?" He listened for a moment, then, "So I hear you quit. *Bloom's*," he added, then listened some more. "Really?" He sent Susie another look, flicking his eyebrows up and down. "Really? You did? I mean... So, okay—*really?* Like, now?" Another pause. "He did? Well, that was nice of him, but I think Susie—"

She shook her head sharply. Rick nodded.

"Yeah. She doesn't know anything much. No, I won't tell her. Okay. Well. Congratulations, I guess." They exchanged good-byes and Rick ended the call.

"What won't you tell me?"

Rick winced, then said, "Your brother Adam is going to quit, too."

Chapter Ten

Julia and Susie arrived at the Bloom Building lobby at the same time, which was surprising since Julia lived only a ten-minute walk away while Susie lived downtown in the East Village. She'd taken an Uber uptown, she told Julia after she entered the building and greeted Tomás, the aging doorman who'd been working the lobby desk for at least twenty years and still called Susie and Julia "my little Bloom *chicas*." He noticed a great deal from his perch near the residence's entrance, but he apparently hadn't noticed that Julia and Susie had aged into adulthood. In his mind, they were still scrappy youngsters racing through the high-ceilinged lobby in pigtails and sneakers, giggling or bickering or sucking on ice pops their mother had bought at the supermarket down the street, because treats from Bloom's were too expensive.

The residential entrance was around the corner from the entrance to the store. After Susie had called Julia, Julia had called her mother and told her they were coming over for a family pow-wow. She'd kept her voice steady, as if she were actually in control of her emotions, but the minute Sondra had said, "Of course, *bubby*, come over," tears had overflowed Julia's eyes and spilled down her cheeks.

Julia's husband Ron was a good man, but he was a man. Noticing that she was crying, he'd held her and hugged her for a solid five seconds, and then said he had to get back to polishing his blog post. "Shit happens," he'd told her. "You'll get over it."

"This isn't just shit. This is my brother stabbing me in the back."

Ron had shrugged. "To tell the truth, I didn't think he had the balls to do something like this."

"By the time I'm done with him, he may not have any balls at all," Julia said between sobs.

She'd waited until she was reasonably sure her little weep-fest had run its course, then washed her face, put on a smear of lipstick to impress her mother, hiked down the stairs of the brownstone where their apartment was located, and strolled in the balmy spring evening the few blocks to the Bloom Building. Outside the store, she'd paused. She so rarely actually looked at the store, and even when she looked at it, she didn't really see it, the way she didn't really see the people she loved anymore. She knew them too well—her family and the store. She saw them with her soul, but not with her eyes.

She studied the store with her eyes now. Susie designed the showcase windows. They were sometimes funny and sometimes weird but always worth stopping for, which, Susie insisted, was the whole point of showcase windows. She had not yet arranged the displays to highlight Passover, and the window nearest the store's entrance featured an array of breads and rolls of varying shapes, resembling odd sculptures or maybe the undulating oil inside a lava lamp—spikes, blobs, and spheres, all of them brown and shiny and delicious-looking. Of course, they were inedible, having been coated with some sort of glossy substance so they wouldn't crumble or get moldy. Susie tended to use breads a lot in her window designs, probably a homage to Casey.

Next to the bread window was a window devoted to desserts. Round tins of Danish butter cookies were balanced sideways to resemble the wheels of a gigantic cart filled with packaged sweets. A toddler-size teddy bear piloted the wagon, wearing a New York Yankees baseball cap, its fleecy paws gripping a canister of the gourmet popcorn Bloom's customers adored despite its obscene price.

The third window featured knives from the second-floor kitchenwares department. Paring knives. Steak knives. Carving knives. Knives big enough to butcher a steer, knives small enough to remove a splinter from a baby's thumb. Julia stared at the knives, imagining which one she would like to use on her brother and her uncle.

She wasn't by nature a violent person. But the fact that they would leave her like this—leave the *store*, she corrected herself... No. It felt as if they were leaving her. Flipping her the bird. Kicking her in the gut.

Bloom's didn't have a gut to kick. It would survive, she assured herself as she peered past the knives to view shadows of activity inside. One of her innovations after taking over the presidency of Bloom's was to offer classes and lectures at the store. Tonight, a food historian was speaking on the history of pastrami. If this lecture was like the others, Bloom's would sell a lot of pastrami afterward.

Bloom's would survive, but would Julia? How could she ever trust her brother again? He'd sat in her office at the meeting that very morning and never said a word about leaving. He'd reluctantly agreed to cover for Uncle Jay, to help Susie out with the website. Neither of them had been thrilled with the extra work, but Julia wasn't thrilled, either. No one, with the possible exception of Uncle Jay, was thrilled about any of this.

Adam had acted as if he was a part of the team, though, joining forces with Julia and everyone else to keep the business functioning until Deirdre and Sondra found a new website manager. And all the while, he had been colluding with their son-of-a-bitch uncle. He'd been planning to leave. He'd been faking it.

She felt betrayed. And furious. And on the verge of fresh tears.

She turned resolutely from the windows and marched to the corner, pausing for a moment to collect herself. Traffic streamed up and down Broadway, engines rumbling, horns honking. Above the roof lines, a crescent moon hung high, stark white against the purplish-blue of the night sky, like a cock-eyed smile. Or maybe a smirk.

Sighing, Julia continued around the corner to the residential entrance, where she saw Susie climbing out of a Prius in need of a good car wash. Entering the lobby and hearing Tomás cry out, "My little Bloom *chicas*!" forced her to rein in her emotions. Maybe Tomás thought she was a little *chica*, but she was the president of Bloom's. She needed to be tough. Strong. Thoughtful. Prepared to cut off her brother's balls with one of those super-sharp knives from kitchenwares.

"So, you heard about this from Rick?" she asked Susie, once Susie and Tomás had finished discussing the weather, the midtown traffic, and how big Susie had grown—which, in fact, was not that big at all. Blooms were not genetically predisposed to be drafted into the NBA. But unlike Julia, Susie wasn't on the verge of tears, and thus was able to engage in idle conversation. She smiled and urged Tomás to try a loaf of Casey's seeded rye bread, insisting that it was just the right amount sour and just the right amount dense. Julia had no idea if Tomás was that discerning about rye bread, but Susie liked to brag about Casey's creations.

By the time they reached the elevators, Susie remembered to answer Julia's question. "Rick phoned his dad, and his dad told him Adam was going to be his partner in this new store. Can you believe it? Adam, a partner?"

"With Uncle Jay, no less," Julia muttered. "The halt leading the blind."

"Thing One and Thing Two," Susie countered. "Except that in *The Cat in the Hat*, Thing One and Thing Two cleaned everything up. Uncle Jay and Adam are making a mess, not cleaning it. But they're both things."

"Where is Rick now?"

"He's still at the apartment with Casey. There's plenty of beer. They'll be fine." The elevator door slid open and Susie reflexively peeked inside before entering. Julia knew she wasn't checking the car for a potential rapist. She was looking to make sure Aunt Martha wasn't in it. Whenever they encountered Aunt Martha in the elevator, she droned on and on to them about how they should attend meetings at her women's club, so they could develop into proper feminists.

As if they weren't already feminists. Yes, Julia was married, but she'd kept her own last name. And she was the president of the best deli in New York, if not the universe. And when she wasn't crying, she was prepared to castrate her brother. What could be more feminist than that?

The car was empty, and they stepped inside and pushed the button for the twenty-fourth floor. "Rick said his father told him not to tell anyone about Adam being a part of this plot," Susie continued. "Rick told me anyway. I think he deserves points for that."

"At the moment, he's my favorite cousin," Julia said. "I can't believe they're going to open a rival store."

"I'm not sure how much of a rival it will be. It's going to be miles away."

"The East Side of Manhattan isn't that far from the West Side. We get lots of customers who live on the East Side. They come across town for Bloom's. I told Adam that. Multiple times." Her voice wavered as a sob threatened to escape. She swallowed it back down.

"Anyway, you're assuming Uncle Jay and Adam know what they're doing. They aren't going to be a rival if they don't understand the business."

"I didn't understand the business when I took over here," Julia pointed out. "I learned by doing."

"Yeah, but you've got a brain. Uncle Jay and Adam? Not exactly candidates for Mensa."

"Adam is definitely a candidate for Mensa," Julia said. "He was going to get a PhD in mathematics, remember?"

"But he didn't. Besides, being math-smart isn't the same as being business-smart."

That argument didn't sound terribly convincing to Julia. Math skills could be mighty useful when it came to running a store.

"Does Mom know what's going on?" Susie asked.

Julia shook her head. "I just told her that we needed to talk to her. I didn't tell her why."

"Well, she'll know soon. And then we'll plot. A Bloom-women plot against Adam...I can get into that. He's such a little shit." Susie's eyes were bright. Her smile was brighter.

How could she be happy? Didn't she realize the threat Adam posed, not just to Bloom's but to the

Blooms? Uncle Jay, too. The two of them were tearing the family apart. And what was Bloom's without the Blooms? The store and the family were one and the same in Julia's mind. If you created a Venn diagram with the Blooms in one circle and Bloom's in the other, it would look like a total eclipse, the moon overlapping the sun.

The elevator stopped on their mother's floor. Once again, Julia and Susie peeked through the open door to make sure Aunt Martha wasn't lurking in the hallway, ready to pounce. Her apartment was on the twenty-fourth floor, too, just down the hall from their mother's. That had come in handy when Julia and Susie were as young as Tomás seemed to think they still were. They often raced down the hall to hang out with their cousins. Susie and Rick liked to pretend they were twins. Rick's older brother Neil was two years older than Julia, and believed himself much too mature to hang out with her, but she'd thought he was the coolest person she'd ever known.

Now he lived near Miami and ran a charter sailing company, ferrying tourists around the Keys. He wasn't a traitor regarding the family business, though, because he'd never worked for Bloom's in the first place. He was still cool—too cool to sell bagels and lox, knishes and kugel to connoisseurs of kosher-style cuisine. Certainly too cool to hang out with Julia or any of the other Blooms on a regular basis.

If Adam had followed through on his plans to attend graduate school, Julia wouldn't have considered him a traitor, either. But he hadn't. He'd joined Bloom's, instead, and initiated innovations, and made himself surprisingly useful and productive. Julia had felt their relationship was evolving. She'd stopped thinking of him as her obnoxious kid brother and instead viewed him as an adult, a *mensch*, an honored member of the tribe. She'd listened to his suggestions, even if she didn't always agree with them. She'd allowed that maybe Bloom's would expand someday, open a satellite store or two—in San Francisco, perhaps, or Chicago, or Austin, Texas. Not on the East Side, where they'd be cannibalizing their own customer base. And not yet. Not while Julia was still figuring out how to run the company.

She'd only just scored a minor victory with her pickle merchant. Opening a Bloom's franchise could wait another year or two.

She and Susie strode down the hall to their mother's apartment. Julia pressed the doorbell. The door swung open almost immediately. "Tomás buzzed me and said you were on your way up," Sondra greeted them as they entered the foyer. She gave each of them a one-armed hug. Her other hand held a martini glass filled with a rosy liquid. "Cosmos," she said before they could ask. "I made a pitcher. You sounded so upset on the phone."

Julia forced a smile. She wasn't a huge fan of Cosmopolitans, but tonight she could probably use a drink. Or two. Or fifty.

"Do you need a haircut, Susie?" her mother went on, leaning back to assess her younger daughter. "You're looking kind of shaggy."

"Casey's hair is longer than mine," Susie pointed out.

"Yes, well..." Sondra nodded, as if Susie had made her argument for her. "So come in and tell me what terrible thing is happening."

Like Susie, Julia's mother didn't seem all that upset. She'd been in the meeting that morning. She knew about Uncle Jay. She'd been assigned the task of hiring a replacement for him. Through their open office doors after the meeting, Julia had heard Deirdre teaching her how to use online hiring sites. This ought to have daunted Sondra—unless she'd off-loaded the job onto Deirdre.

In any case, there was no love lost between Sondra and Uncle Jay. She was probably secretly happy to see him go. Or not so secretly happy.

There was plenty of love between her and Adam, however. By the time Julia informed her of her son's treachery, she might need fifty drinks herself.

She led Julia and Susie down the hall to the kitchen. It was ridiculously large for a New York City apartment, but pre-war buildings often had oversized rooms. The kitchen's square footage was mostly wasted on Sondra, who was even less of a cook than Julia was. She spent half her life on diets, creating meals out of broccoli florets and yogurt-dill dips, low-salt chicken broth, diet cheese that tasted like synthetic rubber and rice cakes that tasted like foam packing material. The other half of her life, when she wasn't on a diet, she ate ice cream and taco chips and fried chicken from the supermarket. Bloom's made delicious rotisserie chickens, but they cost more. They should. The chickens were free-range, antibiotic-free, and kosher. Bloom's customers unflinchingly paid top dollar for those rotisserie chickens. Julia's mother wasn't a Bloom's customer, however. She'd choose the bargain, every time.

A large pitcher of Cosmopolitans stood on the center island. Sondra might not be much of a cook, but she knew her mixed drinks. She immediately filled two more martini glasses with the concoction, then handed one to each of her daughters. "A toast," she said. "To my wonderful children."

Two-thirds of a toast, then, Julia thought. One of those children wasn't so wonderful.

She sipped the cocktail. The dryness of the vodka and the tartness of the cranberry juice made her eyes water. Or else it was just emotion causing her to tear up. She lowered her glass and announced, "We have a crisis."

"I gathered as much," Sondra said, still sounding inappropriately cheerful.

"The reason Uncle Jay left Bloom's..." Julia heard the wobble in her voice. Damn it. She did not want to cry in front of her mother. Ron might not have showered her with sympathy, but Sondra would drown her in it. She'd fuss. She'd dote. She'd make Julia feel like an incompetent toddler.

Susie helpfully completed the sentence Julia had begun. "He's opening a competing deli on the East Side, and he's taking Adam with him."

"What?" Sondra's eyebrows shot up so fast, they nearly collided with her hairline. She set her drink down with a thunk, miraculously not breaking the narrow stem. "A competing deli?"

"He's taking on Bloom's. Food fight!" Susie clearly found something amusing in all this.

"That's ridiculous. Jay barely knows how to tie his shoes."

"Adam knows how to tie his shoes," Susie noted. "And he's leaving with Uncle Jay."

"That's insane!"

"It's awful," Julia said, relieved that her mother recognized how catastrophic this was.

"Jay is a moron. Why on earth would Adam side with him about anything?"

"Well, he did. According to Uncle Jay, anyway." The sob Julia was trying so hard to stifle rose into her throat, clogging it like a wad of wet cotton.

"I need to talk to him." Sondra reached for her cell phone, which lay on the counter.

"We're not supposed to know about this," Susie reminded them. "Uncle Jay swore Rick to secrecy, and then Rick told me. I don't want him getting in trouble."

"If he gets in trouble, I'll pay for his lawyer," Sondra said. "I may start adoption proceedings. He's a better son than Adam. Adam's *leaving*?" She shook her head in shock. "What could he possibly be thinking?"

"He's thinking I said no when he nagged me about expanding Bloom's," Julia guessed. "This is his revenge."

"Because you said no? That's not the way I raised my children."

Julia wasn't sure about that. Sondra had raised her children to negotiate, to wheedle, to use whatever leverage they had to get what they wanted. If Sondra spent too much time working at the store, they'd demand extra ice cream for dessert or an extra hour of TV time before bed. If she experienced a spasm of disciplinary zeal, they'd find a way to rebel—sneaking a joint in Susie's bedroom off the kitchen, or applying mascara once they'd left the house for school. Sondra had banned them from wearing mascara in high school; she'd told them she thought it made them look like cheap raccoons. Julia wasn't sure what an expensive raccoon looked like.

"It's not as if Adam and Uncle Jay are irreplaceable," Julia said. "I mean, everyone is replaceable in some way." The sob built in pressure. She was going to gag on it if she didn't release it soon. The mere thought of how replaceable everyone was—her mother, her beloved husband, her artsy sister, her very self—depressed her. Losing her brother to Uncle Jay depressed her. Her Cosmo depressed her, all that icky, sticky Cointreau, but she tried to sip it anyway, hoping it might erode the swell of tears clogging her windpipe.

"Family is not replaceable," Sondra said with such certainty, Julia gave up and let the sob out.

"Don't cry," Susie said, patting Julia's heaving shoulders. "It's not that bad."

"It's that bad," Julia argued.

As she'd feared, Sondra's maternal instincts kicked into high gear. She wrapped her arms around Julia, forced Julia's head against her shoulder, and rocked back and forth, murmuring, "*Shah, shah*," the way a mommy would comfort a child who'd just fallen off her bicycle and scraped her knee. If only a bright red Band-Aid with white stars on it could make everything all better for Julia.

But how could she heal from her brother's betrayal? How could she heal from the gut-deep fear that she wasn't up to the challenge he and Uncle Jay had thrown at her? What if they opened their store and it was a wild success? What if they lured away all of Bloom's East Side customers? What if Bloom's went bankrupt?

Grandma Ida had trusted Julia to run the business. What if she failed?

Julia didn't fail. She was the perfect child. She was the Wellesley woman, the law school graduate, the Bloom child who never made mistakes. That was why Grandma Ida had trusted her with the presidency of Bloom's. Not flaky Susie. Not arrogant Neil. Not goofy Rick. Not shit-for-brains Adam. Julia was the good Bloom child, the one who made everyone feel better, and she was not supposed to fail.

She probably wasn't supposed to cry, either. But she wept freely into the soft velour of her mother's tunic top. She assumed it was machine washable, because every garment Sondra owned, including the mother-of-the-bride dress she'd worn to Julia's wedding, was machine washable.

She hated herself for weeping. Letting her mother see her fall apart was a bad idea. Sondra kept patting her hair and cooing, "*Shah, shah,*" as if trying to summon Persian royalty.

"I'm okay, Mom, really," she mumbled into her mother's armpit.

"You're overstressed, sweetie. It's okay. Too much pressure on you. You're allowed to fall apart."

Not that she needed Sondra's permission, but she appreciated it. "I'll be okay."

Sondra eased her away from her bosom. "Of course you will. But in the meantime, maybe you need a little breather, am I right? Take a step back. Catch your breath. It's all been too much, too soon."

Julia eyed her mother warily. "What are you talking about?"

"Remember the plan, when Ida decided you would be the next president of Bloom's? You were working for that fancy-schmancy law firm. You didn't want to leave that job. You knew nothing about food retail. Am I right?"

Sondra shot a glance at Susie, who shrugged, then nodded. "You were pretty freaked when Grandma Ida dumped the store on you," she said.

"And we decided, the three of us, that you'd be like a figurehead, and I'd run the business, and we'd just make sure your grandmother didn't find out. Remember?"

Julia remembered. She'd been overwhelmed by Grandma Ida's having chosen her to run Bloom's after her father's death. She'd asked her mother to do the job while she shuttled back and forth between the third-floor office of the Bloom's president and Griffin, McDougal, where she was an associate researching divorce precedents. The arrangement hadn't lasted long, however. Besides the obvious difficulties of trying to be in two places at once, and hating the idea of deceiving her grandmother, Julia had discovered that she actually did want to run Bloom's, and that she could. That she could *hondle* with pickle merchants, and schedule evening lectures about pastrami in the store, and oversee the modernization of the store's inventory management.

Which was Adam's job.

What if her mother was right? What if family was irreplaceable?

She was losing her brother, and she couldn't replace him, and the store's inventory management system was going to regress to what it had been before Julia had taken over—the Myron Finkel method of counting on one's fingers.

More tears flowed. Not a trickle anymore—a spate. A deluge. Niagara Falls.

"Get a grip," Susie said. "It's not the end of the world." She yanked open the refrigerator door, pulled out a zip-locked bag full of sliced green bell peppers and a tub of hummus, and dipped a pepper into the hummus. "Bloom's hummus is better," she announced. "This tastes a little oily."

"Since when are you a hummus maven?" Sondra asked.

"I eat lots of hummus. You don't have any pita chips, do you?"

If sisters were replaceable, Julia would like to replace Susie. How could she be fussing about hummus at a time like this? "All right," she said, if only to shut Susie up before she started spouting hummus recipes. "It's not the end of the world. But it could be the end of *our* world. To have two insiders leave Bloom's and open a competing store? It's like, I don't know, a spy novel. Secret agents fleeing to some other country and capitalizing on everything they learned while they worked at the CIA. Selling our secrets."

"They're going to be selling bagels, not secrets," Susie argued. "And they won't be selling Casey's bagels—at least, they won't be if you sign a solid contract with him. If you don't pay him enough, he'll sell to any deli that will. He's got bills to pay. Rent. Salaries. Insurance."

"Fine. He's got bills to pay. So do I. So does Bloom's. If Uncle Jay undercuts us, the business collapses. That's your future, Susie. I can go back to being a lawyer. What are you going to do? Who's going to pay you for your limericks?"

It was a low blow, and Julia regretted it the moment she'd uttered the words. Susie skewered her with a hostile glare. "I'll write great poetry," she said. "I'll be named poet laureate of the city—or maybe the country. I'll publish bestselling books. People will be shocked that a book of poetry can land on the Times bestseller list, but I'll do it. And I sure as hell won't starve, not with Casey doing all the cooking. And I'll thank Adam every day for having forced me to stop writing stupid limericks for the *Bloom's Bulletin*."

Julia deserved that. But her regret evolved into anger. Anger at Susie for being grateful, of all things, to Adam for precipitating this crisis, and for implying that the *Bloom's Bulletin* was stupid.

And anger at her mother, too, for suggesting that Julia step down from the presidency and let her take over. "You know what?" she said. "I'm going to fix this. I'm going to make it work. I thought I could count on you two for support, but it looks like I'm going to have to do this all by myself. Here." She handed her mother her martini glass. "I don't even like Cosmos. Thanks for the offer, but I'm going to keep running Bloom's. Thank *you*—" she turned to Susie "—for letting me know what Adam was doing. I'm going to leave now." She stormed out of the kitchen, heading for the door.

"Can I have your Cosmo?" Susie called after her.

Julia didn't know if she was joking.

She didn't care.

Chapter Eleven

"What the hell are you doing?" Sondra's voice blasted through the phone.

Adam gave his head a quick shake to clear it. What the hell he was doing was enjoying a post-coital joint with Dulcie. She rarely smoked pot, because she said it gave her acute munchies and, as an aspiring ballerina, she had to watch her weight. Her body was so lean, you could count her ribs through her skin, and her limbs were as thin as drinking straws except for the lemon-shaped bulges of her calf muscles. Her feet were particularly ugly; she'd said on more than one occasion that she expected to have bunions by the time she was thirty.

She wasn't thirty yet. She'd told Adam she was twenty-two, and he chose to believe her, although her face was so dewy and her voice so breathy, he wouldn't be surprised to learn that she was a couple of years younger. She had to be at least eighteen to be in the college-level program at Juilliard, so Adam knew he wasn't in any danger of breaking any sex-with-a-minor laws.

She thought he was cool, which made him wonder a little about her judgment. He definitely wasn't cool, although his apartment—which he'd been subletting from Julia ever since she moved in with Ron—qualified as cool. It was tiny, it was a walk-up, but it was Adam's. According to the lease, it was technically still Julia's, but he was paying her to live there, so it was his, too. He wasn't burdened with obnoxious roommates. The bathroom was big enough to accommodate a full-size tub, and the fire escape wasn't caked with pigeon shit.

His mother apparently didn't think he was cool, at least not at the moment. And he wasn't about to tell her what he was doing. He handed the joint to Dulcie, who pinched it delicately between her thumb and forefinger—everything she did with her hands seemed delicate, even when what she was doing was X-rated—and pushed away from the pillow. "Hi, Mom," he said, signaling to Dulcie that she should remain quiet. He was an adult, and he didn't have to justify his sexual activity to his mother. But Sondra sounded furious, and he saw no reason to drag Dulcie into whatever Sondra was furious about. "What's up?"

"What's up is that you're running off with your idiot uncle to start a new store."

How did she know about that? He hadn't told anyone about it, not even Dulcie, who'd been the one to tell him about the available East Side retail space that made this whole enterprise possible. Uncle Jay had sworn Adam to secrecy, and he'd honored that promise.

He willed the pleasant pot fog, to say nothing of the even more pleasant sex fog, out of his brain and inhaled deeply a few times. Next to him, Dulcie took a final deep drag off the joint and then daintily snubbed it out in the ashtray on the night table beside the bed. *Think*, he ordered himself, shifting so he wouldn't be distracted by the sight of Dulcie's lithe body. *Analyze. Figure this out.*

He hadn't broken his promise to Uncle Jay, but his mother somehow knew about their plans. No point in denying it. Instead, he said, "It's a business opportunity."

"A business opportunity to undercut Bloom's? A business opportunity to stab your sisters in the back, and your grandmother, and me?"

"I'm not stabbing anyone in the back," he said, wincing at the whiny defensiveness coloring his voice. "It's nothing personal."

"Are you joking? Nothing personal? You're going to open a rival store and it's nothing personal?"

"It's no more personal than Julia was being personal every time she shot me and Uncle Jay down when we suggested opening an East Side branch of Bloom's." This was sounding violent. He was stabbing Julia. Julia had shot him down. The image of a duel to the death between him and Julia at the O.K. Corral rose in his mind and made him grin. Obviously, there was still some residual pot-high toying with his brain. He shook his head again and forced himself to stop smiling.

"So this is, what, revenge? Julia was just here at my apartment, sobbing her heart out. That's how much you're hurting her."

Adam's mother was good at inducing guilt. Because she did it so often, Adam had become equally good at deflecting her efforts. If Julia was sobbing her heart out, he assured himself, she didn't have what it took to be a tough business leader. If Bloom's went under, it would be because Julia was a weepy wimp. She wanted him to pick up the slack Uncle Jay's departure had created, and he didn't want to. Let her store go down the tubes. Not his fault.

"I don't want to talk about this right now," he said. "How I choose to make a living is not your business."

"Not my business? I'm the vice-president of Human Resources, in case you forgot. Bloom's is my business, literally. And now I've got to hire someone to replace you, too. I'll put an ad in the paper—or on that LinkedIn thing. *Wanted: a new son.*"

"You do that, Mom," he said. Wearily, not angrily. He didn't want his mother to hate him. He didn't want his sister to sob her heart out. But he was an independent adult. He got to choose his life path. He got to decide whether to spend his days in the basement of Bloom's, monitoring the ebb and flow of the store's inventory, or to become a partner—a *partner!*—in a brand new venture. If Uncle Jay knew how to do everything other than inventory, their store was going to be a grand success.

And it was going to have an ideal location, thanks to the slender dancer who'd drifted into a deep slumber beside him in his bed. She had a pretty loud snore for such a petite girl. He hoped his mother couldn't hear it through the phone. Although if she did, big fucking deal. He was an adult. He got to choose his sexual pleasures along with his life path and his career.

"You'll regret this, Adam," his mother warned before disconnecting the call. Adam sighed, tossed his cell phone onto the night table, and reached for the extinguished joint. It still had a few good tokes on it. He relit it, inhaled deeply, and stared at the ceiling.

A joint in his hand, a naked ballerina in his bed, a new career awaiting him. Life was good, even if his mother was pissed at him.

❧

The real estate was perfect.

Well, not quite; true perfection didn't exist. Dulcie was a perfect girlfriend, except that she snored and was flat-chested and obsessed with her weight, and she didn't read newspapers or understand the first thing about mathematics. Uncle Jay was a perfect uncle, except that he was too full of himself. He talked too much, he bragged too much, he played too much golf, and he wanted to call their venture Jacob Bloom's Delectable Food Emporium. But other than that, he scored pretty high on the near-perfect scale.

And this empty storefront on Lexington Avenue was as close to perfect as Adam could have hoped.

He'd decided to go AWOL from Bloom's the morning after his mother had threatened to hire a new son to take his place. Why bother checking in for work when the secret was out? If he showed up at the store, Julia would probably fire him. He didn't want to get fired. He wanted to quit on his own terms.

Seated on the cross-town bus, staring out the window as Central Park blurred past the smudged pane during a two-block stretch when the bus actually moved faster than ten miles per hour, Adam contemplated whether his sister would actually fire him. If she did, she had to know he'd be unable to pay the rent on the apartment he was subletting from her. She was charging him less than the market rate, losing money every month, which was awfully generous. If he moved out, she might not be able to sublet the place to anyone else—that would depend on the terms of her lease—and the cost of breaking her lease would be an entire month's rent, at least. But still, she could have charged him a lot more, and she hadn't.

He felt kind of bad about that.

But this new store was an opportunity. He'd given his sister so many chances to let him spread his wings a little—or, more accurately, spread Bloom's wings. She'd rejected him every time.

Reminding himself of that made him feel a little less bad.

Hell, Julia would never fire him. She didn't have the guts. Just the thought of his quitting the store had reduced her to tears.

He got off the bus and turned the corner onto Lexington Avenue. It wasn't as crowded as Broadway, but the skimpier flow of pedestrians moving along the sidewalk was an indication of the Upper East Side's classiness. Over on the Upper West Side, huddled masses jammed every square inch of sidewalk, making walking to Bloom's almost impossible.

So their store would be exposed to less foot traffic here on the East Side. But more people would be able to see the windows. More people would be able to access the place. A higher percentage of that foot traffic would enter the store.

Adam wondered whether they should get information on the pedestrian density, on the number of potential customers in the neighborhood in general, and on this block in particular. That seemed like a mathematically sound thing to do.

But then he saw the actual store and thought: *it's perfect.*

It was small compared to Bloom's, but of course it would be. Bloom's stretched an entire block, from corner to corner, while this storefront was one of seven shops on the block. Bloom's hadn't started out so big, he reminded himself. It had begun its life as a pushcart from which his grandparents had sold knishes—he'd heard Grandma Ida recite the origin story too many times to count. When she and Grandpa Isaac had moved their business indoors, it had taken up only a tiny sliver of a shop. And then it had grown. It had expanded like yeasty dough, taking over the adjacent shop, and then the shop next to that one, and the next shop, and the next. Then it had expanded upward. Then the company had purchased the whole building.

Give it time, Adam thought, craning his neck to scrutinize the bland beige apartment building rising above the empty storefront Jacob Bloom's Delectable Food Emporium would soon occupy. Someday, they might own the whole building, too.

Uncle Jay and three other men were just inside the door of the empty store, waiting for Adam. He'd phoned Uncle Jay that morning to say he wanted to see the site, and Uncle Jay told him to come on over. He didn't ask Adam why he wouldn't be working at Bloom's today, pretending he had no intention of leaving. Did Uncle Jay know the news had leaked?

Uncle Jay swung open the door, his face ruddy with pleasure, his apparel—twill slacks and a cotton sweater over a collared polo shirt—as well suited to the golf course as a business engagement. "Adam! Come on in! I want you to meet some people."

Adam was not dressed for the golf course. As usual, he had on a pair of cargo pants, a T-shirt, a hoodie, and sneakers. If he'd known he was going to meet some people, he would have exhumed a button-front shirt from the back of his closet.

Uncle Jay didn't seem to mind Adam's appearance. "Guys, this is my nephew, Adam," he said to the men. "A brilliant kid. He's going to manage our inventory. And probably lots of other stuff, too. He's great."

Adam was unable to keep from smiling. Hype came naturally to Uncle Jay, but Adam still appreciated being the subject of it. When was the last time Julia or his mother, or even Grandma Ida, had said he was great?

"Adam, this—" he gestured toward a young-ish guy in a semi-stylish suit "—is Harold Marzicanti, the realtor in charge of renting this unit. And these two men—" he swept his hand toward the other two, who, like Uncle Jay, were dressed on the upper end of business casual "—are Gil Jenners and Rupert Niles. You may think you and I are important, but they're ten times more important. They're our financial backers."

"Oh. Wow. Nice to meet you," Adam said, shaking their hands and trying to remember which one was Gil and which one was Rupert. They were both middle-aged. One was going bald; the other had reddish hair that rippled in rolling waves, like the corrugated roof shingles on a hacienda.

He wondered how much they were investing in the store, and what they wanted in return for their investment. He also wondered where Uncle Jay had found them, how he knew them.

After shaking Adam's hand, Rupert leaned toward Uncle Jay and said, with a pronounced British accent, "A fine young chap you've got here, Jake."

Adam hardly thought of himself as a chap. Didn't chaps have to wear bowler hats and carry walking sticks? Didn't they have to drink tea? He wasn't a big fan of tea. And why did he call Uncle Jay "Jake"? Was Uncle Jay planning to go by Jacob, his birth name, now? Would Adam have to call him Uncle Jacob?

That sounded all wrong to Adam, but he couldn't very well grill his uncle about it. Instead, he whispered, "Are these guys going to be partners, too?"

"No." Uncle Jay released a booming laugh. "No, Adam, they're just investors." To the two men, Uncle Jay explained, "He wants to know if you're going to be partners in the store."

"Me? Run a store?" The bald one guffawed. His accent screamed Long Island more than British Isles. "No way! We're just investors," he echoed Uncle Jay, giving Adam a broad smile that should have reassured him.

Adam couldn't pinpoint why it didn't. The men looked affluent enough, but they didn't fit his mental image of investors. Investors ought to be old and musty, with checkbooks that looked like loose-leaf notebooks, three checks per page. They ought to sit in oversized leather chairs and peruse the stock charts in the *Wall Street Journal* or *Barron's*. In fact, they ought to be so wealthy, they had agents and brokers who handled their investments for them.

Unless they were investing in something really risky and crazy, like the theater. Then they were supposed to hang out in penthouse apartments, gathering around grand pianos and listening while actors sang the songs of some new show in an effort to convince them it was the next *Oklahoma!* or *Hamilton.*

They weren't supposed to be two guys in middle-age prep attire, checking out an empty storefront. Except, apparently, they were.

Whatever. If they were prepared to invest enough money, Adam could start drawing a salary, and then he could quit his job at Bloom's—if Julia didn't fire him first.

"So, we're just running through the place before we sit down and sign the lease," Uncle Jay went on, as bubbly as champagne. "The way I see it..." He took Adam's elbow and ushered him through the barren store. "We'll have the cheese cases here, right inside the entrance. Along the back wall, the deli department. Hot entrees, cold meats, salads. Right wall will be baked goods. Shelving through the center of the store, with non-perishables. How does that sound?"

It sounded exactly like the layout of Bloom's. Which, Adam had to admit, worked for Bloom's. "Are we going to have kitchenwares on the second floor?"

Uncle Jay grimaced. "Absolutely not. That's something Bloom's would do. Not us. We're completely different."

Okay. For a minute there, Adam had thought Uncle Jay was simply planning to launch a Bloom's franchise under a different name, with different ownership. But this store would obviously be totally unique. Nothing like Bloom's at all, except for the exact layout of the merchandise.

Adam didn't know much about the science of retail displays, anyway. There was probably a logic to the way foods were organized in a store. Maybe customers entered craving cheese, so the cheese had to be right at the front. Maybe they had to toss cheese or meats into their shopping carts in order to be inspired to buy bread. As for the non-perishables on the shelves, they probably needed to be in a certain sequence. What that sequence was, Adam didn't have a clue.

He hoped Uncle Jay knew. Glancing behind him at Gil and Rupert, he doubted they'd be much help.

Susie would know. Somehow, she had an instinct for that kind of thing—how stuff should look, how it should be exhibited, how it could be made enticing. He had no idea where she'd developed that talent. Did they teach Shelving 101 at Bennington? Wherever she'd learned it, she was good at it. The windows she designed for Bloom's were freaky and fun. She understood, in some intuitive way, that certain shapes of pasta should be on a middle shelf and certain other shapes on an upper shelf, that people would bend over to reach some kinds of crackers but not others, that expensive things should go on the end caps because people seemed to think that if something was displayed on an end cap, it was a must-buy.

Shopping carts or baskets? The store was so much smaller than Bloom's. Would they have enough room in the aisles for carts? What if customers bought everything in sight and got fat? Would they have to make the aisles wider? That would be a nice problem to have—not the fat part, but the buy-everything-in-sight part.

He wandered around the open space, visualizing the layout as his uncle described it and picturing Bloom's. Susie had done all that rearranging after Julia had taken over the store. Tweaking, she'd insisted, but she'd moved quite a few things around and sales had picked up. Adam wondered if she would do that for Jacob Bloom's Delectable Food Emporium. Could they hire her as a consultant? Or maybe as a full-time employee?

How much was all this going to cost? How much money were these investors going to cough up?

The visions his brain had conjured as he'd wandered through the empty store—shelves teeming with merchandise, refrigerated cases piled high with cheeses and meats, check-out counters beeping as the scanners racked up sales—dimmed, as if a white mist had settled over the scene. He blinked a few times to clear the mist away. Finance was Uncle Jay's department, not Adam's. Raising the money, kissing up to the investors—not his problem. He would handle inventory. He'd pick Susie's brain. Or—as Uncle Jay had described things—he'd simply mimic what Bloom's was doing. It worked for them. Why shouldn't it work for Jacob Bloom's Delectable Food Emporium?

The business really needed a new name, though. Jacob Bloom's Foods. Jacob Bloom's Emporium. Jacob Bloom's Period.

Better yet: Jacob and Adam Bloom's.

Chapter Twelve

"This poem is called *The Queen*," Susie said. She was standing on a stage so small, she felt like a trained elephant in the circus, balanced on a colorful barrel. On the other side of the rostrum, the café was a midnight blue, crowded with circular tables cluttered with wine goblets, beer bottles, and cocktail glasses. She'd guess that a significant percentage of her audience was either drunk or well on their way, but that was fine with her. There was no prize money tonight. The only pleasure in this poetry slam would come from the act of spewing her most recent poem.

She surveyed the crowd, her gaze snagging on her cousin Rick. He sat alone at their table, smiling encouragingly at her. Anna hadn't come tonight—she was on a date with the second violinist in a string quartet she sometimes played with, but Susie had kindly not shared that fact with Rick. She was glad he'd accompanied her. She wished Casey had come, but of course he was home, probably asleep by now. Probably dreaming of sourdough starter or scones.

She returned Rick's smile, then directed her gaze to the faceless blur of drinkers and ostensible poetry lovers seated around those tables in the gloomy cafe. She unfolded the paper she'd written the poem on—she'd completed it just that afternoon and hadn't memorized it, but with no prize money at stake, she didn't think anyone would mind her reading the words rather than declaiming them from memory. Yet as soon as she leaned toward the microphone and started reciting, the poem came to her in all its anger and hurt and resentment, and she ignored the paper.

> *"Because she is older.*
> *Because she is favored.*
> *Because she doesn't have a tattoo on her ankle.*
> *Because she takes things seriously.*
> *Because she is taken seriously.*
> *Because she views you as a slave or a toady or a personal affront.*
> *Because she went to law school.*
> *Because she spends ninety dollars on a haircut, and the stylist cuts each strand individually, delicately, reverently.*
> *Because she does not live in sin.*
> *Because she is better loved by Grandma.*
> *Because she is important, and mature, and would never waste time writing poetry.*
> *Because she is not you, and you will never be her.*
> *She is the queen.*
> *You are the person who kisses her ring."*

It wasn't Susie's finest opus. It had burst from her, riding a tsunami of emotion, and now it existed, words in a pattern. A poem.

The audience appeared to like it—but again, they seemed fairly stewed. They'd laughed at the line about law school, which Susie supposed was kind of funny.

Once she was done, she gave a self-conscious little curtsy at the smattering of applause, then folded the paper along its creases, stuffed it into the back pocket of her black jeans, and climbed off the pedestal-sized stage. As soon as she reached Rick, she dropped onto her chair and took a long, bracing gulp of the merlot she'd ordered. It was tart and a little acidic. Were those the proper terms for a wine connoisseur? *Tart on the palate, with a finish of battery acid.*

A wine connoisseur would never order this wine.

"Does Julia really spend ninety bucks on a haircut?" Rick asked.

"I don't know." Susie shrugged. "The last time I saw her was at my mother's apartment last week. Mom told me I needed a haircut. Julia's hair was perfect, of course."

"Of course." Rick ruminated on this, rotating his glass as he thought. "I spend, like, twenty bucks on a haircut, not counting the tip."

"You're a cheapskate," Susie said. Reciting the poem hadn't made her feel better. Not that she'd expected it would.

"So you haven't gone to work since then?"

"I've gone, but I haven't seen her. I can avoid her if I want." Another shrug, another slug of wine. "She's acting like such a bitch. I don't want to be near her."

"Why? I mean, stress, sure. My father and your brother dumped her, so yeah, she's in a bad mood. But why would she be taking it out on you?"

"Because she wanted me and Adam to do your father's job, and now Adam is gone, so she wants me to do it myself. But I don't have the time or the energy. Or the interest. It's not like I'm sitting around playing solitaire while I'm at the store. I write the weekly *Bulletin*. I oversee the displays. Then I come back downtown to work at Casey's place, or I go to Nico's for a slice of pizza and write poetry. So no, I'm not going to add your father's job to my to-do list."

"How about Adam's job? Does she want you to do that, too?"

"There's no way I can do inventory." Susie wrinkled her nose. "That's so...dry. So mathematical—which, I guess is why Adam likes it. 'Oh, look, we're running low on cracked pepper. Why are we out of kasha? Who ordered all these pot holders?' I'd go nuts in two seconds flat."

"I think it's a little more involved than how many pot holders you ordered. Adam's supposed to be some kind of genius, right?"

"Adam's an idiot. So's your father, if you don't mind me saying so. Why did he do this? Why did he quit Bloom's?"

It was Rick's turn to shrug. "Your guess is as good as mine."

"No, it's not. All I've got are guesses. You're his son. He could tell you things. I'm not allowed to talk to him. Julia said."

"She can't tell you who you can or can't talk to."

"Sure she can. She's the queen." Susie drained her glass. If she was smart, she'd listen to a couple more poems and then call it a night. She wasn't smart, though, at least not *that* smart. She flagged down a weary-looking waitress and asked for another glass of merlot.

"I thought your poem was terrific," the waitress said without much feeling. If she was kissing up for a better tip, she ought to sound a little more enthusiastic.

Susie waited until the waitress was gone, then sighed and stared at the spot on the table where her empty wine glass had stood. "Is it bad to hate your family? Does that make me evil?"

"You're asking me?" Rick snorted. "My father gave me shit for years because I was trying to make films. Now I'm finally earning money, and he treats me with respect. Hell, I'm probably making more money than he is at the moment."

"We should move down to—where is your brother? Key West? Key Largo?"

"Marathon. It's probably going to be underwater in a few years, with global warming. Why should we move there?"

"He's the only member of the family I don't hate. Other than you."

"Gee, thanks." Rick leaned back in his chair, stretching his legs under the table and kicking Susie's foot. Maybe she hated him, too. He didn't even seem to notice that he'd kicked her. "Neil can be full of himself," he said.

"Like Julia isn't? That's her whole thing—being full of herself. The entire universe depends on her. Everyone is out to screw her. People make decisions for whatever their reasons, and she thinks it's all about her. She's the queen." Her poem might or might not be terrific—probably not—but it was true. "Neil sails around in a boat all day. That sounds like fun. We could join his crew. 'Ahoy, ye maties!'" she chirped. "'Lower the main-sail! Batten down the hatches! Walk the plank!'"

"He's not a pirate. Nobody walks the plank—unless their checks bounce," Rick joked.

"Why do you think he's full of himself?" Susie asked.

"He is. If Julia is the queen, he's the king. Or maybe the overlord. His boat is his world, and he's in charge of it. I went sailing with him once, and he said, about two thousand times, 'Remember—a boat can have only one captain, and I'm it.'"

Susie had to admit that was egotistical. "Should I write a nasty poem about him, too?"

"Besides, he stays down in Florida and ignores all the family shit. Dad quits his job and throws Bloom's into a frenzy, and Neil couldn't care less. Mom decides to eat acorns for dinner, and Neil doesn't give a damn. I'm making commercials for Phat Larry, and Neil doesn't even know who Phat Larry is."

"He's a lucky guy," Susie said. "I wish I didn't know who Phat Larry was. Does your mother really eat acorns?"

"Only if they're organic." Rick laughed. Aunt Martha's diet was heavy on plants and organic stuff, and light on flavor, but Susie was pretty sure he was kidding. Acorns had to be inedible if you weren't a squirrel.

The waitress arrived with a fresh glass of merlot. Susie took a sip. Just as acidic as the last glass. "I just think it would be fun to run away," she said. "The way your dad did. The way your brother did. I mean, just say *sayonara* to the family and head out in a new direction. Or *shalom*."

"What about Casey?" Rick asked. "You'd run out on him?"

"I'd take him with me," Susie said, but she wasn't really sure about that. It was a moot point; he'd never leave his precious gourmet bakery, which was finally beginning to take off, showing a profit more weeks than not.

If he ran away with her, would he still want to go to sleep at nine o'clock?

She could run away from Bloom's without leaving the city—although if she did, Julia would probably hire a hit man to find her and mow her down. And really, Susie didn't want to leave Bloom's. She just wanted to write the *Bloom's Bulletin* and design the showcase windows and shelf displays, and not be asked to do anything else. Before Julia had taken over Bloom's, when their father had still been alive and running the place, Susie had worked at Nico's pizza parlor in the Village, and Nico had let her design the windows for his trattoria. Her windows for him had been quirky, and they'd often included a poem. Nico always said he didn't get what she was doing, but as long as her displays attracted customers, he was happy.

Julia had more or less the same approach. She gave Susie free rein, and Susie came up with some whimsical imagery for the windows, a major change from the staid, dowdy windows the store used to have, filled with merchandise stacked high and sometimes coated with a thin layer of dust because the displays were changed so rarely. Now the displays were fun. People stopped, they smiled, and they wandered into the store. If Susie could just be left alone to do the windows and the *Bulletin*, she'd be happy.

But it was more than just Julia's trying to unload Uncle Jay's job on her. It was Julia's attitude. She acted as if everyone's decision was a personal attack on her. In her view, Uncle Jay and Adam hadn't left because they wanted to start a new store. They'd left because they'd wanted to hurt her. And Mom—sheesh. She was only trying to help, offering to take over some of Julia's responsibilities. Julia acted as if their mother was orchestrating a palace coup.

If Julia and their mother were smart, they'd argue in private. But no, everything on the third floor was done at top volume, hollered from office to office through the open doors. That morning, while Susie was trying, with middling success, to figure out how many orders for Seder-in-a-Box had gone through the website—if only Adam were around, she could ask him, since he was a lot more computer savvy than she was—Julia and Sondra had engaged in a screaming match that resonated throughout the third floor like an over-amped heavy-metal concert. Actually, Susie's mother had done most of the screaming. "I'm not trying to take over!" she had shrieked. "Why do you keep saying that?"

"Because you always wanted to be the president of Bloom's!" Julia had replied, her voice a few decibels softer than Sondra's. "Even before Dad died, you wanted that."

"So, it's against the law to want something?"

"It's against the law to try to take something that isn't yours."

"She's a lawyer, Sondra," Myron Finkel's nasal, raspy voice had drifted out of his office. "You really think you should argue the law with her?"

"Life would be easier if we didn't have families," Susie said to Rick before sipping some more of her caustic merlot. If she didn't have a family, she wouldn't have to worry about Bloom's. She could go to work, leave work, not think much about work one way or another. She could enjoy the aspects of her job that were enjoyable and cope with the aspects that weren't. If her colleagues yelled through open doors, she wouldn't have to cringe, thinking, *I'm related to these people.*

She wasn't related to Myron, at least, or Deirdre. She took some solace in that.

Of course, if she didn't have a family, Rick wouldn't be her cousin. Would she even know him? Would she get stuck attending poetry slams all by herself because she didn't have a cousin to accompany her and her boyfriend went to bed too early?

The guy who'd been reciting—the one who always dressed like a mime; Susie encountered him at a lot of poetry slams—abandoned the itty-bitty platform after reciting a thunderous ode about fungus: "Rootless, faceless, soulless, shameless, the wildness of less-ness..." and was replaced by a round-faced blond woman pretty enough to cause Rick to sit up straighter. He might be madly, resolutely in love with Anna, but he was also male. He couldn't help himself.

"This poem is called *Hearing,*" the blond woman said, and then proceeded to perform what Susie could only assume was a poem in American Sign Language. Her hands swayed and fluttered and shaped the air. Her facial expressions ranged from smiling to frowning to wide-eyed in surprise. Her lips moved but no sound emerged. It was an interesting choreography, but as someone who did not understand ASL, Susie had no idea what the poem was about.

It earned a rousing round of applause, however. If this slam had included a money prize, the cute blonde woman would have won it.

Maybe the Bloom family ought to communicate using sign language. Then they wouldn't scream back and forth from office to office. Even better: they should use sign language without knowing what one another's gestures meant.

Except the one-finger salute. They all knew what that meant. The next time Julia started making demands or moaning about how Adam and Uncle Jay had betrayed her, Susie could use that particular sign language to communicate her sentiments.

"Here's an idea," Rick said. "Let's go uptown and check out the store."

"Now?" Was Rick implying that she shouldn't finish her ghastly glass of wine?

"Tomorrow. My dad told me where it's located. He said Adam found them a perfect storefront for rent."

"Adam couldn't find his own molars if his mouth was closed," Susie muttered. "Someone must have told him about the place."

"Well, we should go have a look. Maybe it's so crappy, your sister won't have to worry about their store surviving." His smile brightened. "Hey, maybe my dad will hire me to direct commercials for the place."

"Whose side are you on, anyway?" Susie faked a scowl. "You're going to make commercials for him?"

"I'd make the commercials for myself. If I bring a new client in to the Glickstein Agency, it could be good for my career."

Susie eyed him over the rim of her glass. She remembered the way he'd been when he was fresh out of NYU's film school, when the career he'd been dreaming of included film festivals and art house theaters and acclaim, Oscars and Césars and Nobel Prizes, if they gave them for films. Now the career he dreamed of was all about climbing the ladder in an ad agency, moving from ads starring a bling-encrusted used car salesman to ads starring his father.

"No, wait, I can't do it tomorrow," Rick said as he studied the screen of his phone. "I've got meetings. How about the day after? I could get away around lunch time."

"Fine." Her cousin, her life-long buddy, practically her twin, had *meetings*. What had happened to Rick? When had he turned into a corporate dweeb?

She glanced toward the rostrum, where a skinny guy with a long, bedraggled pony-tail and a pierced lower lip was reciting a poem about one of those weighted plastic clowns that you could knock over with a punch and it would bounce back upright. As best Susie could figure, the clown was a major metaphor—for what, she wasn't sure, but probably for life.

145

The guy might have had a pierced tongue, too, given his lisp. Droplets of saliva sprayed from his mouth and glittered like airborne dew in the spotlight pinpointing the stage.

Maybe that was a better metaphor for life than the boxing clown that popped back up when you knocked it over. Sometimes when someone knocked you over, you didn't pop back up. There were no guarantees in this world—certainly no guarantees that you could remain standing when life was doing everything in its power to flatten you.

But spit was a good metaphor. Life was full of spit. Sometimes you were the spitter, and sometimes you were the spittee. The best you could hope for was that the metal stud piercing your tongue didn't get in the way when you were drinking wine.

Even if it was a wretched merlot.

Chapter Thirteen

Julia entered her office to find her mother sitting in her chair—the chair Julia had purchased to replace her father's chair, which had been too big for her—and chatting on the phone. "Bernie, *bubby*, come on," Sondra was saying. "You're talking to *me* now. What's the lowest price you can give me for those pickles?"

Sondra was negotiating with Bernie Koplowitz? Bernie, whom Julia had cajoled into giving Bloom's a nice discount on his products? What the hell?

"Mom." Julia strode toward her desk.

Sondra waved her hand in a brush-off motion and swiveled away from Julia. "Forgive me, Bernie, but you're no Murray Schloss," she said into the phone. "You can do better than that."

Julia reached across the desk, yanked the phone from her mother's hand, and lifted it to her ear. "Bernie?" she said, forcing sweetness into her tone. "Hi, it's Julia. Forget what my mother said. We've got a deal. Okay?"

"You all right, sweetheart?" Bernie said in his raspy, Jersey-inflected voice. "Your mom giving you a hard time?"

"She's just joking around," Julia said, glaring at her mother, who leaned back in Julia's chair, lips pursed and hands folded primly on the desk. "I'm in charge

147

of the pickles." That sounded absurd, but it was true. Julia Bloom, the president of Bloom's, was in charge of the pickles.

"Because I offered you a good price."

"I know. We're sticking with that. I'm sorry my mother bothered you."

"Sondra Bloom is never a bother," Bernie assured Julia. "I met her a few times, back when I was fighting Murray for the Bloom's account. I'll tell you this: now that your father's gone, may he rest, I'd go after her. She's a nice-looking gal, smart, aggressive—everything a woman should be. My wife, though... She wouldn't be happy if I started in with your mother."

Julia decided he had to be joking, and she laughed accordingly. "Stick with your wife, Bernie. That's the best policy." As if she, who had tied the knot with Ron less than two years ago, was an expert on marriage.

She said goodbye, pressed the disconnect button, and planted the phone back in its cradle. Then she glowered at her mother. She felt uneasy; being so angry with Sondra contradicted her role as the person who made everyone feel better. But she was furious, and she was getting better at letting her rage-flag fly.

"The pickles are my responsibility," she said, her voice tight but level. "Your responsibility is HR."

"I'm just trying to help," Sondra said, exuding wounded innocence and self-righteous indignation. "I negotiated the pickle contracts when your father was alive. Nobody ever knew that, but I handled the pickles."

"And now *I* handle the pickles," Julia said. "You're supposed to be hiring a website manager and an inventory manager."

"Deirdre is taking care of that," Sondra said.

"It's not her job. It's your job."

Sondra's expression evolved. Her eyebrows quirked up, her lower lip quivered, and her sculpted nostrils, the masterwork of the plastic surgeon who'd performed her rhinoplasty, narrowed. If Julia didn't know better, she would have expected her mother to start crying.

Her mother was too tough to cry, though. She hadn't even cried when she'd received word from Bloom's Eastern Europe buyer that Ben Bloom had died from eating rancid sturgeon in St. Petersburg, Russia.

Even though Sondra wouldn't cry, her tremulous appearance released a surge of guilt within Julia. She'd scolded her mother. She'd *hurt* her mother. That was not the sort of thing Julia did.

"Mom," she said, attempting an ameliorating smile. "The thing is, the biggest help you could give me would be to hire some people to replace Uncle Jay and Adam."

"My son is irreplaceable," she said, words Grandma Ida might have said about Uncle Jay.

"I meant professionally. Of course, he'll always be your son." *He may not be my brother, though.* During her years working as an associate in the family law department at Griffin, McDougal, Julia had done a lot of research on divorce. She'd never stumbled across any case law concerning siblings divorcing one another, but if such a thing were possible, she'd consider divorcing Adam. The traitor. The turd.

"Julia. You're stretched beyond your capacity," Sondra said. She rose regally from Julia's chair. "I don't want to have another fight with you. But you need to think very carefully about who you're pushing aside. You want to be Bloom's president. Fine. It's a fancy title. Keep the title. Let me help you with the job. If you don't, you're going to snap."

Julia recalled the fight Sondra had referred to, when Julia had accused her mother of trying to usurp the power of that fancy title. She would have launched into another full-tilt battle again today, except that with all the doors open, everyone would hear her, the way they'd heard her last time. It wasn't good for the troops to hear their leader chewing out her mother at top volume. As the president, Julia had to maintain her poise. She had to prove she was not snapping.

Even if she was.

"Please, Mom. Leave the pickles to me." She gestured toward her office door. "If you want to help, go find a new inventory manager. That's the most helpful thing you can do."

Lips pursed again, Sondra glided to the door. Her farewell glance clarified for Julia the meaning of the phrase *if looks could kill*. If they could, Ron would have become a widower that moment.

She watched her mother walk back to her own office. Once Sondra was out of view, Julia headed to Susie's tiny office, hoping her sister would help her to calm down. She didn't want to snap. She couldn't afford to snap. But damn, she was close to snapping like a fraying bungee cord, on the verge of dropping some hapless soul to her death in a gorge below.

She was the bungee cord and also the hapless soul.

Entering Susie's office, Julia saw her sister seated cross-legged in her standard-issue chair, her knees pressed against the chair's molded arms, her back curved, her arms arched so her hands rested against the keys of her computer, and her gaze focused on the screen. Dressed, as usual, in black, she looked like a charred pretzel.

"How are our Seder-in-a-Box sales going?" Julia asked with artificial cheer.

The look Susie sent her wasn't lethal, but it extinguished Julia's cheer pretty quickly. "They're going," she said. "I think."

"What do you mean, you think? Can't you tell?"

"The website is not my job," Susie said tersely.

"Can you tell if the sales are rising? I mean, Passover is just a couple of weeks away."

"They're rising."

Susie's taut, gritty tone indicated she was pissed—whether about the sales or Passover or life in general, Julia didn't know. She took a guess. "Grandma Ida will host a Seder," she said. "We'll all go. We'll be together. Everything will be fine."

"Really? You'll sit at the same table as Uncle Jay and Adam?"

Good question. Julia hadn't thought that far ahead. Well, yes, she had thought that far ahead, but she hadn't come up with an answer yet. Grandma Ida did have a long table. Maybe if she sat at one end and her back-stabbing relatives sat at the other…

"I'm writing this week's *Bloom's Bulletin*," Susie said. "I don't give a shit about how many Seders-in-a-Box we sell. I'll put the product on the front page, but Uncle Jay obviously doesn't care about that anymore. Right now, I need a rhyme for matzo."

"Lotsa," Julia said helpfully. "Lotsa matzo."

"Wonderful," Susie said in a tone of voice that implied she didn't think it was the least bit wonderful. Scowling, she hit the delete key and then resumed typing, her fingers dancing on the keys.

Julia wasn't sure she could bear fighting with her mother and her sister at the same time, especially since she was alienated from her brother. She was rapidly running out of loved ones to love. "Susie. Whatever I did to offend you, I'm sorry. Just tell me what it is, and I'll stop."

"Really? You'll stop breathing? Let me know when your face turns blue," Susie said, then hunched over her keyboard and read what she'd written in a tight mutter. "'If you celebrate Passover Seder, take it easy, allow Bloom's to cater. With matzo and wine, your Seder is fine, And save room for some macaroons later.' There," she said, sounding both smug and annoyed. "A *Pesach* limerick. My work here is done." She pounded a key on her computer, leaned back in her chair, and grinned. Not at Julia, though. She wanted Julia to stop breathing and turn blue.

I give up, Julia fumed, although of course, she couldn't give up. She was the president of Bloom's. Grandma Ida had dumped this weighty responsibility on her. She had to keep the business afloat, even if she herself wound up drowning in the process.

She stormed back to her own office, stepped inside, and slammed the door. God, she hated everyone, with the possible exception of Myron and Deirdre, because they weren't her relatives.

All right, she didn't hate Ron, and he was her relative. He'd crawled out of a different gene pool, however. Maybe that was why she still loved him.

She crossed to her desk, not caring if any of the other third-floor denizens viewed her closed door as an ominous sign. It *was* an ominous sign. Julia was feeling homicidal at the moment. If she opened her door, she might be unable to prevent herself from racing to her mother's office and throttling her, and then returning to Susie's office and stabbing her multiple times with a letter opener.

Oh, yes, she was letting her rage-flag fly.

She picked up her cell phone and tapped Ron's number. After two rings, he answered. "Hey, babe, what's up?"

"I'm going to kill my mother and sister," she said. "Will you come and see me in prison?"

"Only if they allow conjugal visits." He laughed at his own wit, then said, "How would you like to be married to a Pulitzer Prize winner?"

If he was going to mock her, she'd mock him back. "Is that your way of saying you want me to leave you and find a new husband?"

He laughed again, evidently considering her as funny as he was. "This article is going to be fabulous," he told her. "Even Kim is psyched. You know she always gives me a hard time. But she read my final draft and actually announced that she's not going to give me a hard time with this one."

Ron insisted that his editor was a hard-driving bitch, but Julia had met Kim a couple of times and thought the woman was quite pleasant. Then again, Julia thought she herself was pleasant, and Susie and her mother probably considered her a hard-driving bitch right now.

"Which article is this?" she asked. She had enough on her mind without keeping track of Ron's work, too.

"About the payday lenders and their scams. They loan money to customers who can't possibly repay their loans, then have the customers take out another loan to pay back the first loan, and it just snowballs. These guys are unscrupulous, and they've got friends in high places. I really think I've nailed this one, Julia. It's going to make me a star."

"That's nice." And really, it was. She was happy for him. She just wasn't happy in general.

He didn't seem to notice. "I'll be on cable news shows. I might have to wear a thousand-dollar suit."

"If you do, I won't recognize you," she warned.

"You'll recognize me if I take off my pants."

Not the most romantic words he'd ever used, but Julia responded anyway. Ron was sexy. That was how he'd reeled her in—by being ridiculously sexy. Who ever thought a journalist specializing in business and finance could be such a turn-on? The only thing that would make Ron sexier would be if he was less aware of how sexy he was.

That, and a thousand-dollar suit, one that he might shed garment by garment in a sultry strip-tease. "My mother wants my job," she told him, deciding that now wasn't the time to contemplate how much she'd like to be at home in bed with him.

"You knew that going in."

"Going in, I wanted her to have my job."

"And now you don't. You'll just have to fight her. You have to establish dominance."

Her mind conjured a nature video she'd seen some years ago, in which two large, antlered mammals—antelopes or rams or gnus—battled to determine which one would be the alpha of the herd. They'd butted heads, emitted loud grunts and squeals, and literally locked horns. Her brow ached in sympathy; if she and her mother had horns, would she have head-butted her mother out of her office? Would this fight for dominance come to that?

"You're the president of Bloom's," Ron reminded her. "Do you know why you're the president of Bloom's?"

"Because I'm brilliant and talented?" she guessed uncertainly.

"Because your grandmother named you the president of Bloom's. Because she wanted you to be president. Because she believed you were the best person for the job." He paused to let that sink in. "Ida is the smartest person in your family, except for you when you're having a good day. She was smart enough to put you in charge. You need to have as much faith in yourself as she has in you."

Julia wondered if that simple wisdom was what professors taught in business school, or perhaps in journalism school. She pondered it for a few seconds, then said, "I'm going to go talk to Grandma Ida."

"You do that," Ron encouraged her. "Tell her your husband is going to win a Pulitzer Prize."

Even when she was fuming, Ron could make her smile. She might have married him because he was sexy, but she stayed married to him because he amused her. She ought to call Bernie Koplowitz up and share that bit of marital advice with him.

Instead, she said goodbye, ended the call, and left her office.

Less than a minute later, she emerged from the elevator on the twenty-fifth floor of the Bloom Building. She had no idea whether Grandma Ida would be home, and if so, whether she would welcome a visit. It didn't matter. Julia was the alpha. She had the biggest antlers. If she needed to confer with her grandmother, she would confer with her.

Lyndon answered the door and smiled. "Well, this is a surprise," he said, welcoming her into the foyer. "I was just fixing your grandmother a mushroom quiche. Would you like a slice?"

"I'd love a slice," Julia said, forgetting her anger as the rich aroma of baking pie crust and melted cheese wafted into the entry from the kitchen.

"Let me tell her you're here. She's watching a show on TV." He strode down the hall, passing the formal dining room and the living room for the bedrooms.

Julia could remain in the entry, inhaling the magnificent fragrance of the quiche, or she could follow him. Feeling alpha, she followed him.

Grandma Ida's apartment was directly above the one Julia had grown up in, with the same floor plan. Her grandmother had turned the bedroom above Julia's childhood bedroom into a den. Two heavy, ugly wingback chairs flanked an even heavier, uglier sofa, all three pieces upholstered in a nubby mustard-hued fabric. Across from the sofa and chairs stood a bulky television set just this side of an antique. It was framed in a fake-wood veneer and its innards bulged out in back, and it was accessorized by an equally outdated VCR player. At least it broadcast in color and had a remote control.

Grandma Ida sat in one of the wingback chairs, dressed in a pilling maroon sweater and a gray skirt, a cup of tea beside the remote control on the end table at her elbow. She glanced up at Julia and her eyes widened slightly beneath the dense black mop of her hair. If she was given to smiling, she might have smiled. "Why aren't you at work?" she asked.

Julia crossed the room, bent over, and kissed her grandmother's cheek. "I am at work. I needed to talk to you, and Lyndon said I could have some quiche."

"Quiche." Grandma Ida shook her head. "Who eats pie for a main course? Pie should be a dessert—and it's a *goyishe* dessert. I never sold pies in Bloom's. Today, they sell quiche down there. Your father started in with the quiche. At least he never sold the kind with ham in it. It's not kosher. I told Lyndon, if he makes me a quiche, he has to make it with mushrooms. No ham."

"And that's what you shall have," Lyndon said, bowing slightly and sending a dimpled grin Julia's way. "I'll go see if it's ready. You ladies can have your confab."

"What's a confab?" Grandma Ida asked.

Julia settled on the sofa and eyed the television. A man and a woman, both with grave expressions, sat behind a semi-circular desk, pontificating on the dismal state of the environment, national politics, and hip-hop. "A confab is something like that," Julia said, gesturing toward the screen.

"I saw this terrible thing last night," Grandma Ida said, then shuddered. "I couldn't sleep, so I came in here to watch some TV, and there was this terrible thing. A fat man with gold chains around his neck. Probably fake. And he was doing that thing they're talking about, the rap music. It's not really music. It's just shouting. He wanted me to buy a cheap car."

"No one needs to own a car in Manhattan," Julia said.

"Your Uncle Jay owns a car."

And look at him, Julia wanted to wail. *He's a traitor.* "What are we going to do about Uncle Jay? He's serious about opening a competing deli on the East Side."

"You're the president," Grandma Ida said. "What are *you* going to do about it?"

"I'm going to ask your advice." Julia peered into her grandmother's face. Grandma Ida looked old, but she never really aged. The creases bracketing her mouth and pleating the outer corners of her eyes hadn't changed in decades. Her jawline was still tight, and her mouth was no more downturned today than it had been in the sepia photos Julia had seen of her when she'd been Julia's age. Her hair, of course, was inky; not a hint of gray glinted through that heavily dyed mane.

Grandma Ida's face was grim, but it was also wise. Julia had never consciously acknowledged her grandmother's wisdom, but she acknowledged it now. Why else would she have used the pronoun *we* instead of *I*?

She wanted Grandma Ida's input. She wanted her support. She wanted them to be a team.

"He was always the naughty one, my Jacob," Grandma Ida said. "Your father was the well-behaved one and Jay was the *kol-boinik*. Like you and your sister."

"Susie isn't a *kol-boinik*," Julia argued, although she wasn't sure what a *kol-boinik* was. It sounded male. "What does that mean, anyway?"

"A rascal," Grandma Ida translated. "A mischief-maker. Never serious. Always doing the fun thing. He thinks running his own store will be fun. You and I could tell him a thing or two."

"Then let's," Julia said. "Let's tell him how much work it's going to be."

"Eh." Grandma Ida flapped her hand, as if swatting at a mosquito. Her bracelets rattled. "He'll learn. I give him a week. By next week, he'll be back."

"Do you think so?" A spark of optimism caught fire inside Julia. Given her mother's apathy about hiring a replacement for Uncle Jay, maybe the best thing would be to wait him out, to have him come back to Bloom's, defeated and overflowing with remorse. If he came back, Adam would come back, too. Adam had grandiose ideas about expanding the Bloom's franchise, but that was all they were. Grandiose ideas.

"He's a fool, my Jacob. But a good man underneath. He'll come back." Grandma Ida reached for her tea and took a sip.

"You know so much," Julia said. "I still have so much to learn. Why did you name me president?"

"Because," Grandma Ida answered, "you're a lawyer."

"Being a lawyer doesn't qualify me to run Bloom's."

"You spent a lot of time in school. You know big words. You can read a contract." Grandma Ida took another sip. "And you don't have a tattoo. Your *meshuge* sister, she has a tattoo. That's not a good thing."

Julia had no opinion one way or the other about the tiny butterfly inked onto the skin of Susie's ankle. "Everyone in the family hates me," she said. "I think they hate me because I'm the president of Bloom's."

"Heavy is the head that wears the crown," Grandma Ida recited. "That's from the Bible."

"Shakespeare," Julia corrected her.

"He wrote the Bible, didn't he? The Christian part of it." She shrugged. "Everyone else in the family, something goes wrong and they fall apart. Not you."

Julia wasn't sure about that. She was falling apart now, wasn't she? Cell by cell, synapse by synapse, she was coming undone. She was afraid her uncle and brother would steal business from her. She worried that the Seder-in-a-Box sales would tank. She was concerned that Susie would do a poor job on the *Bloom's Bulletin*—her limerick about Passover was less than inspired. Julia suspected that her mother would never find people to replace Uncle Jay and Adam, but instead would devote all her energies to undermining Julia. She fretted that Myron would never figure out how to create a spreadsheet.

Her greatest fear was that the business would collapse, and it would be her fault, because she'd fallen apart.

"You have *chutzpah*," Grandma Ida said.

"I don't think so."

"You're wrong. I know from *chutzpah*, and you've got it." Grandma Ida set down her tea, then hollered, "Lyndon? When is lunch?"

"I'm just taking the quiche out of the oven now," he called back. "Come into the dining room and I'll cut it up."

Julia sprang off the sofa and extended her hand. Grandma Ida ignored it, using the arms of her chair to hoist herself to her feet. Then she hooked her fingers around the bend in Julia's elbow, allowing Julia to escort her to the dining room.

"Do you mind if I join you for lunch?" Julia asked.

Grandma Ida glanced at her, quirking her eyebrows. "A person's got to eat," she said. "Thank God for that, or Bloom's wouldn't exist."

Chapter Fourteen

Susie was waiting for Rick when he arrived at the Upper East Side address of his father's new store. She stood with her hands in the hip pockets of her snug black jeans, her hair a messy shag in the breeze stirred up by the traffic cruising along Lexington Avenue. She was staring at the empty building as if it were worthy of intensive study.

As far as Rick could tell, it was just a vacant storefront. He tried framing it with his hands, shaping mirror-image L's with his index fingers and thumbs and peering through the frame, as if he were going to film the building.

Nothing special. Not worth filming.

He sidled up beside Susie. "Sorry I'm late," he said. "There are always meetings. Some Staten Island law firm wants us to handle their advertising. Ah, commerce." He smiled.

Susie didn't return his smile. "You're turning into an ad man," she said.

"It pays the bills." He steered his gaze back to the empty storefront. "So this is the place?"

"Must be. Your father and my brother are inside."

Rick tried to give it the same intense scrutiny Susie had. But intense scrutiny had never been his long suit. That was why he liked movies better than paintings.

Paintings just sat there, doing nothing. Movies moved. If a vision got boring, no worries—the camera would soon transport you to the next vision. You didn't have to linger on an image, searching for subtext and meaning.

Still, this enterprise was his father's big thing, and Rick owed it a fair assessment. As far as he could tell, the store itself wasn't terribly wide. No way would it have the capacity of Bloom's. The front window spanned the width of the unit, and through the glass he could see his father, his cousin Adam, and another man wandering around, talking and pointing. Propped up on a ledge inside the window was a square of cardboard with the words, written in heavy black marker: *Future Home of Jacob Bloom's Delectable Food Emporium.*

"That's stupid," Susie said, pointing to the sign.

"You design much better windows. No argument there."

"No, I mean the name. *Delectable* Food Emporium? Like, what, they're going to sell food that isn't delectable?"

"They're going to sell food that *is* delectable. Hence the name: *Delectable Food Emporium.*"

"Hence? Since when do you use words like hence?" She shook her head in disapproval. "Customers are going to assume that the food will be delectable. If it isn't delectable, they aren't going to go into the store. So the store's name is telling them nothing they haven't already figured out. Unless, of course, the food *isn't* delectable, in which case the store's name is a lie." Another disapproving shake of her head. "It's a stupid name, that's all." With that, she pushed open the glass door and stepped inside.

Adam bounded over to her, as energetic as a puppy who believed she had a doggie biscuit hidden behind her back. "Hey, Susie. Uncle Jay said you guys would be stopping by today."

"We would have gotten here earlier, but Rick had a *meeting*." Susie sent Rick a withering look.

He wondered what she had against meetings. She'd told him that her sister held a staff meeting at Bloom's every Monday morning—and maybe, he realized, that was what she had against them. But he ignored Susie's scornful tone, gave Adam a fist bump, and looked around. "Who's the guy with my dad?" he asked.

"He's going to help us outfit the place. We're working out the layout. We're figuring, refrigerated cases for cheese and dairy, yogurt, stuff like that, as you first come in the door. Along the back, refrigerated cases for deli meats, prepared meals, whatever else needs refrigerating. And freezer cases for ice cream. Gourmet only. The good stuff. Ten percent butterfat minimum, according to Uncle Jay." He gestured toward another blank wall. "Over there, we'll have the bakery section. I'm going to talk to Casey and see if he wants to be a supplier. Then, up the middle, rows of shelving."

"That's the exact same layout as Bloom's first floor," Susie pointed out.

"I know. It's a good layout. Why reinvent the wheel?"

"If you're going to do what they do at Bloom's, why not stay at Bloom's?" Susie asked.

"Because we're on the East Side. It's a different world here. A different clientele. Besides—" he grinned "—this is *ours*. We're partners. It's *ours*."

"Maybe you should get Susie to design your displays," Rick offered.

She sent him another look, this one scathing. "I'm already doing too much stuff for Bloom's and not enough for Casey. And I need time to write poetry."

"Actually," Adam said, giving Susie a smile so sweet, just looking at it made Rick's teeth ache, "I was hoping maybe we could hire you to write our circulars for us, and our website text. You do such a great job with the *Bloom's Bulletin*." Susie opened her mouth to object, but Adam continued before she could speak. "You could turn it into a business of your own. A consulting business. You could specialize in writing clever circulars for businesses. I think you'd be great."

"Or I could write poetry," she retorted.

"That, too. You write poetry for the *Bloom's Bulletin*. Those limericks."

"If you want advertising, hire Rick." She jabbed a finger in Rick's direction. "He can have a meeting. I'm not writing ad copy."

"But the *Bloom's Bulletin*—"

"I'm doing that because I'm a Bloom. The family trust gets a share of the business's profits. *You* get a cut of that, even though you're here. You want to create a trust and pay me dividends from this place? Great. I'll write limericks for you."

Man, she was in a sour mood. Rick wondered if she had PMS or something. He didn't ask, though. He'd learned the hard way that women hated being asked if they had PMS.

"Where are you getting all the money for this?" he asked Adam as he surveyed the vacant store with his gaze. "The rent, the shelving, the refrigerated cases... Did Dad win the lottery or something?"

"Something like that," Adam said, pride brightening his tone. "He's got investors. He says they're bottomless pits of money. They want to spend, spend, spend."

Rick shot his father an awed look. Investors who wanted to spend, spend, spend? Rick wished he knew people like that. If he did, he could quit making commercials starring Phat Larry and return to his original passion: creating films artistic enough to win the *Palme d'Or* at Cannes.

He glanced toward his father, who appeared more animated than Rick had ever seen him before. Words rushed out of him in a torrent, and he waved his hands, sweeping them through the air, pointing here, there, up at the ceiling, with its exposed ducts and pipes, down at the scuffed linoleum floor. He hadn't been this excited since his marriage to Wendy. Maybe not even then.

After all, Wendy didn't pay for his car, or his golf club membership, or his elegant apartment just a few blocks from here. She'd decorated the apartment, but she didn't pay for it. She was more in the category of the apartment itself, or his father's car—something his father paid for, owned, and derived pleasure from.

"He's into fixtures," Adam told Rick and Susie. "That's what he calls everything. Lighting fixtures. Refrigeration fixtures. Shelving fixtures." An impish smile crossed Adam's lips. "Fixtures are cool."

Susie's frown made it clear that she didn't think even refrigeration fixtures were cool. "How much are these investors sinking into all your fixtures?" she asked. "Starting a store isn't cheap."

"Grandma Ida and Grandpa Isaac did it."

"Years ago. Decades. And they did it slowly. Their first shop after the pushcart was, like, one tenth the size of this place."

"They didn't have investors," Adam pointed out. "We do."

"Then I'll repeat my question. How much are they investing?"

Adam shrugged. "That's not my department. I'm in charge of inventory. We're looking at warehouses in the Bronx—cheaper than Brooklyn, and more convenient than Queens or Jersey. If I can get Casey on board, we won't need storage space for the breads. We'll just truck them straight uptown from his bakery. Do you think you could put in a good word for us with him?" he asked Susie, his tone turning plaintive.

"Like I want to help you guys."

"You want your boyfriend to make money, right?"

She sighed and looked away for a moment, then turned back. "Are your investors going to buy trucks for you?"

"That's Uncle Jay's department. I'll figure out what we need and place the orders, and Uncle Jay will pay the bills—with the investor money. But I'm serious, Susie—if you could put in a good word for us with Casey, I'd be in your debt forever."

"You'll be in debt to the investors; you'll be in debt to me. Did it ever occur to you that you should be in debt to Bloom's? If not for Julia giving you the inventory job, you'd be at Purdue right now, studying for a doctorate. A fate worse than death, if you ask me."

"Stop being such a downer," Adam retorted. "This is exciting. You could be a part of the excitement if you wanted. You could write your limericks for us instead of Julia. You don't want to? Fine. Just keep your downer vibes to yourself, okay?" He glanced at Rick. "You get it, don't you? You see why this is so exciting?"

Rick wished he could say yes. His father sure seemed excited. Adam was psyched, too. But really, one store or the other—what difference did it make? Bloom's was already established. The hard work had been done. Now it was a money machine, paying scores of salaries, pouring profits into the family trust, keeping people around the city—around the *world*—well fed. As Adam himself said, why reinvent the wheel?

Because they wanted an East Side store? Or just because?

At last, Rick's father joined them in the center of the room. He gave Rick a robust hug, then reached for Susie, who offered her cheek, deftly avoiding an embrace. Her current grouchiness was apparently aimed at everyone. Yeah, probably PMS.

"What do you think?" Jay asked Rick.

"It looks great," he said, then cringed inwardly at what a ridiculous lie that was. It might look great eventually, if the man who'd been conferring with his father, and was now calculating the room's dimensions with an industrial-size tape measure, outfitted the place with the right fixtures. It would look even greater if Susie oversaw the décor. Rick could appreciate a good shot, a good composition, an aesthetic arrangement of objects in space. But Susie was the one who knew how to arrange those objects, how to compose them in a given space. If he ever had the chance to make his own movies, he'd hire her to be his art director. She could write her poetry on the side.

His father turned to Susie. "I know it's not much to look at right now," he said. "But use your imagination. It's going to be fantastic. Delectable food wherever you look. The best yogurt. The best salamis. Exquisite gourmet chocolates."

"Honey-roasted almonds," Adam added. "Plantain chips."

"Right," Susie muttered. "I've got it. Delectable gourmet food." She tilted her head toward the cardboard sign in the front window. "It's causing a lot of upheaval back at the Mother Ship."

Jay seemed pleased to hear this. "They deserve upheaval," he said. "Not my problem. Right, Adam?"

Adam nodded hesitantly. Maybe he thought the upheaval back at Bloom's was on his list of responsibilities, along with ordering inventory.

"This is going to be huge," Jay said. "People wouldn't want to invest in it if they didn't have faith that it would be a huge success."

Susie shrugged, clearly unconvinced. "I've got to get downtown. I wanted to see what you guys were up to, but I promised Casey I'd cover the counter until closing today."

"I have to get back, too," Rick said. "This Staten Island law firm—we've got more meetings. I think they're going to assign the account to me."

Another crushing hug from his father, another fist bump with Adam, and he followed Susie out of the store. On the sidewalk, she squinted in the glaring midday sunlight, then slipped a pair of sunglasses up her nose.

He could no longer see her eyes, but he could tell from her mouth, from her posture, from the angle of her head, that whatever was bothering her went beyond whether she was plugged up with a tampon. Susie was his buddy, his honorary sister, the closest he would ever come to having a twin. "What?" he asked.

"It's an empty store. What the hell are they thinking?"

"They've got investors."

"Big effing deal. Bloom's has no outside investors. It's all family—and that's what keeps the money in the family. It's good, being a family-owned company—except for the fact that I hate my family at the moment." She peered into the store and shook her head. "They're going to have to pay the investors back, right? They think this is theirs, but it's going to belong to their investors."

Rick chewed that over. "Maybe."

"No maybe. What, you think these investors aren't going to want a return on their investment?"

"I don't know." Finance had never been Rick's strong suit. If he managed to pay all his bills by the end of the month, he was content. Balancing his checkbook was a rare accomplishment, worthy of celebration.

Perhaps he ought to discuss the financing with his father. But what would he say? His father knew more about that stuff than Rick did.

"I've got to go," Susie said, starting down the street. The subway station was a couple of blocks south, visible from where they stood. "You heading back downtown?"

"Not right away," he said, feeling strangely unsettled. Who were these happily spending investors? What promises had they wrung from his father? "I've got to make a call."

"Okay. I'll be in touch."

"Yeah. Say hi to Anna for me if you talk to her," he said, waving Susie off and pulling his cell phone from his pocket. He waited until she was a block away, her back to him, then tucked his phone back into his pocket and turned, walking in the opposite direction.

One block east and two blocks north, he reached the building where his father and Wendy lived. He wasn't sure why he was there, except that he knew Wendy would offer him something to eat—she always did—and he was hungry. Jacob Bloom's Delectable Food Emporium hadn't offered him any ice cream or plantain chips.

Back in his unemployed-filmmaker days, the doormen in his father's building always looked askance at him when he showed up to visit his father and Wendy. The lobby was posh and impeccable, with marble floors and veined mirrors on the walls and sleek leatherette benches. He'd show up ungroomed, unshaven, in fraying jeans held together with patches of duct tape, ragged flannel shirts, and battered Teva sandals. Now that he worked at Glickstein, his apparel was intact and passed for clean, even if he didn't run a load of laundry as often as he should. And he wore sandals only in the summer. Susie had told him wearing sandals with socks was dorky, and his socks got dirty much too quickly for someone who didn't like doing laundry. But back before he started working at Glickstein, his budget hadn't stretched to cover shoes, which cost too damned much.

Despite his greatly improved grooming, the doorman frowned at him, oozing disapproval. The doormen in his father's building seemed to be chosen for their superciliousness—either that, or their ability to look spiffy in a pseudo-military uniform, with a double row of brass buttons down the front of the jacket and gold braiding on the shoulders, trousers with satin stripes down the sides, and a visored police-style hat. Rick told the current doorman his name, even though this guy had seen him here enough times to recognize him by now.

His suspicious gaze never shifting from Rick, the doorman lifted a phone on his console and pressed a button. "Someone named Rick is here," he said, a rather casual announcement given that militaristic hat and those satin-striped pants. The doorman listened for a moment, lowered the phone, and said, with what Rick sensed were grave misgivings, "You can go up."

Smiling, Rick headed for the elevator. He liked Wendy. He was also chronically amused by the fact that she and his father lived on the thirteenth floor of a building that had no thirteenth floor. The builders had skipped right over it—or at least, the elevator buttons did. Jay and Wendy Bloom officially lived in apartment 14D, on the fourteenth floor, but the floor numbers jumped from twelve to fourteen, as if by omitting a button numbered thirteen, the building could avoid having a thirteenth floor. Why thirteen was supposed to be unlucky, Rick wasn't sure—his mother had once provided a lengthy lecture about the number twelve reflecting the twelve Apostles and thirteen being extraneous and therefore bad, which had little relevance if you were Jewish. His mother had made the story sound so boring, he'd lost interest about halfway through.

It didn't matter, though. You couldn't simply make the thirteenth floor disappear by pretending it didn't exist. His father lived on the thirteenth floor, whatever you called it—and he seemed pretty lucky. He had investors who wanted to spend, spend, spend, after all.

Wendy was hovering in the apartment's open doorway when Rick exited the elevator. As always, she was a vision of blond pulchritude, her face as bright as the early spring sunshine outside and the curves of her body emphasized by the clingy Lycra exercise clothing she wore. If she'd been working out, she'd managed to do so without having excreted a single drop of sweat. Her hair was bouncy, her face smooth and dry. Rick suspected she wore exercise clothing not because she exercised but because she wanted people to think she did. But he'd never ask her. She was his stepmother, and merely twelve years older than him, which meant that at one time she could have been his babysitter. You didn't ask your babysitter whether she was faking it with her exercise clothes.

"Hey, there!" she greeted him, then gave him a hug. "What a surprise!" She always seemed thrilled to see him, as if eager to make sure he accepted her into his family. Of course he accepted her. She made his father happy, and she was cheerful and generous. A little empty-headed, but amazingly good-natured.

And she always fed him. His mother fed him, too, but his mother fed him tofu and quinoa and vegetables that were always misshapen and bruised because, she claimed, they were organic. As if the lack of fertilizer caused zucchini to grow crooked.

"I was in the neighborhood," Rick said, pleased that it was the truth.

"Well, come on in. I was about to make myself a peanut butter and marshmallow fluff sandwich. Would you like one?"

"I'd kill for one," he said, following her into the apartment. Turquoise was Wendy's favorite color, and the apartment's living room reverberated with it. Turquoise carpeting. Turquoise velour upholstery on the curved couch and side chairs. A pattern of turquoise, green, and white woven into the drapes. While not crazy about the color, Rick could tolerate it if there was a peanut butter and marshmallow fluff sandwich in it for him. He'd bet good money the peanut butter was homogenized, not the gritty, oily, fresh-ground stuff his mother bought when she wasn't serving sesame seed butter or cashew butter.

Marshmallow fluff was strictly *verboten* in his mother's apartment. All that high-fructose corn syrup! All that refined sugar! All that exquisite sweetness!

"So, what brings you to the neighborhood?" Wendy asked. "Your dad is down at his new store. If he'd known you were coming—"

"His new store was why I was in the neighborhood," Rick said, seeing no reason to lie. He shed his jacket and settled himself at the tiny breakfast table tucked into the corner of the narrow kitchen. The table was adorned with turquoise placemats and a turquoise plastic napkin holder. At least the napkins were white. He pulled a couple from the holder and set them in front of the two chairs.

Wendy bustled about, preparing their sandwiches with as much flair as a *Cordon Bleu* chef preparing a soufflé. She spread the peanut butter in festive swirls on slices of white bread—*white bread*, a food his mother was so contemptuous of, she wouldn't even feed it to the pigeons in Riverside Park—and then crowning the peanut butter with a plush layer of fluff. Her fingernails, Rick noticed, were painted turquoise.

"What do you think of the store?" she asked as she worked. "Your dad is so excited about it."

"I noticed that," Rick said.

"It's all he can talk about." Wendy carried the sandwiches to the table, then filled two tumblers with chocolate milk from the refrigerator and joined Rick. "It's a little bit much, actually. All day long, he goes on and on about crackers. Should he stock these crackers or those crackers? Do customers prefer round crackers or square crackers? And bread sticks. Do you know how many kinds of bread sticks there are? And painting chips. If he wants to paint the walls, he should paint the walls, but why does he go on and on about ordering painting chips?"

"Plantain chips, maybe?" Rick suggested.

"Isn't that what I said?"

He started to explain what plantains were, then decided the effort wasn't worth it. "Does he ever talk about Bloom's?" he asked. "From what Susie tells me, people are pissed off that he left."

"Well, no." Wendy took a bite of her sandwich, chewed daintily, and dabbed her lips with her napkin. "I mean, he loves Bloom's. How can he not love it? He loves his mother, and Bloom's is her baby. Just like *he's* her baby. I guess he thinks of Bloom's as his brother. Now that he doesn't have his other brother..."

Her logic struck Rick as screwy, but Rick let her babble because she'd made this absurdly tasty, gooey sandwich for him.

"Anyway, you know how it is with brothers. You have a brother."

Rick didn't see much of his brother Neil, but he couldn't imagine quitting the guy, even if Neil could be officious and bossy. Behaving officious and bossy was what older siblings did. "I'd never leave Neil," he said, realizing that sounded like the sort of thing you'd say about your lover.

"And maybe Jay wouldn't have left Bloom's, except that the opportunity presented itself. You know how it is with opportunity."

Rick wasn't quite sure. "How is it?"

"It knocks." She took another bite of her sandwich. He realized she was nipping off the bread crusts. Her sandwich was gradually coming to resemble a square of foam rubber, spongy and white. "When it knocks, you've got to open that door. And then these men came along and offered Jay all this money to get his new store off the ground. I mean, how do you say no when a man offers you a lot of money?"

Rick wondered whether offering Wendy a lot of money was how his father had won her hand in marriage. But she'd raised the subject that had been niggling at him, and he was happy to follow up. "Who are his investors? Do you know?"

"I haven't met them." Wendy sipped her chocolate milk and dabbed at her lips again. "He met them at the golf club he belongs to, out on Long Island. Isn't it funny, how you play golf at a golf club and you play golf *with* a golf club?" This philosophical gem was followed by a gust of trilling laughter.

Rick politely laughed along. "I never thought of that," he admitted. "So these guys, Dad knows them? He plays golf with them?"

"Oh, I don't know. Sometimes I'm not sure they even play golf out there. They just get together and sit around the clubhouse, talking man talk. It's like a fraternity, without the Greek letters." She'd finally consumed the last of the crust, and she bit into the body of her sandwich. A deep moan of satisfaction emanated from her. "Whoever invented marshmallow fluff deserves the Noble Prize."

"Nobel," Rick corrected her, then shook his head. "Sorry. You're right. He deserves the Noble Prize."

"Or *she* does." It was Wendy's turn to correct him.

He nodded. "*She.* Definitely. So these guys, these investors—Susie thinks Dad's going to have to pay them back, and that might eat up the store's profits."

"I don't think so. Jay says they're just looking for a place to park their money, and if they want him to, he'll pay them back once the store starts showing a profit. I think that's very nice of them."

More than very nice. Rick wished credit card companies and landlords were that nice. "I guess his membership in the golf club is worth what it costs."

"Does it cost money?" Wendy shrugged. "I just thought he paid when he played, like at a bowling alley." She smiled. She had the whitest teeth Rick had ever seen. "I've talked to one of those investors on the phone a couple of times, but we didn't talk about golf. He asked to talk to Jay, so I passed the phone along. He's got the cutest accent."

"Really? What kind of accent?"

"British, I think. Or maybe it's Irish, or Australian. I can't really tell the difference. It just sounds so cute, though. I'm always expecting him to say he wants a spot of tea. He never does, though. He says, 'Might I have a word with your husband?'" From her attempt at an accent, Rick couldn't tell if it was British, Irish, or Australian. Or possibly French. She was really bad at accents.

"So he's not American?"

"He sure doesn't sound American. He talks like one of those Monty Python actors. I'm always waiting for him to say his parrot is dead."

Why would a Brit want to invest in a glorified grocery store in Manhattan? Didn't London have its own grocery stores?

Then again, according to Adam, this investor wanted to spend, spend, spend. Maybe he'd already invested in a bunch of grocery stores in England—gourmet shops selling Indian curry and Jamaican jerk chicken and Canadian...whatever Canadian cuisine was all about. Maybe this investor, this chap, this bloke, wanted to invest in a store that sold plantain chips to Upper East Side patrons.

Or maybe he didn't care what he invested in. Maybe he just wanted to park his money somewhere.

"How's your sandwich?" Wendy asked.

He realized he'd stopped eating as his brain churned. He took a bite, let the filling coat his tongue—a magnificent blend of pasty peanut butter and sticky marshmallow—and swallowed. "Delicious," he said, although his mind remained miles away, across the pond, wondering how his father would have met a Brit at a Long Island country club where you had to be nominated for membership by other members. He supposed the guy could be an immigrant, living on Long Island but hanging onto his accent. He could be so rich, he owned homes both in the United Kingdom and in the greater New York area.

Rick wondered whether the guy might want to invest in films. He could dig out one of his old screenplays, ask Susie to polish it up for him—she was the talented writer in the family, after all—and then he could present it to this investor who wanted to spend, spend, spend, and see what happened.

If his father could create Jacob Bloom's Delectable Food Emporium, why couldn't Rick create something worthy of the *Palme d'Or* at Cannes?

Chapter Fifteen

"**Y**ou seem frazzled," Martha said as she approached Sondra in the mail alcove off the residential lobby of the Bloom Building.

Sondra *was* frazzled. Her daughter, her first-born, whom she'd spent twenty agonizing hours in labor to deliver into the world, was treating her like a week-old loaf of *challah,* as dry as plasterboard and just as flavorless. All she did was try to help—all she'd ever done, in her entire life, was try to help—and Julia was barely speaking to her. She was actually closing her office door for hours at a time. Or at least minutes at a time, but they felt like hours. To be cut off like that, shut out, cast aside...

Sondra stabbed the little key repeatedly at the slot in the brass door of her mailbox. Why did they make the key the same damned color as the mailbox door? Why was it so damned tiny? Why couldn't she get the damned key into the damned slot?

Because she was frazzled. That was why.

"You need a night out," Martha said.

Sondra sighed and turned to face her sister-in-law. Martha had on a beige canvas coat with a brown corduroy collar—a barn coat, Sondra recalled, as if one was supposed to wear the garment on a farm, while mucking the stalls or chasing bats out of the rafters with a pitchfork. Below the hem of the coat, Martha's corduroy slacks bagged at the knees, an olive-green shade that didn't work with the coat. On her feet, she wore gray raglan socks and Birkenstock sandals. A fashion mistake from head to toe.

"A night out would be nice," Sondra agreed. She'd always done her best to get along with Martha, even though the woman had the personality of a boiled turnip. They were neighbors and fellow in-laws, after all, both of them having lost their Bloom husbands, both of them still Blooms despite that loss. "Do you know any single men?"

Martha smiled. She didn't smile often, so Sondra considered this a victory of some sort. Her daughter might think she was incompetent because she couldn't quite figure out how LinkedIn worked. But she could accomplish this. She could squeeze a smile out of Martha.

"I know something better than single men," Martha said.

"I'm not interested in married men."

Martha hinted at a second smile. "You don't need a man to have a night out. Come with me to my women's club. We talked about this. Remember? I'm just on my way to the meeting."

A night out at Martha's women's club? An evening surrounded by women as dreary as Martha, expounding on the evils of sexism and the joys of sisterhood? Sondra had been observing the dynamic between Julia and Susie lately, a dynamic as toxic as a hair-tearing cat fight on one of those tawdry, family-feuding TV shows where everyone drawled. Sisterhood didn't strike her as particularly joyful.

Then again, Martha's women's club might not be about sisterhood. Maybe they were lesbians. Martha didn't strike Sondra as a lesbian, but who knew what she did in her bedroom, or whom she did it with? The rare times Sondra ventured down the hall to Martha's apartment, she never got near the sleeping quarters. Usually, she and Martha remained in the kitchen, because Martha was always busy soaking beans or watering her alfalfa sprouts or grinding her own tahini.

"What do they do at your women's club?" Sondra asked cautiously. She had nothing against lesbians, but she didn't want to spend the evening watching women with crew-cuts hitting on one another.

"We've got a guest speaker this evening," Martha said. "She's talking about life balance and self-actualization. I told you this, Sondra. You really should come."

Life balance and self-actualization sounded ominous, but also vaguely interesting.

"They serve wine and snacks at the evening meetings, too. Not very good wine. I don't drink it, but..."

Wine? Definitely interesting.

"Come on. I'm walking over there now. We could go, listen to the speaker, and if you'd like, you could come back to my apartment for a bite to eat. I was planning to heat up some leftover cauliflower goulash."

"I'll pass on the dinner, but..." Wine and snacks, and Sondra could come home and indulge in a bowl of ice cream for dessert, because wine and snacks didn't amount to much of a dinner. "All right. I probably need to self-actualize—and I can't seem to get my mailbox open."

"You do need to self-actualize. We all do." Martha smiled yet again, a faint, gray-tinged smile. Sondra dropped her key chain into the side pocket of her purse, lifted the strap over her shoulder, and followed Martha past Tomás and out of the building.

At five o'clock, the sidewalk abutting Bloom's was packed with workers on their way home, many of them detouring into the store en route to pick up some Heat-'N'-Eat entrees or tomorrow morning's bagels. Sondra was glad to see so much foot traffic in the vicinity of the store. Jay's stupid store would never see this kind of foot traffic. Did people on the Upper East Side even walk? Most of them probably commuted to and from work in chauffeur-driven limos. Or, if they did walk, they walked briskly. All those fancy-schmancy professionals were too busy and important to stroll, to pause and gaze into the shop-front windows, to be captivated by some cockamamie arrangement of bread that resembled a lumpy sculpture. Sondra wasn't sure what Susie was trying to convey with her windows, but they did attract attention.

"Where, exactly, are we going?" she asked as Martha threaded a path through the crowds. If she'd known she was going on a long walk, she would have changed her shoes. Not that her ballet flats hurt her feet, but as ugly as they were, Martha's Birkenstocks looked a lot more comfortable.

"The you-you church," Martha said.

It took Sondra a minute to realize she was talking about the Unitarian Universalist Church. "Ida wouldn't like the thought of us attending a meeting at a church," she remarked.

"I'm not sure it's truly a church," Martha responded. "Unitarians are too open-minded. They don't have enough rules to be a real religion. Anyway, Ida doesn't like me. I don't care what she thinks."

That sounded like self-actualization to Sondra. A spark of anticipation flickered inside her. Attending this meeting might not be such a bad idea.

And there would be wine.

As it turned out, the meeting wasn't in the chapel, so Ida couldn't blow a gasket over the possibility that her daughters-in-law were converting to Christianity. Martha led Sondra into a community room, the sort of space where people might drag their chairs into a circle and declare that they're alcoholics. The chairs here were set up in rows, however. A long table against one wall held bowls of crackers and platters of cheese cut into cubes and drying a little along the edges. Beside the cheese platters was a stack of plastic cups, beside the cups several boxes with taps protruding from them and pictures of goblets, some filled with white wine and some with red, illustrating their flat surfaces. The boxes didn't bode well, but wine was wine. Sondra kept her eye on those boxes as Martha called greetings to some of the women milling around near the table.

These were her friends, Sondra realized. Martha actually had friends.

They didn't look like lesbians, although looks could be deceiving. Some appeared to be middle-aged, but most were a bit grayer and more wrinkled than Martha and Sondra. The other women dressed as unstylishly as Martha, in jeans or cords or twill slacks and blousy tops that failed to hide their thick waistlines. A few had the grizzled look of mountain climbers or marathon runners, but many of them landed somewhere on the border between plump and fat.

Sondra ought to attend these meetings more often. The chubby women made her feel svelte by comparison. Her daughters—lucky girls—had inherited their father's metabolism, as well as his reasonable nose. Sondra had inherited her own family's hawk's-beak of a nose and well-insulated *tuchas*. She liked to think her tunic-length tops concealed not her mid-section girth, which wasn't really that girthy, but the generous proportions of her rear end.

As ample as her tush was, it was definitely one of the smaller tushes at this gathering. Martha was thin, and Sondra supposed she herself would be a bit thinner if she was willing to eat all that organic vegetarian crap Martha dined on. Cauliflower goulash? The very idea made Sondra shudder.

Before she could pluck a plastic cup from the stack and fill it with wine—white or red, it probably didn't matter because they'd both taste blah—Martha started introducing her to other attendees. "Jean, this is my sister-in-law, Sondra. Sondra, this is Jean. And this is Norma. Norma, my sister-in-law, Sondra..."

The names came at her in a blur. Someone wrote "Sandra" on a sticky rectangle of paper and glued it to Sondra's shoulder, explaining that newcomers always wore an identifying name tag. Sondra didn't bother to correct the spelling on the tag. She felt more incognito this way.

The women Martha introduced her to were all pleasant enough in their way. None of them ranted about the percentage of females in the House of Representatives or sexual harassment in the workplace or the difficulty of finding a properly fitting bra for under forty dollars. Who knew? Maybe they weren't wearing bras. They didn't appear too floppy, but it *was* a woman's club, and they *might* be lesbians.

Instead, they talked about normal, apolitical things: landlord hassles, subway delays, homicidal cyclists, suicidal cyclists, obnoxious squirrels in Central Park, and some Cantonese-language film playing at an art house near Columbia University. "The subtitles were incompetent," a short, round woman with slate-colored hair babbled. "I had no idea what they were talking about. But the nuances! I never saw such amazing nuances in a film before."

Sondra inched closer to the wine boxes.

"Why don't we get started?" a woman called out. She looked oddly like Margaret Thatcher, her wavy, champagne-blond coif brushed back from her face, her fire-plug body clad in a royal blue suit, and a string of pearls the size of garbanzo beans looped around her neck. She had fat ankles, Sondra noted, peering past the chairs to where the woman stood by a lectern.

"I'm going to get some wine," Sondra whispered to Martha, deciding she had to assert herself. Asserting herself ought to go over big at a gathering like this.

Martha nodded and accompanied her to the snack table. After filling a glass with white wine the color of lemon juice, Sondra loaded a paper plate with cheese and crackers. She, after all, didn't have a Tupperware container of cauliflower goulash waiting for her at home.

They sat in the back row, which Sondra appreciated because it kept her closer to the snack table, in case she needed to refill her glass or her plate as the program progressed. Also, if the speaker was boring, Sondra would be able to yawn without being too conspicuous about it.

The Margaret Thatcher woman remained at the lectern, wearing a stern expression as the yammering crowd of women settled into the chairs. "Good evening," she greeted them once everyone was seated and the chatter had died down. Her voice boomed metallically through a microphone attached to the lectern. "Let's dispense with the business portion of our meeting quickly, so we can introduce our guest speaker."

The business portion had to do with dues and expenditures, an announcement about the room's thermostat settings from the church's management, and a fervent debate about a book club, which Sondra deduced was a sub-group within the club. "They refuse to choose books written by men," Martha whispered to Sondra. "I find that a bit close-minded. What if a man is transgender? He might have started life as a woman. How can you refuse to read his book?"

Sondra doubted that many books would fall into that particular category. But she nodded sympathetically and sipped her wine. Not great, but not wretched. The cheese was as non-denominational as the church, sort of mildly Havarti-ish and rubbery in texture. Whatever it was, it hadn't been purchased at Bloom's, where the cheeses were strong and fresh and sometimes smelled like dirty gym socks. This cheese had no scent at all, which wasn't necessarily a bad thing.

After the debate about the book club selections died down, the Margaret Thatcher woman smiled thinly. "Let's get on with our speaker, shall we?" she said. "Inga Vinderson is an adjunct professor at the New School and the author of three books on self-actualization. She'll have copies for sale after the meeting, cash only."

"Signed copies," the woman standing next to the Margaret Thatcher woman added. She wore a ribbed turtleneck sweater, a camel-colored wool blazer, and black slacks. Her hair was short and straight, a blend of gray and black that reminded Sondra of tarnished sterling silver. If the woman washed her hair with silver polish, would the black disappear?

"Signed copies," the Margaret Thatcher woman obliged. "We're very happy to have her here with us this evening. Inga, I'll turn this over to you."

The audience applauded. Sondra balanced her plate on her knees and clapped carefully to avoid splashing wine out of her glass. The speaker spent several long seconds adjusting the microphone and arranging sheets of paper inside a black folder on the lectern's surface. Sondra strained to see how many pages there were so she could estimate how long her speech would be. But seated in the back row, she couldn't view much.

"Thank you for having me," Inga Vinderson said in a voice that sounded like a crow's caw and didn't require the amplification of the microphone to reach Sondra. "I'm here tonight to talk about self-actualization. What is self-actualization? It is becoming your true self."

Sondra drank some wine. The more she drank, the better it tasted. If she drank enough, it might start to taste like Dom Pérignon.

"Who is your true self?" Inga asked rhetorically. "How do you know? What questions do you ask?"

The wine, unfortunately, didn't make the cheese taste any better. Sondra bit into a cracker, which crunched loudly. Thank God she was in the back row, where her noisy food wouldn't distract the speaker.

"It's important to dig deep into your heart, your soul, your psyche, to find the answers to your questions. *Who are you?* More important, *whom do you want to be?* And finally, *how do you get to be that person? How do you reach that ideal you? What do you need to do to actualize yourself?*"

Sondra didn't have to dig all that deeply. She wasn't sure what actualizing herself meant, but she knew who she wanted to be: the president of Bloom's. Also, a good mother, even if her children were ingrates who didn't trust her, didn't confide in her, didn't rely on her, and shut their office doors. They didn't deserve a mother as wonderful as she was, but she hoped that, somewhere in their selfish little hearts, they occasionally thanked God or fate or luck that she and not, for instance, Martha was their mother. Sondra might not be the world's greatest cook, but she never fed her kids cauliflower goulash.

"Once you've come up with answers—and those answers can and should change as you grow and change—you need to map out a route to actualize those answers. *How do you get from here to there? What changes do you have to make?* Because—and this is the hard part—you cannot self-actualize without changing. And change is always difficult."

Sondra wished she knew exactly what Inga meant by self-actualize. She kept using the phrase without really defining it. It was one of those amorphous terms that sounded both jargonish and optimistic. Sure, everyone wanted to self-actualize. Who *wouldn't* want to self-actualize? But what the hell did it mean?

Maybe a little more wine would make things clearer for her.

She sipped, nibbled on a cracker, and contemplated the questions. Okay, so assume she wanted to become the president of Bloom's. How to get from here to there? Murder Ida. Shove Julia out of the way. The second step was ugly, the first illegal.

She could do what Jay was doing: leave Bloom's and open her own store. Except that she didn't want to be the president of some other store. She wanted to be the president of Bloom's, because by marrying Ben Bloom and taking his name as her own, she had become a Bloom. She'd lived pretty much her entire adult life as Ben's wife, she'd worked hand-in-glove with him at the store, and she *knew* Bloom's. She *knew* the pickle merchants and the cheese importers and the ladies who prepared kugel and knishes in the basement kitchens. Susie knew Casey, who baked Bloom's bagels, better than Sondra did, but Susie wasn't competing to become the president of Bloom's. If they ever got married, Casey would be Sondra's son-in-law, and she'd know him. She already knew Morty Sugarman, who managed the bread and bagel department. She'd known him longer than Julia had been alive.

"Expand your mind," Inga continued in her avian voice. "Don't start by thinking about what you do. Start by thinking about who you are. Do you define yourself as a mother? That's fine if you're raising your children, but what if you aren't anymore? Who are you *now*? So many women become depressed when their children grow up and leave home, because they're still defining themselves as mommy. It's time to be someone else! Who is that someone?"

Not mommy, Sondra thought. She couldn't believe Susie was her favorite child at the moment. Julia and Adam had been her successful creations, Ivy-Leaguers, Julia going on to graduate from one of the top law schools in the country and Adam accepted to a doctoral program. Had he followed through on that, she would have attained what every Jewish mother supposedly wanted: to be able to say, "My son, the doctor." Even if he was a doctor of mathematics, rather than a *real* doctor. He used to tell her that PhDs were the real doctors, and MDs were merely technicians, no more exalted than a plumber. Urologists *were* plumbers, in a way, and when you called a plumber at three a.m. on a Sunday because water was shooting out of your toilet like Old Faithful, you could expect to pay that plumber a hell of a lot more than you paid Dr. Whoever at the local clinic.

But Julia wasn't a lawyer, and Adam wasn't a doctor. Julia was running the business Sondra ought to be self-actually running, and Adam had aligned himself with Jay, running another business.

Susie, though... Susie might write poetry and live with a tall, blond *goy* and have a tattoo on her ankle, but she was self-actualized. She was who she was supposed to be, who she *wanted* to be.

Also, she seemed to be furious with both Julia and Adam. Sondra could relate to that.

So, okay. She was no longer a mommy. She was no longer a wife. She had a career—not the career she ought to have, or at least not the title, but she did work. Did Jean and Norma and any of these other rah-rah-sisterhood members of Martha's women's club have jobs?

They were club women, not career women. Martha brimmed with fiery feminism—but look at her. She didn't have a career. When Jay had first met her, she'd been working as an administrative assistant in the public defender's office. A file clerk, basically, but Jay had watched a lot of cop shows on TV and thought she was something special. As soon as they were married, she got pregnant, and she decided to quit her job and become an earth mother. Not working wasn't a problem for her; Jay could support her on what Bloom's and the Bloom Family Trust paid him. Even when Sondra worked side by side at Bloom's with Ben, they were living only on Ben's salary and the trust money, because Ida had been too cheap to pay Sondra a salary of her own.

These days, Martha kept busy with volunteer activities—reading newspapers to blind people at a neighborhood senior center, helping out now and then at a food co-op, where, Sondra supposed, she stocked up on quinoa and kale and all those other healthy, yucky foods she loved. But she didn't *work*. She was still living on Bloom family money.

Sondra worked. She was the most feminist feminist in this room.

But who was she? What was she?

What did she want to be?

She wanted to be someone who got to enjoy a night out—with a man, not with her dowdy sister-in-law and all her dowdy sister-in-law's dowdy friends. She wanted to be courted, wooed, romanced. She wanted to be worshipped by a man who admired her, respected her, didn't cheat on her. Someone who didn't take her for granted. Someone who thought she was wonderful.

Someone who was smart and funny and generous. Someone who—all right, he didn't have to be movie-star handsome. But attractive. Fit. A full head of hair would be nice, but if he was bald, he should have a nice-shaped skull. Not a skull that made him look like that Dr. Seuss illustration of "Yertle the Turtle," with a few stray hairs sprouting from the top of his scalp. Not someone who shaved off all his hair and his head looked like a giant thumb.

I want to date, she thought. *I want to be the belle of the ball. The head cheerleader. A feminist femme fatale.*

Not, of course, if it meant she had to lose twenty pounds. That was not part of her self-actualization plan. But her face... She'd have to look younger. A head cheerleader was not supposed to look fifty-three years old.

Her nose was already as good as it would ever be, thanks to the plastic surgery she'd undergone as a teenager. Her mouth had always been nicely shaped. Her cheekbones were passable, and she could contour them with blusher. Her forehead...a bit wrinkled. Too many lines running horizontally from temple to temple. She'd frowned too much over the years. She'd had reason to frown—and she had even more reason to frown now, because she wasn't self-actualized.

Inga Vinderson was lecturing her audience to figure out how to get from here to there. A few Botox injections would get Sondra to self-actualization.

Why the hell not? Why devote all her energy to Bloom's, to helping her daughter succeed and bringing *nachus* to her bitchy old mother-in-law? Why not actualize *herself* for a change? Smooth out that forehead, buy some high-end cosmetics, maybe go to a professional cosmetologist for a real makeover, and then put herself out there. The world was full of men. Surely at least a few high-quality men would fall for her.

The room erupted in applause, startling her. Was the talk over? What had she missed?

Nothing important, she realized, joining the hand-clapping and spattering a little wine on her knee. She was glad she'd chosen white wine. It wouldn't stain.

"She made some interesting points," Martha murmured. "Particularly what she had to say about self-expression as a handmaiden of self-actualization."

When had Inga said that? Sondra had missed it.

No matter. She would self-express by getting the creases in her forehead ironed out. "I liked what she had to say about knowing who you are and then mapping a route to get there," Sondra murmured back.

"Well, yes. Kind of obvious, but it's something we need to be reminded of from time to time."

Sondra hadn't thought it was obvious. For her, this had been an epiphany. She might even consider buying one of Inga's books and having her sign it, except then she'd feel obligated to read it, and who had time for that? She was going to be way too busy self-actualizing.

Chapter Sixteen

"Maybe we should have a baby," Julia said. Ron glanced up from his laptop, which was perched on his knees. Weren't men supposed to have ugly knees? Stretched out beside her in bed, clad in fleece shorts and a wrinkled T-shirt featuring a silk-screened image of Bart Simpson skateboarding, he had his legs on full display. The hair on his calves was too curly. His feet were large and bony, typical male feet. But his knees were actually quite lovely, two matching ovals covered by taut, smooth skin.

Curly hair notwithstanding, Ron had ridiculously appealing legs. Everything about Ron's appearance was ridiculously appealing, with the possible exception of that silly T-shirt. Two years into this marriage, Julia still found herself astonished at times that a guy as hot as Ron Joffe could have fallen in love with her.

Usually, she felt comfortable, even a bit smug, about having wed such a gorgeous guy. But she was suffering from insecurity these days. Insecurity about the job she was doing, the business she might be failing, and the love she wasn't feeling from her family slopped over into insecurity about her marriage.

If they had a baby, it would cement their connubial bond. Also, she could take a maternity leave and forget about Bloom's for a few months. Maybe she could extend her maternity leave, take off for a year...and by the time she was ready to return to work, Grandma Ida would have named someone else to run the place and Julia could just stay unemployed.

Or she could go back to Griffin, McDougal and become a law associate once more, researching prenup agreements and divorce settlements, helping marriages that were falling apart to fall apart a little more thoroughly.

She didn't want her own marriage to fall apart. Even if Ron's knees had been knobby and oddly angled, and his eyes hadn't been the color of rich dark chocolate, and his smile didn't cut adorable dimples into his cheeks, she would still want to be married to him.

But a baby would strengthen the glue that held them together. She was staring down her thirtieth birthday. Maybe she ought to find out if she was better at raising children than she was at running Bloom's.

"We'd have to move," Ron pointed out. "We can't have a baby here."

True enough. They were living in Ron's one-bedroom apartment in a brownstone a few blocks from the store. It was bigger than the apartment she'd lived in before they'd gotten married, but most coffins were bigger than that apartment. Both apartments were walk-ups, too. She supposed people had babies in walk-ups, but schlepping a stroller up and down the stairs wouldn't be easy.

"Do you want to move?" she asked Ron.

The look he gave her reflected a blend of amusement and exasperation. "I mean, sure, if you want to have a baby, I'm not opposed. Having a baby involves sex, so I'm good with that." He tapped a key on his laptop, evidently saving whatever he'd been doing. "But if you want to have a baby just because you're pissed at your mother, I don't think that's a good reason."

"I'm not pissed at my mother," Julia argued, although of course she was extremely pissed at Sondra. "My mother would be thrilled if we had a baby."

"Do you want to thrill her?"

Julia sighed. No, she didn't want to thrill her mother. She wanted to convince her mother that hiring trained, capable people to replace Adam and Uncle Jay was absolutely the most useful thing Sondra could possibly do. But she'd tried to convince Sondra of that for a week, and she'd failed. Just one more black mark next to Julia's name, one more piece of evidence that she was incompetent.

Her cell phone rang. "That's probably your mother right now, calling to tell you how thrilled she is," Ron said before steering his gaze back to his laptop.

Sighing, Julia tossed aside the book she'd been trying to read—she was a failure at reading, too, because her mind wouldn't remain on the pages in front of her, but kept wandering back to Bloom's—and reached for her phone. Not her mother, she noted as she saw the name on the screen. She swiped and lifted the phone to her ear. "Susie?"

"I've got bad news for you," Susie said.

Wonderful. She was probably calling to tell Julia she'd decided to abandon Bloom's and work for Uncle Jay, too. Or go back to waitressing at Nico's. Or she'd won a MacArthur Genius Grant and was going to write poetry full-time, which meant she would no longer write the *Bloom's Bulletin* and design the store's windows. That would qualify as tragic. "Should I be sitting down?" Julia asked, even though she was already sitting.

"Uncle Jay has investors."

Julia took a moment to digest this. "Okay," she said slowly. She hadn't thought much about how he was financing his new venture. She'd assumed Adam hadn't chipped in much, since he didn't have much to chip in. She knew Grandma Ida wouldn't have given Uncle Jay any money. Uncle Jay had received his Bloom's salary and he'd received his share of the business's profits, but he seemed to enjoy spending money more than saving it. She'd figured he didn't have enough to bankroll a new business. He would have had to finance it some other way—with a loan, or with investors.

"Bottomless pits of money," Susie elaborated. "I don't know why I'm telling you this. Maybe just because I'm the nicest person in our family."

"Who are these investors?" Julia asked. "Does Uncle Jay actually know people who are bottomless pits of money?"

"Uncle Jay doesn't share his social life with me," Susie said. "Rick asked Wendy and she said one of them has a British accent. Or maybe an Irish accent. She can't tell the difference."

That was Wendy. For years, the family referred to her as The Bimbette, because she was too cute and sweet to be a bimbo, but too buxom and vacuous to be anything but a bimbo. If they ever explained this behind-her-back nickname to her, she might actually take it as a compliment—because she was a bimbo.

"Rick told you this?"

"We went over to check out the store. Adam offered me a consulting job. Treat me better, or I might take him up on it."

"You wouldn't." Julia heard the pleading and panic in her voice.

"That's what you said when I told you I was getting a tattoo, and I got a tattoo."

True enough. Susie didn't listen to Julia. She never had.

"Just stop being so bossy, okay? I'm tired of you taking all your shit out on me."

"I don't take my shit out on you," Julia protested.

"You take it out on me, instead," Ron muttered next to her. She gave him a kick, not to hurt him but hard enough that he'd know it was deliberate.

"You do," Susie said. "And I'm sorry Bloom's is falling apart and no one is talking to anyone, but it's not my fault. If you want to whine to someone, whine to Mom."

"I can't whine to her. She's trying to steal my job."

"Then whine to Grandma Ida."

"She's upset enough, as it is."

"I'm upset enough, too."

"All right. I'm sorry." Julia wasn't sure what she was apologizing for, but she was touched that Susie would share this scrap of information about Jay's financial backers, even though she had no idea what to do with it. Susie was still her sister. They were still family. If Julia's saying she was sorry made Susie feel better, Julia would say it. "What did Uncle Jay's store look like?" she asked Susie.

"It looked like nothing. An empty storefront. They've come up with a real dandy name for the place, though: Jacob Bloom's Delectable Food Emporium."

"You're kidding."

"Stupid, right? They're such schmucks. Okay, I've got to go. Casey is setting the alarm clock. I hate alarm clocks. He should just use his freaking phone."

"Either way, it would wake you up," Julia pointed out.

"Either way, I'm still mad at you," Susie declared before disconnecting the call.

Julia stared at her phone for a minute, enjoying the warm bubble of gratitude that swelled inside her. She was thankful not just for the information Susie had shared, but for the recognition that Susie hadn't abandoned her.

Yet. She still might leave, if Julia didn't treat her better. A tricky proposition, because Julia believed she was already treating her well.

Another thought overtook that one: *Jacob Bloom's Delectable Food Emporium.*

"Bloom's," she murmured.

"Hmm?" Ron typed something, then turned to her.

"Bloom's. Damn it, I wish I'd paid more attention in that class on intellectual property law."

"What?"

"Trademark infringement. Damn it!" Her mind was whirling now, churning the way it used to churn when she'd been at the law firm, digging through records and precedents in search of something, anything, that would stack the odds in favor of a client.

"What?" Ron asked again.

Energy buzzed through her. She leaped off the bed and paced around the room, trying to burn it off, trying to stay focused. "He's planning to name his store Jacob Bloom's Delectable Food Emporium."

"That's a stupid name."

"Not only is it stupid," she said, "but...*Bloom's.* He's trading on our store's name, its reputation. We're Bloom's. He can't call his store Bloom's."

"He's calling it Jacob Bloom's...whatever. Delicious Delicatessen."

"Delectable Food Emporium. God, you're right. It's a really stupid name."

"But *his* name is Jacob Bloom. You can't keep him from using his own legal name."

"I can if he's using it to trade on our reputation." She stubbed her pinkie toe on one of Ron's sneakers— he had a bad habit of leaving them in the middle of the bedroom floor, which, she supposed, was an improvement over his former bad habit of leaving them in the middle of the living room floor. But she was too excited to get upset about his slovenliness or her pinkie toe pain. "I don't think Bloom's is trademarked, but there are common law trademarks. Everyone knows Bloom's, right? They hear Bloom's, they think of our store. It's been in existence for more than fifty years, almost sixty years. It's established. You hear Bloom's, you think Bloom's. Right?"

Ron shrugged. "I don't know, maybe some people think of flowers."

"Don't be difficult." She hopped over to the bed, sat on the edge, and rubbed the ache out of her toe. "I have to research the law." Another burst of energy overtook her and she rose again, carrying his sneakers to the closet as she paced. "Even if common law trademark doesn't pertain, Uncle Jay doesn't have to know that. I can write a threatening letter full of legal jargon. One of my old buddies at Griffin, McDougal can sign her name to it and send it out under their letterhead. We can scare the shit out of Uncle Jay."

"Do you want to scare the shit out of him?"

She grinned and flung herself back onto the bed. Suddenly, she felt enormously competent. More than competent—triumphant. Euphoric. Superior.

Of course Ron had fallen in love with her. She was Julia Bloom. A goddess.

"Put your laptop away," she said, lifting it off his lap and replacing it with herself. "Time to celebrate."

Ron looked bemused but pleased. What she was about to do with him involved sex, so he was good with it.

Chapter Seventeen

Susie wasn't used to Julia being so nice to her. It made her uncomfortable, all Julia's praise over Susie's latest limerick in the *Bloom's Bulletin,* and the little gift bag she'd given Susie filled with Belgian truffles—the chocolate kind, not the mushroom kind. Bloom's sold both kinds, but Susie much preferred the kind that wild boars didn't dig out of the ground with their snouts.

Julia actually seemed cheerier over the past few days, too. Maybe because, as far as Susie could tell, their mother wasn't trying to replace her as the president of Bloom's. Sondra was keeping a low profile, arriving late at the office and leaving early, only rarely shouting something to Deirdre through her open office door. She seemed obsessed with the tea towels the store stocked on the second floor, in kitchenwares. The tea towels were an ongoing issue; for two weeks, now, Sondra had been discussing them with Deirdre loudly enough for everyone on the third floor to hear, even if—like Susie—they didn't want to. But another thing Susie didn't want to hear was arguments between her mother and her sister, and she hadn't heard any of those lately, either.

She sat in her minuscule office, proofreading the latest *Bloom's Bulletin* while she munched on a chocolate truffle. Really, rhyming "briskets" with "biscuits" was not a huge stretch. But Julia couldn't seem to heap enough praise on Susie. And she'd stopped asking Susie how Seder-in-a-Box sales were going.

Clearly, Julia wanted something from Susie.

"Come upstairs with me," Julia announced, startling Susie. She hadn't heard her sister's approach, but there Julia stood, filling Susie's office doorway.

"To see Mom? Isn't she in her office?"

"To see Grandma Ida."

So that was what Julia wanted. "Why?"

"I have to discuss something with her."

"What do you need me there for?"

"Moral support?" Julia gave Susie a beseeching smile.

Susie laughed. "Right. Like I could provide that. Grandma Ida hates me."

"She doesn't hate you."

"She likes you better."

Julia couldn't argue that. "I need you with me. I've figured out a way to—well, if not stop Uncle Jay, at least thwart him. I want to run it past her."

"Why? You're the president. She gave you the power. You don't have to get her okay to do anything."

"She's still the chairman of the board. I'd rather not do this behind her back."

"You like getting her approval," Susie guessed. Julia's smile faltered slightly. Susie had obviously guessed right.

"It's a tricky plan. I want to stop Uncle Jay, but.... Well, he's Grandma Ida's only surviving son."

"What, you're going to kill him?"

"No. Just cut him off at the knees. Come on. Maybe Lyndon will feed us something delicious."

Susie looked at the chocolate smear on her thumb, a residue of the truffle she'd just consumed. She licked it off, then sighed. The *Bloom's Bulletin* didn't need more proofreading. "Briskets" rhymed with "biscuits." Done. She could go upstairs, let Lyndon treat her to a snack—something as tasty as, but more filling than, a chocolate truffle—and then head downtown to Casey's, even if she wasn't really sure she wanted to do counter duty at his bakery that afternoon. She and Casey had blown up at each other yesterday evening, when she'd told him she thought his storefront window was boring and she wanted to redesign it, and he'd told her he'd have to run the idea past Mose first. Mose might be his best friend, and Mose might have an advanced degree in business, but Susie knew a few things, too—like how to grab attention. That was what a store's window was supposed to do.

Casey was being an asshole, giving Mose's opinions priority over hers. Casey needed her a lot more than he let on, and not just because of her afternoon shifts behind the counter at his bakery. He might be the love of her life, but at the moment, she'd prefer indulging in a nosh prepared by Lyndon to competing with Mose for Casey's attention.

"All right," she said, pushing away from her computer. Her chair hit the wall behind her, and she swiveled around to free her knees from the desk. "Let's go."

They rode the elevator to the twenty-fifth floor in silence. Julia's lips moved as if she was rehearsing a speech. Susie checked her fingers to make sure there was no more truffle residue on them. Her fingernails were painted black. The thought of how much Grandma Ida was going to hate Susie's manicure made her smile.

When the elevator stopped and the door slid open, Susie and Julia both reflexively peeked out into the hall to make sure Aunt Martha wasn't lying in wait. A young-ish woman pushing a stroller that appeared as technologically elaborate as a space shuttle was approaching the elevator, and Julia courteously held the door open for her. The woman thanked Julia as she wheeled the stroller into the car. The instant the door began to glide shut, the toddler in the stroller let out a shriek louder than a fire alarm.

"I hate kids," Susie said. At least, she hated them when they were shrieking.

Julia smiled her phony, grateful-for-your-moral-support smile, led the way down the hall to Grandma Ida's apartment, and rang the bell. Susie lurked behind her. Like trying to evade Aunt Martha, hiding behind Julia was an instinct Susie obeyed whenever they entered Grandma Ida's apartment. If Grandma Ida remained focused on Julia, she'd be less likely to criticize Susie's tattoo, or her apparel, or her nail enamel, or every other item on her long list of what she considered Susie's shortcomings.

Lyndon answered the door. As always, he was dressed nattily—Susie had always been amused by the fact that her grandmother's cook-slash-housekeeper dressed better than her grandmother did. His surprise at seeing Julia and Susie registered with a sharp lift of his eyebrows. "Well, hello! Is your grandmother expecting you?"

"I didn't call ahead," Julia said. "I want to talk to Grandma Ida about something, and I decided it would be best if I came upstairs."

"I don't want to talk to her," Susie added. "I'm just here because Julia promised me you'd give us a snack."

"Well, I don't want to make a liar out of Julia," Lyndon said, leading them through the entrance hall. "I'll see what I can rustle up."

"Don't go to any bother," Julia said.

"No. Please, go to any bother," Susie contradicted her. Lyndon laughed.

They followed Lyndon into the living room, where they found Grandma Ida ensconced in her favorite easy chair, reading. A cup of tea sat on the end table next to her chair, and a pair of ugly horn-rimmed reading glasses perched on her nose. Glancing up at their entrance, she looked less surprised than Lyndon had.

"Look who's here," he announced.

"Thank God. This book is awful." She held the book up so Julia and Susie could see the cover. Henry James's *The Portrait of a Lady*.

"Why are you reading that?" Julia asked, giving Grandma Ida's cheek a kiss before she settled onto the couch. Susie followed suit, pecking her grandmother on the cheek and then dropping onto the couch, relieved that Julia was occupying the seat closest to Grandma Ida's chair. "It's so boring. I had to read it in college."

"So did I," Susie said.

"I didn't go to college." Grandma Ida slid a scrap of paper into the book to hold her place, and then folded the book shut. She set it on the end table next to her tea, and set her reading glasses down on top of it. "Lyndon's friend Howard gave it to me. He said it was a classic. What do I know from classics? I decided to read more and watch TV less. Every time I get insomnia, I turn on the TV, and there's that horrible man with the chains around his neck, screaming at me to buy a used car."

"Fat Larry's Auto Mart?" Susie grinned. "Rick makes those ads."

"He does?" Julia asked.

Susie nodded.

Grandma Ida scowled more deeply than her everyday scowl. "*Oy gevalt.* Better he should be broke than make *drek* like that. The man screams, stupid rhymes. And all that jewelry he wears, it's terrible. Lyndon and Howard don't wear so much jewelry, and they're *faygelas*."

Lyndon returned to the living room carrying a tray that held two cups—more tea, Susie supposed, since that was what Grandma Ida was drinking—and a plate of plump, nubbly macaroons. "We're getting in the spirit," Lyndon said. "Passover is just around the corner."

"Did you make these yourself?" Julia gazed lustfully at the coconut blobs.

"No. I bought them downstairs. They're delicious."

"You make good macaroons," Grandma Ida chided him. "You should make some."

"Don't be so demanding," Lyndon teased. "Bloom's macaroons are much better than mine." He winked at Julia. "Tell me who your supplier is, and I'll be in your debt forever."

"I'm already in your debt forever," Julia teased back. "We'll talk. I'm sure we can negotiate a deal."

"Save your negotiating a deal for the *gonifs* we do business with," Grandma Ida snapped. "I'll take one of those macaroons, since you're having."

Julia dutifully passed Grandma Ida the plate, then passed it to Susie, who helped herself to two. Such a nourishing day—chocolate truffles and macaroons. Maybe she should write a diet book based on today's intake. *The Bloom's Diet*—all sweets, all the time.

Lyndon left them chewing on the moist, gooey cookies. Once Julia had swallowed, she began to speak. "I've got a plan for dealing with Uncle Jay's store," she said. "I wanted you both to hear it, because you're the only two people in the family I trust anymore."

"You don't trust your mother?" Grandma Ida asked. Fortunately, she drowned out Susie's mumble about how Julia probably shouldn't trust her sister, either.

"Not at the moment," Julia said, ignoring Susie. "Here's the thing. Susie told me Uncle Jay plans to name his store Jacob Bloom's Delectable Food Emporium."

"That's a *farkakte* name."

"Yes—but it's more than that," Julia explained. "He's using 'Bloom's' in his name. It's trademark infringement."

"What are you talking, trademark infringement? It's his name."

"Yes, but Bloom's has been in existence for more than fifty years. Our store has a common law claim on the trademark. We can legally contest Uncle Jay's use of the name Bloom's for a store that's basically duplicating what we're doing. If he were opening a clothing store, or a hardware store, or a hair salon, maybe we could allow him to use Bloom's in the name of his business. But he's opening a store that will be in direct competition with Bloom's. We can sue him to keep him from using the name."

"Sue him? You want to sue my son?"

"Well, just threaten him. I'm hoping it will scare him enough to give him pause."

"But sue him? And the whole world would know you sued him? It would be a *shandeh* for the family."

"I hope it wouldn't come to that, Grandma," Julia said. "I was thinking I could just have someone from my old law firm write a letter. It might scare him."

"I don't want him scared. I just want him back here, working for the store."

The store. As if Bloom's was the only store in the world. Susie supposed that in Grandma Ida's world, it *was* the only store.

Julie twisted on the couch to look at Susie. "What do you think?"

"I think Grandma should phone Uncle Jay and tell him to grow up and stop this shit. Excuse me, Grandma—this nonsense," she edited herself. "He's your son. You're his mother. Call him up and yell at him. It's what mothers do."

"I already called him, twice," Grandma Ida said. "I told him we need him here, at the store. He told me his mind was made up, he was starting his own store. He said—" she looked both exasperated and kind of proud "—I was an inspiration to him. I started a store. Now he wants to start a store."

"Those were different times," Julia said. "When you and Grandpa Isaac started your store, I mean. It's not so easy to start a store these days."

"It wasn't easy then," Grandma Ida argued. "But your grandfather and I, we knew how to work hard. Jay, I don't know. I thought he'd give up by now."

"Well, he hasn't given up," Julia said.

"He's an idiot," Susie said. "I wish he was doing his job here, because I sure as hell don't want to be doing it. I think you should threaten him, Julia. Tell him you're going to sue him. If it gets him back here, I'm all for it."

"It'll get him back here angry," Grandma Ida said. "And scared. You want him working for you angry and scared?"

Susie's gaze sharpened on Grandma Ida. The woman had made a valid point. Susie wasn't used to expecting shrewd observations from Grandma Ida. Judgment, yes. Criticism, constantly. But thoughtful analysis of a complicated family dilemma? Who knew she could do that?

"She makes a good point," Susie said to Julia.

"He's the one who made things ugly by leaving—and taking our brother with him. I'm just trying to keep him from making things even uglier." Julia turned back to Grandma Ida. "If there's a Bloom's delicatessen here, and a Jacob Bloom's delicatessen on the East Side, people are going to assume they're the same store."

"Which is what Uncle Jay and Adam wanted in the first place," Susie reminded her. "They wanted to open a branch of Bloom's."

"No East Side branch," Grandma Ida said, reverting to her usual domineering behavior. "This is a West Side store. We talked about this already. No opening a Bloom's branch over there, where all the hotsy-totsy people live."

"Exactly. But if he calls his place Bloom's—"

"A silly name. What was it? Jacob Bloom's Delicious Food?"

"Delectable Food Emporium," Susie and Julia corrected her in unison.

"It's *farkakte*. Delectable? I don't even know what that means."

"It's definitely a bad name," Julia agreed.

"So, you tell him he can't call it that, he'll come up with a better name. And then his store will be a success, and he'll never come back." Grandma Ida leaned back in her chair, her lips downturned, her eyes looking oddly glassy. A few tears leaked from them, funneling into the narrow wrinkles that webbed her cheeks.

Susie had never seen Grandma Ida cry before, not even when Grandpa Isaac or Susie's father died. But she was crying now. The sight shattered Susie. She had to look away.

"Do you think I should let him go ahead and fail?" Julia asked.

"I don't want my son to be a failure." Grandma Ida sniffed deeply, blinked several times, and composed herself. "I don't want him to be sued. I want him to come to his senses. Does he have any senses?"

"I don't think so," Julia muttered.

"He married that blond *shiksa*. Not sensible. But then, he married Martha, and that wasn't so sensible, either. He plays golf. Is golf a sensible game? I don't know."

"Some people enjoy it."

"Hitting a ball around in the grass? *Meshugena*." Grandma Ida shook her head, sniffled damply, and reached for her tea. "You want to threaten him? It's up to you, Julia. You're the president. But it breaks my heart."

Susie hadn't realized Grandma Ida had a heart. After today, though, she'd concede the woman had a brain. A pretty high-functioning brain for someone in shouting distance of her ninetieth birthday. And yes, a heart, too. And tear ducts.

"You figure it out, Julia," Grandma Ida said. "You trust me, I trust you. Figure out a way to stop him before he breaks my heart any more."

Julia rolled her eyes. "That's a tall order. I'll do what I can."

She pushed herself to stand, and Susie stood, too, snatching another macaroon on her way. Grandma Ida's eyes lost their bleariness and narrowed on her. "You're wearing black nail polish? What are you, *meshuge?*"

"Yes," Susie said defiantly. "I'm *meshuge*."

"*Oy*. A poet. A golfer. And now I have to read this book." She lifted her eyeglasses, put them on, and picked up the book. "I'll tell you this," she said, waving the thick volume at Susie and Julia. "She's no lady, this woman. All that money she inherits, and she marries a *putz*."

Susie and Julia called out a farewell to Lyndon as they left the apartment. Out in the hall—no sign of Aunt Martha, thank God—they raced to the elevator, pressed the button, and waited. "What do you think?" Julia asked Susie. "Should I threaten to sue him?"

"I think you should torch his store as soon as it opens," Susie suggested. "He can get an insurance settlement so he won't feel like a failure."

"Seriously."

"Seriously?" Susie mulled over what Grandma Ida had said. "Seriously, I think an angry, resentful Uncle Jay is not who you want to have working for the store. She made a good point."

"I know." Julia looked dismayed.

"Forget him. Hire a replacement and let him sink or swim."

"If he calls his store Bloom's, it can cause repercussions here. People will shop there, thinking they're shopping at Bloom's. We'll confuse customers. We'll lose customers."

"Dog eat dog," Susie said. "That's why I'd rather write poetry than run a business."

"That business pays you enough money so you can afford to write poetry," Julia reminded her.

"Yeah," Susie said as the elevator arrived and she stepped into the car. "Bloom's is my bottomless pit of money." She watched the door slide shut and jabbed the third-floor button with her black-tipped index finger. The entire subject tired her out. Let Julia come up with a strategy to get Uncle Jay and Adam back. Let her repair the family. Susie had Casey and his boring window display waiting for her downtown. She'd go, she'd work for him, but she'd be angry and resentful.

Grandma Ida would say that was a bad thing.

She'd be right.

Chapter Eighteen

A dam was having some misgivings.

He woke up alone in bed. After yanking on a pair of sweat pants, he staggered into the kitchen, where he found Dulcie balanced on one foot, her other leg propped on the kitchen table and her torso bent at the waist so she looked as if she were kissing her knee. The toe of her propped foot stuck straight out, pointed so sharply he could imagine it piercing a hole in the atmosphere. Her arms were curved and her fingers appeared boneless as they framed her narrow ankle. She was dressed in pale pink leggings and a leotard top so tight it molded to her skeleton like a second skin. Adam never knew how much he loved leotards until he started dating ballet students.

Some people rose in the morning and did stretches. Adam rose in the morning and scrounged for coffee.

His bones felt as rubbery as hers looked. A little too much weed last night, he figured. She'd taken only a few hits, not wanting to get the munchies and, God forbid, satisfy them by devouring something salty and crunchy and fattening. Adam had wolfed down most of a party-size bag of Cheese Doodles, and he didn't feel any fatter this morning. Just a little bleary.

And a little apprehensive.

Yesterday, Uncle Jay had ordered furnishings for the store as if he anticipated a dire shortage of shelving and refrigerator units over the next decade. "We don't have enough room for all those shelves," Adam had objected.

"We'll need the shelves for storage," Uncle Jay had argued. "We'll put some up in the back room and some in the basement."

"Do we have access to the basement? Is that part of our lease here?"

"I think so," Uncle Jay had said, sounding less than positive.

"How are we paying for all this stuff?" Adam had asked, skimming the order forms Uncle Jay had filled out with the decorator.

"The investors will cover it."

"I'd like to sit down and talk to them, see what they have in mind for us," Adam had said. "I only met them for a few minutes that one time."

Uncle Jay had stared at him with eyes as hard as shotgun pellets. "You're in charge of inventory," he'd lectured Adam. "I'm in charge of finance. You don't have to sit down and talk to the investors. What you have to do is find warehouse space for us to rent. Cheaply. I don't want to burn through all their money at once."

What if the investors don't have that much money? Adam had wondered. It was a stupid thought. If they truly didn't want to spend, spend, spend, as Uncle Jay swore they did, he wouldn't be ordering all those fixtures. He sure wouldn't want to drain his own bank accounts to pay for them.

Still, if Adam was a partner, why shouldn't he get to know the investors? Wouldn't the investors want to get to know him?

Dulcie lifted her foot off the table, swung her leg around and behind her, and folded herself forward so her chest was pressed to her thigh and her dangerously sharp foot pointed at the ceiling. All while balanced on the other foot. Maybe this was ballet. Maybe it was yoga. Maybe she was a contortionist.

Whatever she was, her pointed-toe routine was a hell of a way to start the day. Adam preferred to keep both feet on the floor and his head focused on his goal, which was to get food. Despite all the Cheese Doodles he'd eaten last night, he was starving.

He prepared a pot of coffee, clicked the machine to "brew," and rummaged through the refrigerator for breakfast. Since leaving Bloom's, he was too embarrassed to shop there—and also, since leaving Bloom's, he was no longer entitled to an employee discount. So rather than buying some of Casey's gourmet bagels, he'd settled for a package of prepacked bagels from the supermarket. They tasted like mealy torus-shaped bread. No shiny crust. No chewy texture. None of the exotic flavors Casey specialized in: pesto and sun-dried tomato bagels, raisin and honey bagels, black olive and garlic bagels. The cellophane package Adam pulled from the refrigerator contained just plain bagels, bland and boring. He'd bought some chive-flavored cream cheese to jazz the bagels up, but it didn't taste anywhere near as good as Bloom's flavored cream cheeses.

"Can I toast you a bagel?" he asked Dulcie as he pulled a couple of bagels from the package.

"No, thanks." Her voice sounded normal, even though her lips were practically jammed into her knee.

"I've got some Cheerios," he offered. "Some granola bars. Some—" he swung the refrigerator door open again, slid out a cardboard carton, and flipped open the top "—correction, *one* egg."

Dulcie lifted her head, lowered her leg, and gave him a sweet smile. Her cheeks were barely flushed. "I'll pass, thanks."

"You've got to eat something for breakfast."

"I never eat breakfast."

"It's the most important meal of the day." Shit. He sounded like his mother.

"Do you have any grapes?" Her hair was mussed. It looked sexy that way. Maybe she should turn herself upside-down more often. "I'd eat a grape."

"A grape? A single grape?" Adam's outrage was tempered by the fact that he didn't have any grapes. "Do you ever worry that you're borderline anorexic?"

Laughing, Dulcie closed the distance between them and balanced her skinny arms on his shoulders in a semi-hug. "I'm a ballerina. We're all anorexic."

"You need to eat."

"I eat enough."

"I should drag you through Bloom's," he said. "You should see all the food there. It might make you want to eat. A grape," he muttered, shaking his head and breaking from her so he could return the egg to the refrigerator. How on earth could he, a member of the family that had created the best food store in New York—or, if you asked Grandma Ida, the world—be sleeping with a girl who didn't eat? It was as outrageous as Catherine the Great sleeping with a horse, which Adam wasn't sure actually happened, although his girlfriend back at Cornell insisted it had.

He sliced the bagels and fought off a pang of regret that he couldn't drag Dulcie through Bloom's because he no longer worked there. He no longer had a place there. He was no longer welcome there.

He might feel better about that if he could sit down and crunch numbers with Uncle Jay's investors. If he could see for himself that this Jacob Bloom's Delectable Food Emporium venture was a real thing, funded by real money. Sure, the storefront they'd leased was real. The order forms for the shelving were real. But the money? How real was that?

Not only did Adam want to make sure the investors were serious about sinking all that money into Uncle Jay's store—Uncle Jay's and *his* store, he reminded himself—but he wanted to ask them for an advance on his income from the store. Without his Bloom's salary, he was burning through his meager savings way too fast. If he rented directly from a landlord, he could delay a rent payment without too much hassle. It would take a landlord months to evict him, and he'd be drawing an income well before an eviction could wind through the legal system. But he didn't rent from a landlord. He sublet this apartment from Julia. And she wasn't going to give him months. She'd kick him out if he was more than a few days late with his rent. She hated his guts.

He hated that Julia hated his guts. He wondered if Susie hated his guts, too. Or, for that matter, his mother. Grandma Ida probably did. Hating people seemed to be her default setting.

Dulcie left the kitchen for the bedroom, giving him nothing better to look at than his bagels darkening from pasty white to tolerable tan in the toaster oven. Since watching bagels toast was right up there with watching grass grow and watching paint dry on the fascinating scale, he directed his thoughts elsewhere, analyzing his situation the way he used to analyze mathematical puzzles, back when he'd been a student.

His analysis: He felt isolated. He felt enslaved. He was allegedly a partner in this new business, yet all he did was what Uncle Jay told him to do: Find retail space. Find storage space. Work up inventory lists. Much the

same shit he'd done at Bloom's, but at least he'd gotten paid for it there, and he'd gotten to work with people. He'd known all the delivery guys. He'd known all
the kitchen workers, and they'd frequently sneaked
him a misshapen blintz or a dollop of chopped liver
on a plastic spoon. He'd been a part of something at
Bloom's—not just a business but a family.

What would it mean if his family, with the lone exception of Uncle Jay, hated his guts? How did you survive something like that?

By reminding yourself of why you left. He'd left
because Julia had shot him down every time he'd suggested expanding Bloom's. He'd left because he felt
she was wrong about the business. He'd left because,
even there, he was still a glorified drudge. A decently
paid drudge, but a drudge nonetheless.

Passover was coming soon. Grandma Ida would
host it, as she did every year, and Adam wondered if
he would be invited to attend. What if he wasn't? What
if he wound up spending the night of the first Seder
alone, nibbling on supermarket bagels and then be-
latedly realizing that he wasn't supposed to eat leav-
ened bread products for the eight days of the holiday?
Was he going to have to buy that tasteless matzo they
sold in the same supermarket where they sold the
tasteless bagels? The Passover matzo sold at Bloom's
had a robust, wheaty flavor. It was baked on flat stones
and came out a little inconsistent in shape and a little
uneven in color, and it was the most delicious matzo
Adam had ever eaten.

He supposed he could order himself a Seder-in-a-
Box, a creation which had convinced him that Uncle
Jay, who had come up with the concept, was a marketing genius. The Seder-in-a-Box contained pretty
much everything you needed to make a Seder dinner:

matzo, bitter herbs, *charoseth*, a large tub of Bloom's chicken soup with matzo balls, Haggadah books, and even some cheap yarmulkes, although Adam still had a blue velvet yarmulke from his bar mitzvah with his name and the date of the event printed on the satin lining. The promo slogan for the Seder-in-a-Box was "Just add wine and serve." You'd probably have to add hard-boiled eggs and some meat, too—chicken or pot roast. But if he was booted from his family and all by himself on Passover, he could skip the meat, or open a can of tuna. He had no idea how to prepare a pot roast.

Maybe Uncle Jay would also be booted from the family, and they could celebrate Passover together. Somehow, Adam doubted that Wendy knew how to prepare a pot roast. When you were as pretty and blond as she was, you didn't have to know how to cook.

The toaster oven dinged, and he opened the door and arranged the sliced bagels on a plate. As Dulcie returned to the kitchen, wearing a baggy sweater almost as long as a dress over her leotard and tights and lugging her canvas tote, which probably weighed more than she did, he cut one of the bagel halves into two semi-circles and put one on a separate plate. "Here," he said, handing it to Dulcie. "You can have this for breakfast."

"A half a bagel?" she looked aghast.

"That's a quarter of a bagel," Adam corrected her. "I sliced the bagel in half, and then I sliced the half in half..." He tapered off, aware that she'd lifted her gaze from the plate to him. She looked bewildered, either by the notion of eating more than a single grape for breakfast or by the basic math he was explaining.

If he'd stuck to his original path in life, he would be working on his PhD in mathematics at Purdue right now, hanging out with women who might not be as dainty or flexible as Dulcie, but who would know the difference between a half bagel and a quarter bagel, and who would eat more than a grape for breakfast. He would be paid—much less than he was earning at Bloom's but more than he was currently earning. Of course, if he panhandled at Penn Station, he'd also earn more than he was currently earning. But he wouldn't be worrying about whether his family hated him or where he was going to spend Passover. And he'd be with people who knew basic geometry.

He watched as Dulcie tore a piece no bigger than her thumb from the bagel section he'd given her. She took a knife, dabbed the tip into the tub of cream cheese, and touched the knife to the bagel. If she'd actually added cream cheese to the piece, he couldn't see it. She popped it into her mouth, chewed, and swallowed. "There. Are you happy?"

No, he thought, but then she kissed him, and that made him marginally happier. She set her tote on a chair and dug through it to find her sneakers, which she wiggled her feet into without bothering to untie the laces. He could see the odd lumps and bumps of the bag's contents as she shifted them around. She kept two pairs of ballet slippers in there, and her purse, and a hoodie, and some notebooks, and who knew what else? He'd peeked into the bag a few times, but he'd never dumped out its contents to see what she schlepped around. He told himself this was out of respect for her privacy, but it might also be because he really didn't want to know.

"I've got to go," she said. "I've got a class."

He should have offered to walk her the few blocks to Juilliard, but if he did, he'd have to get dressed. And he was hungry. In all honesty, he'd rather eat his bagel than walk Dulcie to her class.

"I'll text you," she said, brushing another kiss onto his lips and then sweeping out the door, walking with her toes pointed outward, like a thin, graceful, female Charlie Chaplin.

He liked her. He especially liked her when they were naked in bed. But...what did it mean when he'd rather eat a bagel than walk down to Lincoln Center and deliver her to her ballet class?

She didn't need an escort. It was sunny out, and she was twenty years old, and she'd grown up in Manhattan. She still lived with her parents on East 86th Street when she wasn't spending the night with Adam. That was how she'd stumbled across the storefront for rent that would soon be the home of Jacob Bloom's Delectable Food Emporium—and a hell of a lot of shelving.

But still...

He'd rather eat a bagel.

He slathered a thick layer of cream cheese on his bagel halves, poured a cup of coffee, and settled at the table where she'd been stretching just minutes ago. The bagel didn't taste particularly good, but it was food. He needed to eat. He needed to think.

He needed to talk to the investors.

He needed to locate affordable warehouse space for the store's inventory.

He needed to find out whether he'd be welcome at Grandma Ida's Seder.

He needed to know whether his family hated him.

He chewed, swallowed, and sighed. Getting a PhD in mathematics would have been a lot easier.

Chapter Nineteen

Susie stared at the page of lined notebook paper. She'd scrawled a few words on those lines: *Floating. Lost. Horny. Alone. Bereft.*

Where was the poem?

Some poems came to her fully formed. With others, she wrote words, then stared at them, studied them, absorbed them until they started to take shape, or a poem would ooze out from the spaces between them. Right now, the only word that carried any weight with her was *bereft*. It was such a strange word. Spoken aloud, it sounded weird. Be. Reft.

It was late. She was tired. Casey had gone to bed hours ago, memories of their argument still vibrating in the air. Of course, she'd done most of the arguing. Casey was too reserved to argue. Too nice. Too Catholic.

"I know you do the windows for Bloom's," he'd said. "But my bakery isn't Bloom's. It isn't a world-renowned deli where bourgeois liberals and tourists go to buy pickled artichokes. It's a small downtown operation."

"It isn't an operation," Susie had retorted. "It's a store. Who told you it was an operation? Is that one of Mose's business school terms?"

Casey had opened his mouth, then shut it, apparently opting to cool off before he responded. Susie hadn't wanted him to cool off. She'd wanted him to be

219

as furious as she was. But no, he'd had to be calm and reasonable. "Mose did go to business school. He has an MBA, and I think he knows what he's talking about. He's given me good advice so far. And he says the window should be safe and familiar. Like bread."

"There's nothing safe and familiar about your bread," Susie had railed. "Your bread is special. You need a special window."

"I really think I'm going to go with Mose on this. Leave the window the way it is. You can do whatever you want with the Bloom's windows, but my window— we're going to keep it safe and familiar."

"*Your* window? Or yours and Mose's?"

"Come on, Susie." Casey had tried to cajole her with a dazzling smile. Usually that smile could heat her insides and dampen her panties. But not tonight. Not once he'd added, "Mose is my best friend. I trust his judgment on this."

"Oh, you trust *his* judgment. You don't trust *my* judgment. I'm not your best friend. I just live here and have sex with you in the early evening, because you have to be asleep by nine. Do you dream about Mose when you sleep? Or do you just dream about bread?"

Once again, Casey had refused to respond. He'd withdrawn, which really wasn't fair. How could she fight with him if he wouldn't fight back?

Paradoxically, he'd won the fight by not fighting. He'd shut down, walked into the bedroom—not stormed, not raced, not stomped, but walked—and closed the door. Without slamming it.

She'd stared at that unslammed door for a long time. Then she'd filled a glass with wine, gathered her pad and pen, and curled up on the futon sofa in the apartment's main room. And seethed. And waited for a poem to come to her.

The futon sat against the wall beneath the room's only window, which was covered by an ugly venetian blind that the previous tenant had left. Susie had contemplated replacing the blind, but with what? A drape? Accordion-pleat shades? At least with venetian blinds, she could adjust the slats to gaze down at the street below, straight ahead at the reclaimed tenements huddled across the street, or up at a tiny sliver of sky.

She twisted the knob to angle the slats so she could gaze up. The sky was foggy, but she could see the moon through filmy layers of cloud. It was nearly full, a lopsided, gray-white disk with gauzy edges.

When she'd been younger, she'd believed that the moon held the night together, like a big thumbtack pinning the cosmos in place. She used to sneak up onto the roof of the Bloom Building so she could see the sky. Once she'd moved out of Julia's bedroom and into the maid's room off the kitchen, her window had offered only a view of an air shaft; maids obviously weren't supposed to spend time gazing at the moon and the stars. But the advantage of the maid's room was that Susie could sneak out of the apartment through the service door off the kitchen without anyone seeing her. She would scamper up the stairs, past the twenty-fifth floor and onto the roof, and she would absorb the great, dark dome of the night sky arching above her.

The moon held it all together.

During a new moon phase, she would worry. Would the sky fall? Would the stars drift away? But then, a couple of nights later, a slender crescent would appear, and then it would grow bigger and bigger until it was a full silver circle, and she'd believe the world was stable once more.

The full moon wasn't for lunatics. It didn't turn people into werewolves. She didn't want to howl at it.

She just wanted to bask in it, to feel its solidity, its security.

Despite the fact that the moon was almost full tonight, nothing felt solid or secure right now. What would hold everything together?

She lowered her eyes to the spiral notebook balanced on her knees. *Bereft* was too weird a word. She crossed it out and wrote *moon*.

Moon, she thought. *It's dark, it's late, I'm alone with the moon. My companion moon. My lover moon. My family moon.*

Who was holding the family together? Who was holding *her* together?

Not Casey, that was for sure. He'd said Mose was his best friend, which meant Susie *wasn't* his best friend. And Casey thought Mose knew more about window displays than Susie did. What, did they give classes in window displays in business school?

Mose knew nothing about windows. But he was the person Casey trusted. Susie was just a chick who worked behind the counter and slept in Casey's bed.

Everything was falling apart: her relationship with Casey. Her family. Her life. Nothing was dependable anymore.

Grandma Ida, for instance. Seeing her cry had shaken Susie from her scalp to her tattooed ankle. Grandma Ida never cried. How had Uncle Jay reduced Grandma Ida to tears? It wasn't as if Grandma Ida was stuck running the website and the mail orders in his absence. If anyone ought to be crying, it should be Susie. Everything got dumped on her.

To her surprise, she felt the sting of tears pinching her eyes. She blinked them a couple of times, chasing the tears away.

Like Grandma Ida, Susie never cried—not unless her tears might get her something she desired. Tears could be useful if she was looking for attention or sympathy, or if she wanted to make someone feel guilty. But they didn't flow spontaneously for her. She had a high threshold of pain; cuts and bruises didn't faze her. She didn't care much about possessions; if she lost or broke something, no big deal. As far as heartache, what was the point of crying? Rage was a lot more effective than sorrow. If a guy dumped Susie, she brushed herself off, wished him a lifetime of suffering and failure and humiliating impotence, and got on with her life. If her mother scolded her, or her grandmother gave her shit, or her brother acted like a jackass, she figured their attitude was their problem, not hers. When her father died, she'd been upset, but honestly, he'd never paid all that much attention to her when he'd been alive. The night after she'd learned about his death, the moon had been three-quarters full and the sky hadn't fallen, literally or otherwise.

She didn't do *bereft*.

But tonight...

Not bereft, she told herself. She was frustrated, because she was creatively constipated, unable to find a poem in the smattering of words she'd scribbled across the notebook page. She was vexed because her grandmother had cried. She was hurt because Casey had basically told her she wasn't as important to him as his buddy Mose, and then he'd gone to sleep without her.

If she were a smoker, now would be the moment she'd light a cigarette. If she had some chocolate handy, she would have devoured it. Thank God she had a glass of wine within reach.

Casey was determined to make his bakery succeed. That was his top priority, which was fine. She wanted the bakery to succeed as much as he did. But she wanted him to respect her. To listen to her. To freaking *trust* her.

If he'd listened to her, if he'd trusted her, she would have told him he needed a logo. An image. Some visual signal that people entering his store were entering his world, a special, magical world filled with staggeringly delicious bread and rolls and bagels and muffins. A world so amazing, they didn't mind making an extra stop and paying extra money to buy what he had produced.

He had Linus, a six-foot-tall faded plastic lobster, standing inside the bakery. Susie and Rick had found Linus by the side of the road during a film-making trip to Maine a year ago. They'd sort of bought, sort of stolen the statue, used it in the movie, and brought it back to New York, where it had somehow wound up in Susie's possession.

Linus made Casey's customers smile. Little kids visiting Casey's Gourmet Breads with their parents shrieked with delight when they saw him, and talked to him, and offered him tastes of their bagels. Teenagers took selfies with him. But he wasn't a logo. He didn't *say* something, didn't communicate an idea about crusty sourdough that felt almost dry on the tongue, or dense, chewy pumpernickel, or challah as golden as corn, or corn bread even more golden than that. Or the world's best bagels.

A moon, Susie thought. Just like her, the store needed a moon to hold everything together.

She flipped the page in her notebook and started to sketch.

Chapter Twenty

Stuart Pinsky liked big steaks cooked so rare, Jay almost expected to hear moos of protest when Stuart sliced into them. He favored one particular steak house where the steaks were as big and red as lobsters, which he claimed he'd never tasted because lobsters were *treyf*. Jay didn't give a damn about the laws of *kashruth*, but he'd choose a steak over a lobster any day. Meat was meat.

He always felt a little effeminate ordering the queen-size steak at this restaurant, but the queen-size steak was a full twelve ounces—plenty enough, especially for lunch. Unlike Stuart, Jay was married to a gorgeous blonde young enough to be his daughter if he'd been a sexually precocious teenager, and he didn't want to develop a paunch like Stuart's. Stuart's wife, Kim, was svelte—Jay would bet she didn't eat at this restaurant very often—but she was also well into middle age. She was the editor-in-chief of *Gotham Magazine*, where Julia's husband Ron worked. In a roundabout way, Jay had been responsible for bringing those two together. You'd think Julia would be grateful.

Maybe she was. But she wasn't grateful enough to open a Bloom's franchise on the Upper East Side, let alone step aside and tell Jay he deserved to be the president of Bloom's.

Stuart had been Jay's attorney for years. He was one of those nuts-and-bolts lawyers who knew enough to be able to handle everything Jay threw his way. While impressed by the trappings of big, fancy law firms like the one where Julia had worked before Jay's mother had stabbed her sole surviving son in the back by handing Bloom's presidency to Julia, Jay preferred the personal relationship he had with Stuart. They golfed together at Emerald View. They analyzed the annual draft picks of the New York Giants with equal passion, and they nearly always agreed on whom the Giants should have selected but didn't. Stuart had ushered Jay through the legal minefield of his divorce in such a way that he and Martha could still interact civilly. Jay suspected Martha behaved civilly toward him because of the generous alimony he paid her. But then, as Stuart had pointed out, you didn't leave your wife for someone like Wendy with the expectation of saving money. It cost, but you paid the price willingly, because...well, *Wendy*.

Another thing he liked about having Stuart as his lawyer was that they could meet to talk shop over meals like this one—massive, artery-clogging feasts accompanied by top-of-the-line liquor. Today they were drinking eighteen-year-old Glenlivet, which Jay felt negated the queen-size steak he'd ordered in terms of projecting his masculinity. He'd also ordered a wedge salad slathered in Roquefort dressing and sprinkled with bacon chips, and his baked potato was crowned with a generous scoop of sour cream dotted with chives. Nothing queen-ish about that.

If Martha saw him eating a meal like this—for lunch, no less—she'd have a heart attack. Then again, if he ate lunches like this on a regular basis, he'd probably have a heart attack, too. But what the hell. Stuart, as usual, was treating. And Wendy wouldn't care what Jay ate. She was so blessedly agreeable.

"So," Stuart said as he sliced into the king-size slab of beef on his plate, releasing a flood of bright red juice. Jay had eaten sushi that had been cooked longer than Stuart's steak. "I've looked over the paperwork your investors provided. They belong to Emerald View? Really?"

"That's where I met them," Jay said, cutting into his own steak. These days, medium meant pink, which was the way Jay liked it. Tender, juicy, but not oozing blood like Stuart's. "Marshall Wynn hooked me up with them."

"I never encountered them at the club," Stuart said. "I guess we golf at different times." He washed down his meat with a slug of scotch. "I'll be frank with you, Jay. I don't like these guys."

"What are you talking about?" Jay lowered his fork and stared at Stuart. "You just said you've never met them. How can you not like someone you never met?"

"They're not kosher, Jay."

"They're not Jewish. Why should they be kosher?"

Stuart ignored the joke. "I did some checking. As your lawyer, that's my job, right?" His eyes glowed behind his stylish half-rimmed eyeglasses. "This guy, Jenners? He owns a Midtown condo priced at fourteen million."

"I thought he lived in Sands Point."

"Maybe he does. His condo is empty."

"What do you mean, empty?"

"I mean, he didn't buy it to live in it. He bought it to launder money."

"What money? How do you know this?"

"I did some research. It's what you pay me the big bucks for." Stuart grinned. Jay forced a smile, although he didn't find anything amusing in this discussion. True, he paid Stuart the big bucks, but in return he preferred that Stuart tell him only what he wanted to hear. He sure as hell didn't want to hear *this*. "The other one, Rupert Niles?" Stuart continued. "He works for an LLC owned by a Russian mining executive."

The piece of meat in Jay's mouth suddenly seemed dry. It irritated his throat when he swallowed. "I thought Rupert was British."

"His nation of origin is not in question. He's an agent for this Russian oligarch. These guys are money launderers, Jay. They're investing in your new business because they need to get money out of Russia and scrub it clean."

Jay lifted his glass, jiggled it, listened to the ice cubes clink against the crystal. It was a pretty sound, a hopeful sound. If ice could sound so charming, Jay had no reason to be discouraged. "Okay, so they're money launderers. Their money is still legal tender, right? They want to invest in my store. If the condo developer could take their money, why can't I?"

"You could take their money. You could open a store. You could stand on your head," Stuart said, which puzzled Jay because standing on his head was one thing he definitely couldn't do. "I'm just saying, these are not gentlemen you want to do business with. I'm not even sure they're gentlemen."

"Like, what? They forge checks? They hire hit men to kill their competitors? What are we talking about, Stuart?"

"We're talking about money launderers," Stuart said. He sounded so calm and reasonable, Jay had trouble believing there was actually something bad about money laundering. "These guys are taking money out of Russia and investing it in your store because they need to do something with it. Then, at some point, the oligarch decides he wants to leave Russia—because, let's face it, who wants to live in Russia? It's cold all the time, and they drink cheap vodka, and everyone's talking Russian, am I right? My grandparents came from Russia. They wanted to get out of there. Pogroms, corruption, all that craziness."

"Fine. Your grandparents left Russia and came to America. What would stop them from investing money in my business?"

"Nothing, other than the fact that they had no money. This oligarch has lots of money, and when he decides he wants to move someplace where they've got better booze and it doesn't snow three hundred fifty days a year, he doesn't want to leave his money behind. He probably hasn't paid taxes on that money. Maybe he hasn't paid his creditors. Maybe he's got a *nudnik* ex-wife like Martha, but unlike you, he doesn't want to hand half his money over to her."

"I don't want to hand half my money over to Martha, either."

"And you don't," Stuart pointed out. "You gave her the apartment. She could have demanded a lot more alimony, but I saved your ass. I'm trying to save your ass again. So listen to me."

"I'm listening," Jay said, although Stuart's words hurt his ears. Not just his ears—his heart. His stomach. His balls and his bowels. Everything ached. "My investors—Gil and Rupert—it's all dollars. Not rubles."

"Of course. The money goes through some international bank, one of those sleazy banks that deals with large quantities of cash and doesn't ask questions. The rubles are converted into dollars. Or who knows? Maybe these guys are using cryptocurrency. That hasn't got a nationality."

What little Jay knew about cryptocurrency was enough to convince him he didn't want to know more. It was too technical, too confusing. Adam might understand it; he was a math genius. But how could Jay ask Adam to figure out whether the investors were planning to cover the store's rent and pay for the décor in bitcoins, whatever the hell they were? Jay had kept Adam away from the investors, because they'd wanted things *sub rosa.* They'd agreed to meet Adam once, so Adam would be convinced that they existed, but they didn't want to meet him again. They wanted to deal only with Jay. There was a secretiveness about them.

Jay had thought their secretiveness was glamorous, proof that they were thinking in big numbers and didn't want news of their wealth bandied about. People with a lot of money had to be cautious. Word got out that you were sitting on a mountain of cash and everyone would come to you with their hands out. Every *schnorrer* would want to be your best friend.

"And here's the thing," Stuart went on. He was clearly enjoying his meal a lot more than Jay. Half his steak was gone, and he was cutting his baked potato into bite-size chunks. He popped one chunk into his mouth, skin and all, and chewed slowly, leaving Jay to wonder what *the thing* was.

"The thing is," Stuart finally said, "sooner or later, the oligarch is going to leave Russia, and he's going to want to access his money. Maybe he'll sell the condo, or maybe he'll live there. But he isn't going to want to be the silent partner in a neighborhood delicatessen."

"It's not going to be just a neighborhood delicatessen," Jay protested. "It's going to be a delectable food emporium."

"Regardless. Whenever this guy says the word, your investors are going to pull his money out of the place. And then it's gone."

"But by then," Jay said hopefully, "the store will be making a profit. I'll be able to pay them back."

"They're investing, what, a million dollars? Two million? How long is it going to take for you to earn that kind of profit? New businesses don't succeed overnight. You're not talking about some high-tech unicorn, Jay. If you went to a bank and signed for a loan, they'd charge you interest and work out a re-payment plan. These guys aren't doing that. They're just handing you the money. It's because they're crooked. Legitimate businessmen don't hand over money like that."

Jay reached for his glass. The clinking ice cubes no longer sounded cheerful to him. They sounded like knells, doleful chimes announcing the death of something.

His store. His dream. His chance to show his mother that he wasn't the fuck-up she apparently thought he was. His chance to run a store, to own his own business, to be the head honcho, the boss man, the lord of all he surveyed. The success.

He wanted to argue with Stuart, but he couldn't. If he'd ever stopped to think about Gil and Rupert's largesse, their nonchalance, their fast talk and *sub rosa* crap and their general slipperiness, he would have been forced to acknowledge there was something not kosher about them, to use Stuart's term. He hadn't wanted to acknowledge that, so he hadn't stopped to think.

Not thinking had always come easily to Jay. But damn it, his lawyer was forcing him to think.

"I don't know what to do," he said.

"You know what to do." Stuart lifted his glass. "You tell Jenners and Niles, 'Thanks but no thanks.' You scale back your plans, go to a bank, and get a loan." He punctuated this advice with a lusty sip of scotch.

And pay all that interest. And know, every day, that he didn't actually own the business himself. The bank did. It would take him years to repay the loan, years during which he would be just an employee, a name above a door, but not the lord of all he surveyed.

And really, all he'd ever wanted—other than to be a lord—was for Bloom's to open a branch on the East Side.

Not even that. What he'd wanted was to be taken as seriously as Ben had been, as Julia was. He didn't want to be the Susie of his family, the flake who was dismissed because she had a tattoo on her ankle. Not that Jay had a tattoo, but Susie wasn't lord-of-all-she-surveyed material and everyone knew it. The only difference was that Susie didn't care.

Jay cared.

"I'll go to the bank," he said, then took a deep swig of scotch. Liquid courage, he thought. He was going to need a lot of courage to get through this crisis, so he might as well start by drinking some.

Chapter Twenty-One

Felicity Calabrese was driving Rick crazy.

Phat Larry had brought his wife with him to watch him record his new ad because, he claimed, she had a great eye. Gazing at her, Rick wouldn't say her eyes were all that great. First place for her greatest feature would be a tie between her boobs, on proud display in a snug V-neck sweater, and her hair, which was the color of radioactive mayonnaise, except for the dark roots. It stuck out around her face like a saint's halo in a Renaissance painting, big and round and blinding.

Her jewelry was also blinding. Her ears were adorned with diamonds the size of hazelnuts, and a hammered gold snake with a ruby eye coiled around her left wrist. Not that you could miss her cleavage in the tight sweater, but just in case, she wore a clunky diamond-studded necklace which acted like a beacon, directing Rick's attention to that spectacular part of her anatomy.

Of course, all those huge, glittering stones could be cubic zirconias.

Her face wasn't bad, although she looked as if she'd applied her eyeliner with a felt-tip marker. But her voice was coy and squeaky. And she was using her grating little-girl voice to lecture Rick on everything her great eye was telling her about this latest commercial.

"I don't think he should stand in front of a green screen," she complained. "It's boring."

"It won't be a green screen in the final version," Rick explained as patiently as he could, because although Phat Larry was rehearsing his lines and pinching the bridge of his nose in deep concentration, he was also listening in on Rick's conversation with Felicity. Rick had to remain polite and reasonable with the woman. He couldn't risk antagonizing a client by being rude to the client's wife. "The green screen won't show in the commercial. I'll project pictures of his car lot and the building onto it, and a few featured cars that he wants highlighted. We use special effects."

"Special effects? Like what, aliens shooting laser beams?"

"Special effects, like green-screen technology. The screen doesn't record an image. We edit in that image later. We'll include the shots of his sales lot, like I said, and a few of the cars." He glanced at his notes. "He's got a classic Mustang, a Jag with very low mileage, a Karmann Ghia, and a vintage T-bird. Right, Larry?"

"The T-bird is not for sale," Felicity said.

Phat Larry broke character to shout, "It's for sale. I'm not giving you that car, Fel."

"It's not for sale," Felicity confided to Rick, just loud enough for Phat Larry to hear.

"Sweetheart," Larry said, his voice coated in enough venom to flatten an elephant. "The profit I make when I sell that baby will buy you that ring you had your eye on, the one with the pineapple on it made out of yellow sapphires and diamonds. Remember?"

Felicity's face softened. Evidently, she did remember.

Rick, on the other hand, could not begin to envision a ring featuring a pineapple made out of yellow sapphires and diamonds. To be sure, he couldn't quite picture yellow sapphires. Maybe they looked like pineapples.

"Renee?" he hollered for his assistant. "Is the teleprompter ready?"

Renee pulled a brush and a jar of loose facial powder from her industrial box of cosmetics and carried them to Phat Larry, whose face and scalp were already shiny with sweat, even though Rick hadn't yet begun filming. Today, Renee wore a T-shirt reading, "Don't Freak With Me." "Teleprompter's ready," she called over her shoulder as she puffed powder across Larry's glistening forehead. When she was done, she jabbed the handle of her brush into his well-padded belly and said, "Stop sweating already."

"I can't help it," Larry moaned. "It's hot in here."

It was actually fairly chilly. Despite the fact that Glickstein paid a generous rental fee, the owner of the studio set the thermostat as low as he legally could to save money. But Rick didn't mind working in the cold atmosphere. He only wished it would keep Larry from getting *schvitzed*. Once Larry started rapping and dancing, he'd probably sweat as if his glands were the human equivalent of Niagara Falls.

"All right," Rick said. "Let's do a run-through, okay?" He discreetly switched his camera to record as Phat Larry took his place in front of the green screen. Felicity lurked somewhere behind Rick. He couldn't see her, but he could feel waves of disapproval radiating from her. It took abundant quantities of willpower not to spin around and tell her to take a hike—preferably across the Fifty-Ninth Street Bridge into Manhattan—or else to direct the damned commercial herself.

Renee started the thumping background music and Larry launched into one of his flailing dances. His warm-up suit was a royal blue velvet which actually contrasted nicely with the green screen. His scalp was no longer gleaming, thanks to Renee's skillful application of powder, but his gold Corvette pendant burned the lens of Rick's camera whenever the Fresnel lights glinted off it.

> *It's Phat Larry here, and I got news for you.*
> *We got cars galore, at bargain prices, too!*
> *You want a sedan, you want a coupe,*
> *Come on in—I'll give you the scoop.*
> *We got SUVs and vans and wagons.*
> *We got every kind of vehicle, and I ain't braggin'!*
> *We got a classic 'Stang and a Karmann Ghia.*
> *We got a gorgeous Jag-ee-war right hee-ah...*

At this line, he jabbed his thumb over his shoulder at the screen, where Rick would edit in the picture of the Jaguar.

> *So come to Fat Larry's Auto Mart.*
> *I'll sell you a car that'll steal your heart.*

Larry was perspiring as his dance wound down, his face glossy but his smile bright with hope. "What do you think?" he asked Rick.

What Rick thought was that he'd have to coordinate the background shots differently than he'd planned. "You didn't mention the T-bird in your rap."

"I couldn't think of anything that rhymes with T-bird," Larry explained.

"Free bird," Felicity said. "Drive a T-bird, you'll feel like a free bird. He's not selling that car," she added. "He's gonna give it to me."

"I'm selling it," Larry snapped.

"The fate of the T-bird is between the two of you," Rick interjected, hoping to stop a major fight before it started. "I'll just splice in the background differently."

Felicity scowled. "He looks like a chicken flapping its wings when he dances," she remarked. "Maybe I should choreograph his dance."

"We've got the studio only until four," Rick pointed out, glancing at his watch. If Felicity decided to give Larry a dance lesson, Rick wouldn't have time to film any more takes. Not that he really needed to. None of them would be any better than what he'd already recorded while Larry thought he was just doing a warm-up.

Renee, bless her heart, mentioned a desperate need for coffee and snacks and asked Felicity to accompany her down the street to the bodega on the corner. "I can't handle all the snacks and the coffee myself," she said. "You boys will have to carry on without us."

"They'll carry on, all right," Felicity muttered.

"Bitch," Larry called after her as she followed Renee out of the studio. To Rick, he snarled, "I'm not giving her that T-bird."

An hour, a cup of heavily creamed coffee, and a stale granola bar later, Rick called it a wrap and waved the Calabreses off. They were still arguing about the T-bird as they exited, flinging F-bombs at each other like guests tossing rice at a wedding. Renee shook her head. "I considered pushing her into the path of a speeding car while we were out buying the snacks," she said, tossing the leftover granola bars into her cosmetics case. "But there were no speeding cars. Just a really slow car. It wouldn't have put a dent in her."

"I appreciate the sentiment," Rick said as he packed up his gear. "I also appreciate that you're not going to be charged with murder. But if you do ever want to kill Felicity, I'll testify on your behalf in court. Same goes if you kill Larry."

"I'll keep that in mind," Renee said as she snapped her cosmetics case shut. "*Ciao.*"

He followed her out of the studio, locking up behind them and carrying the key downstairs to the manager's office. Once outside, he stood for a moment on the sidewalk, breathing in the fresh air. A hint of springtime filtered through it, a solid promise of warmth.

The studio was in an industrial part of Queens—concrete buildings that resembled children's building blocks. Most people would find the neighborhood ugly, but Rick liked the geometry of it, all those right angles, all those flat façades, some presenting blank canvases and others blotchy with graffiti. If he were a true filmmaker, an auteur entering his masterpieces into competition at Sundance and Cannes, he'd film some scenes here, catching the slope of the sunlight, the corrugated metal of garage doors, the mysteries that could be lurking just around the corner.

He loved the money he was earning at Glickstein, even if it wasn't exactly making him rich. But the job? Dealing with clowns like Larry Calabrese and his shrewish wife? He sure as hell didn't love that.

He strode down the sidewalk toward the subway station, struggling not to sink into self-pity. Jobs weren't supposed to be loved, he reminded himself. Jobs were supposed to be tolerated, endured, survived. Did he know anyone who actually loved his job?

Most of his classmates from film school were pursuing career paths as uninspiring as his own. He recalled one job he had, working Camera Three for a TV show that was recorded here in the city. He had NYU friends doing similar gigs out in L.A. And other NYU friends filming commercials, like what he was doing now. One friend was teaching video technique at a high school and producing local-access talk shows somewhere in South Dakota. Rick hadn't realized they had studios in South Dakota. For that matter, he hadn't realized they had electricity there. His classmate called him an ignorant New York asshole in their emails. Rick couldn't argue the point.

Rick's brother Neil seemed content sailing tourists on his boat around the Florida Keys, but he often complained about marina fees and obnoxious passengers and how much time and energy he had to spend repairing things on the boat. Sometimes he ran short of cash at the end of the month, if the weather had been particularly crappy. He drank a lot during hurricane season.

Susie's boyfriend Casey enjoyed running his gourmet bakery. But he had to get up before dawn to bake his inventory, which meant he had to go to bed when the city was just shifting into high gear for the night. Not ideal. Susie herself ricocheted back and forth between Bloom's and Casey's bakery and didn't seem happy about trying to meet the demands of both jobs.

Rick's father, though... He seemed truly excited about his new venture. Of course, everything always seemed exciting at its birth. It was one hundred percent potentiality and zero percent actuality. At the start of a new project, your dreams were still intact. They hadn't been destroyed yet.

That was what Rick wanted. Enthusiasm like his father's. Joy at the prospect of waking up and going to work. Maybe his father's joy would dissipate when he was actually running his store—stocking shelves, negotiating with suppliers, firing employees who spent too much time vaping in the alley behind the building. But now, in the planning stages, he was feeling joy in his professional choice.

Rick wanted that joy.

He'd never asked his father for career advice—which wasn't to say his father had never given him career advice. Back before Rick started at Glickstein, when he was surviving on odd jobs and stale slices of pizza Susie sneaked him at Nico's, his father had been full of advice: "Get real employment, something that pays. Sit at a desk like a *mensch* and earn a salary." The thought of spending his days seated at a desk had given Rick more heartburn than Nico's pizza.

He did like earning a salary, and much as he loved pizza, he'd rather eat Casey's cooking than anything Susie had ever smuggled to him at Nico's. Maybe he'd feel joy if he had financiers spend-spend-spending on him. Hell, if he had that, he wouldn't need his Glickstein salary. He'd be filming these austere warehouse buildings and the sloping shadows they cast, tracking some ambient music, and entering competitions. No more snarky comments from Susie about his meetings—not if his meetings were with producers and distributors and A-list actors.

Yeah, that would make him feel joy.

His cell phone vibrated. He pulled it out of his pocket and tilted the screen to minimize the glare. *U up for a drink?* Adam texted.

Rick was always up for a drink, but he was especially up for a drink right now, when he was feeling sorry for himself. *Sure,* he texted back.

Adam texted him the name of a bar near Lincoln Center.

C U there, Rick typed, then headed down the stairs to the subway.

Adam was already at the bar when Rick arrived, his fingers wrapped around a sweating bottle of beer. "I hope you don't mind," he said, holding the beer up. "I was thirsty."

"I'm thirsty, too." At not quite five o'clock, the after-work crowd hadn't crammed into the bar yet, and Rick had no trouble catching the bartender's eye and requesting a bottle of Stella Artois. He couldn't taste much difference between it and a cheap domestic beer, but he liked the name, and he liked the fact that he could now afford to buy imported beer. It made him feel successful—which was exactly what it was supposed to do. He'd worked in advertising long enough to have learned that with certain products—like beer—the ad was selling attitude more than taste. And he'd been living with himself long enough to know he was a sucker for that kind of attitudinal persuasion.

He and Adam found a small table in a dark corner against the wall and settled into their chairs with their beers and a bowl of some sort of bar snack that looked like a mix of pebbles and twigs harvested from a hiking trail. "So," he asked casually, "how are things going with Jacob Bloom's Phenomenal Gourmet Foods?"

"Delectable," Adam corrected him, not sounding too thrilled. "Not phenomenal. Delectable."

"Delectable makes me think of cute girls," Rick said. "You still seeing that ballerina?"

"Which one?" Adam grinned. "I'm on my third ballerina."

"Good for you." Rick suppressed a spasm of jealousy. Adam was four years younger than him and a math nerd, and he was already on his third ballerina. Rick had never had one ballerina, let alone three.

Then again, what did he need a ballerina for, when there were women like Anna Wong gliding through the universe? Not that he had her, but he would someday, hopefully. She was much more tolerant of him lately than she'd been even a year ago, thanks to ass-wipes like Phat Larry who paid money to the Glickstein Agency, which in turn paid money to Rick.

Adam, he noted hadn't answered his question. "How are things at the delectable place, then?"

"Fine," Adam said, then took a hard slug of his beer.

Rick might not be the most observant guy in New York, but Adam's tone of voice didn't say *fine*, and his chug-a-lugging his drink didn't say *fine*, either. Besides sensitivity, another of Rick's weak areas was subtlety. He'd used up his supply of tact dealing with Felicity Calabrese all afternoon. "How bad is it?" he asked his cousin.

Adam looked startled. He lowered his bottle and said, "It's a mess." Then he raised his bottle and wiggled it at a passing server, signaling that he wanted another.

A mess was not a tragedy. Any new enterprise was bound to be a mess. The store didn't have its shelves yet. It didn't have its fancy flooring and lighting fixtures. The place probably reeked of that tangy chemical fresh-paint smell. In fact, Rick thought messes were conducive to creativity. He was pretty sloppy, and he was creative.

"The money's dried up," Adam said. The server, a skinny woman in stretch jeans and a long-sleeved white T-shirt that hung on her like clean laundry on a clothes line, placed a fresh bottle in front of Adam and swept his empty away. Adam took a quick, deep gulp of beer.

Had the money dried up because Adam had a drinking problem? "I thought those investors were throwing money at you."

"Your dad said he conferred with his lawyer and concluded that just because they were throwing money at us didn't mean we had to catch it. He's decided that we're not taking their money." Adam shook his head. "I'm supposed to be his partner, but he doesn't give me a vote. He just tells me we're not working with the investors anymore."

"Why not?"

"Who the hell knows? I'm the partner he tells nothing to." Bitterness colored Adam's voice. "He's visited three banks to discuss loans. So far, he hasn't accepted the terms any of them offered."

"What terms?"

"They charge interest."

"Well...yeah. That's what banks do."

Adam sighed and shook his head. His eyelids were half-lowered, as if he were rationing the amount of light he'd expose his eyes to. Not that the bar was particularly well lit. "I think this whole thing is going down the tubes."

"Really? Jacob Bloom's Delectable Food Emporium?"

"It was a stupid name. Maybe that's what jinxed us."

Rick didn't believe in jinxes, but he couldn't argue. Jacob Bloom's Delectable Food Emporium was a stupid name.

"What am I going to do, Rick? Should I go to Purdue and get a PhD?"

"Is that still an option?"

"I don't know. I'd have to see if they had money to fund me." Adam drank some more beer, then sighed again. "I don't want to go to Purdue. I *liked* managing inventory at Bloom's. But—I mean, bridges were burned. Julia will never take me back. And it's not like I could walk into some other store and ask them to hire me to do inventory. They don't know me from Adam." He snorted a humorless laugh. "Maybe I should change my name."

"If my father's talking to banks, he hasn't given up. You shouldn't give up, either." Why was Rick saying this? His father and Adam *should* give up, go back to Bloom's, get their old jobs back. Unless, as Adam said, bridges had been burned.

They had been, of course. But bridges could be rebuilt. Decades ago, when the George Washington Bridge couldn't handle all the traffic traveling across it, engineers built a second roadway underneath the first roadway, thus creating two traffic-jammed arteries where before there had been only one. Anything was possible.

"I'm broke." Adam gave Rick a hang-dog look. "I haven't received a paycheck since I left Bloom's, and it's not like I can live off my savings. I mean, it's not like I actually *have* savings. I hope you don't mind paying for the drinks."

Rick shrugged.

"I'm a formula guy, right? A proofs guy. I like things laid out logically. I like to be able to run through the problem and get an answer that makes sense. Your dad is a dreamer. He's not a big fan of details. I guess I'm the details partner. When he kept saying he didn't want me to talk to the investors, I got suspicious. But... you know? I ignored my suspicions. I stifled my doubts. I wanted to buy into the dream."

"Okay, so..." Rick sipped his pricy imported beer and sorted his thoughts. Barely an hour ago, he'd been feeling oddly envious of his father for living his dream, pursuing it, making it come true. Having investors throwing money at him—and catching the money with both hands and maybe his teeth. He'd imagined his father surfing on waves of joy as he created his emporium. And now, it turned out, his father was having to hustle—begging banks to loan him money at cheap interest rates when his only real credential, in terms of business, was that his last name happened to be Bloom. The guy must be pissed off beyond belief.

Rick indulged in a fleeting moment of amusement as he visualized himself giving his father career advice for a change. The role-reversal scenario faded, but he still might have to give career advice to Adam, if not his father. Rick was the elder cousin, after all. He was the wise man at this table, if for no other reason than that he was paying for the beers.

"You like doing inventory?" he said. "You want to go back to Bloom's? Go back. Crawl. Grovel. Beg Julia's forgiveness. And Grandma Ida's, too, I guess. I'm not really sure who's in charge over there, but I bet it's Grandma Ida."

"She might forgive me," Adam allowed. "Julia won't, though. My mother probably won't, either. And what about your dad? Am I supposed to crawl back to Bloom's while he's still trying to open his store? I was his partner. I can't just dump him, can I?"

Rick pondered some more, then shrugged. "Whatever you do, it's going to suck."

Adam nodded glumly.

"Sometimes life just throws shit at you. But sometimes it throws rainbows. Get through the shit and take pictures of the rainbows."

"That's your philosophy of life?"

Rick hadn't really thought about it until he'd given voice to it, but yes. It was a good, workable philosophy of life. "Put on your waders, pinch your nose, and wade through the shit."

"What if I don't see any rainbows? How am I going to take pictures of them?"

"You've got a ballerina," Rick reminded him. "Your third ballerina. I'd call that a rainbow."

Adam smiled shyly. "Three rainbows," he said.

Chapter Twenty-Two

Susie arrived at her old apartment carrying her sack-sized purse, a duffel bag filled with spare clothes, and a box of Casey's assorted muffins which hadn't sold and were otherwise destined, along with that day's other unsold but edible merchandise, for a soup kitchen near the Manhattan Bridge. She might be leaving him, but that didn't mean she couldn't help herself to some goodies on her way out the door.

The apartment she'd shared with Anna and Caitlin had only one bedroom which could fit—barely—two narrow beds. When all three women had lived there, they used to rotate among the beds and the couch in the main room, although Caitlin tended to spend enough of her nights with other people—friends, lovers, hook-ups—that Anna and Susie had both gotten to use the beds most of the time.

Susie would be sleeping on the couch tonight. It wasn't particularly comfortable, but she planned to stay up late enough that when she finally stretched out on the lumpy upholstery, she'd be too tired to care.

"Did you bring us doughnuts?" Caitlin asked eagerly. She was wearing lounge pants with little polar bears patterned on them, a baggy Henley shirt, and strips of paper towel woven between her bare toes in preparation for a pedicure. As she shook a bottle of scarlet nail polish, she eyed the box hungrily.

Susie set it on the tiny table next to the kitchen alcove and dropped onto one of the chairs. "Muffins," she said. "Casey doesn't make doughnuts. But the muffins are really good."

Anna was barefoot, too. Susie wondered whether they were doing a better job of keeping the floor vacuumed than they had when she'd lived there. Then she noticed Anna's yoga mat rolled up and leaning against a wall, and realized Anna must have just finished her yoga. Which could explain why she was wearing yoga pants.

Anna pried open the box's lid, peered inside, and smiled. "You want something to drink," she said. It wasn't a question.

"What do you have?"

"Wine," Anna said.

"And tequila," Caitlin added, settling onto another chair and propping her feet on the edge of the seat so she could rest her chin on her knees. She peered into the box, nodded her approval, and then proceeded to polish her toenails.

"Tequila. Sounds good," Susie said.

Anna pulled three glasses from the cabinet above the sink. Susie recognized them; she'd bought them at a job-lot schlock house in the neighborhood for fifty cents a glass. They were ugly, with narrow ridges etched into them that reminded Susie of corduroy, and she'd had no qualms about leaving them behind when she and Casey had moved in together. But she was here now, not with him, and it seemed right that she should be drinking tequila from an ugly glass.

Anna poured an inch into each glass, then sat across from Susie and tossed back her long, straight hair. Rick was obsessed with Anna's hair. He always raved about how it was so black it looked blue, and confessed that he dreamed of raveling his fingers through it and discovering that it felt as soft as it looked. In all honesty, Susie thought Anna would look a lot cooler if she chopped it off. At least six inches shorter, maybe eight. And added bangs.

But Anna's hair didn't matter. She was a true friend, and so was Caitlin. Without a moment's hesitation, they'd urged Susie to come and stay with them when she'd sent them the cryptic text: *Casey trouble.* They understood what that meant. It meant she needed friends and a place to stay. And tequila.

She took a sip of the liquor and felt it burn past her throat, down her esophagus, into her stomach. God, that stuff tasted awful. She took another sip.

Lowering her glass, she saw Anna gazing expectantly at her. Caitlin was dabbing polish on her final nail, and then she screwed the cap back onto the bottle of polish, set it on the table, and lifted her gaze to Susie, too.

"Well?" Anna prompted her.

"We had a fight," Susie said. As fights went, it hadn't been much—but in her mind and her heart, it had been huge, partly because she and Casey fought so rarely. They disagreed, and they discussed things, and they occasionally sulked. But this time, this fight... it hadn't just been a disagreement or a discussion.

"The window of his store is boring," she told Caitlin and Anna. "I came up with a much better design. It's not like I don't know what I'm doing. I design the Bloom's windows, right? I used to design the window at Nico's. So I came up with this fabulous design for Casey's bakery window. It had a big crescent moon, and lots of stars, and then some loaves displayed below, and a few loaves sort of floating in the air among the stars. Because bread is magic."

"Okay," Anna said carefully.

Caitlin's eyes widened. "Wow. He didn't like that?"

"I don't even know if he liked it or not. He said he had to check with his best friend, Mose, and Mose didn't like it."

"His best friend?" Anna sounded indignant. "Aren't you his best friend?"

"That's exactly it. I'm supposed to be his best friend. I'm his woman. His lover. I live with him. *Lived*," she added, although using the past tense sounded so sad. What if they never made up? What if this disagreement was the one that destroyed their relationship forever?

It wasn't about the window, really. It was about trust, and best-friendship, and whom Casey chose to listen to in his life. "He's known Mose a lot longer than he's known me," she said, wondering why she was rationalizing Casey's rejection of her ideas. "They met when they were told they weren't good enough to join the St. John's basketball team as walk-ons their freshman year."

"St. John's?" Caitlin had a way of latching onto the unimportant details. "I thought Casey went to the Culinary Institute of America."

"He went to St. John's, and then to the C.I.A." Calling the culinary school the C.I.A. that was one of Casey and Susie's jokes. He was the antithesis of a spy, after all—so absurdly straightforward he drove her crazy sometimes. "Mose has an MBA, so Casey acts as if Mose is the world's expert in everything. And Mose said having stars and moons and bread floating through the sky like UFOs made no sense."

"It doesn't have to make sense," Anna said.

"That's why I love you," Susie said. "A window doesn't have to make sense. It just has to grab the attention of passers-by. It has to captivate them and then lure them inside. You understand that." She raised her glass in a toast to Anna and took a drink. With each sip, it tasted a little less vile. It was probably anesthetizing her taste buds. "The moon holds everything together. The stars represent magic, but the moon represents solidity. Security. Beauty and illumination."

"What does the floating bread represent?" Caitlin asked.

"It represents bread," Susie said. "It tells the world, 'This is what we're selling.' I tried to explain this to Casey, but he said Mose knows about store windows because of his frickin' MBA. Casey took Mose's side over mine. And that hurts." A sob bubbled up at the back of her mouth, but she swallowed it back down.

"Maybe it's just a guy thing," Caitlin said as she reached for a muffin. "Bros stick together. No girls allowed in the clubhouse, and all that bullshit. Or maybe Casey thinks you're a poet and he wants a hard-headed business person figuring out his window. What is this, anyway? Does it have raisins in it?"

Susie leaned across the table and squinted at the muffin, hoping to identify it by its appearance. "Walnuts," she said. "That's an oat bran muffin. So healthy, it'll add ten years to your life."

"Yeah, right." Caitlin took a bite and swallowed. "A little stale, but delicious."

"These were the unsold ones. If they don't sell within two days of being baked, they get discounted. If they don't sell at the discounted price, Casey donates them to a soup kitchen—or the staff can take them."

"I remember when you said Casey was Godiva dark chocolate," Anna remarked.

Susie nodded. She remembered, too. Back in her single days, she and Anna and Caitlin used to compare the men in their lives to chocolate. The guy she'd been dating before she met Casey was a Snickers. Caitlin had told Susie her most recent boyfriend was a Twix, neither here nor there. The second violinist Anna had been seeing lately was, according to her, a Hershey's bar—solid, reliable, but not terribly interesting. She also said she thought Rick was licorice, which wasn't chocolate but seemed about right.

When Susie had first met Casey, he'd definitely been Godiva dark chocolate, gourmet-rich, a complex of sweet and bitter and mysterious. She'd been as infatuated with him as she was with that imported Belgian confection. He'd seemed so unusual. Exotic, almost—tall and blond and eerily placid, from the distant land of Queens, New York. He'd been working with Morty Sugarman, baking and selling bagels at Bloom's, and his bagels, then as now, were the best bagels she had ever tasted. She'd all but thrown herself at him, and he'd insisted that he wouldn't sleep with her until he got to know her better, which was something no man had ever done with her before. For a while, she'd thought he might be a virgin, or possibly gay.

He most definitely wasn't either of those things. He was phenomenal in bed—or he had been, before he'd started falling asleep at nine p.m.

"He's turned into M&M's," she told her friends. "Sweet, but with a hard shell that won't melt."

"I love M&M's," Anna said. "M&M peanuts, though. Not the plain chocolate ones."

"He could be one of those new M&M flavors," Caitlin said. "Mint, or peanut butter, or pretzel."

"There's an M&M pretzel flavor?" Anna looked stunned.

The discussion was veering off course. Susie steered it back. "He should respect me as much as he respects Mose, right? Like you said, I should be his best friend. He should trust me. I'm not an idiot."

"Of course you're not," Anna said.

"You're a genius," Caitlin added, which seemed a bit over the top, but Susie appreciated the compliment.

"Here we are, living together," Susie continued. "He's asked me to marry him a bunch of times. But I can't confide in him, because he's too busy confiding in Mose."

"You can confide in us," Anna said, patting her hand in reassurance before lifting her glass to drink.

Susie drank, too. So did Caitlin. She loved these friends, maybe even loved them more than she loved Casey at the moment. Maybe loved them more than he loved Mose.

But he was only the biggest of her long list of problems. "I can't even talk to him about all the other stuff going on in my life," she said, hearing a wobble in her voice as the incipient sob threatened to break free once more. "Half the time he's home, he's sleeping. When he's awake, he's worrying about the store."

"Well, it's still kind of new," Caitlin said reasonably. "He wants it to succeed."

"It's doing fine," Susie said. "He earns a small fortune just from his bagel account with Bloom's." Saying *Bloom's* fueled the sob, making it swell until she was afraid she'd choke on it. It was so weird, this urge to cry. She wasn't used to it. She took a swig of tequila and felt the incipient sob slide back down her throat. "Everything at Bloom's is a mess," she reported. "My sister is freaking out because my uncle is trying to compete with her by opening a deli of his own. I haven't talked to my mother in days—which maybe isn't such a terrible thing. My brother has gone to the dark side with my uncle. My grandmother cried in front of me. I didn't know she could cry, but I definitely saw tears run down her cheeks. I've known her my entire life, and I never saw her cry until Julia threatened to sue Uncle Jay."

"Ooh." Caitlin wrinkled her freckled nose. "That's always a bad thing, when family members sue each other."

Anna agreed with a nod.

"And I can't even talk to Casey about any of this. He's so preoccupied with his store, and payroll, and health inspections, and blah-blah-blah. And whatever Mose tells him."

"Casey doesn't know any of this is going on?"

"He knows," Susie conceded. "But he just tells me everything will be okay, and I'm the strongest Bloom in the family, and I should just ride out the storm. It's, I don't know. Patronizing."

"He's right," Anna said. "You *are* the strongest Bloom." Not that she was an expert on Susie's family.

"I don't feel strong."

Caitlin broke off a chunk of her muffin and handed it to Susie. "Eat this. It'll make you strong."

"It'll put hair on your chest," Anna chimed in, helping herself to a date-bran muffin.

Susie laughed. One thing she didn't want was a hairy chest.

"Everything will work out however it's supposed to work out," Caitlin said. That was the extent of her philosophy of life, but it kept her going. Nothing ever flattened her. She'd get knocked down, she'd weep buckets or rage like a tornado, and then she'd shrug and say, "Well, I guess that was the way it was supposed to work out," and she'd move on. Anna did yoga, but Caitlin was, in her own loud way, the most Zen of the three of them.

Susie didn't do yoga. Holding poses, taking slow breaths... She lacked the patience for all that. Her philosophy of life was basically: when things are good, enjoy them for all they're worth. When things are bad, write a poem about them. Also—with a nod to Shakespeare—to your own self be true.

Her truth right now was that she had lost her anchors. Her main anchor, Casey, valued his friend Mose more than he valued her. Her other anchor, her family, was corroded and crumbling, as if it had spent too much time submerged in a salty, polluted sea.

But she had Anna and Caitlin, and the living room couch, and tequila. And stale muffins.

She might not be the strongest Bloom, but she'd survive.

She reached into the box and pulled out a pumpkin-pecan muffin. For strength, she told herself. For strength, and to soak up the tequila.

Chapter Twenty-Three

"Are you having a meeting?" Grandma Ida asked.

She stood in Julia's open office doorway, Lyndon hovering behind her. Julia met his gaze and he shrugged, as if to say Grandma Ida's visit to the office was her own idea, not his.

Julia wasn't having a meeting. It wasn't Monday. On rare occasions, she might call a meeting on a day other than Monday, but Myron Finkel was the only attendee happy about those extra meetings, because Deirdre always catered them with bagels from the store. The rest of the third-floor staff didn't like the meetings even on Mondays, so Julia did her best not to schedule them more often than once a week.

Of course, in times of crisis, a meeting might be called at any time. And this was a time of crisis. She'd actually thought about conferring with her team about whether to threaten to sue Uncle Jay for trademark infringement, but imagining the tumult that suggestion might cause made her hesitate.

It was a bad idea to threaten something if you weren't prepared to follow through on the threat, although lawyers made idle threats all the time. At some point during the past two years that she'd been running Bloom's, she had stopped thinking like a lawyer. Yet every time she contemplated sending Uncle Jay a letter filled with scary legal jargon about trademark infringement, copyright law, and intellectual property, she'd felt a twinge of excitement not unlike what she'd felt when she'd first met Ron and had no idea what this reporter who intended to write a story about Bloom's for *Gotham Magazine* might really want with her.

What he'd wanted, as it had turned out, was sex. And love. And also a story for his magazine.

Lawyers made threats. They also mapped out all the possible consequences of an act. When Julia thought about threatening Uncle Jay, the map that spread before her gave her pause. If she threatened to sue Uncle Jay, Grandma Ida would be furious, or devastated, or both. She'd actually wept when Julia had suggested the idea. At her age, a notion she found so terribly traumatic might shatter her. Julia couldn't imagine Grandma Ida ever dying, but...she *was* old.

A different possible outcome, if Julia threatened to sue Uncle Jay, was that he might decide simply to change the name of his store. Then he would no longer be in breach of trademark law.

Or he might feel compelled to return to his position at Bloom's, which would be wonderful, except that he would labor under a cloud of seething resentment. He would hate Julia. His hatred and resentment would lead him to shirk his responsibilities.

Adam would likely seethe and shirk, too.

She didn't want Uncle Jay and Adam to hate her. She was supposed to make everyone feel good, not resentful.

"No meeting," she told her grandmother. "Were you on your way downstairs?"

"No. I want to talk to the family."

"If I was having a meeting, it would be more than the family. Myron, and Deirdre—"

"Just the family. Your mother and sister and you. *Oy*," Grandma Ida added with a sorrowful shake of her head. "It's only half the family. Where's the other half of my family?"

Some are dead, and the rest are on the East Side, Julia almost answered. "Come on in," she said instead. "Have a seat. I'll get them."

"Lyndon can stay," Grandma Ida said as she entered Julia's office and headed straight for the couch. Lyndon followed her in and shrugged again. Evidently, he had no idea what she was up to.

Julia stood but didn't approach the door. Her mother and sister would be able to hear her if she shouted. "Mom? Susie? Can you come here for a minute?"

She hadn't seen her mother since her regular meeting that past Monday. At the time, Sondra had been uncharacteristically chipper. She'd actually hummed while she'd smeared cream cheese on her poppy-seed bagel. At the end of the meeting, she'd said she had a doctor's appointment at noon and wouldn't be back afterward.

"Is everything all right?" Julia had asked. Most people weren't so cheerful about a doctor's appointment.

"Everything is great," Sondra had assured her.

As far as Julia knew, everything *was* great for Sondra, more or less. Julia knew her mother was spending time in her office because she heard her hollering back and forth with Deirdre about the stock of egg beaters and egg timers on the second floor, and of course her latest obsession, the tea towels. Also, Deirdre reported regularly to Julia on her and Sondra's efforts to hire a new website and mail-order manager. According to Deirdre, the search was not going well. "People are reluctant to work for a family-owned business," Deirdre had informed Julia. "They worry about nepotism. They worry that they won't be able to rise beyond a certain point in the corporate hierarchy because family members will be blocking the path."

"You've risen," Julia had pointed out, then conceded, "You're practically family."

Deirdre had nodded. Julia wondered, sometimes, whether Deirdre knew that Julia knew that Deirdre and her father had had a long-time affair. The expression "office wife" could have been applied to Deirdre almost literally, except for the fact that her father's actual wife worked for the store, too. How he and Deirdre had managed to carry on when Sondra was always coming and going was one of the great mysteries of Julia's life. Someday, she would like to get Deirdre drunk and ask her.

Grandma Ida evidently didn't think Deirdre was family enough to be included in today's impromptu meeting. Just people named Bloom. Susie entered Julia's office first, looking more funereal than usual. She was dressed in her standard black apparel, effecting a combined goth/cool-urban look, but her face was drawn, her eyes puffy and slightly bloodshot. Either she wasn't sleeping well, she'd contracted a severe case of conjunctivitis, or she'd started her day by smoking a joint. That last possibility seemed more Adam's style than Susie's. Susie preferred to drink her intoxicants, not inhale them.

She nodded at Julia and flinched slightly when she turned and saw Grandma Ida seated on the sofa, clad in one of her dowdy skirts and pilled cardigans. Susie quickly recovered from her surprise and gave Grandma Ida a dutiful kiss on the cheek before hoisting herself onto the old wooden desk where she always sat during meetings.

"Mom?" Julia shouted again.

"I'm coming." Sondra swept into the room, looking startled. Seeing Grandma Ida might have surprised her as it had surprised Susie, but she looked startled before turning toward the couch, where Grandma Ida and Lyndon sat. Her startled expression was directed at Julia.

Why on earth would she be surprised to see Julia standing by her desk in her office? Did Sondra still pine for that desk? Did she believe so deeply that the desk ought to be hers that the vision of Julia—Bloom's effing president, for God's sake—standing beside the president's desk in the president's office jolted her?

Then Julia realized that her mother's shock wasn't just directed at Julia. She turned and acknowledged Susie, Grandma Ida, and Lyndon with nods, and her expression didn't change at all. Her eyes remained wide, her brows arched, her smile stiff and tenuous. "What's going on?" she asked as she moved toward the couch and sat at one end, allowing Lyndon to position himself between her and Grandma Ida on the cracked leather cushions. She turned back to Julia, staring at her with that same eerie, wide-eyed look.

"Grandma Ida has something she wants to talk to us about," Julia said, resting her hips against her desk and tilting her head toward her grandmother.

They all looked at Grandma Ida. "*Pesach*," she said.

"Right. Passover. It's next week," Julia concurred.

"I'm hosting the Seder," Grandma Ida said. "I always do, and I'm hosting it this year, too. Lyndon—" she patted his hand "—and his friend Howard will do the cooking. They make a delicious Seder."

"They do," Sondra agreed. Of course, Sondra had never prepared a Seder at all—or at least hadn't prepared one in Julia's lifetime. Cooking had never much interested her.

"Howard does most of it," Lyndon said. "He was born to it, after all." Which was Lyndon's way of reminding them all that his partner was Jewish.

"I like his matzo balls," Susie chimed in. "They're not too heavy, not too light. The Seder-in-a-Box sales are good," she added, eyeing Julia. "I *think*. The way Uncle Jay set up the website, it's kind of hard to figure out. But the orders have really picked up this week. I put Seder-in-a-Box promo all over the latest *Bloom's Bulletin*, so I guess that's not a big surprise."

"So," Grandma Ida said. "I already told Martha. Neil is coming up from wherever he is, sailing around in that cockamamie boat. It's not what a normal person should be doing, but..." She shrugged. "He'll be there. Also Ricky. I have to talk to him about that screaming man with the car around his neck."

"What screaming man?" Sondra's voice sounded perplexed. She still wore that startled expression.

"From one of the commercials Rick made," Susie explained."

"He wears a car around his neck?"

"It's a necklace."

"It's a terrible thing, this commercial," Grandma Ida said. "The man screams. Rhyming screams, late at night."

"What on earth is he selling?"

"Cars," Susie said.

"I would never buy a car from that man. He's *farkakte*. So Ricky will come." Grandma Ida paused dramatically. "Jacob and Adam won't be there."

Silence smothered the room for a long minute. Julia finally cleared her throat. "Have you asked them? Do they want to come?"

"I haven't asked them. I wanted you should all know first. I have always hosted *Pesach*, it's a time for family. But they betrayed us. They did this terrible thing, leaving the business, competing with us. On the Upper East Side," she concluded, as if she considered the location of Uncle Jay's new store the greatest betrayal of all. "You can't sue them," she added, shooting Julia a sharp look. "But they aren't welcome at my Seder."

"Sue them?" Sondra blurted out, directing her frozen-in-shock expression toward Julia. "You were going to sue them? For what?"

"It doesn't matter. I'm not going to do it," Julia said regretfully. "Grandma Ida vetoed the idea."

"What would you sue them for?" Sondra persisted. "Being idiots? Is that a crime you can be sued for these days?" Her eyes remained wide and round, her forehead as flat as a wall.

Grandma Ida leaned forward, peering around Lyndon at Sondra. "She's not going to do it," she said. "You don't sue family. It's not right."

"I agree," Sondra said with an emphatic nod.

That must be a first, Julia thought, her mother and grandmother actually agreeing about something. She glanced toward Susie, who was gazing at their mother but looking as if her mind were many miles away.

Maybe Julia ought to sue them all. "You don't sue family, but it's all right not to include family in your Seder?" she challenged Grandma Ida. She never questioned Grandma Ida's decisions and edicts, but she was questioning this one—partly because she thought Grandma Ida was wrong to forbid her from suing Uncle Jay, and partly because a Seder without the whole family present seemed impossible. Neil was coming all the way from southern Florida. If family was so sacrosanct you couldn't sue one another, how could you exclude some of the family from the Seder?

"They've broken my heart, those two," Grandma said. "A lawsuit, with courts and judges and newspapers, it's all so public." She shook her head and clicked her tongue. "No. But a holiday, a *yontif,* that's private."

"Grandma, are you sure this is a good idea? Lyndon, what do you think?" Julia asked, shifting her gaze to the one man in the room. His eyebrows spiked and he shrugged. Obviously, he didn't know what he thought.

Bloom family dynamics probably seemed incomprehensible to him. As far as Julia knew, his family was normal. He had a sister who was a nurse at Maimonides Medical Center, and a brother who pushed papers in the city's Sanitation Department. According to Lyndon, they all got along well enough, even though his family wasn't crazy about Howard. "They don't care that I'm gay," he'd once told Julia, "but I think they would have preferred that I hadn't crossed the racial line. My sister's always asking me why I can't settle down with a black man."

"The heart wants what it wants," Julia had commiserated, thinking at the time that her heart wanted Lyndon, except for the fact that he was gay. She loved Ron. But Lyndon was so serene and patient. And he was a much better cook than Ron, even if Howard would be doing much of the food preparation for the Seder.

"I think your family is *meshugena,*" Lyndon said now, then grinned. He'd worked for Grandma Ida long enough to have picked up a fair amount of Yiddish. Then again, most people who lived in New York picked up a bit of Yiddish. "But it's up to your grandmother. We don't want her heart broken any more than it already is."

"Lyndon is *klug,*" Grandma Ida said. "You know what that means?"

Julia didn't know. Nor, apparently, did anyone else. "Is it a kind of shoe?" Lyndon asked, which got a laugh out of Susie.

"*Klug*. It means wise. That's you, Lyndon. Sondra, if your son asks you about the Seder, tell him he broke his grandmother's heart and he's not welcome."

Julia would have expected her mother to roll her eyes and sigh. She hated when Grandma Ida ordered her around. But she only stared blankly at her.

"All right, then. Lyndon, let's go downstairs," Grandma Ida said, using one hand on the arm of the sofa and the other on Lyndon's knee to push herself to her feet. "It's a nice day. We're going to the park to watch those people roll the balls around."

"Soccer?" Susie asked.

"Bocce," Lyndon told her.

"It's a nice sport," Grandma Ida said. "Very quiet. No one yells. Not like that crazy man with the car around his neck."

Julia, her mother, and her sister watched while Lyndon escorted Grandma out of the office. Grandma Ida called a greeting to Myron as she passed his open door, and then said, "Is that a TV? They have a show about solitaire?"

"You can play solitaire on a computer," Lyndon explained to her.

"It helps you learn how to use a computer," Myron added. "That's what Jay told me."

"It helps you to waste time," Julia grumbled. Although he wasted time and still didn't know quite how to use a computer, she wasn't going to fire Myron. Given Deirdre's difficulty trying to hire someone to fill Uncle Jay's position, it would be foolish to create an additional third-floor vacancy that Deirdre would have to fill. Of course, as vice-president of HR, Sondra ought to be having that difficulty, not Deirdre.

Sondra peered out the door, watching Grandma Ida's progress toward the elevators. Then she sighed.

"I hate when she gives me orders. Who does she think she is?"

"The matriarch of the family," Julia said. "The CEO of the company."

"She always bosses everyone around." Sondra's words were bitter, but her expression remained pleasantly bland. "I think barring Adam from her Seder is nasty. Jay, who cares? He can have a *shiksa* Seder with Wendy. But Adam... He may be her grandson, but he's my son."

"He abandoned Bloom's," Julia reminded her mother. "He broke her heart."

"I didn't even know she had a heart." Sondra sighed.

"I'll call Adam and tell him he can't come," Susie volunteered as she hoisted herself off the desk. "I don't care."

"Good. You call him." Sondra assessed Susie with her gaze. "You still haven't gotten a haircut, have you. You look bedraggled."

Susie scowled. "Thanks."

"You need money? I'll pay for a haircut. Where do you get your hair done?" she asked Julia.

"She said she's going to call Adam. Don't give her a hard time."

"Right," Susie agreed. "Don't give me a hard time."

"All I'm saying is, you're a beautiful girl, and you'd be even more beautiful if your hair was shaped a little."

"I don't want my hair shaped," Susie retorted. "It's exactly the shape I want it."

"Okay. I love you girls. Now I've got work to do. Or maybe I should just play some solitaire," she added with a faint grin.

Susie crossed the room to stand with Julia while they watched their mother exit. Then they looked at each other. "I wish she'd stop criticizing my hair," Susie said.

"What was wrong with her? She looked weird."

"You think so?"

"Her face was all stiff. Oh, no." Julia sank against her desk. "What's that condition called, where your face gets paralyzed? Bell's palsy? She had a doctor's appointment on Monday—"

"I don't think she has that. It usually just affects one side of your face. She looked pretty symmetrical to me."

"You noticed it, too?" Julia was relieved to hear she hadn't just imagined her mother's odd appearance. "She looked...I don't know. Blank."

"She looked like someone who got Botox injections," Susie said.

"Botox?" Julia gazed out the door through which their mother had vanished. "Oh, my God. You're right. Her forehead was so smooth." Julia frowned, grateful to feel her eyebrows dipping and her forehead contracting. "Why would she do that?"

Susie stated the obvious. "To look younger."

"She didn't look younger. She just looked stiff."

"Whatever. I should see if I can reach Adam," Susie said, starting for the door. "As far as I know, he and I are still talking."

Julia snagged Susie's arm and pulled her back. "Okay, so Mom looked stiff and blank. You look—well, not bedraggled, but..." Julia studied her sister. "Miserable."

"I'm fine."

"You're not fine."

Susie blinked resolutely. "Casey and I are having some problems, that's all. Not a big thing."

"What problems?"

Susie sighed. She had gotten Julia through so many ups and downs in the early days of her relationship with Ron, and with the losers she'd been with before him. Although Julia was two years older than Susie, Susie had been more...well, *promiscuous* sounded judgmental. More experienced with men sounded better. More relaxed about them. Less intense. Less blinded by notions of passion and romance and happily-ever-after.

If, for once, Julia was the one in the stable, healthy relationship and Susie was the one caught up in a relationship crisis, Julia had to help her. She admitted she felt kind of good about being the one giving advice rather than receiving it. "What did he do?"

"He didn't do anything," Susie said. "He just wouldn't let me design the window at his store, because his best friend didn't like the design I came up with. He trusts Mose more than he trusts me."

"I'm sure he trusts you," Julia said.

"Not with his store window."

"Do you want me to talk to him? I could tell him how much people love your windows here at Bloom's."

"No," Susie said quickly. "It's between him and me." She sighed again. "It's about trust, not about the window."

That sounded so mature to Julia. So deep. So wise. What was that word Grandma Ida had used to describe Lyndon? So *klug*.

"I'm fine, really," Susie said. "Mom, I'm not so sure. I mean, a nose job is one thing. But injecting poison into your face? That's kind of scary."

"Maybe the Botox makes her feel prettier."

"She'd be a lot prettier if she could smile like a normal person," Susie said, giving Julia a smile. A pretty smile, a normal smile, but also a poignant one, tinged with sorrow.

"Come talk to Mom with me," she urged Susie. "I don't want to talk to her alone."

"What are we talking about? Her immobile forehead?"

"Yes." Julia took Susie's arm again, this time not to keep her from leaving but to escort her out of this office and into their mother's office. As usual, Sondra's office door was open, so she'd be able to shout at the other third-floor denizens at will. Julia didn't have to knock before entering.

Sondra was seated at her desk, thumbing through a catalog of small kitchen appliances. She glanced up at Julia and Susie and gave them one of her inanimate smiles. "Hi, girls."

"We wanted to talk to you," Julia said.

"*Julia* wanted to talk to you," Susie corrected her. "She just dragged me along for company."

"If it's about hiring Jay's replacement, I delegated that to Deirdre. She's much better at navigating those hiring websites than I am."

Better wasn't good enough, Julia thought. Better wasn't finding Bloom's the replacement they needed. At least Deirdre was trying, though.

Her mother was trying, too—in a completely different definition of the word. "Are you doing Botox?" she asked.

"I am," Sondra said. "You noticed?"

"Yes."

"I look fabulous, don't I?"

"You do," Julia said. It was what her mother wanted to hear.

Susie never felt the need to make people feel good. "You look like you've just seen a ghost," she said.

"No, she doesn't," Julia argued. "She looks very... smooth."

"Can you blink?" Susie asked Sondra.

"Of course I can blink." Sondra gave Susie a peeved look—or as peeved a look as she could, given that her face, from the artificially narrow bridge of her nose up, was petrified.

"I've seen ads for Botox on TV," Susie said. "They list about a million possible bad side effects."

"I haven't had any of them," Sondra said.

Apparently, being unable to move your forehead wasn't considered a bad side effect. "How long does it take to wear off?" she asked.

"A few months, but then I'll probably get another round. I'm really pleased. I think I look ten years younger."

She looked ten years more astounded, for sure. Julia kept that thought to herself.

"You looked nice before," Susie said, earning another attempted glower from Sondra. "Why did you do this?"

"I don't have to explain my decisions to you," Sondra said sharply. She leaned back to include Julia. "It's time for me to start dating again. Your father has been gone for three years, now. I had always imagined myself continuing his legacy here at the store, fulfilling his dreams for Bloom's. But I'm not doing that, am I. I'm sitting here trying to find a replacement for his brother."

Actually, Deirdre was doing that, but once again, Julia didn't verbalize her thoughts. "You're helping with the second-floor inventory," she said, gesturing toward the catalog. "Are those some new electric can openers? Are we going to start ordering in some different makes and models?"

"I don't care about electric can openers," Susie said. "I care that my mother wants to date the kind of men who judge a woman by whether she's got some creases in her forehead. Any guy who considers that important is a superficial asshole. But what do I know? My hair isn't shaped right." She flung her hands in the air, shot Julia a look, and strode to the door. "I've got a limerick to write, and then I've got a brother I have to tell he can't come to Grandma Ida's Seder. Good luck. I hope your brain doesn't get paralyzed." With that, she stormed out of the office.

Sondra gazed after her for a moment, then turned back to Julia, who was scrambling to think of a way to make her mother feel better after Susie's obnoxious little hissy-fit. "She's having problems with Casey," Julia said by way of explanation.

Her mother didn't look sorry. She didn't look hurt, or angry, or vexed. She didn't look anything at all. "Casey's a nice young man, but he's a *baker*. Why she can't find someone a little more respectable, I don't know. But that's her problem, not mine."

Maybe her brain *was* paralyzed. She certainly didn't sound the least bit concerned about Susie's crisis. She didn't sound engaged at all.

"So, you're dating?" Julia asked.

"Not yet, but I hope to be, soon. There's this other website which is even more confusing than that LinkedIn site. I keep forgetting whether I'm supposed to swipe left or right."

"Mom. A lot of the guys on those websites are just looking for sex."

"Who can blame them? It's what men do." Her mother shrugged. At least her shoulders still worked. "If I can't run Bloom's, I may as well do some looking, myself. I'm not too old for sex. And—" the smile taking hold of the lower half of her face looked smug "—I don't look too old for it, either."

"Just...be careful," Julia warned.

Her mother glanced toward the doorway, then back to Julia. "Susie doesn't use those dating websites, does she?"

"She's been living with Casey for the past year. Why would she be going on dating websites?"

"Good." Sondra flipped a page in the catalog. "I lost the presidency of Bloom's to one daughter. I'd hate to lose some prospective suitors to my other daughter."

Julia might have assured her mother that Susie would want nothing to do with anyone who considered himself a suitor. She might have warned that the men who hung out on many of the dating websites wouldn't consider themselves suitors, either. But she was too irked by her mother's words, the competition inherent in them.

The presidency of Bloom's had never been Sondra's to lose. And Julia had never competed with her mother for it. It was what it was.

But she wasn't going to give it up just to make Sondra happy.

So she'd tell her mother she looked fabulous. Maybe that would make her, if not happy, a little less unhappy about not being the president of Bloom's. That would be something.

Chapter Twenty-Four

Jay had never been to Ron Joffe's office before. True, Ron's boss, the editor-in-chief of *Gotham Magazine*, was the wife of Jay's attorney. But Kim Pinsky was kind of a ball-buster. Jay had encountered her at a few social events and found her intimidating and kind of bitchy. Certainly not someone he'd want to pay a call on while she was at work.

And he'd never had any other reason to visit *Gotham's* headquarters. Any advertising Bloom's did in the magazine was handled over the phone and through email.

But what he had to discuss with Julia's husband couldn't be handled over the phone or via email. He was coming to Ron humbled, weak, needy. Begging for help from a distance was easier but less effective than getting in the face of the person you were begging. You needed a favor, you asked in person.

Fortunately, Ron was in his office when Jay arrived. A receptionist buzzed Ron, and evidently he'd said he would see Jay, because she put down her phone and pointed to a hallway on the other side of the small, quiet cubicle cluster that extended beyond her reception desk. "Third door on the left," she said.

Gotham's headquarters disappointed Jay. He had thought the nerve center of one of New York City's most popular magazines—one of the nation's most popular magazines, in fact—would be spacious and bustling. He'd expected not a cubicle farm but a newsroom humming with high-octane energy and importance, like what he'd seen in movies about the *Washington Post*. In those movies, most of the reporters worked in a big, open area crowded with desks and lit by rectangles of fluorescent light imbedded in the ceiling, with all the important folks—the editors and such—ensconced in glass-walled offices that allowed them to gaze out at their underlings, as if the reporters were tunneling their way through some huge, human ant farm.

Then again, *Gotham* was a magazine, not a newspaper. Jay supposed many of the reporters worked on location, so there was no need for a spacious room filled with desks occupied by hard-bitten journalists, yammering on telephones and pounding away on clattering typewriters.

Ron rose from his desk as Jay approached his open door. He looked surprised to see Jay, but not hostile. Jay took this as a promising sign. They shook hands, and Ron gestured toward the two chairs facing his desk, an invitation for Jay to sit. The office was small, but it was decorated with striking posters of wild animals: a lion rippling with strength, a couple of pandas oozing adorableness, an orangutan with floppy lips, looking as if it wanted to plant a big wet one on whoever had photographed it.

Jay took a seat. Ron circled behind the desk, nudged his computer monitor aside so it wouldn't block his view of his visitor, and settled into his chair. "So," he said. "How are things?"

Loaded question. "You tell me," Jay replied. "Passover is just around the corner, and my mother never called me about the Seder. I finally called her. Lyndon answered and told me I wasn't invited."

"I think there are some ruffled feathers," Ron said.

Jay snorted. Ruffled feathers made him think of pigeons competing for bread crumbs in Central Park. Not getting invited to his mother's Seder was more on a par with that Hitchcock movie where the birds slaughtered people with their beaks and claws.

"Look," he said. No need to play coy. He was here on a mission. He might as well get on with it. "There are hurt feelings on both sides. But now, maybe, it's time for us all to slap on some Band-Aids and heal." Not that Jay felt the hurt on one side equaled the hurt on the other. Julia's nose was out of joint because Jay had tried to take the initiative professionally, to launch something new, to expand his horizons. Jay's gut was wrenched because his mother had barred him from her Seder—and for what? His initiative had failed. His launch was sinking. He was losing on all fronts.

He had an ego. He had his pride. He also had an expensive apartment, an expensive wife, expensive expenses. If he couldn't make Jacob Bloom's Delectable Food Emporium happen, he needed to return to Bloom's. Passover, family, money—it all came together in some way.

If only that way wasn't blocked by a ten-foot-high wall with concertina wire coiled along the top.

"The thing is," he said, "I never would have left Bloom's if your wife had green-lighted an East Side Bloom's franchise."

"That's between you and Julia—and your mother," Ron said. "I'm not a part of it."

"Right. You're just a modest reporter, making the world safe for democracy." Jay wasn't sure if his words had been an attempt at humor or just his bitterness and disappointment spilling out. Ron's tenuous smile indicated he wasn't sure, either. "Maybe you can make the world a little safer for me. How bad is it? How much does Julia hate me?"

Ron shrugged. "She's been thinking about suing you, but your mother won't let her."

"Suing me? For what? Quitting my job?"

"Trademark violation. You can't have the word 'Bloom's' in your store's name. I'm giving you a heads-up here, Jay. Change the name of your store. Get rid of the 'Bloom's.' Nobody wants a lawsuit."

For God's sake. Jay's name was Jacob Bloom. You couldn't sue someone for using his own name. If this was what they taught in that prestigious law school Julia had gone to...

He sighed. Screw the lawsuit. Screw the name of his store. He'd come here not to fight with his family but to figure out a way back into their good graces. "The store isn't going to happen," he admitted, feeling his chest contract, as if the air was leaking out of his lungs. Or maybe his soul was leaking out of his body.

Ron leaned back in his chair, tapped his fingers together, and scrutinized Jay. He said nothing. The silence swelled, making Jay uncomfortable. Ron was a journalist. Shouldn't he be asking questions?

Actually, Jay acknowledged, Ron was an expert at his job. He knew his silence would become intolerable if it lasted long enough, and Jay would feel compelled to answer questions Ron didn't even have to ask. "I can't get the funding I need," Jay said. "We had some financiers backing the store, but that fell through. I've gone to several banks, but their terms are ridiculous. I mean, really. Like something out of...what was that play? With the pound of flesh?"

"*The Merchant of Venice,*" Ron told him.

"Right. Whatever." Jay sighed, feeling his chest contract even more, as if a pound of his fleshy organs was shriveling into dust. "No one wants to give me a loan with reasonable interest. They don't think I'm a good risk. Can you believe it? I'm a Bloom. I've worked at Bloom's my whole life. I want to start a store like Bloom's. How can they think I'm a bad risk?"

"Did you present them with a solid business plan?"

"I told them what I intended to do, and they said they wanted this and that, details I didn't have. The financiers didn't demand any of that stuff." Jay faltered. Of course Gil and Rupert didn't demand any of that stuff. They didn't care whether his business succeeded or failed. They were just interested in parking their dirty rubles somewhere.

Ron stared at him again. The corners of his mouth barely twitched upward, but it was enough of a smile to cut dimples into his cheeks. Was he amused by Jay? Laughing at him?

He shouldn't have come here. But he was desperate. He needed to get back to where he'd been, and he wasn't sure how to make that journey. He was even less sure, now that Ron told him Julia was planning to sue him for using his own damned name.

As far as Jay knew, Julia adored Ron. Jay believed the guy was his best bet, someone who could crack open a door in that ten-foot-high wall and usher Jay through it.

If Ron was telling the truth about Julia's plan to drag Jay through the courts, that door might be hard to reach—if a door even existed. "Maybe I should just call my lawyer and tell him to prepare to countersue Julia," he muttered. "Is that what I should do?"

Ron did laugh at this. "That would be kind of incestuous, wouldn't it? Your lawyer is married to my editor. I'm married to your niece." Still smiling, he shook his head. "She's not going to sue you. Ida won't let her."

"My mother won't let me come to her Seder, either."

"She's upset. According to Julia, you broke her heart by leaving Bloom's."

"I can't even phone my mother. She's got her damned sidekick Lyndon running interference." Jay considered the situation. "You think I should just show up at the Seder uninvited? I could bring your brother-in-law with me, use him as a human shield."

That joke worked. Ron's smile widened. "What do you really want, Jay? You want me to run interference?"

That was exactly what Jay wanted. "Would you? Would you tell Julia I want my old job back? Adam probably wants his job back, too. He's been whining about how he gave up a PhD for this—and it's all shot to hell. We want to go back to Bloom's. We're willing to abandon our dream. The least they could do is forgive us."

Ron's smile grew hard and cold, his gaze harder and colder. "As I said, it's between you and your family. I don't want to be in the middle of it."

"Julia's your wife. What does *she* want?" One thing Jay knew was how to please his wife—at least one of his wives. He assumed Ron knew how to do that, too. "Does she really not want me at Bloom's? Has she replaced me already? Has she found someone who can come up with ideas like the Seder-in-a-Box?" When Ron said nothing, Jay added, "She wants to sue me for being a Bloom. That's the whole point, isn't it? I'm a Bloom."

"What happened with your financiers?" Ron asked.

"According to your editor's husband, they're money launderers. They work for some Russian billionaire.

He advised me not to touch their money. We don't know where it's been."

Ron leaned forward, the ice melting from his gaze. "I did a piece last year on Russian oligarchs funneling money into the city to get it out of Russia and convert it to US dollars. Who are these guys you were working with?"

Jay caught himself before uttering their names. "I don't want to get in trouble with them. They could be dangerous."

"They aren't dangerous," Ron assured him. "Their boss might be, but he's in Russia. They're just agents handling his money." Ron was definitely warming up. He leaned forward, as if he wanted to leap across his desk, wrap his hands around Jay's gut, and wring information out of him. "Names?"

"I can't. They'd know I told you, and…I don't know. They'd come after me."

"I'll keep you out of it," Ron promised. "I've probably already got them in my files. You'd just be confirming what I already know."

"They belong to my golf club. What would happen if I ran into them in the club's lounge while they were sitting there, drinking Dewar's?"

Ron swiveled away from Jay and began gliding his computer mouse across his desk, tapping the buttons, his eyes on his monitor. "What's the name of your club?"

"Emerald View, but—"

"Okay." He tapped his mouse a few more times, read his screen, and snorted. "Rupert Niles? The phony Brit?"

"You know him?"

"He's popped up before. I did a lot of research for that article last year."

"He's phony? He's not from England?"

"Robert Nelson, from Piscataway, New Jersey. He spent time in London after college. I guess he thought the accent made him seem classy."

He was right. Jay had considered him extremely classy.

"He and his buddy—" Ron read from his monitor for a moment "—Gilbert Jenners tried to buy Emerald View last year. They had Russian money to burn. The club wasn't for sale, though."

"Thank God for that. If they bought it and then pulled out once the money was laundered, that could have been the end of the club."

"Could have been." Ron shifted his attention from his monitor back to Jay. "This is good info. I've been posting updates on the story in my blog. I'll keep your name out of it. Don't worry. I know how to protect my sources."

Jay tried really hard to believe that.

"I tell you what." Apparently, Ron sensed Jay's doubt and his worry. "I'll talk to Julia. I'll talk to Ida, too. I'll even talk to Lyndon. I'll see if I can get you an invitation to the Seder."

Just the hope that he might find his way back to his family made Jay feel marginally safer. "Do you think they'll forgive me?"

"No promises." Ron stood, indicating it was time for Jay to leave. "But I'll do what I can."

Ron wasn't a bad guy, Jay decided as he rose from his chair. He should probably dress a little better—he was wearing blue jeans and sneakers with an off-the-rack oxford shirt—but he was smart and sharp, and he had his own office rather than a cubicle out by the receptionist's desk. A little hard to read, but he was clearly tough enough to survive working for Stuart's wife.

Was he tough enough to persuade Julia and Jay's mother to allow Jay back into the family and the business? Kim Pinsky might be a ball-buster, but Julia and Ida Bloom?

They could be brutal.

Chapter Twenty-Five

"You know, I've got to work in the morning," Rick muttered.

Susie shushed him, although she didn't have to. His voice rose barely above a whisper.

Besides, there was no one around to hear them. At two in the morning, the block where Casey's Gourmet Breads was located stood empty and dark, except for a few street lamps and the flashlight Susie had given Rick to hold. She wore a backpack filled with equipment, and her arms hugged a bag of out-of-date breads and rolls. She'd volunteered to do the soup-kitchen run yesterday, and none of her co-workers had challenged her. Schlepping the leftovers to churches and shelters in the Bowery was no one's favorite chore, even if they all felt suitably noble after making the donation.

Susie hadn't made the donation. She didn't feel particularly noble, either. But damn it, she was going to create a window for Casey.

She had no idea if they were going to get back together. They'd been carefully avoiding each other during her shifts at his store. Casey sent her occasional texts telling her, in his gentle, non-histrionic way, that she should get over herself and acknowledge that Mose just might know more about storefront marketing than she did. According to Caitlin, Casey's texts were classic passive-aggressive behavior. Susie wasn't sure about that, but then, she wasn't sure about what classic passive-aggressive behavior was, either.

For her, the bottom line was that Casey hadn't apologized to her. He hadn't told her she was more important to him than Mose. He hadn't declared his respect for her creativity and vision. He hadn't said he trusted her judgment.

She missed him. She missed snuggling up to his long, lean body when she drifted off to sleep. She missed joking with him, eating with him, confiding in him. Screwing him, even if that had to happen much too early in the evening. But as long as he continued to rely on Mose more than her, she saw no way of fixing their relationship.

If it was over, however, she was going to end it in a spectacular way.

She shifted the bulging sack to her left hand so she could dig her keys to the shop out of the pocket of her jeans. "You broke up with him and didn't give him back his keys?" Rick asked.

"First of all, we didn't exactly break up." Semantics, Susie knew, but he *was* still texting her and she *was* still working with him. It was certainly possible that at some point, he would emerge from the bakery's kitchen, walk down the counter to where she was ringing up an order, drop to his knees, and beg her forgiveness. Actually, he could skip the knees part and just beg. If he did, she'd forgive him in a nano-second, and they'd be back together.

But so far, he wasn't begging or kneeling. He was only texting. If he thought that was the way to repair their romance, he was an idiot.

"You didn't break up, but you're not living with him anymore," Rick pointed out. "You're not talking to him. You're pissed as hell at him. Sounds like you've broken up to me."

"Maybe we have," Susie said, hearing bleak disappointment in her tone. "Anyway, I still work here. So I need a key." She used that key to unlock the two deadbolts and the doorknob, jiggling and twisting the key until the door swung open.

Behind her, Rick sighed. "Other than holding the flashlight, why am I here?" he asked.

"I didn't want to be alone on the street at this hour."

"But why me? Why couldn't Anna accompany you?"

Susie pushed the door wider, pocketed her key ring, and turned to glare at him. "Two women at two a.m.? That just doubles the target of any creep who might go after us."

"So I'm your bodyguard." Rick didn't seem pleased.

"You're winning points with Anna by doing this," Susie told him.

His frown faded. Let him think he was a macho hero, protecting his poor, defenseless cousin from whatever thugs and perverts might be roaming the East Village in the middle of the night. Susie doubted he'd need to defend her against any sex fiends or homicidal maniacs. But walking down a dark city street late at night with a man next to her reduced her vulnerability by a hell of a lot.

Once they were inside the store, she bolted the door, set down her gear, and moved the stale loaves of bread already in the window to one side. They'd been lined up in a boring formation, about as inspiring as the hash marks on a ruler. Love it or hate it, Susie was going to transform this window.

She'd planned everything out. She'd shellacked the stale breads and rolls yesterday evening after work.

She'd purchased fish wire. She'd borrowed a spare music stand from Anna so she wouldn't have to buy an easel. She'd had her poem printed on a placard, white letters on a black background, and decorated it with silver stars. She'd created a crescent moon by covering a cardboard cut-out with aluminum foil.

"So, Casey didn't like this design?" Rick asked as Susie unfolded the music stand and stood it on the side of the window furthest from the door.

"He never saw the design. I described the concept and he threw a fit. Or he would have thrown a fit if he were the sort of person who threw fits. He just said he thought the current window arrangement was fine." Actually, he'd said Mose thought the current window arrangement was fine, which had hurt her far more than if he'd told her he himself was madly in love with the current window. "I don't want to talk about it," she added, more brusque than she'd intended. But she *didn't* want to talk about it. If she talked about it, she might cry, and she definitely didn't want to do that.

Instead, she began threading the fish wire through the stale, shiny rolls and muffins and loaves, and stringing them at different heights from the top of the window. "You're going to Grandma Ida's Seder?" she asked him, hoping to get her mind off Casey even as she commandeered his window.

"I have to. Neil's coming all the way from Florida."

"Is Glickstein giving you the day off? Oh, I guess they are," she said, realizing that with a name like Glickstein, the ad agency's founder was likely Jewish himself.

"I guess Casey won't be coming," Rick said, sounding rueful.

So much for keeping her mind off Casey. "I guess not," she said, forcing herself to sound nonchalant. "I told Adam he couldn't come. He sounded depressed."

"Of course he'd be depressed. Grandma Ida's Seder is..."

"Boring," Susie said.

"But the food is good. Last time I talked to my father, he said he was hoping he'd be there," Rick told Susie. "With Wendy. She loves Seders. She thinks the Moses story is cute."

For a moment, Susie thought he'd said *Mose's* story. She supposed Casey's best friend's full name was Moses, although she'd never thought to ask. He was just plain Mose, the guy with the MBA who didn't know squat about window displays. "The Moses story isn't cute. It's a story about survival, and escape, and magic. And plagues."

"You don't have to tell me," Rick argued. "I had a bar mitzvah. I know that stuff."

"I'm just saying—it isn't cute. And last I heard, Grandma Ida didn't want your father at the Seder, either."

"He really wants to go, though. Maybe he can convince Grandma Ida. You can fight about your work and your business but still be family, right?"

"I don't know. Can you?"

"You and Casey still work together," Rick said.

"That's the exact opposite. We aren't family, but we don't fight about work and business. Except for the window." She almost explained that what they were really fighting about was friendship and trust and love, not a stupid window. But she shoved that thought aside, determined not to start sobbing. She hated how weepy her situation with Casey made her. She didn't *do* weepy.

As she hung a glossy croissant far enough from the moon that no one would confuse the two, she forced her mind back to the subject of Grandma Ida's Seder.

She didn't think the Passover story was cute. It was, as she'd said, a story about fleeing oppression. About freedom. About escape.

Many times in her life, she had wanted to escape. She'd tried to escape the proper behavior her parents and Grandma Ida tried to impose on her. She'd endeavored to escape everyone's expectations of her. She'd hoped to escape commitments like the one Casey asked of her every time he brought up the subject of marriage.

And she had. They wouldn't get married. Not when he wouldn't even trust her with his goddamn window. And damn it, even ordering herself to forget about Casey and focus on Passover, she still wound up thinking about Casey.

She'd show him. She'd revamp his window and blow his mind, and if he didn't see how right she was, he could stop texting her and they could officially call it quits.

Like the Jews fleeing Egypt in the Passover story, she'd survive.

Rick dutifully trained the flashlight's beam on Susie's hands so she could see what she was doing. Different bread items at different heights, spaced randomly. More bread items lining the bottom surface of the window, a terrain of various browns and tans, all glossy with polyurethane. The silver crescent moon on the right, twisting slowly in an invisible air current. The music stand, draped in black fabric so it wouldn't look so much like a music stand. And lastly, the poem, propped against the music stand.

She'd labored over that poem. Sweated over it. Shed a couple of tears over it, which bothered her, but at least no one had seen her actually crying, because she'd worked on the poem in solitude, in spare minutes and moments. She'd scribbled ideas on napkins at work here in the store, and on her computer uptown at Bloom's when she was supposed to be writing the *Bloom's Bulletin,* and late into the night on the lumpy sofa in Anna and Caitlin's apartment. She'd brought the poem to a printing shop near the NYU campus, and they'd done a good job transferring it to the placard, with print big and clear enough to read through the glass. She'd added the silver stars herself.

Rick aimed the flashlight on the placard, and Susie gave it a final review:

> *Moon—*
> *You are there, always there,*
> *A sliver, a crescent, a sphere.*
> *Your glow holds the world together,*
> *As bread holds a meal together*
> *And makes it complete,*
> *A tasty treasure on the plate.*
> *A joy to eat.*
> *Celebrate the moon.*
> *Celebrate the bread.*
> *Celebrate togetherness.*

"Nice," Rick said. "You should recite that at a poetry slam."

"No need. It's here, where everyone can see it." Would everyone who saw it understand that it was about more than bread, more than the moon? That it was about holding things together, about the world, about joy?

Hell, even she didn't know if it was about all those things. When she read it as it stood displayed on the music stand in the window, she realized it was about bread. Casey's Fucking Gourmet Bread.

"Too bad we can't eat bread at the Seder," Rick remarked. "Our plates won't hold together."

A humorless laugh escaped Susie. She loaded her scissors, her extra fish wire, and the empty sack from the leftover bread into her backpack and hoisted it onto her shoulder. "That's it. Let's check it from outside to see how it looks."

They couldn't really see it, given the darkness of the hour. Susie took the flashlight from Rick and panned its beam from left to right across the window. Mostly what she saw was the light's reflection against the glass.

"I guess it works," she said.

"Let me take some pictures of it." Rick pulled out his cell phone, adjusted the flashlight's angle to reduce the glare a little, and then snapped some photos. Then he filmed the window, panning the phone the way Susie had panned the flashlight beam. He tapped the phone's screen to end the recording, and said, "It's cool."

"Either that or it's ridiculous." Mose would think it was ridiculous. And Susie told herself, for the hundredth unconvincing time, that she didn't care what Casey would think.

❧

He texted her early the next morning, the buzz of her phone jarring her from sleep: *What the hell did you do?*

She didn't bother to answer. Fortunately, she wasn't on the schedule to work behind the counter at Casey's Gourmet Breads today. Two hours after Casey had awakened her with his text, she was in her office at Bloom's, compiling the Seder-in-a-Box sales figures that Uncle Jay should have been compiling, and dumping them into a shared file for Julia and Deirdre. Myron could access them, too, if he managed to overcome his panic about Excel spreadsheets. He'd still be adding on an abacus if he had a choice in the matter.

Julia hollered to Susie that, if the numbers were accurate, Seder-in-a-Box sales were down from a year ago. Rather than holler back that she'd promoted Seder-in-a-Boxes—or was it Seders-in-a-Box?—in the *Bloom's Bulletin* the same amount this year as last, and that maybe Uncle Jay had inflated last year's numbers to make himself look important, Susie left her office and trudged to Julia's open doorway. "I bet Uncle Jay sabotaged the website on his way out the door. He wanted to make sure sales dropped after he was gone, so we'd think he was indispensable."

"Maybe he is indispensable," Julia said.

Susie's eyes widened so much her brows ached. "Are we talking about the same Uncle Jay?"

"Close the door," Julia said.

Susie was intrigued enough to forget about Casey and the window for a moment. She shut Julia's office door and dropped onto the couch. "What's going on?"

Julia sat on the couch next to her. "He's not opening his East Side store," she said. "He wants to come back to Bloom's."

Susie took a moment to absorb this. "What about Adam?"

"He wants to come back, too. Their excellent adventure went down the tubes."

Susie supposed she shouldn't have been surprised. Uncle Jay wasn't exactly a business whiz, and Adam's smarts, while immense, were pretty specific. Still, the news that they had crashed and burned before they'd even taxied down the runway, let alone taken to the air, stunned Susie. "Did Uncle Jay tell you about this failure?"

Julia shook her head. "He was afraid to, so he told Ron instead. And Ron told me. Ron also told me they want to come to the Seder."

Susie recalled what Rick had told her last night, about Uncle Jay's hoping to attend. "Does Grandma Ida know about this?"

"Not yet." Julia leaned back into the cracked leather upholstery and stared at the ceiling. "I don't know. A part of me is so furious with Uncle Jay, I want him banned from the family forever. I can't believe he put us through all this shit."

"You could still sue him," Susie said optimistically. "Maybe not about the name of his store, since that's kaput, but you could think of something."

"The thing is, if I let him and Adam come back, it would solve a lot of problems."

"And it would make Grandma Ida happy. You just love making Grandma Ida happy."

"I do," Julia admitted.

"Mom won't be happy, though. She hates Uncle Jay." Julia nodded.

"Then again, even if she was happy, she wouldn't be able to smile with her face half-paralyzed."

"Just her forehead. I think her mouth muscles still work," Julia said. "Maybe the Seder is the best place for everyone to hash out their differences and make up. We'll all be together. We can talk it through."

Susie tried to envision such a gathering. Mom would be resentful and stiff-browed. Grandma Ida might start crying again. Aunt Martha would tell Wendy she'd married a loser who couldn't launch his own business, and Wendy should join her women's club. Adam would snivel and indulge in self-pity. Neil would be arrogant, so proud of himself for having escaped the family business and all the *tsorris* that came with it.

Casey wouldn't be there.

The Seder was going to be awful. Susie's only hope was that Lyndon and his friend Howard would make such a delicious feast, she would be able to lose herself in a stupor of culinary bliss. And a stupor of wine. She'd drink a lot. That would help.

❧

Back in her office, reading Casey's text yet again—as if it was so long and convoluted and difficult to interpret that she had to review it multiple times—she wished she was in a wine stupor right now. Should she respond to him? What would she say? *Drop dead.* Or: *Tell Mose he can redo your fucking window.* Or: *I hope the window attracts thousands of customers to your store, and you'll realize what a dick you are and what a brilliant person I am, and you'll regret having not trusted me. You'll regret it for the rest of your life, and you'll suffer and grieve and miss me and plead with me to take charge of your window forevermore.*

A little too long for a text, she acknowledged. So she didn't respond at all.

By noon, she realized he wasn't going to send her another text, let alone offer her complete control of his window. The silence of her phone abraded her nerves. Was he too busy cutting down the stars and discarding the varnished breads and rolls to contact her? Or was he too busy handling the high volume of traffic the window had attracted to the store?

Or was he in the kitchen at the back of the store, baking batches of sourdough and rye and ignoring the window altogether?

How was she going to survive the Seder without him? Their very first almost-sort-of-date had been to Grandma Ida's Seder two years ago. He had never attended a Seder before, and he'd looked comically adorable wearing the yarmulke she'd scared up for him, which barely stayed in place atop his wavy blond hair. He'd been eager to learn about the symbolic foods, and he'd followed along in the Haggadah. The books Grandma Ida used were mostly in English and provided transliterations of the prayers everyone was supposed to say together in Hebrew. Casey had dutifully stumbled over the prayers, mispronouncing words. He might have been a nice Catholic boy from Queens, but he'd been game, and although Susie hadn't realized it at the time, he'd been in love with her.

Now he was out of love with her, because she'd done his window.

Fine. She was out of love with him, too.

Unable to concentrate on the post-Passover *Bloom's Bulletin* she was supposed to be writing, she abandoned her desk. Bypassing the elevators for the stairwell, she stormed two flights down to the first floor and entered the store through the staff-only door. She bee-lined for the bagel counter, where Morty Sugarman stood, big and beefy in his spotless white apron, schmoozing with customers as they asked him to fill their orders. This one had to cut back on her salt, so which bagels had the least salt in them? That one wanted two onion bagels, two garlic bagels, and three everything bagels, and could Morty charge him only for half a dozen? Another one said the sun-dried tomato and basil bagels were disgusting and then asked for five of them. Yet another wanted half a dozen dill bagels, which she used in place of hamburger rolls. "It's like having your burger and your pickle all rolled into one."

When Morty spotted Susie, he ignored the line of customers, pulled a waxed tissue from the box behind the counter, and handed Susie an egg bagel. He knew the egg bagels were her favorites. "Go," he'd ordered her. "Enjoy."

She insisted on paying for the bagel, even though she was a Bloom. If she didn't pay for it, it would feel like a gift from Casey. She wanted nothing from him.

Except regret. And remorse. And pleading.

Back at her desk upstairs, she checked her phone again. No messages.

"Asshole," she muttered under her breath before tearing off a chunk of bagel and popping it into her mouth. Why did Casey have to be the best bagel baker in the city? Why did this bagel have to taste so good? Why did it have to taste like joy?

She hoped his shop went out of business. She hoped he'd go bankrupt and move back to Queens, where he could hang out with Mose and do odd jobs with that catering company he used to work for before he became the bagel baker for Bloom's.

Because he'd never come back to Bloom's. Julia might want to take Uncle Jay and Adam back, but Susie would make sure Casey was never rehired. She'd tell Julia that if Bloom's brought Casey back, Susie would move to California and join a cult. They'd believe her.

Men, she thought with a huff. So stupid. She wondered if it was too late to become a lesbian.

Chapter Twenty-Six

"Come upstairs with me," Julia asked Susie.

Susie was at her desk, munching on a bagel and staring at her monitor. She looked more goth than usual, not because she was wearing heavier eyeliner but because her complexion was so pale. She really ought to stop wearing so much black clothing. It made her look like a member of the Addams family.

But she was a member of the Bloom family, and right now Julia needed familial support. "I'm going upstairs to tell Grandma Ida about Uncle Jay and Adam," she said. "Why don't you join me?"

"You don't need me there," Susie argued. "This is going to make her happy."

"Which is exactly why I want you with me. It's going to be a happy visit, not like the last visit." That time, she'd told Grandma Ida she wanted to sue Uncle Jay. Not a happy visit at all.

"I'll pass," Susie said.

"Lyndon might have macaroons." Julia sing-songed, doing her best to sound enticing. Susie needed macaroons. She needed cheering. She seemed so glum.

Susie waved her half-eaten bagel at Julia. "I'm good. Go and have fun with Grandma Ida yourself."

Julia conceded with a sigh. She would have entered Susie's office and given her a hug, but given Susie's mood, that could backfire. Susie might interpret it as patronizing or pitying—which, Julia had to admit, it was. She was so happy right now, happy that Uncle Jay would come back and Deirdre could stop searching for someone to take his place. Happy that Adam would be back in the fold, too. Since he was subletting her apartment, she liked knowing what he was up to and, more important, how much he was earning.

She wished Susie was as happy as she was. She ought to be at least a little happier, cheered by the prospect of Uncle Jay taking the website off her hands. "Just think," Julia said, desperate to boost Susie's spirits. "Once Uncle Jay comes back, you'll have more time to work on your poetry."

"Oh, fun. I'll be able to write better limericks for the *Bulletin*. We have that special on British cheeses coming up, and you know what rhymes with cheeses? Jesus."

"Sneezes," Julia suggested. "We're a Jewish-style deli. I don't think Jesus will work."

"I don't think sneezes will work, either."

"Wheezes?"

"*Pleases,*" Susie said, tapping her keyboard. "Or— here we go: *Stock up on our cheeses, for your nephews and nieces.*"

"That's good," Julia said, even though the line didn't blow her away. Encouraging Susie might make her feel better, and it wouldn't seem quite as patronizing as giving her a hug.

"*Our imported cheddar is Britishly better,*" Susie muttered, ignoring Julia as she typed.

Britishly? Well, why not? If *Britishly* worked for Susie, Julia wouldn't question her.

With another sigh, she left Susie's doorway and headed out of the office suite. She hoped she'd do a

better job making Grandma Ida feel good than she'd
done with Susie. She'd expected news of Uncle Jay's return to thrill Susie, who had so deeply resented having
to add some of his responsibilities to her own. Didn't
she want to write poetry? Didn't she want to do slams?

The elevator door slid open, and Julia reflexively
peeked inside before she entered, to make sure neither
a rapist nor Aunt Martha was lurking inside. The elevator swept her up to the twenty-fifth floor. The corridor
was silent—no screaming toddler this time—and the
carpeted floor muffled her steps.

She really wished Susie was with her.

Lyndon answered the door when Julia pressed the
buzzer. "What's the point of living in a doorman building if folks like you can sneak up here without being
announced?" he teased, giving Julia a wide grin as he
ushered her into the apartment.

"Half the fun is surprising her," Julia said. "Is she here?"

"Where else would she be? It's a drizzly day. No
watching bocce today. She's in the den, reading that
book Howard gave her."

"Then she'll be glad to see me." Julia returned Lyndon's infectious smile and strolled down the hall to the
den.

Grandma Ida sat in her armchair, *The Portrait of a
Lady* open face down on her lap. Her eyes were closed
behind her reading glasses. She looked old, Julia
thought, taking in her grandmother's weathered face,
the deep creases framing her mouth, the age spots on
her hands, the wrinkled skin of her throat, and her in-
congruously black hair.

Julia assured herself that her grandmother wasn't
that old. Most people looked old, weak, and vulnera-
ble when they napped. Especially if they fell asleep sitting up, with a book open across their laps.

Julia crossed the room and gave her grandmother a gentle kiss. Grandma Ida batted her eyes open, squinted up at Julia, then pulled off her reading glasses and batted her eyes again. "Was I sleeping?" she asked. "This book is so boring. It knocks me out better than a glass of schnapps."

"You napped because you needed a nap," Julia said. "Your body was tired."

"Because I'm up half the night with insomnia. I saw that horrible man on the TV again last night, screaming and dancing, and all the cars, and the chains around his neck. I can't believe our Ricky has anything to do with that."

"Well." Julia sat on the couch, angled to face her grandmother. "I come with news about another grandson of yours. And your son."

Grandma Ida pressed a hand to her chest, her bracelets jangling. "*Oy*. What have they done now?"

"What they've done is decided not to open their store across town. They want to come back to Bloom's."

Grandma Ida stared at Julia. She looked shocked, almost as pale as Susie. "Why? What happened?"

"I don't know. All I know is that Ron told me Uncle Jay visited him and said he couldn't go through with the store, and he wanted to know if we would take him back."

"*Oy*," Grandma Ida said again. Julia had thought she'd be pleased, even ecstatic. But she looked oddly alarmed. "What happened? Did something bad happen?"

"Not that I know of. I think something *good* is happening. They're coming back."

"My Jacob, he would come back only if something bad happened. Is he all right? He isn't sick, is he? And Adam? He's okay?"

It hadn't occurred to Julia that something dire might have occurred to force them to abandon their store. "I think they just came to their senses, Grandma," she said. She'd seen her grandmother shed tears over Uncle Jay's betrayal. Why couldn't she smile, now that he was doing something right?

"That boy, leaving, then coming back. And you with the lawsuits. And your brother, so smart and such a *schmendrik*. The two of them, threats, quitting, and then—" she shrugged her shoulders and spread her hands, palm up "—'never mind.'" She shook her head, clearly disappointed. "That's not how you do business. You want to sell knishes, you get a pushcart and you make your knishes and you sell them. And you grow. You build. You create a business, the best knish-selling business in the world. Those two, Jay and Adam, here and there, coming and going. They're going to give me a heart attack."

"You're not going to have a heart attack," Julia said. "I think you should welcome them home."

Grandma Ida looked dubious. "Why didn't Jay tell me this himself?"

"He's probably afraid of you," Julia said, a sentiment she could relate to. Grandma Ida could be awfully scary. "You're so much tougher than he is."

"I'm not so tough." Grandma Ida rolled her eyes, as if she herself didn't believe what she'd just said. "He should have told me himself."

"Why don't you invite him to your Seder?" Julia sweetened her voice in an effort to soothe her grandmother. "We can all be together as a family and reconcile."

"Reconcile? What, like balancing the checkbook?"

"Kind of. Balancing our family."

Grandma Ida mulled over Julia's suggestion. "I'll tell Lyndon to call Jay. You can tell Adam. Tell him they're driving me crazy. They're breaking my heart."

"They'll mend your heart when they come back," Julia said. "It will be a good Seder. Uncle Jay will take over the website and online sales again, and Adam will go back to doing inventory management. It'll be just like it was before they left."

"No." Grandma Ida didn't cry, but she looked terribly sad. "It won't be like it was. They may be here, but they'll be wishing they were somewhere else. Like a dog yanking on a leash. It can pull your arm out of the socket."

"I think they'll be grateful to be back," Julia argued gently. "They went off to try something, and they discovered that what they'd left was far better than what they'd hoped to find. So they came back. They came home."

Grandma Ida still didn't look convinced. If Julia thought about it, she wasn't so sure she was convinced, either. She had no idea what had convinced Uncle Jay to abandon his dream. She'd asked Ron, and he'd shrugged and said, "You'll have to ask him yourself," which could mean he hadn't told Ron, or it could mean he'd told Ron and sworn him to secrecy, or it could mean something else. Julia didn't know.

Nor did she know if he'd turn into a wild dog, yanking on its leash and dislocating her shoulder.

But she was determined to make her grandmother feel better. That was what she did, beyond running Bloom's. She made everyone feel better. It was her most important job.

"Having Adam and Uncle Jay back is going to be great," Julia said. "You'll see."

"I should live so long," Grandma Ida muttered. "*Meshugena,* all of them." She picked up her book and scowled. "This book is *meshugena*, too. If this is what it means to be a lady, I don't want to be a lady. I don't even want to be a portrait of one. Why do they even call it a portrait? Why not a picture?"

"You don't have to read it if you don't want to." Telling Grandma Ida about Uncle Jay's return hadn't cheered her the way Julia had thought it would. Maybe giving her permission to put the book down and watch some TV instead would do the trick.

But then, she might turn on the TV and see one of Rick's obnoxious ads for Fat Larry's Auto Mart.

Sometimes, no matter how hard you tried, you simply couldn't make a person feel better.

Chapter Twenty-Seven

"Which outfit should I wear?" Wendy asked, holding two dresses up on their hangers, one to her right, one to her left, as if they were drapes and she was a window.

They both looked fine to Jay. They both had low-cut necklines; they both ended above her knees; and they both were turquoise. One had buttons down the front and the other didn't, but other than that, they were interchangeable, as far as he was concerned. Wendy would look fantastic in either of them. His mother would hate them both.

His mother probably hated him these days, too. She hadn't even invited him to the Seder herself. She'd had Lyndon do it.

What did she want from Jay? He'd groveled to get back into Bloom's—well, maybe not to her, but to her grandson-in-law. That ought to have won him some points with his mother.

Even before he'd left Bloom's, however, she hadn't been his biggest fan. Neither had Martha, he acknowledged. Nor had Sondra, not that he gave a damn what she thought of him. And Julia...well, she was his boss and he supposed it would benefit him to cultivate a better relationship with her. He still resented the hell out of her for being his boss, though.

At least he had one woman in his life who adored him—a spectacularly gorgeous woman who looked magnificent in any dress she wore, and looked even better when she wasn't wearing a dress at all.

She was waiting for an answer. "You'll look great in either of them," he said.

She smiled like a school girl discovering all As and Bs on her report card. He loved making her smile. He'd have to get her some of those Italian chocolates from the store. She always smiled when he surprised her with a package of chocolates, especially the Italian ones. Once he was back at Bloom's, he'd be able to supply her with all the imported chocolates available at the store.

"I'll go get dressed," Wendy said, waltzing down the hall to the bedroom. "This is going to be the most fun Seder ever."

Yeah, right, he thought, watching her until she closed the bedroom door and he could no longer see her. This was going to be the most awkward Seder ever. He still wasn't sure if his mother was talking to him, or his niece. Adam might talk to him, but Adam was going to be welcomed back into the fold in a way Jay suspected he himself wouldn't be. Adam had told Jay that Julia had invited him to the Seder, and then his mother had invited him after Julia had. Evidently, he wasn't as tarnished as Jay. His weeks-long defection could be explained away. He was young; he was foolish; he'd been led astray by his nefarious uncle. He hadn't known any better. He was smart but not shrewd, and he'd made a mistake, and all was forgiven.

Jay was pretty sure he hadn't been forgiven. When you got invited to a family gathering not by a family member but by a paid assistant, you were clearly on the family's shit list.

Julia had told Jay he could return to his old job, but she'd said it coolly, in a snooty voice she must have cultivated at Wellesley. He'd told her he and Wendy would be at the Seder, and she'd said she was looking forward to seeing Wendy. Not him.

But he thanked her for offering him his job back. He needed the work. He needed the income. He needed access to those imported Italian chocolates.

It pained him to admit that he needed his family, but he did.

He pulled his cell phone from the back pocket of his trousers and stepped into the guest bathroom, shutting the door behind him. He didn't want Wendy to overhear this phone call. She knew his East Side store was dead on arrival, or more accurately dead before arrival, but he hadn't told her why, other than that it just wasn't going to happen. He didn't want to admit to her that he'd been romanced by a couple of crooked guys, that he should have talked to Stuart Pinsky before he'd talked to rental agents and decorators and his *schnooky* nephew. He'd just told her he'd decided to return to Bloom's, and she'd said, "Okay!"

She was so blessedly agreeable. Why couldn't everyone in his life be as agreeable as she was?

He scrolled through his contacts list until he found Ron Joffe's number. Ron's phone rang twice, and then he answered. "Jay? What's up?"

"I'm going to be at the Seder," he said.

"So I've heard. Julia and I are getting ready to head over to Ida's apartment right now. I really can't talk."

Jay lowered the toilet lid and sat. Wendy had attached a fluffy turquoise cover to the lid, an oval shag rug of sorts. He thought it looked ridiculous, but it did make sitting on the lid a bit more comfortable. He stared at the turquoise and white towels on the brass towel rack across from the toilet, then at the elliptical vessel sink with its stylized faucets and spout, then at the shower tub with its white and turquoise curtain, a layer of fabric over a layer of waterproof plastic. Impressive how much plumbing and décor could be packed into such a tiny space.

He closed his eyes against the onslaught of turquoise and spoke into the phone. "I just want to know—are they going to spit on me when I walk in the door? Am I welcome there, or is it going to be unpleasant?"

After a moment's thought, Ron said, "It's the Bloom family. The odds of something unpleasant happening are probably fifty-fifty. But yes, everyone is expecting you to be there."

"And Wendy?"

"Of course, Wendy."

"I don't want anyone to be unpleasant to her," Jay said. "That's all. Can you just, maybe, spread the word that if people have to be unpleasant to me, okay, but they should be nice to her."

"I don't know—"

"Julia sets the tone for everything," Jay pointed out, recalling her snippy Wellesley voice. "She's your wife. Just tell her I want this to be a pleasant Seder. Can you do that?"

"I'll talk to Julia, but no promises." Ron sighed. "Sometimes I wonder why I married into this family. Wendy must wonder that sometimes, too."

"No, she never does." Partly because she was crazy about Jay, partly because she could be charmingly oblivious, but mostly because he protected her from all the fights and tensions and craziness that passed for love among the Blooms. "I appreciate everything you've done for me, Ron. I just want to say that."

"Let's see how this family celebration goes before you thank me," Ron said. Jay detected laughter in his tone, although that might have been wishful thinking on his part. "We'll see you at Ida's."

"See you there. *Gut yontif.*"

"The same to you," Ron said before ending the call.

Jay remained shut inside the bathroom for a moment. He thought about his beautiful wife. He thought about his two sons. Neil, handsome and carefree and in New York at the moment, staying at his mother's apartment in the Bloom Building and planning to accompany her to the Seder. Rick, finally getting his act together, a steady job, a decent haircut, shoes instead of those ratty sandals he used to wear year-round, back when he aspired to be a brilliant film director but didn't have a pot to piss in. He hadn't hit Jay up for money in months.

Jay could survive this. He could survive the failure, his mother's wrath, his niece's bossiness. All he really needed was for his boys to be doing well; and his pretty wife to be smiling; and a decent income so he could afford to buy that pretty wife anything her heart desired, as well as his membership at the country club and the upkeep on his BMW—and the damned cost of the garage where the Beemer sat when he wasn't driving it.

He would drive it to the Bloom Building today. The sun was out; spring was warming the air. He and Wendy would cruise across town in the Z3, with the wind in their hair and the city's energy all around them.

If worse came to worst, if the Seder was a disaster and his family humiliated him, or rejected him, or shunned him, at least he'd have the drive home to look forward to.

Chapter Twenty-Eight

When Julia entered Grandma Ida's apartment, the familiar fragrance of Passover wafted around her, overpowering the apartment's usual scent—a blend of lemon furniture polish and hot tea. She inhaled the glorious aromas of the holiday's foods: savory brisket, salty chicken, onions, horseradish, apples, wine. While she and Ron had walked the few blocks from their apartment to the Bloom Building, anxiety about this family gathering had eroded her appetite. But the seductive perfume of the feast Lyndon and Howard had prepared perked her appetite right back up. She wanted to race directly to the kitchen and start gorging on all that magnificent food.

But of course, her first obligation was to make Grandma Ida happy. Julia had insisted that she and Ron arrive early, a good half hour before the sun would officially set and the Seder could begin. She wanted to be the first one there, to help Grandma Ida set the tone—whatever tone Grandma Ida had in mind. Julia hoped it wouldn't be a bloodletting, revenge-is-mine tone.

Not that she'd mind taking revenge on her uncle and brother. But not today. Not at the Seder.

Grandma Ida was in the living room, dressed as always in a skirt, blouse, and cardigan, her copy of *The*

Portrait of a Lady open in her lap. "Howard is here, so I have to pretend I'm reading it," she explained as Julia bent to kiss her cheek.

Ron kissed her, too. "How are you doing, Ida?"

"How should I be doing?" She shrugged.

"Are you sure we should be having this Seder?" Julia asked, recalling Grandma Ida's behavior a week ago, when Julia had told her about Uncle Jay and Adam returning to Bloom's. Julia had thought she'd be thrilled, but she'd only looked drained.

"How can you not have a Seder?" Grandma Ida patted her hand. "It's *Pesach*. At *Pesach* you have a Seder."

"I just want to make sure you're okay," Julia said.

"I'm okay. Just a little tired. Those two *nudniks* tired me out."

"They tired everyone out." Julia gave her grandmother another kiss, her lips brushing Grandma Ida's tar-black hair. "But that's all behind us, right?"

"Eh. It's behind us until the next time someone does something stupid."

Julia forced a smile. It wasn't like Grandma Ida to be so negative—except maybe it *was* like her. On the walk over to the Bloom Building, Julia had shared her concern with Ron. "I thought she'd be so happy that the family was back together. But she doesn't seem happy."

"Old people are allowed to be grouches," Ron had assured her.

Fine. Grandma Ida was a grouch. She'd always been a grouch, even before she'd gotten so old. Couldn't she be happy and grouchy at the same time?

"I'm going to go give Lyndon a hug," Julia said now. Trying to make Grandma Ida happy tired her out as much as the two *nudniks* tired Grandma Ida out. "Ron, you want to visit with my grandmother?"

"There's nothing I'd rather do," Ron said, dropping onto the sofa. He launched into a monologue about his own painful experiences reading Henry James in college. That might prove more boring than the book itself, but Grandma Ida was fond of Ron. He'd married her favorite grandchild, after all, and he was polite and smart and lacking a tattoo.

En route to the kitchen, Julia paused at the doorway to the dining room. With all its leaves added, the table was a good ten feet long, and it was covered with a heavy damask table cloth. The places were set with Grandma Ida's Passover dishes, circles of thick glass that, at least theoretically, had never been touched by any food that contained leavening. At the center of the table, a round platter held all the symbolic *Pesach* foods: a roasted shank, a heaping mound of *charoseth*, and a matching mound of white horseradish that cleared Julia's sinuses even from several feet away. A bowl of salt water, representing the tears shed by the enslaved Jews. A shrub-sized heap of fresh parsley. A roasted egg. And beside it all, a silver goblet of wine and a plate of matzo covered with a linen napkin embroidered with some Hebrew letters. Julia had no idea what those letters conveyed. She had been bat mitzvahed one morning in her thirteenth year, and by the reception that evening, she'd forgotten everything she'd ever learned in Hebrew School.

She proceeded to the kitchen, where the smell of cooking food was stronger and more tantalizing than the scent of the horseradish. A cauldron of chicken soup simmered on the stove, filled with bobbing beige matzo balls. On the counter next to the fridge sat a serving plate laden with slabs of gefilte fish swimming in clear jelly and garnished with slivers of pickled carrots. Lyndon was fussing at the open oven, stirring the brisket drippings, while Howard peeled hard-boiled eggs. A plate of matzo sat on the table—homemade matzo, round and uneven in color. Bloom's sold matzo year-round, but only special hand-crafted matzo during Passover. Susie had written a mouth-watering essay about how the homemade matzo was prepared in the most recent *Bloom's Bulletin.*

"I want to live here, in this kitchen," Julia said, inhaling the aromas and holding her breath, as if she could get high on them. She probably could. She could get even higher if she filched one of the wine bottles lined up on the counter. Grandma Ida insisted on serving sweet wine at Passover. Today, any wine would do, as long as it had a decent alcohol content.

Lyndon turned from the oven to give her a hug. He and Howard were wearing dueling green aprons with "I'm the Chef" silkscreened in white block letters across the bibs. Howard greeted Julia with a grin and continued to peel eggs. Lyndon tapped his cooking spoon against the roasting pan and slid the brisket back into the oven. "I don't know where you'd fit a bed," he pointed out.

"It doesn't always smell like this," Howard reminded her.

"Wherever you guys are cooking, that's where I want to live. If you ever decide to quit working for Grandma Ida," she added to Lyndon, "I'll hire you for the Bloom's kitchen."

"Oh, I'd really fit in there," Lyndon said with a laugh. She supposed he was right—all those yammering women and a tall, dread-locked, gay black man, gathered around the prep tables, stuffing derma and stewing kasha varnishkes. "Everything I know about Jewish cooking, I learned from Howard. Hire him."

"I like my job," Howard protested.

Julia delicately plucked a carrot from the gefilte fish plate and popped it into her mouth, earning her a light rap on the knuckles from Lyndon. She chewed, swallowed, and asked, "How is my grandmother doing? I mean, with all the family *tsorris*. Was it really a good idea to invite Uncle Jay and Adam to this thing?"

"They're family," Lyndon said, as if that justified everything.

Perhaps it did. She wasn't so sure, though. "Everybody in the family hates everybody."

"I hate everyone in my family," Howard said, "and we always have a great time when we get together."

Voices drifted down the hall to the kitchen. Someone else must have arrived. Julia was not going to be able to live in the kitchen, so she shored up her courage and bade the two chefs goodbye. Closer to the living room, she heard Aunt Martha's voice. That would probably mean Neil was here, too. Julia hadn't seen him since last September, when he'd come to New York for Rosh Hashanah. That time, his skin had been a radiant tan, but so had everyone else's—if not radiant, at least tan. Now, they all had winter pallors, but not Neil. As she stepped into the living room, she saw that his complexion was a glowing gold. Julia comforted herself by noting that even though Neil was only two years older than her, all that Florida sunshine had etched faint crow's feet at the outer corners of his eyes.

Of course, on guys, crow's feet looked cool. On women, no.

Ron stood chatting with Neil, who gave Julia an obligatory hug and kiss before returning his attention to Ron to discuss manly stuff: sailing, baseball, hedge funds, and the like. Martha, the epitome of frumpiness in a shapeless sack of a dress and shoes that had to be comfortable because they were so ugly, was yam-

mering at Grandma Ida, who looked even less cheerful than she'd looked when Julia had arrived. "Henry
James is one of the great literary stylists of English language," Martha pontificated.

"A stylist? He does hair?" Grandma Ida touched
her storm-cloud coiffure.

"A *literary* stylist," Martha said, enunciating each
syllable as if she thought Grandma Ida was deaf, or
possibly senile.

Grandma Ida sent Julia a pleading look. "I think
Grandma Ida is pulling your leg," Julia told Martha. It
might not be true, but she was willing to provide cover
for her grandmother.

More voices at the door, and then Sondra swept
into the living room. Her hair was pleasantly fluffy, and
she wore slim-fitting trousers and a drapey silk tunic
that fluttered around her torso. She looked happier
than she'd ever looked before while in the presence of
Grandma Ida. Julia tried not to stare at her immobile
forehead.

"Happy Passover, everybody!" she greeted them,
as if it were Christmas and she expected to drink a lot
of spiked eggnog and receive some lovely presents.

"Hey, Aunt Sondra!" Neil gave Julia's mother a
warmer greeting than he'd given Julia.

Sondra hugged Neil back, having to reach up to do
so, and then swooped down on Grandma Ida and gave
her a perfunctory kiss on the crown of her head. "Happy Passover, Ida."

"Look at you." Grandma Ida squinted up at Sondra. "You look different. A real glamour-puss."

Sondra's smile grew even wider, although her brow
remained frozen.

"It's because she's started coming to my women's
club," Aunt Martha announced. From everything Aunt

Martha had ever told Julia about her women's club, Julia would never have guessed that cosmetic procedures were a crucial element of the club's mission. Aunt Martha confirmed this when she added, "We're having an excellent program next week—a member of the mayor's mass-transit task force. She's going to speak on the history of the IRT line. That's the system's oldest subway line—and it's our line, here on the Upper West Side."

"It certainly acts like the city's oldest subway line," Ron muttered. Julia sent him a faint smile to let him know she heard him. Through the living room's towering windows, she could see the daylight dimming. Had the sun set yet? Could they start eating all that fabulous food Lyndon and Howard had prepared? Even better, could they get through the Seder before Adam and Uncle Jay showed up?

Not that she wanted to start before Susie arrived. As if Julia had magically conjured her sister, Susie appeared in the arched doorway to the living room, Rick by her side. Susie looked like crap to Julia, but marginally better crap than she'd looked the past few days. Rick looked like a guy being tugged in two directions. His clothing shouted up-and-coming ad man, but his hair was unkempt, and either he'd forgotten to shave or he'd decided to try for a beard. A couple of years back, when he dreamed of becoming the next Truffaut or Scorsese or Kubrick, he'd attempted to grow a beard. He'd looked as shaggy as a coconut, but as far as Julia knew, the closest he'd come to making a movie was a short documentary he'd filmed to promote Bloom's. It had costarred Susie and the large plastic lobster which currently resided in Casey's bakery. The documentary had had glimmers of wit and artistry. Rick's beard had had neither.

"Hey, Neil." Rick and his brother bumped fists, slapped each other's backs, and bumped fists again in a clumsy fraternal choreography. Then Rick kissed his mother.

Susie gravitated to Julia's side. She was wearing an actual skirt. Julia hadn't known Susie owned such a garment. It was black, of course, and she'd paired it with a black shirt and black tights, making her resemble her own shadow. She'd skipped make-up, but her eyes were dark, anyway, rimmed with sorrow. "Things still bad with Casey?" Julia whispered.

Before Susie could answer, Grandma Ida blurted out, "Where's your boyfriend? Where's my favorite bagel maker?"

"He couldn't come," Susie answered, attempting a smile. Then she turned back to Julia. "Grandma Ida likes Casey better than me."

"We all do," Julia teased. When Susie's smile faded, Julia gave her a hug. None of that fist-bumping and back-slapping for them. "Grandma Ida just likes Casey because he covered for her when she was stealing bagels and donating them to disabled shut-ins," she reminded Susie.

"Right." Susie glanced around. "When can we start drinking the wine?"

"Now wouldn't be soon enough," Julia said.

"So that commercial," Grandma Ida complained to Rick. "It's terrible."

"What commercial, Grandma?"

"With that loud fat man screaming about cars. In rhyme, no less. It gives me heartburn. You made that commercial?"

"It's what the Glickstein Agency pays me to do."

"It's terrible. It gives me nightmares." She shook her head. "All that shouting, cockamamie poetry."

"It sounds special," Neil said with a smirk. "I'd love to see it."

"Don't pick on your brother," Grandma Ida scolded Neil. "He's got a real job, like a *mensch*. He isn't sailing around the tropics in a boat."

"Florida isn't the tropics," Neil corrected her.

"*Nu*? Where's my son? Where's Jay?" Grandma Ida asked no one in particular.

"Maybe he decided not to come," Sondra said hopefully. "I think the sun has set, so we should probably get started without him."

"Where's *your* son?" Grandma Ida asked Sondra, her tone sharp with accusation.

"I don't keep tabs on my children," Sondra shot back in a lofty voice. "They're adults. They don't check in with me."

"I'm here," Adam called from the entry. "Everyone's here." He entered the living room, followed by Uncle Jay and Wendy.

Aunt Martha's already dim expression lost what little wattage it had, while Wendy, clad in a bright turquoise mini-dress and silver high-heel mules, blinded Julia with the radiance she emanated. "We're here!" she exclaimed, as if this was the most thrilling thing in the world. "We met Adam in the lobby. What a coincidence!"

Not really a coincidence, since they'd all been invited to the same place at the same time, but Julia didn't mention that.

"Good," Grandma Ida said, glowering at Adam. "We need you here. You're the youngest. You have to ask the four questions." The four questions were a part of the Passover service, and the youngest person at the table was supposed to ask them. From the moment of his birth, Adam had been the youngest.

"It's supposed to be asked by a child," Adam said. "I think I've outgrown the role."

"You're the youngest," Grandma Ida said, sparing Julia from having to point out that despite having achieved legal adulthood several years ago, Adam remained an immature brat. He'd rejoined Bloom's, he was back in the family, but if that fact hadn't made Grandma Ida happy—and apparently it hadn't—Julia wasn't sure she was ready to forgive him for all the heartache he and Uncle Jay had caused.

Wendy seemed unaware of the undercurrent of anger and resentment flowing through the living room. She continued to beam as if she'd just won a free trip to Bermuda, if not the Holy Land—she'd undoubtedly prefer Bermuda, but the Seder traditionally ended with everyone saying, "Next year in Jerusalem." Standing next to her, Uncle Jay looked solemn. He wore crisp khakis and a pink oxford shirt, an outfit that would have served him well at Julia's old law firm, where most of the attorneys had dressed like prep school graduates at a twentieth-year reunion. He glanced so fleetingly at Julia, she didn't have a chance to greet him. Just as well, since she was no longer in a forgiving mood.

He edged over to the chair where Grandma Ida sat and hunkered down next to her. "Hello, Mom," he said.

Grandma Ida glowered at him, then at Wendy. "Her shoes hurt my eyes," she said.

Wendy laughed. "They hurt my feet," she said, making it sound like a boast. "I guess that makes us even."

"Even with what?" Grandma frowned at Uncle Jay, as if expecting him to explain Wendy's comment.

Not that it could be explained. "Thank you for inviting us to your Seder," he said.

"Eh. We get together at *Pesach*. It's what families do. The sun rises; the sun sets. We gather for *Pesach*."

That might be as close as Grandma Ida ever got to saying Uncle Jay was welcome and she absolved him. Julia hoped he'd accept that and not press Grandma Ida for more loving words. Loving words didn't come naturally to Grandma Ida.

"Speaking of the sun setting," Lyndon called from the doorway, "the sun has officially set." Julia assumed that was his way of saying the brisket was done and they'd better all gather around the table and get the meal underway. With all the readings, the ceremonial tastings, the appetizers and main courses and negotiations over the dessert matzo, the Seder would last for hours. By the time they got around to saying, "Next year in Jerusalem," the moon would probably be setting.

"Who's going to lead the Seder?" Rick asked. He shot Neil a look. Neil shook his head. He might be older than Rick, but evidently he felt unqualified.

Not that any of the other men in the room was particularly prepared to preside over the ritual meal. Ron could probably fake it if he had to, but he wasn't a Bloom, and Grandma Ida tended to reject people who had merely married into the family when it came to important duties—like running Bloom's, as Sondra had learned to her great annoyance.

"Jay will lead it," Grandma Ida announced.

Uncle Jay blanched. In years past, he'd asked to lead it, but Grandma Ida had insisted on leading it herself, with Aunt Martha cheering her on as an exemplar of feminism.

Ron pulled a yarmulke from the pocket of his jacket and planted it on his head. Rick and Neil each donned their own yarmulkes. Uncle Jay groped futilely in the pockets of his trousers. "I don't have a yarmulke," he said, sounding plaintive.

"Lyndon has spares," Grandma Ida said.

"You've always wanted to lead the Seder," Wendy cooed, gazing proudly at her husband. "This will be fun."

"I don't think so. I'm so rusty. Mom, why don't you lead it?"

"You should, Ida," Martha chimed in. "On behalf of the oppressed—"

"No one here is oppressed, Martha," Sondra cut her off, doing her best to grin. She obviously wanted Uncle Jay to lead the Seder, no doubt because she expected him to botch it.

"Jay will lead," Grandma Ida said with finality. "Lyndon, get him a yarmulke."

The family filed out of the living room and into the dining room, Sondra chattering with Aunt Martha, Rick and Neil walking side by side but somehow managing not to touch, Adam and Susie both looking forlorn for their own personal reasons, Uncle Jay muttering to himself and Wendy radiating a smile that belonged on a billboard advertising an orthodontist's services. Julia held back, and Ron did, too, offering his arm to Grandma Ida as she moved in her slow, slightly shuffling gait toward the doorway.

"I'm fine," she said, but she took Ron's arm anyway. If Julia couldn't make her grandmother happy, maybe her husband could. Seeing them ambling together toward the dining room filled her with warmth. If the family still had some rips and snags in their fabric, at least they were beginning to mend. And it was thanks to Ron. He'd been the one Uncle Jay had asked for help returning to the fold. Ron had folded him back in.

She preceded Ron and Grandma Ida into the dining room in time to see Lyndon hand Uncle Jay a yarmulke. Everyone milled around the table, eyeing one another, calculating whom they wished to sit next to and whom they wished to avoid.

"Sit, sit," Grandma Ida barked. Susie took her place beside Rick. Sondra sat next to Aunt Martha. Julia grabbed a chair at the opposite end of the table from Uncle Jay, who hesitated before pulling out the armed chair at the head of the table, the throne where Grandma Ida usually sat. He didn't seem to be enjoying his leader-of-the-Seder status at all. Was he really that embarrassed about his Hebrew pronunciation? The family had always conducted most of the Seder in English, anyway.

"It's an honor," Julia finally scolded him, her voice carrying the length of the table. "Leading the Seder is an honor, Uncle Jay."

"I know." Wendy practically bounced on the toes of her painful silver shoes. "Sit at the head of the table, Jay."

"That's my mother's seat," he argued.

"Just sit already," Grandma Ida snapped. "We can't have a Seder standing up. It says in the *Haggadah* we're supposed to recline."

With that, her legs buckled under her, and she reclined herself straight down to the patterned rug, dragging Ron to his knees beside her. She pressed her hand to her chest, gave him a panicked look, and moaned, "*Oy!*"

Chapter Twenty-Nine

A dam sat quietly on a vinyl-upholstered chair in one corner of the waiting lounge outside Mount Sinai St. Luke's ER. Roosevelt Hospital's ER might have been a few blocks closer to the Bloom Building, but Grandma Ida had insisted on being taken to Mount Sinai St. Luke's, because it sounded more Jewish. Adam felt St. Luke negated Mount Sinai, but Grandma Ida had argued that Mount Sinai was where God had given Moses the Ten Commandments, which, as she put it, was like the Passover sequel. Son of Seder, he supposed.

She'd seemed pretty feisty for someone in the grip of a heart attack—unless it was a stroke, or perhaps just vertigo. Who knew? Lyndon had dialed 911 while Ron had dropped to his knees on the dining room floor and tried to perform CPR on Grandma Ida. She'd barked that he was hurting her, all that thumping and pounding on her chest. "I'm trying to keep you alive," Ron had said, to which Grandma Ida had responded, "Don't try so hard."

Did that mean she wanted to die? Or just that Ron was bruising her ribs? She was pretty old, after all.

Adam stared at his cell phone, his thumb skimming the screen. He wanted to call Dulcie, but what would he say to her? "Our Seder has gone off the rails"

sounded kind of bizarre, and it was also an understate-
ment. "Hey, guess what? I don't have to recite the frickin' four questions" sounded ungracious, but it came
closer to his genuine sentiments.

Although he wasn't particularly religious, or optimistic, he'd had high hopes about this Seder. It was
supposed to be his chance to reconcile with the family. His chance to assure his mother and sisters he was
back on board, the rebel tearing off his armband and
pledging allegiance to the Bloom flag. He'd been so
bummed when Uncle Jay had told him their East Side
store wasn't going to happen, and so joyful when Julia
had phoned to invite him to the Seder. He was losing
a dream and gaining a reality. Not necessarily a fun
trade, but a good, solid one.

His family hadn't exactly embraced him, though.
He'd expected some kisses, or at least some hugs,
when he'd walked into Grandma Ida's living room.
His mother had smiled at him, but it had been a weird
smile, as if something wasn't functioning properly in
her facial muscles. Julia had just nodded at him, treating him like an employee or a tenant—which he was,
but he was also her brother. Susie had looked like shit.
Grandma Ida had looked like someone who'd eaten
too many prunes, or too few prunes, or who was turning into a prune herself. In retrospect, he realized, she
might have been in the early stages of a heart attack or
a stroke, or whatever it was that had happened to her
on the dining room floor.

He still didn't know precisely why Uncle Jay had
pulled the plug on their store. It was about a lack of
funding, but Uncle Jay hadn't told him what was wrong
with their financiers who wanted to spend, spend,
spend. Did they suddenly not want to spend, spend,
spend? Was the money they wanted to spend, spend,

spend counterfeit? When he'd asked, Uncle Jay had mumbled something about *sub rosa*, which made no sense. And then the banks weren't offering low-rate loans, and the company that owned the building had another retailer interested in renting the storefront, and Uncle Jay had said, "Let's just go back to Bloom's."

Thank God Bloom's let them come back. Adam was religious enough to offer a modest prayer of thanks for that.

Had their arrival at the Seder caused Grandma Ida to collapse? If she died, would it be their fault?

The hospital's waiting lounge echoed with a constant din—nurses, doctors, and technicians conferring, striding purposefully, pushing wheelchairs and carts and gurneys. An infant fussed on its mother's lap. A flat-screen TV fastened to the wall in one corner broadcast a Yankees game along with a stream of unnecessary commentary from the sportscasters. But most of the noise came from Blooms and Bloom-in-laws. His entire family had migrated from Grandma Ida's apartment to the hospital.

On his left, his mother yammered to Wendy about some beauty procedure she'd had done. "I think I want to start dating again," she told Wendy. "Does that make me a bad person?"

"Of course not," Wendy assured her. "You're a very good person."

"And I want to look my best. Does that make me vain?"

"I don't think you're vain," Wendy said. "We all want to look our best. What do you think of my dress? It's new. Isn't it cute?"

Adam disagreed with Wendy—not about her dress, which was definitely cute, but about his mother, who was definitely vain. However, if she wanted to date, she should date. Dating might keep her too busy to call Adam at awkward times, like when he was stoned or having sex with a ballerina, and ask him what he was doing.

On his other side, Susie and Rick sat together on a vinyl sofa, Rick eyeing the Yankees game and Susie moping, her head resting on Rick's shoulder. Across the lounge, Julia was demanding that the receptionist tell her what was going on with Grandma Ida. Ron stood beside Julia, his hand resting on her shoulder. Whether he was comforting her or holding her back so she wouldn't lunge across the receptionist's desk and attack the woman, Adam couldn't say.

"They're probably running tests," the receptionist said.

"Probably? *Probably?* The woman collapsed in her dining room!"

"I'm sure she's being taken care of."

"I should be in there with her," Julia said, gesturing toward the swinging doors that led from the lounge to the examining rooms.

"Not right now," the receptionist said, the epitome of patience. "Your grandmother is very busy right now."

"Busy lying on a stretcher and being frightened?"

"Nothing frightens Ida," Ron remarked.

"How do you know? She collapsed in her dining room!" As if the location of Grandma Ida's collapse was all that relevant. "She shouldn't be alone in there."

"She's not alone," Ron said. "There are doctors and nurses in there with her."

"And phlebotomists," the receptionist added.

Uncle Jay paced the length of the lounge, visibly agitated. Adam had no idea whether he was agitated about his mother's collapse or the demise of Jacob

Bloom's Delectable Food Emporium, or something totally unrelated. One of his precious golf clubs might be dinged, or the engine of his beloved BMW might have made a funny noise while he was driving uptown to the hospital. He and Wendy had come to the Seder by car, and while the rest of the family had made their way to the hospital on the subway, accompanied by Aunt Martha's tedious lecture about the history of the IRT line, Uncle Jay and Wendy had cruised uptown in his hot little coupe. Despite their swifter transportation, they'd entered the emergency room after everyone else, because while the trip had taken them little time, finding a parking space near the hospital had consumed a half hour.

Not surprisingly, Grandma Ida had arrived at the hospital way ahead of everyone else. Adam concluded that the most efficient way to travel around Manhattan was by ambulance.

Tuning out the babble of the sportscasters on the TV, he closed his eyes and tried to burst the bubble of guilt that swelled through his body. It was his fault Grandma Ida had collapsed. His fault the family was so fractured. His fault that he preferred Dulcie to Tasha, his fiercely righteous girlfriend in college, whose thighs had been much fatter than Dulcie's but who was dedicated to saving the planet. What was Adam dedicated to? Maintaining inventories of pickled herring and smoked salmon and gourmet imported chocolates?

This was what he'd been reduced to. Not a doctoral candidate in mathematics. Not the boyfriend of a woman willing to sleep in a hammock in a tree to keep it from getting chopped down. Not a devoted son, a loyal brother, a true family member.

A guy who wanted to smoke pot, *schtup* ballerinas, and quantify jars of pickled herring. A guy who wanted to be a partner in something. A guy who wanted his grandmother to think of him as more than just the kid who asked the Four Questions because he was the youngest.

"I'm a piece of shit," he said aloud.

Susie glanced over at him. "No kidding," she said.

"You're supposed to argue with me."

"I'd be happy to oblige. What do you want to argue about?"

"My being a piece of shit."

She smiled sadly. "Sorry. I can't argue that."

He noticed tears shimmering along the edges of her eyelids, getting trapped in her lashes. That he noticed her tears was a good sign, he thought. He might still have some humanity inside him, some brotherly sensitivity. "What's wrong?"

"Casey," she said. "I don't want to talk about it."

"You don't want to talk about Casey?"

"Yeah." She sighed shakily. "He's a piece of shit. Or maybe I am. Maybe we all are."

That sounded pretty accurate to Adam.

❧

Sarcasm wasn't in Casey's nature, so when he said, "Thank you for calling," Susie knew he really meant it.

He'd left her three messages since she'd redesigned the window of his store. Her plan had been to wait until he'd left five messages before responding; fewer than five didn't seem like enough of an effort on his part. But after the third message, he'd gone silent, which she'd interpreted to mean he really didn't want her to get back to him, after all.

But if Adam, of all people, could see how upset she was, she realized she needed to let Casey know. "I'm

upset," she said into her phone, two words that actually distracted Rick from the game being broadcast
on the TV in the lounge. He glanced at her, and she
rose from the sofa and strode to the vestibule through
which the whole family had paraded fifteen minutes
ago. She shouldn't have called Casey in a busy waiting
room with so many people within earshot. The vestibule contained a row of wheelchairs along one wall,
but no one was sitting in them. She had the place to
herself.

Fortunately, the cell phone reception was clear in
the vestibule. "I'm upset, too," Casey said, sounding
not the least bit upset. After a long pause, he added,
"The window is attracting attention."

"Of course it is. That's what windows are supposed
to do."

"People stop and stare at it. They don't necessarily
come in and buy bread, but they stop and stare."

"Good. If they don't even stop, they aren't going to
go into the store. Stopping is the first step."

Another long silence. "I want them to stop. I want
them to look. But all that stuff—the moon and the
poem... It's a beautiful poem, Susie. I mean that. But
it's *you*. That poem isn't me. It's *you*."

She wasn't Casey. He wasn't her. She got that. She
wouldn't want to be in a relationship with someone
who was just like her. Hell, no. Someone like her would
drive her crazy.

Had she driven Casey crazy? He didn't seem crazy.
If anything, he seemed too sane most of the time.

"I'm not sure what I'm going to do about the window, Susie. It's just...I mean, it's beautiful, but it's just
not..." He fell silent.

"It's not what?"

"Right."

"Okay. Fine. Take the damned window apart. Smash it to pieces. Do what you want." Let him have his sane, boring, Mose-approved window. Let him have his sane, boring bread and his sane, boring life. Let him move back to Queens. What did she care? "I need the music stand back," she said. "I borrowed it from Anna."

"I'd like to see you," he said. "We should talk about this in person."

"Well, I can't see you now. I'm in the hospital."

"You're in the hospital?" He sounded aghast. "What happened?"

"It's not me. I'm not in the hospital. Well, I am, but just in the emergency room." That didn't sound good, either. "Actually, my grandmother is the one in the emergency room. I'm just hanging out here with a bunch of empty wheelchairs."

"My God. Is Ida all right?"

"She collapsed." That sounded even worse. "She never lost consciousness or anything," Susie explained, hoping to reassure Casey. "In fact, she kept ordering everyone around, even the EMTs. She didn't like their gurney. She said the wheels were too squeaky. I guess her hearing is still okay." She realized she was rambling and reined herself in. "We don't know what's wrong with her. She's inside with the doctors, and we're all outside in the waiting area. They aren't letting anyone in to be with her." Susie recalled the discussion she'd overheard between Julia and the receptionist. "They've got a phlebotomist," she said. "I'm not sure what that is."

"I think they're the people who take blood tests," Casey said helpfully.

"Great. So they're sticking her with needles."

"Today's Passover, isn't it? What about your Seder?"

"What about it? I'm famished, and all that food is sitting in her apartment, going to waste." Closing her eyes, she inhaled, trying to replace the antiseptic smell of the hospital with her memory of the aromas at her grandmother's apartment. The chicken soup. The roast brisket. The gefilte fish. The syrup-sweet wine. Her stomach twinged with hunger pangs. She might collapse from starvation, waiting to find out how Grandma Ida was.

If she was going to collapse, she supposed, a hospital ER was an excellent place to do it. Much better than collapsing in Grandma Ida's dining room.

"You should be with your family," Casey said. "Let me know how Ida makes out."

"Sure." That he cared about Grandma Ida was a plus. That he cared more about Grandma Ida than he did about Susie was a minus. But she was too wrung out to do the math. He hated her window. He didn't appreciate it. He didn't *get* it. It wasn't *right*. He was going to destroy the display and come up with something safe and uninspiring. He was going to trust Mose's judgment.

Maybe she'd let him know how Grandma Ida made out. Maybe she wouldn't. He could call Julia if he wanted an update. All Susie wanted was to climb to the roof of the Bloom Building, thirty blocks away, and see if the moon was above her, holding things up. Because right now, it felt as if the sky was falling.

❧

Julia remained by the receptionist's desk, as if standing there, as solid and unavoidable as an oak even if she was only five-five and on the thin side, would force the receptionist to let her through those doors to where Grandma Ida was being poked and prodded and—

God only knew—resuscitated with electric shocks that made her fragile octogenarian body levitate off the examining table.

The receptionist ignored her.

Someone ought to be with Grandma Ida. If doctors were questioning her, barking orders at her, asking her about what she'd eaten and where it hurt and whether she was allergic to penicillin, someone ought to be there to help her through the interview. Not that Julia knew the answers to any of those questions, but she could hold Grandma Ida's hand and encourage her, and murmur to her that everyone out in the waiting area loved her and wanted her back on her feet, even if their primary motivation was to return to her apartment and have their Seder.

But the bitch behind the desk refused to let Julia be with her ailing grandmother.

She surveyed the waiting area. Her mother, Aunt Martha, and Wendy were currently schmoozing like best friends. Neil was sprawled out on a chair, his legs extended across the floor, perfectly positioned to trip anyone who might wander by. Susie was hovering near the ER entry and chatting on her phone, Rick was watching the television, and Ron had joined Adam and Uncle Jay. They stood in a huddle, their voices inaudible from across the lounge.

Since the receptionist was ignoring Julia, she decided to find out what they were talking about so intently. When she was just a few feet from them, Ron noticed her and broke from the others. "Hey," he said, giving her his dimpled, sexy smile.

"Do you know what's going on back there?" She gestured toward the swinging doors.

Ron shook his head. "They'd tell you before they'd tell me."

"I just thought—the way you all were talking, and you all looked so worried..."

"I'm not worried. A bit concerned, that's all." He took Julia's arm and led her away from her brother and uncle. "We were talking about their store. I was giving them some statistics about how many small businesses fail within the first year so they wouldn't feel so bad."

"Their business didn't fail. It didn't even get off the ground."

"They feel like failures." Ron shrugged. "Be gentle with them."

"They stabbed us in the back. *They're* the ones who should be gentle with us. They're lucky I let them come back to Bloom's."

Ron was still smiling, but his eyes were stern. "Number one, they know they're lucky. Number two, you're lucky, too. You couldn't find replacements for them. Susie was ready to mutiny because you stuck her with Jay's portfolio." He glanced toward Susie, who wandered back to her chair next to Rick. Her brow was furrowed, her lips twisted into a pout. "She still looks mutinous."

"She and Casey are on the rocks," Julia said. "Maybe off the rocks and underwater at this point."

"I guess you'll have to be gentle with her, too."

"Oh, God." Julia sighed dramatically. "I don't know if I have that much gentleness in me."

"You do." Ron kissed her forehead, then nudged her back toward the receptionist. "Don't be gentle with her. Torture her until you can get some info on your grandmother."

As if by magic, the receptionist bellowed, "Is Julia Bloom here?"

Evidently, torture would not be necessary. Julia bolted across the room to her desk. "Yes?"

"Come with me." The receptionist rose and headed for the swinging doors. Julia sent Ron a quick look, half panic and half relief, and raced after the receptionist.

Beyond the doors, the ER was divided into small examining rooms partitioned by walls and privacy curtains. The air smelled of caustic cleansers and alcohol, a sharp, sterile scent. The receptionist led Julia to one of the drawn curtains and slid it open. "She asked for you," the receptionist said before stalking away, back to her desk to perform the sacred duty of blocking anyone else who attempted to breach the inner sanctum of the ER.

Julia stepped around the curtain to find her grandmother clad in a hospital johnny, the back of her bed tilted up so she could sit. Her clothing was piled neatly on a chair, and a tangle of wires rose from the neckline of the johnny and plugged into a screen above her bed. A jagged green line sped from left to right across the screen. "I'm fine," Grandma Ida said. "They should let me go home."

"Really?" Relief washed through Julia, warm and fluid. "You're fine?"

"She's fine," a man behind her said, "but we're not going to let her go home."

Julia turned to see a compact man in a white coat swing past the curtain and enter the room. He had dark hair and dark-framed eyeglasses, and he carried a clipboard. He looked to be about Julia's age. Was he old enough to be taking care of her grandmother?

He extended his hand. "I'm Dr. Popkin, the cardiology resident on call tonight. Your grandmother is going to be fine."

"But she can't go home?"

"She's got AFib. Atrial fibrillation. Her heartbeat is erratic." He pointed to the jagged line on the monitor. "It's irregular and rapid."

"That doesn't sound fine," Julia said.

"Well, yes." Dr. Popkin seemed much too calm. "It's a problem. That's why she fell. Fortunately, she didn't hurt herself in the fall. But this condition can cause dizziness, light-headedness—and if untreated, it can cause a stroke."

"A stroke!"

"I didn't have a stroke," Grandma Ida called from the bed. "I'm fine. Tell him to let me go home."

Dr. Popkin ignored Grandma Ida. "We can treat this in two ways. One way is to give her heart a little electric shock. I'd rather not do that, though, given your grandmother's age."

"I'm right here," Grandma Ida shouted at him. "Don't talk about me like I'm not here. I can hear every word you say. I'm not deaf."

"I'm sorry." Dr. Popkin smiled weakly. "I don't want to give you electrical cardioversion. That's where we give the heart a little shock—"

"I'm not deaf," Grandma Ida repeated. "I heard you, a little shock, and I'm old. I already knew that. It's not a secret. I'm old."

The doctor's smile grew wider. "We don't say old here. We say elderly."

"Elderly, *schmelderly*. I'm old, and I want to go home."

"The treatment I'm recommending is to get your heart under control with several anti-arrhythmic drugs. We have to monitor you while we administer these drugs to make sure they're doing what we need them to do. That's why I'm admitting you to the hospital. Just to get your heart back to a healthy rhythm."

Grandma Ida gave him a hard look. Then she turned to Julia. "Tell him I want to go home."

"He's not deaf either, Grandma. He knows you want to go home. But they have to monitor you while they give you this medicine."

"What about the Seder? Everyone's having a Seder, and I'm supposed to be here with these things stuck to me?" She plucked at the wires fastened to her chest with sticky square pads.

Julia nudged Grandma Ida's hand away, just in case she'd intended to yank off the pads. "Everyone's here," she said. "We all left the Seder and came here."

"Everyone?"

"Everyone but Lyndon and Howard. We left them packing up the food so it wouldn't go bad."

"Jay is out there?" She peered past Julia at the curtain, as if she could see beyond it, into the waiting lounge. "My Jacob?"

"Yes, of course. He and Wendy drove to the hospital in his hot little sports car."

"That car." Grandma Ida clicked her tongue. "He loves it like another son." She thought for a minute. "He should be in here, too. He came back. He should hear what this doctor is saying." She turned back to Dr. Popkin. "Him, you have to talk to loudly. He's a little deaf."

"He is not," Julia chided her grandmother.

"He doesn't always listen," Grandma Ida pointed out.

True enough. "I'll go get him." Julia left the examining room, hurried to the swinging door, and inched it open. "Can you get my Uncle Jay?" she called to the receptionist.

The receptionist seemed irked by the request, but she dutifully hollered, "Uncle Jay?"

"Jacob Bloom," Julia said, feeling foolish for having not given the woman Jay's real name. But before the receptionist could holler again, Uncle Jay had charged over to the swinging door. Julia held it open for him, and he crossed the threshold.

He looked worried and worn, none of his usual swagger in evidence. "She's okay," Julia informed him as she led him to Grandma Ida's examining room. "But they want to admit her, and she doesn't want to stay."

Uncle Jay nodded, but Julia wasn't sure how much he'd heard. Maybe he was a little deaf, after all.

She pulled back the curtain, and he pushed past it. One long stride brought him to her bedside. He gripped the bed's aluminum side rail and peered down at her. "Mom. You're okay." He studied her intently. "You look good."

"Eh. I'd look better if I was home. Tell this *boychik* who's pretending to be a doctor to let me go home."

Dr. Popkin stepped forward and introduced himself. "She needs to stay here so we can monitor her," he said, and launched into his spiel about atrial fibrillation and anti-arrhythmic cardioversion.

"Are you old enough to be practicing medicine?" Uncle Jay asked.

"I am. I'm a third-year resident in cardiology. Columbia Medical School."

"Ivy League," Jay said, clearly impressed. "You look very young."

"Your mother looks young, too," Dr. Popkin said.

"I look old," Grandma Ida argued. "This doctor, he said a shock can make this happen, what I have. The *meshugena* heartbeat."

"I said it could be a triggering event," Dr. Popkin corrected her.

"And you gave me a shock, Jacob. A disappointment. A heartbreak. Did you know a shock can make people's hair turn gray overnight?"

That wasn't likely to happen as long as Grandma Ida kept going to her god-awful hairdresser and getting her hair dyed black, Julia thought.

"You're saying *I* caused you to collapse?" Uncle Jay's voice rasped. "That can't be true, Dr.—what did you say your name was again?"

"Popkin. I'm not saying anything you did caused this. Your mother has probably had AFib for a while. But a shock can exacerbate it. Obviously, her heart went a little haywire earlier this evening, which is why she fell."

"You left Bloom's, Jay. You turned from me, from your family, you left us. It broke my heart. Ask Julia, she'll tell you. You broke my heart."

Julia raised her hands in protest. She wasn't going to join in this mother-and-son bearing of souls.

"It wasn't that I wanted to leave the store," Uncle Jay insisted. "I wanted to *lead* the store. You gave it to Julia to run." He shot Julia a resentful glare, then turned back to his mother. "I felt extraneous."

"I gave it to her to run because she's a lawyer. You need a lawyer to do certain things. But you do certain things, too. So you're back. And maybe no more shocks for me, no more heartbreak."

"I can't live my life for you, Mom. I didn't mean to break your heart, but...I have to do what's right for me. That's how you raised me—to be independent."

"Eh. I raised you to work for Bloom's, and now you're working for Bloom's. You want to lead? Lead the Seder. Lyndon and his boyfriend made all that food. Go and eat."

"But you—"

"I'll get leftovers. I can eat leftovers, can't I?" she asked the doctor.

"I don't see why not," he assured her. "Once we release you. They should keep until then."

"Go," Grandma Ida said. "Be a *mensch*. Lead the Seder."

Uncle Jay glanced Julia's way again. He no longer looked resentful. He no longer looked afraid. He didn't exactly look happy, either. Resigned, mostly. "She wants me to lead the Seder."

"I'm right here," Grandma Ida said. "I'm not deaf."

"She wanted you to lead the Seder before all this happened," Julia reminded him, gesturing toward the squiggly line on the monitor above Grandma Ida's bed. "Maybe if you'd just said, 'Sure, Mom, I'd love to,' she wouldn't have collapsed."

"It's not my fault. She's probably had this condition for years. Maybe it was a good thing we finally found out about it and got her diagnosed."

"Sure. It's a good thing. Go lead the Seder, Jay."

He eyed his mother, Dr. Popkin, the heart monitor, and then Julia again. "My Hebrew sucks."

"No one will care."

"I don't know why you don't ask Julia to lead the Seder, Mom." His tone was petulant. He sounded almost as sulky as Susie looked. "You asked her to run the store."

"My Hebrew sucks worse than yours," Julia said.

His gaze swung back to Julia and he almost smiled. "I'm better than you at some things, right? My Hebrew sucks less." He sighed. "I guess we should tell everyone what's going on. You want us to tell everyone, Mom?"

Grandma waved her hand, a sweeping motion sending them out of the examining room. Together, they walked through the swinging doors and into the lounge.

Sondra and Aunt Martha rose as Julia and Uncle Jay moved toward them, and Wendy scampered to Uncle Jay's side, tottering only the slightest bit on the high heels of her glittering shoes. Neil stuffed his phone into his pocket. Rick's attention lingered on the television for a moment, watching the end of a play before he turned to Julia and his father. Adam had his arm around Susie's shoulders. They looked like a brother and sister. A brother comforting a sister. Julia hadn't known Adam could be that considerate. Maybe he was growing up.

Ron moved behind Julia and gave her shoulder a squeeze.

"Grandma Ida's going to be okay," she announced.

"Of course she is," Sondra said. "That woman is indestructible."

Julia and Uncle Jay filled them in. They used all the fancy terms Dr. Popkin had used—atrial fibrillation, anti-arrhythmic cardioversion, blah-blah-blah. Uncle Jay made sure everyone knew the doctor was a Columbia Medical School graduate.

"Mom wants us to go back to her apartment and have the Seder," he said. "I'll be leading the Seder. It's what she wants."

"I'll stay here with her," Julia said, surprising Jay but apparently no one else. "You all go and celebrate Passover. I'll join you later. I want to be with Grandma Ida until she's admitted and settled in a room for the night."

"I'm going to take the subway back to the apartment," Wendy told Uncle Jay. "Martha was telling me about the history of the IRT."

"Can you handle the subway stairs in those shoes?" Sondra asked.

"If Wendy takes the subway," Rick said, "I'll ride in the car with you, Dad."

"Hey, no," Neil said. "I'll ride in the car."

Uncle Jay paid no attention to them. "Really?" he asked Wendy. "You'd rather take the subway than come in the car with me?"

"It's a smart choice, Wendy," Aunt Martha said. "You need to view the mosaics in the station up close. The effort they put into those tiles, the craftsmanship— you don't see that anymore. Newer isn't always better. Handcrafted mosaics in subway stations have been replaced with what? Flat-screen TVs?"

"Also modern medicine." Julia swept her hand through the air, indicating the hospital in which they were gathered.

"Still, the old ways weren't always bad," Aunt Martha argued. "Bloom's sells food prepared the old ways."

True. But the store also maintained an active website and a profitable online business. Uncle Jay deserved a point for that, even if he was a jerk.

He might be a jerk, but he was also her uncle. He was family. They all were.

"You own a car," Rick said to Neil, practically an accusation. "You ride in cars all the time."

"You're here all the time. You can ride in Dad's Beemer whenever you want."

"No, I can't."

They continued the argument as the family swarmed into the vestibule and then through the door to the street. Julia accompanied them, eager to return to Grandma Ida's side but also wistful about waving everyone off. They'd be returning to Grandma Ida's apartment, to that long dining room table laden with soup and gefilte fish, matzo and wine. It was what families did on Passover, and she and Grandma Ida wouldn't be with them.

She watched the Blooms parade down the block toward the subway station and wherever Uncle Jay had parked his car, Neil and Rick continuing to bicker as they trailed behind him. The sun had set more than an hour ago, back when they'd been about to begin their

Seder. Now the sky was a rich, dark blue and the moon had risen above the buildings lining Amsterdam Avenue. Not a full moon, but bright and white, smiling down onto the city.

She wished she could smile, too, but the moon was happier than she was. She wished she could be at the Seder with Grandma Ida. She wished this atrial fibrillation episode had never happened. She wished Uncle Jay had never left the store, taking Adam with him, and then come crawling back. She wished Casey and Susie were happy together.

She wished she could make everyone feel better. But she couldn't.

Sighing, she reentered the building, stalked across the lounge without acknowledging the receptionist, and pushed through the swinging doors into the ER. She heard voices emanating from Grandma Ida's examination room, and laughter. Grandma Ida never laughed—but she was laughing now.

Julia pushed back the curtain to find her grandmother and Dr. Popkin grinning. "I was just telling your grandmother how much I love Bloom's," he said. "I grew up eating food from Bloom's. My father would take the subway from Park Slope in Brooklyn all the way to Bloom's, just to buy bagels and lox for Sunday brunch. And the knishes! Man, I loved those knishes."

"That's how we started," Grandma Ida said. "With a pushcart, selling knishes."

Julia braced herself for the likelihood that Grandma Ida would launch into the Bloom's origin story, a tale she loved sharing. But Dr. Popkin cut her off before she could get started. "When I was in medical school, we'd get the Seder-in-a-Box for Passover, even though we were here in the city. We didn't have time to prepare a Seder. So my classmates and I would order the Seder-in-a-Box. Everyone—the Jews and the gentiles—we all loved those boxes."

"You should have told Jay when he was here," Julia said, feeling generous. "The Seder-in-a-Box was his idea."

"He's not stupid, my son," Grandma Ida said. "He just does stupid things."

"I'm going to see if they've got a bed for you upstairs in the cardiac unit," Dr. Popkin said. "I'll be right back." He left the room, the curtain fluttering in his wake.

"He seems so young," Grandma Ida said. "Is he married?"

"I don't know. Why?"

"I'm thinking Susie. Things aren't good with her and Casey, am I right? She didn't bring him to the Seder."

"No. Things aren't good."

"So find out if this Dr. Popkin is married."

Julia smiled in spite of herself. "Susie would never forgive me if I set her up with a doctor."

"You never know," Grandma Ida sing-songed. She seemed in an awfully good mood for someone in an ER with a heart ailment.

The curtain fluttered again, and Dr. Popkin entered, carrying a soft-sided pouch, one of those insulated lunch totes. "They should have a bed ready for you in about a half hour," he reported.

"It takes a half hour to throw on a sheet and a pillow case?" Grandma Ida clicked her tongue.

"It's a little more complicated than that. But…" He unzipped his bag and pulled out a small stack of matzos wrapped in plastic. "Since I'm on duty here at the hospital for Passover, I brought my Seder with me. It's not Seder-in-a-Box—and it can't be a real Seder, because we can't drink wine in the hospital. But if you'd each like a piece of matzo, we could say a *brucha*."

"That's not Bloom's matzo," Grandma Ida clucked as Dr. Popkin broke a square of matzo into three small pieces. "This time of year, we sell round sheets. Hand-made."

"I know. I was rushing when I packed my lunch bag. I took the cheap matzo."

"A lunch bag? It's too late for lunch. This is dinner."

"Yes, but this is my lunch bag," he said, lifting the container. "Here." He handed Julia and Grandma Ida each a piece of matzo. Then he recited the prayer, in much better Hebrew than Julia could have managed.

She chewed the dry matzo, wishing it was gourmet Bloom's matzo slathered in *charoseth*, wishing platters of fish and meat and wine and honey cake and macaroons would follow. Wishing she was with her family.

She was with Grandma Ida. That was family. And at that moment, Dr. Popkin was family, too. Family was whoever you broke bread—or matzo—with. Whoever you laughed with.

Whoever kept your heart beating through the night.

❧

Acknowledgments

Writing a novel is like having a baby. I gestated it, I nurtured it, and I gave birth to it—but I couldn't have done so without the help and support of others. At the top of the list of people I must thank is Lou Aronica, my brilliant editor (and favorite karaoke partner), who pushed me to make this book stronger and deeper and so much better. Thanks, as well, to Stacy Mathewson and the entire Story Plant team, and to Steven Manchester for his invaluable advice. I could not have survived as a writer without my fellow writer-friends, in particular my Romex sisters and the Smart-and-Savvies. Finally, thanks to my parents, who introduced me to delicious delicatessen food and never tried to talk me out of pursuing my dreams; my husband, who has always had more faith in me than I have in myself; and my sons, who have taught me that you can survive pretty much anything if you know how to laugh.

About the Author

Judith Arnold is the bestselling, award-winning author of more than one hundred novels and several plays. A New York native, she lives with her husband near Boston in a house with four guitars, three pianos, a violin, a kazoo, a balalaika, and a set of bongo drums. She treasures good books, good music, good chocolate, and good wine—although she will settle for mediocre wine if good wine isn't available. You can learn more about her at her website: www.juditharnold.com.